Mercy's Peril

by

Virginia Barlow

Calhan Brides

Cover Art by *Tina Lynn Stout*

The Wild Rose Press, Inc.
PO Box 708
Adams Basin, NY 14410-0708
Visit us at www.thewildrosepress.com

Publishing History
First Edition, 2026
Trade Paperback Print ISBN 978-1-5092-6400-1
Digital ISBN 978-1-5092-6401-8

Calhan Brides
Published in the United States of America

Dedication

For my brother Roy, because you have always been there for me…

Chapter One

Richmond, Virginia, 1857

Tonight, I gave birth to a fragile miracle, a daughter. She arrived feet first, and Dr. Perry urged me to surrender to death, but Mammy, through her courage and faith, turned the child. For two long hours, I clung to life while Mammy fought beside me, and when it was over, my daughter's tiny fingers curled around mine, bringing tears of gratitude.

Percival sent a cruel message condemning me for my failure to produce a son and vowed to take my gilded chest as punishment. He demanded I name her Rue, for regret. But I will not let his darkness define her. I call her Mercy, for she is my salvation, a light in this house of shadows, and a reminder that grace can bloom even in sorrow. She will grow strong and pure, a light undimmed by her father's shadow. –Grace Bennett

****

New York, New York, January 1876

The hand came out of nowhere.

Mercy Elenna Jackson froze, every muscle coiled tight as a scream clawed its way up her throat. She swallowed, caught between panic and the impulse to run. She wasn't alone.

Her heart plummeted to the depths of her scuffed boots, and a cold sheen of terror slicked her brow. Uncle Justice assured her the warehouse would be empty.

1

Silence pressed down, deafening beneath her thundering pulse.

Finding the names of her mother's other killers, clearing Mama's memory, and recovering the precious gold box were all that mattered.

She could not fail.

"Well, well. You came after all."

A low, menacing voice spoke inches from her ear. His hot, disturbing breath skimmed the nape of her neck, sending icy tendrils of fear spiraling down her spine.

Swathed in the darkness, Mercy weighed her dwindling options. The document she sought lay tucked in the upper right-hand drawer of the black desk, mere feet away. Should she dive for the prize, bolt for the door, or try bluffing her way out?

The shipping office's owner, Connor Calhan, left for the evening. His carriage disappeared into the night before she picked the warehouse lock. She wouldn't have entered otherwise.

The hand on her shoulder squeezed, and bluffing her way out won.

Drawing a slow, steady breath, Mercy shifted her weight, adopting the coarse, hardened tone of a dockworker. "Expecting company, are ye?" Cloaked in shadow, she could be anyone, unknowable and unpredictable. The less this man knew, the better.

"Indeed, I am." The man's voice held a tinge of dark amusement. "Punctuality is a virtue most hosts appreciate. Willing or otherwise. And since you've graced me with your prompt arrival, I see no reason to delay our unhappy business."

Mercy swallowed and tilted her head in mock defiance. "What unhappy business? I've done nothing wrong."

His derisive snort ruffled her hair, and a rock dropped in her stomach. "The fact you picked the lock, scaled the stairs, and navigated straight to my desk in the dark with unerring precision suggests otherwise. Who sent you?"

His voice cut through the darkness with surgical precision. *His desk?* The implication hit Mercy like a blow. *He couldn't be…*

She swallowed hard, loathing the way her body betrayed her, the fine hairs on the back of her neck rising in alarm. Forcing a brittle laugh, she pretended her knees were not shaking like wind chimes in a gale.

"No one." Keeping her tone light, she shrugged as if she broke into shipping offices every other day. "It's freezing outside, and my fingers were numb. I came inside to get warm."

His silence stretched until the rock in her stomach grew into a boulder.

Lacing every word with disdain, he gave a mirthless chuckle. "And you know nothing of a certain document tucked in my desk drawer, is that it? Strange, considering your gaze hasn't wavered from the spot."

Mercy's breath hitched. *How does he know?* A flicker of unease slithered through her. Testing his grip, she shifted her shoulder, calculating her chances of escape. "I don't know what you mean." Her laugh came out sharper than she wanted, and her heart hammered against her ribs. "As I said, I—"

The words died on her lips as he released her shoulder and yanked her around to face him. Numb with surreal fascination, she gulped back her cry of pain as she came face-to-face with Connor Calhan.

The moonlight streaming through the tall window etched his frame in stark relief, highlighting the imperious tilt of his head and the cruel curve of his lips. Recognition hit her like a thunderclap.

"Damn." *Of all the cursed luck.*

Hatred and fury surged through her. She had never been caught until tonight, and the fact that Connor Calhan had been the one to do it made her mad as hell. Making a fist, she swung at his face with all the rage she could muster, hoping to knock him on his ass.

Connor didn't flinch when her blow landed with a sickening thud.

His counterstrike came swift and unrelenting, a crushing blow hurling her into the opposite wall. The impact rattled her bones, sending a violent jolt of pain radiating through her body like a lightning strike.

Mercy crumpled to the floor, her limbs unresponsive, her breath shallow and labored. She teetered on the edge of consciousness. "Bloody hell." For a fleeting moment, she wondered if she had died.

But raw, searing pain confirmed otherwise. She forced her body to respond, assessing each limb with care. Relief trickled through her as her appendages obeyed, though every movement brought sharp agony.

Connor's mocking voice cut through the haze. "There's only one way out, and it's past me. Shall we see if you're brave enough to try?"

She froze, and her failure settled like a stone in her chest. Uncle Justice would never forgive her for getting caught, and the five hundred dollars he promised for stealing the document would come to naught.

The money would pay for Aunt Charity to see a doctor, and the document would bring revenge. Her failure to acquire what she set out for left a bitter taste in her mouth.

Squinting at Connor through a haze of pain, she calculated the distance between them. Movement sent fresh waves of torment coursing through her, and she groaned.

A flickering lantern on the wall cast shadows across his towering frame, highlighting every chiseled feature.

As her vision wavered, his piercing blue eyes seemed to multiply, doubling like some terrible, two-headed beast.

"Buggering hell, they sent a boy." Connor's tone dripped with censure. He approached with slow deliberation like a predator closing in on its prey. With a limp.

Mercy narrowed her gaze. She had not noticed he favored his right leg before. But the injury did not make him less dangerous.

He loomed larger than life, standing well over six feet, his broad shoulders and square jaw giving him an air of ruthless authority.

"Let me help you up." Crouching beside her, he extended his hand.

"No." One did not hold hands with the devil. Rage tightened her chest as she stared back at the man who ruined her life. She had not expected him to be handsome and frowned when her belly fluttered with unease.

His starched linen shirt strained over broad shoulders, while fawn breeches clung to his muscular legs, tucked into polished boots. Wealth and power radiated from him, making Mercy want to retch on the luxurious brown carpet beneath her.

His office walls were swaddled in cream silk, a

marble hearth stood along one wall, and his grand mahogany desk taunted her a few feet away. The room reeked of opulence and control.

Mercy wrinkled her nose. *Who could work in such suffocating perfection?* Leaning away to put more space between them, she grimaced, but she wasn't done fighting. Not yet.

His stern gaze pinned her in place, his frown tightening the knot in her stomach.

"Who are you? Who sent you?" His clipped voice took on smooth indifference as he repeated his question.

As if she would tell a Calhan a damn thing. Mercy blinked hard, willing her double vision to clear. "No one. I came to get warm." She pushed her body upright, wincing as pain lanced through her shoulder. Lord, she'd be black and blue by morning.

"A liar and a thief." His deep voice held a hint of steel, demanding answers. "I will ask one more time. For whom do you work?"

Perched at his feet, she felt as exposed as a roasted chicken trussed up on a brown woolen platter. His expression betrayed nothing, and his silence unnerved her more than his words.

Moistening her dry lips, she shrugged. "I came of my own accord. A fellow could freeze in this weather." Her cap concealed her hair, her breasts bound tight to avoid scrutiny. If he mistook her for a boy, what did she care?

Connor's sharp gaze roved over her, lingering too long where her disguise faltered. With a flick of his wrist, he sent her cap tumbling to the floor. Her thick brown braid spilled free, a damning betrayal.

A feral smile curved his lips. "But you're not a boy,

are you?" His warm, peppermint-laced breath brushed her cheek. "Let's start with your name."

His eyes dropped to her lips, making her stomach twist with apprehension and nausea rise in her throat.

"I suggest you tell the truth his time." He leaned closer, his eyes mere slits.

Mercy forced a shrug and glanced away. "Elenna Jackson." Thank goodness lying to this bastard didn't come with her usual prick of conscience.

Connor's smile sharpened. "And the reason you are in my warehouse?"

The heat of his body stifled her, and she leaned further back. "My friends and I were playing Questions and Commands. I didn't like their questions, so I picked a Command. They require an ink pen from your desk. Proof, you see." She shrugged again, feigning nonchalance. "*And* it's cold."

"Dressing as an urchin to play your little game is customary?" His dry tone suggested he knew otherwise.

Mercy scrambled for an answer, and another lie slipped out like smoke over silk. "These are all I own. My brother died last year, and we can't afford better. People think I'm a boy when I wear the hat, and it keeps me safe."

Connor studied her, his piercing blue eyes peeling back her layers of deception. "I see." His words feigned understanding, but his sharp gaze betrayed his doubt.

Mercy bit the inside of her cheek, forcing her expression to remain neutral. A quick glance at his desk fueled her resolve. The parchment lay so close it tantalized her, and she had to secure it, no matter what the cost.

"Did The Phantom send you?" His question sliced

through her thoughts, sharp and probing.

Surprised, her breath caught, and she glanced up. "Who? I know no one by that name."

Aunt Charity had long suspected The Phantom's shadowy hand in her mother's death. *"Only God and your mother's diary know the truth."*

But Mercy had her mother's diary, and although the name appeared like breadcrumbs amid cryptic entries, it revealed little.

Connor's icy gaze remained on her. "Then why sneak into my warehouse? We both know you aren't here for a writing instrument."

Before she could respond, he grabbed her arm and hauled her to her feet, his touch fueling her simmering resentment. *Damn the man to hell and back.*

Jerking her arm free, she glared. "You do not believe me? Have you decided I am not cold, too?"

Connor's narrowed eyes bored into hers. "You could have sought shelter elsewhere. My desk and office are not sources of heat. I know someone sent you." His lip curled in a faint, derisive smile. "I baited a trap to catch a rat, and here you are."

Mercy's mouth gaped open. *After all his sins, he dared call her a rat?* She hoped to bluff her way out, but now…

Slipping her hand into her pocket to grasp her knife, she took a deep breath to steady her nerves. At this range, she could do real damage. "At least I do not have innocent—" Choking back the words, she bit her lip to keep her anger under control. Her knowledge of his sins would not help her get the document.

Connor frowned, his tone suspicious. "Innocent…what?"

Think fast, my girl. Her gaze shifted to the opulent silk walls behind him, disgust curling her lip. "Do you ever see the hungry and helpless as you pass in your gilded carriage?"

His expression hardened. "You know nothing." He studied her with intense scrutiny. "If you are hungry and helpless, there are honorable ways to survive. Send a male relative to me, and I will give him a job."

Male relative. The hypocrisy of his words twisted her stomach. She had no male family left but Uncle Justice, and he would never stoop to work for a Calhan. Her hand moved in a flash of fury, wielding the knife she kept in her pocket for emergencies. And this situation qualified.

But Connor moved faster, knocking the knife from her grip with infuriating ease, sending it to the floor. In an instant, he had her against the wall, his solid frame imprisoning her.

"What is this?" He murmured into her ear, his voice low and predatory. "I offer you honest work, and you try to stab me?"

His body pinned hers, their chests and hips pressed together, his hand locking both her wrists above her head. Her heart thundered, and the sting of failure burned in her eyes. Her last vestige of hope, her weapon, lay discarded at her feet.

Mercy swallowed hard and lifted her chin, allowing her hatred to burn in her eyes. "I would not work for you or take your coins if my life depended on it."

Connor arched an eyebrow, his piercing gaze unyielding. "Indeed? But you would steal from me. Shall we recount your accomplishments tonight? Breaking and entering. Attempted robbery. Assault. All premeditated crimes can result in years behind bars. Tell me, why not earn your living the right way and keep your freedom?"

Because I need that document as much as I need air to breathe. Mercy forced a smile, her heart pounding in her chest. His word against hers. She shrugged, feigning indifference. "All I did was pick a lock."

His proximity suffocated her, his iron-hard body pressed against hers, radiating with heat, making her nauseous. Leaning down, his breath brushed her cheek. "I could summon an officer right now and have you arrested. And we both know it."

Cold dread coiled in her stomach. Aunt Charity's face flashed in her mind, frail, helpless, and sick. Mercy swallowed the lump in her throat.

His lips tightened. "This is no game. The men who sent you will stop at nothing, even if it means taking your life. Lies won't shield you from a bullet or a blade. My advice? Run far and fast before you end up dead."

His words lanced through her, but the intensity of his gaze rooted her to the spot. His eyes dipped to her lips, and for a fleeting moment, she thought he might kiss her.

Mercy shoved him with all her strength, forcing him to step back.

Connor's jaw tightened as he ran a hand through his hair. "What made you come here alone? An innocent like you should be home in bed. And where the hell is your maid? You could be ruined, or worse. Do you not understand the danger?"

Her lips twisted into a bitter smile. "My maid does not like the docks, and I had no choice." Aunt Charity could not afford a maid, but he did not need to know. Lying to this devil got easier by the second.

Their gazes locked, a silent battle of wills. After a tense pause, he motioned toward the open door. "Then go. But the next man you encounter might not offer you mercy."

She didn't wait for him to change his mind and fled into the dark corridor, her bravado crumbling with every step. Racing down the stairs, across the open space, and into the cool night air, she shivered. Remnants of terror clung to her like a second skin. Relief and fury warred within her as she hastened down the alley toward her waiting mare.

"Damn Connor Calhan to hell." Her voice shook with rage. *A trap?* Uncle Justice swore Connor would be preoccupied tonight.

Annoyed at this unexpected turn mingled with concern over her uncle's reaction to her failure, Mercy kicked the cobblestones with a heavy heart. Wiping the sweat from her brow, she cast a wary glance back at the formidable facade of Calhan Shipping, which loomed ominously in the dim light. "I will be back." She needed that cursed document more by the second.

With a defiant jerk of her chin, Mercy buttoned her jacket and swung into her saddle, her movements sharp with irritation. He may claim victory tonight, but it was a mere battle in a much larger war. A war she would win. Connor Calhan may think he won, but soon, he would learn just how relentless she could be.

Chapter Two

New York, New York, June 1859

Today, I sat in a chamber thick with tension, surrounded by senators from across the North as we confronted the nation's deepest wound: slavery. It does not merely bind men in chains—it shackles the soul of the republic. The debate roared, shaking the very foundation of our Union. Lincoln's stance against slavery's expansion stirs both hope and fear. Should he win the presidency, I worry the fragile ties holding this nation together will snap, plunging us into war. Southern senators grow bolder, cloaking their threats in calls for western expansion.

*Some speak of gentler masters, but I cannot ignore the cruelty whispered behind closed doors—the suffering accepted as custom. Even dressed in civility, slavery remains a moral blight. If war becomes the price of its end, so be it. One man owning another defiles every founding ideal. I will stand for justice, for a future where no man kneels in chains and every soul breathes free. So long as I draw breath, I will fight for that America. –
Major Jonathon Calhan*

****

Connor leaned back in his leather chair, the creak of its worn seams audible over the crackle of the fire in the hearth. His brow furrowed as he massaged the scar on the outer side of his right thigh. On cold nights, a slow, dragging ache settled in, gnawing from the inside, as if the shrapnel buried deep in his flesh remembered how it got there. He had been walking beside the supply train when the shell struck. A cracking roar as if the sky split open, followed by a thud, and a high-pitched ringing in his ears. The explosion blinded him. Dirt, splinters of wood, and metal shards whistled through the air. The air smelled of burned metal, gun powder, and blood. Hot burning hellfire ripped his thigh apart, and he fell face down in the mud while sweat and fear pressed around him. Even now, he could taste the blood, see the smoke, and hear the screams. One whiff of burned black powder and he was back in the mud, wondering if he was alive or dying.

Benson, his butler, stepped into the study, startling Connor from his memories.

He wore a frown of disapproval and carried a tray. His immaculate black linen uniform in sharp contrast to his gray hair and white shirt. "I am happy to see you took my advice to rest your leg. We both know what happens when there is a chill. I brought willow bark tea for the pain and a hot compress, sir. Cook has dinner ready, and I informed her you will be eating in here tonight."

"Thank you." Connor accepted a cup of tea and sighed when the older man laid the compress against his thigh. The heat took the edge off the pain. "Someone had to be at the office to see if our trap worked. My leg is less important than catching the bastard."

"Did your evening adventure bring about the desired result?" The older man had been with Connor since before the war and knew the situation.

Connor shook his head and related the details of Miss Elenna Jackson's attempted robbery of the document in his desk, leaving out the way her silky brown hair framed a heart-shaped face, how her emerald-green eyes gleamed with beguiling innocence, concealing the cunning mind behind them. Even dressed in ill-fitting breeches and a baggy shirt, she exuded a sensual allure that no amount of rough clothing could hide. God must have a wicked sense of humor to gift such beauty to a liar and a thief.

Benson's eyebrow rose. "The Phantom sent a young woman to collect a document revealing the names of the Knights of the Confederacy and his identity? How absurd. He has never involved a woman before. Why would he do such a thing now?" Benson's brow wrinkled as he studied his face. "And a pretty one, judging from the gleam in your eye."

Connor frowned and ignored his last comment. "I do not know. I prepared for a seasoned spy and entertained a girl. She navigated my warehouse in the dark with familiarity. Which tells me someone drew her a map, and she practiced her entry. She counted the steps as she walked from the door to my desk with unerring accuracy." He did not like the thought that someone he trusted had connections to the man who orchestrated his father's murder.

A slight knock on the door announced the arrival of a footman bearing a tray with Connor's dinner.

"Set it there, John." Benson waved him toward the table sitting by Connor's knees.

They waited until the man left before continuing.

"I will discover who sent her, and who gave her the details of my warehouse. Jefferson Swift followed her when she left. There is a traitor somewhere with access to my property, and I do not like the situation."

"Have you considered Francios Blanchart and his daughter?" Benson's haughty sniff of disdain rivaled any noblemen.

Connor's mind whirled. "Francios is out of town for another day, and Gabrielle refuses to soil her boots with the warehouse's wooden floors. Neither one has been inside my place of business." Casting a side glance at his butler as he served dinner, he grimaced. "You want to believe Gabrielle is involved because you do not like her."

"Guilty, sir. And with good reason. There is something about her that does not ring true. I do not know why you insist on escorting her when the terms of your agreement with her father have been met. Her little scandal with an alleged lover no longer blackens her reputation, thanks to your good name and constant companionship. No Dame would dare cross you, and I would be delighted if she never darkened our door again." His nose rose an inch higher. "There is greed in her eyes, and you do not love her, sir. Despite her campaign to convince the world your escort means more than a gentleman's agreement with her father. Calhan Shipping is safe from Mr. Blanchart's subterfuge, and Miss Gabrielle's social life is flourishing. All is well. Why continue?"

Connor sighed. "Because I require her presence to attend social events. Going alone will draw more attention than Gabrielle's high-pitched laughter. The Phantom has slipped through my fingers for a decade, and now he has resurfaced; I must not fail. General Cooper thinks he is a man of circumstance and will be in attendance at important social events. Gabrielle makes it easy to study the men present while all eyes are on her. I will continue to tighten the noose."

His butler sniffed. "As you wish, sir. But dare I hope you will court a gentle woman when this is over? It would do my heart good to see children running through the halls."

Connor's snort echoed around the room. "And dirty your walls and floors?" He chuckled, delighted at the thought, but then sobered. Marriage, as an institution, held no allure. The arrangement he struck with Francois Blanchart now weighed as heavy as an anchor around his neck, dragging him into the abyss.

"I would think you had enough to do with my nieces and nephews running around. Lord knows there are plenty of them with two more on the way. Max and Reese couldn't be any prouder if they tried. Max acts like a lovestruck fool. Hell, they all do, and it's downright nauseating." Shaking his head, his sigh came from the bottom of his soul. "But to answer your question, no. I will never marry, and it is for the best. If a woman were to look past my scars, she would see my bloody past, the lives I took, and the things I have done. I cannot sleep at night because of the faces of the dead haunting me. I hear the cries and see the blood. The explosions ring in my head, and my thigh reminds me of things I wish I could forget. Why inflict my pain and nightmares on an innocent when I can have all the joy of children and family through my brothers?"

Benson's sigh rivaled his. "Because you deserve to be as happy as they are."

Connor disagreed. "I swore an oath over my father's grave, and I will not stop until it is fulfilled. I cannot afford to put a wife and children in danger. The cost is unacceptable."

Benson nodded, his disappointment evident. "Would you care for wine with your dinner, sir?"

The older man had a unique way of changing the subject when irritated, but Conner knew how to deal with him.

"I will relent on one condition. When every last member of the Knights of the Confederacy and The Phantom are either dead or imprisoned, if I find a woman who can see past everything I have done, and if she is amenable, I will court her. Is that satisfactory, Benson?"

The old man gave a stiff nod and turned away.

"And yes, I will have wine with my dinner."

With his good humor restored, Benson smiled. "I will hold you to your word, sir. I plan to make a note of it in my journal for future reference."

Connor's brow rose. "No need. What good is a man if he has no honor?"

"Quite right." Snapping his fingers at the footmen, Benson ordered the next course to be brought in and the empty dishes removed. "Cook made apple tarts for dessert, and for a moment, while you babbled about your scars, I debated whether or not to tell you." Straightening his jacket and brushing imaginary lint from his sleeve, the older man resumed his position behind Connor, and dinner continued.

He allowed Benson to be familiar because of their years together, but not to mention tarts because he disagreed, reeked with traitorous tendencies. "I am happy you came to your senses, or you would be job hunting tomorrow."

They both knew he lied, and with a cheeky grin, dinner continued.

Later, Connor stood beside the long-paned window

of his study, staring into the inky darkness, his jaw set in grim determination. His thoughts turned to their conversation and his unfulfilled oath sworn over his father's grave. Until he dismantled the knight's entire web of corruption and power, he would remain focused and unyielding despite Benson's nudging.

His scowl deepened as he turned from the window to the fire crackling in the hearth. A man with his secrets and sins could never be a good husband, or a good father. Not for anyone. Not even for a mythical soulmate.

The word made him sneer. Soulmate. Did such a creature even exist? His brothers' wives were dazzling women, each one intelligent and strong, who could inspire a seed to sprout beneath the permafrost.

What if only three perfect women walked the earth, and his brothers married them? Where did that leave him?

The wind howled through the chimney, a mournful, haunting sound. Connor nodded in grim agreement with the gale's phantom voice. "Exactly where I should be. Doing my job to keep my family and the country safe."

He turned back to the fire, its glow casting long, flickering shadows on the wall. It was better this way and safer for everyone.

Rattling windowpanes jolted Connor from his thoughts, pulling him back to the cold, stark reality of the moment. He sighed, rose from his chair, and closed the damper on the hearth. Turning down the oil lamp, he allowed the room to fall into a shroud of shadows, the faint glow of orange coals casting a ghostly light across the walls. Sinking back into his worn leather chair, he leaned into its embrace, the silence pressing against him like a second skin.

General Cooper, his director, remained optimistic that the infamous Phantom, leader of the shadowy Knights of the Confederacy, would soon fall into their grasp.

A hope Connor did not share. For eight long years following the war, he hunted the Knights, dismantling their ranks piece by piece, while their leader eluded him like a shadow in the night.

And then, two years ago, The Phantom reemerged with fury. A wave of audacious plots followed his reappearance, including plans to rob Lincoln's grave, assassinate senators, burn Washington to the ground, and kill the president.

Frustrated, General Cooper held a long, heated meeting wherein he determined the only way to lure the devil into the open was a decade-old document scrawled in a cryptic, indecipherable code. Connor's father entrusted the parchment to General Cooper before his death, convinced it held the identities of the Knights and their leader.

"That parchment is our only lead to the bastard." General Cooper's voice hung heavy with conviction. "We don't need to read it. We need to make him believe we can and are closing in."

Connor frowned at the general's plan. "He's a careful man, and the war ended ten years ago. Any man with a lick of sense would question why we haven't come forward before this."

Cooper shrugged with a wry smile. "It's not what you know, son. It's what they think you know that counts. Spread the word that we've discovered the cipher and are decoding the parchment. Ensure everyone understands we are drawing up charges for a decade of crimes."

And Connor did, which led to Miss Elenna Jackson breaking into his warehouse. His lips curled into a grim smile. Cooper had been right about tonight's visitor, and he would be hard to live with.

At twenty-four, with the Civil War's scars fresh on his soul, Connor discovered his father's secret association with the Unified Intelligence Agency while the weight of his grieving mother, his sister, and three younger brothers pressed like an anvil on his shoulders, already bowed by the horrors of war.

Rage consumed him then, a fire burning so hot he wanted to mount a horse, ride into Virginia, and exact bloody vengeance on every rebel in sight. But General Cooper intervened, pulling him back from the brink of reckless fury.

"Think it through, son." Cooper's steady voice soothed his rage. "We can catch every damn one of the sons of bitches if we move smart. But it takes patience. No mistakes."

With reluctance. Connor agreed, swallowing his thirst for vengeance and stepping into his father's shoes as a spy. He swore allegiance to the Unified Intelligence Agency, vowing to serve the cause of justice for God and country. To those looking on, he oversaw the family's shipping business, a dutiful son shouldering the mantle of responsibility. But in truth, the shipping empire served a far more dangerous purpose, funding and concealing his covert activities for the agency.

Chapter Three

Richmond, Virginia, April 1861
Tensions in Richmond have reached a breaking point as debates over slavery and the Union's surrender of Fort Sumter dominate every conversation. Though many neighbors once hoped for compromise, President Lincoln's call for seventy-five thousand volunteers shifted sentiment. At a public meeting last night, Virginia voted to join the Confederacy under Jefferson Davis. My husband, Percival, ever proud and certain, claims war is inevitable. His cold smile at the thought of victory sends a chill through me. I long to visit my father in the North while travel is still possible, but I fear the roads may soon be too dangerous.

Life at home grows darker by the day. The house, once quiet, now echoes with the voices of Percival's nightly guests, men who drink, argue, and speak of violence. I am not allowed downstairs after dinner, but the servants whisper of flaring tempers and drunken boasts. I thank God for the sturdy latch on my bedroom door. But I worry about my daughter. How can I raise her to be kind and honest in a world unraveling with hatred? There must be a way to hold onto goodness amid the madness. –Grace Bennett

****

Connor did not sleep well as memories of the war danced in his head like demons, followed by sensual, arousing dreams of…her.

They were alone in the semidarkness of his office at the warehouse. The light of the fire flickered across Elenna's beautiful face while he questioned her about The Phantom. Her falsehoods flowed like honey in the summer heat, but the flicker of guilt in her gaze betrayed her. She knew more about The Phantom than she pretended.

"I have come for the parchment." Her beguiling green eyes lingered on the top right-hand drawer of his desk. "What must I do to convince you to give it to me?" Her voice dropped as soft as velvet.

"It will never be yours." Connor stared as she unbuttoned her jacket.

"Never?" The set of her chin challenged him, as did the green fire in her eyes.

She stepped closer, her warm scent settled over him like a lover's caress, exciting, intoxicating, and seductive.

He studied her through half-closed eyes, every nerve raw and waiting.

With slow, deliberate grace, she tugged the cap from her head, and silken strands of chestnut tumbled free, cascading down her back like a river of midnight. The fire caught the edges, turning her hair to molten gold, and for a heartbeat, Connor forgot how to breathe.

Their breaths mingled in the charged space between them. Then, her hand rose to his chest, right above his heart, where it slammed against his ribs like a caged animal.

He ached to touch her, to stroke her silken skin, and taste her soft lips.

Her eyes held his, unblinking, unreadable. Seconds

stretched into eternity before she rose onto her toes and brushed her lips against his in tentative, tantalizing strokes, holding whispers of delights to come, melting into him like she belonged there.

Connor caught her around the waist, dragging her flush to his body as his mouth claimed hers in hot, ravenous kisses.

Her husky moan broke his self-control and desire uncoiled like a snake as he gave in to the need building inside him.

Backing her against the desk, he drank from her lips like a starving man, each kiss more delicious than the last.

Elenna arched her spine, grinding her hips into his, and he groaned. Her breath came fast, her lips opening for his invasion.

The kiss consumed him, making him burn. He wanted to tear off her shirt, push her down on the desk, and drown in her.

A heartbeat later, she whispered against his mouth: "You want to ruin me, don't you?"

The words slammed into him like a fist, jarring him to the core. Breaking the kiss, Connor staggered back.

She stood there, lips swollen, eyes wide and accusing. "Say you want to ruin me, Connor."

He stared in horror. His lack of honor and restraint twisted his gut. Had he lost all reason and decency? No Calhan ruined a woman. Not even a thief.

Not after nine months of escorting Gabrielle through salons and garden parties, rebuilding her reputation inch by painful inch. Not after swearing never to be the kind of man who took because he could. God, what had he been thinking?

Connor jolted awake, breath ragged, chest aching like he had been dragged back to reality with a chain. His bed linen twisted around his legs like shackles, damp with sweat. The fire in the hearth burned low, the heat stifling as he sat up, swiping a hand across his beaded brow.

His thigh burned like hell, but it dimmed compared to the searing heat coursing through his veins. The seductive press of her body, the maddening sweetness of her kiss lingering on his lips, and the sound of her throaty moan. God, what a nightmare of a dream.

He knew nothing of her except that she came to steal from him.

And already she haunted him.

Dragging a hand through his hair, he clenched his jaw so tight it ached. What sort of man dreamed about a woman he should have handed over to the authorities?

He spent his life measured, disciplined, and ruled by duty. His honor had been his shield, and yet in a single night, with a single kiss, she broke through his barriers.

Disgusted, he threw the covers aside and rose, wincing as his leg protested. Rolling his shoulders, he stretched the stiffness from his muscles, willing away the heat still crawling beneath his skin. Ellenna Jackson was dangerous.

The parchment would have to be moved. Those watching would suspect a trap if he did not move it after Elenna's attempt to steal it. The best place would be here in his office at home with Benson helping him keep an eye open. Connor's resolve hardened. He hadn't spent the last decade chasing a ghost, sacrificing his peace, and burying his grief, just to let a deceitful thief deter him. He would uncover every detail about her and her family.

Somewhere in her past, a thread connected her to the shadowy figure that haunted his life for over a decade. Connor would find it and pull that thread until the entire web unraveled, no matter how deep it ran. Or who stood in his way. Lusty or not.

****

The first fingers of dawn filtered through the curtains as Mercy peered into her looking glass and gasped. A dark, grotesque bruise sprawled across half her face, its bluish-purple hues matching the discolored shadows blooming across her left arm and thigh, acquired following her flight into Connor Calhan's office wall. Yet these injuries paled beside the ones her uncle inflicted later, branding her back and knees with their searing reminders of failure.

The symphony of aches coursing through her body was muted by liniment and the bittersweet sting of opium dissolved in her morning tea. Her face was another matter altogether. After probing the tender, swollen skin and finding no permanent damage, a sigh of relief escaped. With trembling hands, she reached for her jar of face powder, dabbing it on with painstaking precision.

As long as she remembered to keep her left side turned away from Aunt Charity's sharp eyes, her movements deliberate and controlled, and the opium within reach, she would avoid any awkward questions.

Mercy hurried to the kitchen to prepare her aunt's breakfast. When steam rose like a ghostly veil from the teapot on the stove, she added tea leaves and inhaled the sweet, enticing scent. There is much to be said about the healing benefits of a well-steeped cup of tea, and for a minute, the bitter tang of her bruises dimmed.

Coddled eggs and fresh biscuits added a hot buttery

aroma to the kitchen, and Mercy's mouth watered. Charity's coughing fits echoed through the corridor late into the night, leaving her with little doubt her aunt would not rise before mid-morning. *Poor dear.*

Balancing the tray, Mercy tapped on the bedroom door before easing it open. Careful to keep her left side angled away from her aunt's piercing gaze, she placed the tray on the bedside table. "I've brought you breakfast, Auntie."

From the bed, a white-capped head stirred before Aunt Charity sat upright with a gasp. "What time is it? Oh, Mercy, forgive me! I must have overslept." Pale and thin, her aunt threw back the bedclothes and slid her legs over the side.

Mercy stood at her side in an instant, her tone firm yet soothing. "You didn't sleep at all, Auntie. Now, stay where you are and eat. I insist."

Despite protests of the impropriety of eating breakfast in bed, Mercy coaxed the older woman back against a mound of plumped pillows and positioned the tray on her aunt's knees with the care of someone who'd long since mastered the art of appeasing fragile tempers.

As her aunt sipped her tea and murmured her gratitude, Mercy's thoughts wandered, the taste of opium bitter on her tongue and the bruises burning like an unspoken confession. *I must get the parchment. Should I go back tonight? Or will Connor anticipate a repeat visit and call the constable?*

Aunt Charity sighed, bringing her attention back to the bed. "I should be up and doing."

Mercy responded with a soft smile, smoothing the bedclothes over the older woman's knees. "You can work to your heart's content once you've eaten and rested, Auntie. On this, I will not yield." Her eyes flickered downward, catching the stark crimson of a bloodied kerchief lying beside the bed. It must have fallen when she adjusted the covers. The sight sent a sharp pang through her chest, and her gaze darted to Aunt Charity's pale, ashen face, the delicate lines of age etched deeper by illness. Cursing beneath her breath, Mercy vowed she would get the old woman to a doctor if she had to raid the parish strongbox to do so.

As if sensing her thoughts, Aunt Charity's eyes narrowed with uncanny perception. "Mercy, you will abandon whatever diabolical plan crossed your mind a moment ago." Her tone sharpened with suspicion. "And while you are at it, explain where you disappeared to last night after checking on me."

Mercy's pulse quickened, her heart clawing its way to her throat. She fumbled for an answer, her voice catching. "Nowhere." Another lie and spoken with too much haste to be convincing.

"I know better." Aunt Charity's frail hand lifted a cracked teacup to her lips as she stared into her niece's face. "You left the cottage, and judging by the bruise on your face, you've taken such care to conceal, you've been meddling in trouble again. Now, I will hear the truth, young lady. And do not bother concocting any nonsense."

Glancing down at the worn carpet beneath the bed, she licked her lips, stalling for time. "I had an errand."

Aunt Charity's eyes flashed, sharp as glass. "And did my brother send you on this mysterious errand?" Her words were clipped, her green eyes alive with conviction. "You should not trust Justice, Mercy. Although I love my brother, I put no store in what he says. If he cared as much as he claimed, he would not send you into danger for his gain."

She opened her mouth, but Aunt Charity raised a hand to silence her. "Don't bother defending him. I know what you will say. He gives you money for things you cannot afford, and you believe you are doing good. And you are, though it pains me to admit it. But at what cost, Mercy?"

The knock at the front door interrupted their conversation, breaking the tension-thickened air.

Mercy rose, smoothing her skirt as she turned to her aunt. "Eat your breakfast, Auntie. I'll see who it is."

She made her way to the door, her steps cautious and deliberate, as she favored her left side.

The cottage, nestled beside the church where Aunt Charity spent all her time, drew visitors searching for counsel or charity. Expecting another parishioner to inquire after her aunt's wisdom or aid, she opened the door and froze.

The last person she ever wanted to see stood on the stoop.

Connor Calhan.

His lips curled into a half-smile, but his eyes betrayed no warmth. They were cold, calculating, and unreadable. Clad in fitted black trousers, a royal blue vest gleaming like polished silk, and a black woolen jacket tailored to perfection, he cut a figure so striking her breath caught in her throat. His golden hair shimmered in the morning light, every strand in impeccable order, and he offered a mock bow portraying more derision than deference. As he straightened, a speculative glint sparked in his ice-blue eyes. The air between them thickened with the intoxicating blend of tonka bean, sandalwood, and citrus.

The scent curled around Mercy, stiffening her resolve even as her nose twitched with appreciation.

God help her, he smelled divine.

The urge to slam the door in his face surged, but before she could act, he put his expensive leather boot in the way.

"What are you doing here?" Sharp with irritation, her voice hung between them.

"Good morning, Miss Elenna Jackson." His intense scrutiny swept her from head to toe. His eyes lingered on her dark blue woolen gown, complete with several patches, before traveling down to the frayed edge of her stockings peeking out beneath the hem. Rising, his attention settled on her thick curly hair, escaping the confines of her hasty chignon.

The contrast between them would be humorous if the stakes weren't so high. His refined elegance mocked her threadbare reality.

At that precise moment, the unruly knot of hair atop her head slid free to dangle behind her right ear. Heat surged up her neck, blooming across her cheeks. Standing before him, Mercy felt every bit the scrappy urchin she resembled next to his immaculate, aristocratic presence.

A knowing smirk tugged at his lips. "Only a fool would mistake you for a man."

Mercy blew a stray wisp of hair from her eyes and crossed her arms. "Only a simpleton would mistake you for a gentleman."

His smirk vanished, and his expression darkened as his attention drifted to the left side of her face. He lingered there, his penetrating stare pinning her in place.

"I offer my sincerest apologies for the injury." His low tone sounded regretful. "Had the room not been so dark, I would never have struck you."

Mercy snorted and narrowed her gaze. She knew the truth about him and would not be swayed by his veneer of civility. "Indeed." The word dripped with sarcasm.

His lips twitched.

"How did you find me?" She glanced behind him, wondering if he brought company.

Leaning against the doorframe, he studied her as though he relished her ire. "I have my ways."

A faint scraping noise came from the other room, and Mercy stiffened. Aunt Charity. Her aunt could not see him here. Not now, not ever.

"You must go." He had to leave before the older woman came to investigate. She cast a panicked glance over her shoulder. "I don't know why you're here, but this is not the time. We can trade insults another day. Right now, I have more important things to do."

Her eyes darted past him to the road to see if anyone noticed his presence, and she frowned in alarm. He drew stares like a harlot in a monastery, and her stomach clenched. Fine carriages and wealthy gentlemen did not visit the Lower East Side of Manhattan unless they were lost or seeking trouble. Did he want to be robbed and murdered for God's sake?

On second thought, why should she care? Such an outcome would solve several of her problems.

Yet as she stepped back, the heady aroma of his cologne curled around her again, stealing her breath. Her mouth went dry. Lord, she underestimated his allure the night before, and in the full light of day, he made her weak in the knees. Damn his black soul.

The crunch of carriage wheels shattered her fleeting composure as a new worry crossed her mind. What if Uncle Justice drove past while Connor Calhan stood on her doorstep? The thought sent ice through her veins. Another whipping would be the least of her concerns. Her failed mission would become irrevocable, and any hope of collecting the promised gold would vanish like smoke.

She glanced down the street, and her knees buckled when a dark carriage, similar to her uncle's, rumbled toward them. Panic coiled in her chest, tight and suffocating. For a breathless moment, she stood paralyzed as nausea rose in her throat.

But self-preservation kicked in. Without a second thought, she grabbed Connor by the lapel of his expertly tailored jacket and yanked him inside. "Get in here before someone sees you."

One eyebrow quirked when she tugged on his jacket, but he didn't resist and stepped inside, stopping mere inches from her trembling body, far too close for comfort.

"And here I thought you planned to slam the door in my face." His deep voice sent a shiver to the bottom of her threadbare stockings.

She slammed the door behind him and leaned against the wall for support, her legs trembling beneath her skirt. "Be still and let me think." She snapped, trying to ignore his towering presence, the erratic rhythm of her own heart, and the unsettling weakness of her knees.

"Shall I remove my boots, or do you plan to carry me to the drawing room as well?"

His breath brushed her cheek, warm and intoxicating, carrying the faint bite of peppermint and the maddening allure of his cologne. Her stomach knotted as she shot him a glare. "I want to toss you out. So don't tempt me. Don't breathe, don't move, and for God's sake don't talk." God, he irritated her.

If anything, her tremors grew more pronounced when his deep voice rumbled up his chest in a low chuckle. Quivering with nerves, she stepped back, ignoring him, and focusing on the approaching clatter of hooves and wheels outside.

The carriage grew louder and closer, until its very presence suffocated her. A cold sweat beaded her brow as her mind raced through a desperate litany of options. Connor Calhan wouldn't fit behind the settee. He certainly wouldn't fit under her narrow bed. Her gaze flicked to the kitchen. Would he fit in the larder? Wiping clammy hands on the sides of her worn woolen skirt, she bit her lip, her breath coming in shallow gasps as the rattling equipage slowed. The sound drew even with the door, and her heart stalled.

And then it passed.

Relief crashed over her like an icy Atlantic wave, leaving her boneless and trembling. "Thank all the saints and angels." Her breath rushed out in a litany of fevered gratitude but faltered when her gaze lifted to Connor.

He stood motionless, studying her with such intensity, her defenses melted away. His expression, though unreadable, gleamed with something she couldn't quite name. Morbid fascination?

Dabbing at the cold sweat on her brow, Mercy straightened her spine, forcing composure into her trembling frame. She had no time to wonder what he thought, and what's more, she didn't care. With a practiced neutrality, she lifted her chin to face the man who filled the cramped space of her entrance hall with his commanding presence.

His raised eyebrows and watchful eyes only deepened her agitation.

"Feeling a little guilty this morning, Miss Jackson?" He studied her with infuriating confidence.

Fearing Aunt Charity's arrival snapped her out of her flustered haze, and she fixed him with a glare. "Why are you here? I thought we said all we had to say last night."

"Did we?" He tilted his head, the movement casual yet calculated. "I can think of several subjects demanding…further exploration."

His words were as deliberate as his presence. Broad shoulders and powerful thighs filled the tiny hall, and the top of his head brushed the sloped ceiling.

Feeling cornered, Mercy retreated into the living area, desperate to put some distance between them. Even there, the heat of his presence reached her, wrapping her in an unwelcome awareness she loathed. Nausea swirled in her stomach. The sooner he left, the better.

Crossing her arms over her chest, she tapped her foot with frustration. "Well, I can't. Whatever you came for, please leave."

His low, rich chuckle rolled through the room, setting her nerves aflame.

"Thrown out already? My, how quickly your enthusiasm fades."

His sarcastic tone set her teeth on edge, and her glare hardened. "You arrived uninvited and barged into my home. You've overstayed your welcome, and I want you to go. I have nothing more to say to you."

He shrugged, unbothered by her ire, and made no

move to leave. "Do you throw all your unwanted guests inside before dismissing them? Or am I the lucky one? I am here for answers, Miss Elenna, and I'm not leaving until I get them."

His casual ultimatum delivered in a matter-of-fact tone made her blood boil. "I've given all the answers you are going to get." Her lips thinned while her ears strained for any sound from Aunt Charity's room. Her stomach knotted tighter with every second he lingered.

"I'm beginning to think you don't want anyone to know I'm here," he mused. "Who are you hiding me from? Let me guess. Whoever he is, he doesn't know about last night, does he?" His eyes gleamed with a wicked light. "This could get very interesting."

Mercy's heart sank as her gaze skidded over the stubborn set of his jaw. He wouldn't leave until he got what he wanted. And she lacked the strength and the leverage to force him out. "What makes you think it's a man?"

"I wonder if The Phantom lurks in your bed chamber like a coward. If you do not answer my questions, I shall have no choice but to investigate. He is the one I am after, not you."

A slow, satisfied smile spread across his face when she groaned.

"I will answer your questions, but keep your voice down." She threw another glance over her shoulder toward the corridor, hoping she had closed her aunt's heavy bedroom door when she left. "Come into the sitting room."

Crossing her fingers behind her back, she sent a silent plea heavenward, promising a week of fasting to atone for the lies she intended to tell.

His brows lifted at her sudden capitulation, and his voice went soft with suspicion. "Why the change of heart? *Is* The Phantom back there?"

"No—" The word froze in her throat as a sharp sound interrupted her.

From the corner of her eye, she saw Aunt Charity shuffle into view, her frail frame wrapped in a shawl, her face pale with disbelief.

"Good Lord God Almighty." The older woman shrieked and clutched the doorframe for support. Her gaze locked on Connor with a mix of shock and terror. "There's a *Calhan* in my home!"

The force of her exclamation nearly toppled her over, and Mercy could do nothing but brace for the storm sure to follow.

Chapter Four

New York, New York – June 1861
War has come. With the fall of Fort Sumter and
Major Anderson's surrender, four more states, Virginia,
Arkansas, Tennessee, and North Carolina, joined the
Confederacy. Many blame Lincoln's call for 75,000
volunteers, but the true cause remains slavery. General
Cooper believes we can end this swiftly. Our troops head
to Virginia with confidence, determined to crush the
rebellion before more blood is shed. With superior
numbers, industry, and infrastructure, and the justice of
our cause, I believe we will prevail.

Tonight, I depart for Washington with our sons at
my side. Connor, Max, and Reese march under General
Cooper. Though worry weighs heavy on my heart, I trust
in their strength. I held Maggie close before leaving and
promised her I'd return safely, with our boys beside me.
Her quiet fear lingers in my chest. But uncertainty is the
enemy of faith. I choose to believe in our mission and in
a swift, righteous victory. –Major Jonathon Calhan
****

Mercy wanted to melt into a puddle on the floor and
disappear between the floorboards.

How in the hell could she get Connor Calhan out of
the house, and more importantly, away from Aunt
Charity before they had a conversation?

The man loomed in the foyer like he owned it, his

smug presence sapping the air from the room. Mercy glared at him with all the fire she could muster, her voice dropping to a venomous hiss. "I hope you're pleased. You've woken my aunt, and whatever shred of willingness I had to finish this conversation just vanished."

Connor replied with a maddening shrug as if the situation amused him. "You may not be willing, but she might be."

Mercy's heart stuttered. *Oh no.* A cold prickle ran down her spine as she turned to note her aunt's interest in their visitor. The older woman teetered in the doorframe, her face alight with curiosity and the dangerous energy of a woman who planned to get answers.

Mercy swallowed hard, panic clawing at her throat. This situation had the potential of a lit fuse hurtling toward a keg of dynamite, and her aunt held the match. She couldn't let this happen.

"Auntie." Her voice came out high and tight. In dismay, she cleared her throat. "What are you doing out of bed? You need your rest. Let's get you tucked back in before you catch a chill."

But Aunt Charity waved her off with surprising force, her thin shoulders squaring with a resolve Mercy recognized all too well. "Remember your manners, child." Her aunt's voice held a thread of steel determination. "It's not every day we find a man in our home, and I'd very much like to know *why*. And the fact that he is a Calhan makes it more interesting."

Mercy's stomach dropped as Aunt Charity turned to inspect Connor Calhan. She took her time, too, studying him with a sharp, assessing gaze sweeping from the crown of his golden hair to the polished tips of his expensive boots. And then she smiled.

Oh Lord, not the smile. That half-curtsey-half-bow, awkward yet charming dip her aunt granted their visitor meant one thing. She planned to interrogate him.

"I am Miss Charity Jackson." With the flair of a stage performer, she lifted her chin high, her voice as light as spun silk. "And you, sir, are Connor Calhan. I've read quite a bit about you in the papers. Some accounts describe you as a paragon of virtue, a gentleman of extraordinary character." Her head tilted, and her smile turned wicked. "Others, however, call you a thief, a murderer, and a ruffian." She paused, a girlish twitter escaping her lips as she surveyed him with unsettling appreciation. "I have wished on several occasions to have a private conversation with you. Though I must say, you are far too handsome to be everything the newspapers claim. I can see why my sis—"

Mercy sprang into action, grasping her aunt's arm with a grip that would have stopped a lesser woman. "Come along, Auntie." The words rushed out in a near-desperate plea, and her cheeks burned when her overpowering visitor cocked an eyebrow. Tugging on her aunt's elbow, she cast Connor a final, scathing look, blaming him for every bit of this unfolding disaster. If her aunt spoke one more word, their secrets would be scattered like glass shards on a marble floor, impossible to pick up and far too dangerous to ignore.

"Not now, Mercy. I wish to speak to Mr. Calhan. There are a few questions I'd like to ask him." Aunt Charity's voice, though faint, cut through Mercy's frantic attempts to steer her away.

Of course, she did. And they were all questions she

would do anything to avoid. Her pulse quickened as panic slithered up her spine, and she tightened her grip on her aunt's cold, fragile arm. "You are like ice, Auntie. Why don't you wait until you're feeling stronger? Mr. Calhan can answer your questions another time."

Aunt Charity, slight and frail though she appeared, twisted free with surprising strength. "By then, he'll be gone, and I feel up to questioning him now. How often does one get the opportunity to speak with a Calhan?"

Her words rang like a bell, tolling doom as she turned, unwavering, toward their uninvited guest. Mercy stood paralyzed, her thoughts whirling. Now what? She had to get control of the situation fast.

Aunt Charity's sharp gaze narrowed. "What do you want with us, young man?" She demanded an answer, her tone both weary and sharp.

The words barely left her lips before her body betrayed her. Her thin chest heaved, a wheezing cough shattering the air. The sharp sound rattled as if something scraped her lungs and broke free. Alarmed, Mercy tightened her grip, dread curling in her gut. *The blood on the kerchief...*

Before she could act, Aunt Charity's trembling hand lifted toward Connor. "Help me to the sitting room." She wheezed between coughs.

Mercy cast a gaze at Connor, certain his true character would come forth, and he would deny her aunt's request.

To her astonishment, the smug defiance in his expression melted away like mist under a rising sun. The fierce sharpness of his posture softened, replaced by an easy grace far too natural to be feigned. His eyes, though cool and unreadable moments before, now held warmth, and when he stepped forward, his movements were deliberate, careful, and gentle.

"I am delighted to be of assistance, Miss Jackson." His voice turned silky smooth and steady. A gentle smile curved his mouth, and for a moment, she gaped at his transformation. Connor Calhan turned from a smug, aloof icicle into a tender, charming gentleman in the flash of a wink.

What the hell was he up to?

Mercy wrung her hands as their uninvited visitor took Aunt Charity's arm and guided her down the corridor with slow, careful steps, as though escorting a queen. The older woman leaned on him too much for comfort and clung to him as he lowered her onto the threadbare settee in the sitting room.

Hovering by the door and feeling as useless as a candle in a hurricane, Mercy's pulse beat a frantic tick as Connor crouched and tucked the cushion behind Aunt Charity's thin frame.

The care he took unsettled her. He performed the act like he belonged here, like he'd done this a thousand times before. Plucking a cushion from the other end of the settee to prop beneath her feet, he lifted the shawl, draped over the armrest, and covered the older woman's knees.

When he stepped back with his hands loose at his sides, he stood at ease in this house where he did not belong.

She chewed the inside of her lip, wishing she could collect her gun and shoot him. Her aunt wouldn't let her, of course, but a girl had to have dreams.

Glancing at Aunt Charity, she noted her labored breaths were steadier, and color returning to her cheeks.

Thanking him for his assistance would be the proper thing to do, but she never claimed to be a lady.

"Thank you, Mr. Calhan." Her aunt lifted her chin with the regal poise of a woman who knew she held the upper hand. A glint of steel flashed in her tired eyes as she looked at their unwelcome guest. "I feel better now…and I will have my explanation. Why are you here?"

The room fell silent, the air taut with anticipation. Mercy stood motionless, her heart in her throat, praying for a miracle.

Connor studied the older woman's face for several long seconds before he nodded. "Miss Elenna broke into my warehouse last night to steal from me." He explained about the parchment and his desk before continuing. "When I questioned her, she told one lie after another while her gaze remained glued to my desk. And in answer to your earlier concerns about my character, let me be clear. I may be many things, but a thief, a murderer, or a ruffian, I am not. Nor do I lay hands on women in cruelty. I did not anticipate the men I pursued would send a woman to do their thievery for them. I confess I am the one who left the mark on your niece's cheek. In the dark, I assumed her to be a man, an intruder, and acted in accordance. I have since apologized to her, and now I extend my deepest regrets to you. Rest assured, Madam, you and your niece have nothing to fear from me."

Splendid. Mercy scoffed, folding her arms across her chest, her lips curling in a sardonic smile. *He is not a thief, a murderer, or a ruffian, but a polished gentleman who punches women in the dark.* How noble of him to apologize, but she did possess a bruise across her cheek, nevertheless. Risking a glance at her aunt, her heart plummeted.

Judging by Aunt Charity's shocked expression, Mercy would never hear the end of this. Theft, lying, and adultery were her aunt's favorite sermon topics, and she had committed two of the forbidden three. The Bible quotes alone would drive her crazy. Closing her eyes, she sucked in a breath of fortitude and waited for the repercussions.

Aunt Charity's voice rose, trembling with equal parts disbelief and fervor. "May the angels and saints deliver us! Did you break into Mr. Calhan's warehouse? To *steal*? Have you lost all sense of decency, Mercy? Surely you know what the Good Book says about such wickedness!"

Yes, she knew. And she intended to sin again at her next opportunity.

Connor's brow arched, his voice cutting through her aunt's tirade like the blade of a knife. "Your name is Mercy? You told me Elenna last night."

His tone dripped with censure, and she wanted to wipe the sanctimonious grin from his face.

Lifting her chin, she met his icy stare with an unrepentant grin. "Yes. I use whatever name is more appropriate for the situation." Using her sweetest voice, she tilted her head to mock him. "Next time I break into your warehouse and get punched in the face, I will no doubt give you a third name. I owe you nothing."

His jaw tightened, and his eyes narrowed to mere slits. The man's face could have been chiseled from granite. "Is that right?"

Aunt Charity sat bolt upright, her sharp tone slicing into her niece like a scythe. "You may feel no duty to explain your actions to Mr. Calhan, but you owe me the truth, and I will have your explanation. Start at the beginning and spare me no detail."

Mercy hesitated, swallowing the instinct to lie. But her aunt's expression burned with resolve, and she knew no half-measure would suffice. With a deep breath, she straightened her spine and began recounting the barest facts, skimming over the more damning details, and leaving out the part about her uncle.

Charity's countenance turned grim, her voice growing sharper with each word. When Mercy fell silent, her aunt sighed, the sound laden with heavy disappointment. "As I suspected. Your uncle put you up to this. You refused to answer this morning, but I see it now. The truth is written plain as day in your expression."

Mercy's lips parted, but no defense came out. She hated disappointing the woman who took her in when she had no one, and the pain of regret cut deep.

Her aunt's weary sigh broke into a violent coughing fit, the spasms wracking her small frame. Gasping for air and sitting ramrod straight, she wheezed until Mercy couldn't bear the sound. Dropping to her knees beside her aunt, her hand hovered, unsure if a pat would soothe or hinder.

But Connor moved faster. Kneeling on the older woman's other side, he offered her his kerchief. Sliding a strong arm behind her, he held her trembling body upright against him and whispered soft words of encouragement into her ear. "There now, Miss Charity. Lean on me. I've got you."

Aunt Charity blinked and gave in to his ministrations without a fuss, clutching his arm as she allowed the traitor to give her aid.

Mercy snapped her mouth closed, her jaw tight with indignation, and crossed her arms over her chest. Of all the conniving, rotten tricks to pull. She scowled, her voice a low mutter, laced with fury. "What in thunder are you doing?"

Calhans were killers, thieves, villains of the basest sort, and not gentlemen. Not caretakers. And not this. When her aunt laid her head on his arm, the urge to kick Connor Calhan in both shins boiled in her veins, but she couldn't, not with Aunt Charity three feet away.

"Giving aid to an ailing woman." Connor, unperturbed by her simmering glare, focused on her aunt.

His voice, deep and soothing as he murmured to her aunt, infuriated her.

"Breathe in deep, Madam. That's it, just one breath at a time. You're doing well. And another. Now, lean on me."

Mercy narrowed her eyes, focusing on his face. She wanted him to know she saw through his elaborate charade of care and concern. Feigning compassion for a frail, coughing woman? How…Calhan of him.

Jealousy took over when her aunt smiled up at him through her coughing fit.

Not to be outdone, Mercy slid closer, clutching her aunt's arm with a determined grip. She matched Connor's every gesture, patting and murmuring her reassurances in tandem, though her tone carried an edge of competitive vigor. Her pats grew firmer, almost brisk, to ensure Aunt Charity would feel the difference and know who her true champion was.

As the coughing subsided, Aunt Charity leaned against Connor with a final, shuddering breath. A glistening sheen of perspiration covered her pale, wrinkled face as she turned to Mercy with a weary shake of her head. "Child, stop your fretting. I don't know if you're trying to pound air into me or crack my ribs, but either way, I'll be black and blue by morning." Exasperation and weariness laced her tone.

Mercy's cheeks flamed with guilt, the heat spreading to the tips of her ears. "I wanted to help." The words escaped her like the petulant defense of a scolded child. At nineteen, she hated the way it sounded, small, impotent, and unconvincing.

Her scorn turned to Connor, the source of all this turmoil. Rising to her feet, she refolded her arms across her chest and pinched her lips into a defiant line. "Helping my aunt won't change my opinion of you, Mr. Calhan." With a sharp, steady voice, she pointed toward the door, her finger trembling with agitation. "Now get out. You've upset her enough, and I will not allow your presence to provoke another coughing fit."

Aunt Charity, still leaning against Connor's solid frame, let out a long sigh. "He didn't upset me half as much as your evening activities, Mercy." Her expression sharpened, pinning her niece with a mixture of bewilderment and disappointment. "I cannot fathom what possessed you to do what you did. He *is* a Calhan, after all. And you know better."

Mercy gaped in disbelief. "*Me?*"

"Yes, you." Aunt Charity replied, her tone clipped and unwavering. Straightening, she continued. "I raised you to be kind, gentle, and God-fearing, not a thief, and not a liar." Her sharp gaze dropped to the faint bruise on Mercy's cheek. "I shudder to think what your mother would say about all of this."

The mention of her mother fueled the rebellion in Mercy's chest. Aunt Charity didn't understand the importance of last night, nor could she. The woman's faith in forgiveness, meekness, and other useless virtues did not hold up in the face of reality.

Mercy squared her shoulders, fire blazing in her eyes. "Yes, I admit I picked the lock and entered his warehouse without permission. But how can you compare *my* paltry sins to his? As *you* said, Aunt Charity, he's a Calhan."

The older woman's tone sharpened, her voice cutting through the tension like a blade. "Mind your tongue, Mercy. We do not yet know the full truth of what transpired."

Connor, unflustered by the rebuke or Mercy's simmering fury, adjusted Aunt Charity's shawl with careful precision. Rising to his full height, his lips curved into a sardonic smile, softening his otherwise severe expression. "I am pleased to see you feeling better, Madame." The sincerity in his tone in jarring contrast to the glint of steel in his eyes.

His eyes flicked to Mercy, lingering just long enough to catch the tremor in her hands before returning to Aunt Charity.

Mercy cursed under her breath, shoving her rebellious hands behind her back to hide their weakness from his probing scrutiny

"It seems my presence unsettles your niece." He delivered his dry observation with a touch of amusement. "And so, as she has requested, I shall take my leave."

He turned as if to depart, but stopped, and reaching into the pocket of his tailored jacket, he retrieved a neat stack of coins. With deliberate care, he placed them on the tea table beside Aunt Charity's knees.

"These are for you, Miss Charity. Seek the care of a doctor. There is no honor in enduring when help is at hand. I'll send my physician, Doctor Trumble, to call on you early next week. This cough cannot be ignored. We both know it will only worsen."

Though his words carried a veneer of kindness, the victorious glint in his eye made Mercy's temper surge like a rising tide. Clenching her fists, her anger rushed out in a torrent.

"You…you *bloody* rat!" Her voice cracked with fury. "How dare you stand here and pretend to help when you are responsible for my—" She stopped short and bit her tongue before she revealed too much. "We don't want your help! Not your bribes, not your guilt, or your blood-soaked coins. They cannot buy absolution, and they sure won't wash the sins from your soul." Her chest heaved, and her hands shook. "I would rather starve in the street, shiver in the dark from cold and beg for crumbs with bare hands before I ever take one cursed coin from you."

Aunt Charity's audible gasp filled the silence, her expression horrified. "Mercy!"

Connor's response cut deep with its calm delivery. "But would you rather see your aunt suffer? Two coughing fits within minutes of each other cannot be ignored. The coins are for her, after all."

The smug confidence in his tone made her rage burn hotter. Mercy bit back her scathing retort, tasting the bitter tang of blood. "No." The word scraped against her pride like a shard of glass.

Connor's face softened, though his eyes gleamed with satisfaction. "I thought not." Turning back to Aunt

Charity, his voice dipped into a gentler tone. "Take care, Miss Charity. If you require further assistance, do not hesitate to send word. I am at your service, day or night."

He glanced back at Mercy with a sardonic smile. "As for you, Miss Mercy, my unwelcome generosity serves a dual purpose. First, to assist your aunt, of course. The second should be apparent, though I suspect you'll find it less agreeable. If your needs are met, dare I hope you'll refrain from trespassing onto my property again?"

Mercy met his stare with unflinching defiance, lifting her chin. "Of course." The lie slipped from her lips without hesitation. Somehow, lying to Connor felt less like a sin and more like justice.

The corner of his mouth twitched, as though he could see through her deceit.

Aunt Charity cleared her throat, interrupting their silent battle. "Thank you, Mr. Calhan. You've been most understanding and merciful, given my niece's misguided actions last night. I accept your generosity and will send for a doctor straight away." She nudged Mercy's foot with her own, a pointed reminder.

Mercy swallowed her indignation, casting her aunt a desperate glance. But the determined gleam in her aunt's eye left her no room to argue. She forced the words out, each syllable dripping with reluctant disdain. "Thank you."

Connor's smile deepened, a mockery of triumph. "My pleasure. You sound as though you've swallowed a frog, Miss Mercy."

Turning to the door, he offered one final bow to Aunt Charity and a word of counsel to Mercy. "Do try to stay out of trouble. The next man might not be as forgiving as I."

As his footsteps retreated and the carriage wheels rumbled away, Mercy seethed. Glaring at the closed entry door, her mind raced with plans. Whatever it took, she would not fail again.

Chapter Five

Richmond, Virginia – August 1861

Percival marched off under General Beauregard in July and returned weeks later, eager to recount every gruesome detail of the Battle of Bull Run. Though the Union Army advanced early on, Confederate reinforcements under General Jackson turned the tide by evening, forcing a retreat to Washington. Percival relives the battle daily, and I've taken to keeping young Mercy upstairs, occupied and shielded from his talk. She's precocious, curious about everything, and a welcome distraction from the horrors of war.

Percival believes victory for the Confederacy is inevitable, but I remain unconvinced. The Union's retreat is more of a regrouping than a defeat. I know the Northern spirit; they will not yield so easily, no matter what my husband says about their lack of fortitude. My heart aches for all who've lost someone, on either side. Right or wrong, we are burying fathers and sons. How did our nation come to this? –Grace Bennett

****

Connor guided the carriage away from the ramshackle little cottage, the wheels crunching on cobblestones as his mind sifted through the revelations of his unexpected visit. Though the two women hadn't realized it, their words and silences revealed more than they intended. Within minutes of stepping into their meager home, he uncovered the truth. The frail aunt and her evident lack of medical care were Mercy's Achilles' heel, the lever her uncle used to bind her.

A wry chuckle escaped as he recalled the fiery blaze in her eyes when he tossed the coins onto their battered table. That flash of pure, unbridled outrage lit her entire being. For a fleeting moment, he imagined offering a small fortune in gold, just to provoke her again and see how bright her rage would burn.

Lord, she had been magnificent in her fury. Why the thought brought him such unexplainable joy, he couldn't say, but it warmed a corner of his soul long left cold.

The memory transported him to a distant echo of his past and his sister Madelaine's shriek of rage when he severed one of her braids. Her cries of indignation ricocheted through their family home until their mother appeared to investigate. And, of course, to administer swift justice. But the warmth of that innocent memory dimmed, replaced by the hard edges of the present.

The city unfolded before him, a relentless sprawl of decay and despair. The Lower East Side stretched like a wound refusing to heal, its peeling facades and shattered windows mirroring the broken spirits of those who dwelled there. Weary, hollow-eyed faces drifted past with their burdens etched into the stoop of their shoulders. The weight of it all pressed against Connor's chest, an ache he had long since grown accustomed to. He couldn't save everyone, but he could fight to make this cruel world a little less dangerous.

Ten years in the shadows as a spy, dozens of criminals either buried in the ground or rotting in cells, and yet the tide of villainy surged on. Every victory felt like a fleeting ripple in an endless sea of darkness. The

Phantom, a specter of cunning and cruelty, loomed in his thoughts. Catching him would be the pinnacle of his career. Once he had the bastard, it would be enough. But even as the thought formed, the hollow ache grew.

His mother's voice drifted through his mind, soft and pleading from their last meeting. *"Get married, son, and make me a grandmother."* The words clung to him like cobwebs, delicate but inescapable.

He grinned then and teased her. "My brothers give you grandbabies by the dozen. What more could you want?"

Her response struck a chord deep within him. *"I want you to be happy, Connor. And holding your child, born of love, would make my world complete."* Her blue eyes, brimming with sincerity, pierced through his defenses, twisting his gut in ways he couldn't explain.

He kissed her cheek and turned away, unable to tell the truth. She didn't know about the vow he had made over his father's lifeless body, nor the dangers shadowing his every step. To tell her would only break her heart, and so he bore her quiet disappointment in silence.

Shaking off the lingering regret, his thoughts returned to Mercy Jackson. Her sharp tongue and unwavering certainty, as she called him a rascal and murderer, lingered in his mind like an itch he couldn't scratch. Too many criminals swore vengeance as he brought them to justice. If one of them uncovered his true identity, his entire family would be at risk.

His brothers, all skilled lawmen, had their ghosts and battles to fight. They understood the stakes and guarded their families with fierce devotion. But his mother and Madelaine? They lived alone and refused to share his or his brothers' roofs, leaving the women vulnerable in ways that made his heart clench.

As the city's grim shadows closed in around him, Connor resolved one thing: if protecting those he loved meant staying in the darkness, then so be it. For the first time since leaving the cottage, the fire in Mercy's eyes wasn't what haunted him, but the knowledge the stakes had never been higher.

Connor resolved to speak with General Cooper. Since the women refused the sanctuary of his home and that of his brothers, an additional operative or two embedded among the servants would provide additional protection. It was a long shot, but better than leaving them vulnerable. His countless attempts to sway them met with continual disappointment.

The carriage jolted, snapping him from his thoughts. His attention drifted to the window, and narrowed when an unusual dark carriage rolled past. Its wheels, driver, and even the drapes cloaking the windows were shrouded in somber black. The entire vehicle exuded an eerie dullness, a perfect instrument for espionage under the veil of night. It bore none of the polished gleam betraying most carriages in the moonlight.

Connor leaned forward for a better look, his brow furrowing. They were nearing the wharf, with its salty air and bustling chaos. He leaned further out, catching another fleeting glimpse before sinking back into his seat. The vehicle was an affront to good sense, a harbinger of death and despair, as if a storm cloud followed in its wake, shielding its inhabitants from any trace of light.

Theories flitted through his mind. A thief's covert transport? A medical examiner ferrying bodies? Or a

Phantom in route to meet his shadowy conspirators. Connor bolted upright, his pulse quickening.

Without hesitation, he rapped on the carriage roof. "Turn around. Follow that carriage."

His driver obeyed, the wheels creaking as they pivoted to give chase. Pulling back the velvet drapes, Connor scoured both sides of the street, his eyes flitting from alleyways to bustling storefronts. But the black carriage had vanished, slipping into the city like a ghost dissolving into mist. For hours, they prowled the waterfront's labyrinth of streets and alleys, their search growing more desperate as the minutes ticked by.

By the time his gold watch chimed noon, frustration burned through him. The Phantom's carriage, or whatever unholy equipage he chased, disappeared, swallowed by the crowded streets as if it never existed. Glancing at his gold watch, he bit out a sharp expletive and clenched his jaw. He had no time to continue the hunt. An appointment with General Cooper awaited, and the previous night's events required his full attention.

As the carriage veered toward home, Connor cursed under his breath. His anger didn't fade when they arrived at the mansion, and his driver stopped behind a gilded driving coach. The ornate wheels gleamed in the sunlight, and a name sprang to his mind.

Gabrielle. Damn.

Bounding up the steps of his two-story brick mansion, he masked his frustration with a cool, deliberate stride.

The heavy oak door creaked open, and Benson stood waiting. With a practiced air, the butler extended his hands, ready to take Connor's hat and coat. "Welcome home, sir."

The older man's voice carried a weight of decorum and unspoken judgment. A slight frown etched his weathered face, the sunlight from the open door catching the silver threading through his meticulous hair. Stepping forward, he closed the heavy oak door with quiet finality. Dressed in a formal black uniform with satin wing collars, a starched white shirt, and sharply creased trousers, Benson presented the epitome of restraint and propriety. His disapproving glance toward the staircase betrayed his unspoken thoughts.

"The young lady has arrived."

His clipped and deliberate tone accompanied a slight tilt of his chin, raising his nose to a condescending height. "She came unannounced and lingered for over an hour, sir. I sat her in the blue salon and asked her to wait. When I returned with refreshments, she could not be found. Mary discovered her on the second floor, in your old room." Disdain coated his words, leaving no doubt about his opinion of the guest's audacity.

Connor's mouth twitched. If Benson had his way, he would chase Gabrielle out with a fire poker, dignity be damned.

"I shall manage the matter, Benson. Thank you." Connor replied, his tone dry and measured.

Curiosity and irritation mingled as he ascended the stairs two at a time. Gabrielle's midday visit baffled him, but her choice to trespass on the second floor added a layer of intrigue. Whatever brought her here would be trouble wrapped in silk and mischief.

He strode down the corridor, his footsteps brisk against the polished wood. Reaching the doorway, he halted.

Inside, Gabrielle lounged in his favorite leather

chair, her posture languid, her expression wistful as she stared out the window. The golden light outlined her figure in a halo, a serene image at odds with his simmering annoyance. Her maid, Prudence, a dour-faced older woman with a sharp nose, glared from her position behind the chair.

"Good afternoon, Gabrielle." His voice, sharp as a blade, sliced through the quiet. "This is a surprise, and an even greater one to find you on the second floor of my home, uninvited."

One eyebrow arched as he studied her.

She turned toward him, her smile a blend of charm and mischief. "Why wouldn't I be?" Her lilting tone treated his reproach as little more than idle banter. "We'll refinish this room as a nursery once we're wed."

Her blue eyes sparkled beneath thick lashes, and her red lips curved into a wide smile. She wore a pale blue day dress mirroring the color of her eyes, her vibrant red hair piled high beneath a jaunty blue-and-white hat. With deliberate grace, she uncrossed her legs and rose, her movements fluid as she strolled toward him.

"I waited forever, darling. I'm so pleased you've come home." Purring like a kitten with a bowl of cream, she wrapped her hands around his arm.

"Mr. Calhan, I will thank you to remove your hand from my mistress at once." Prudence advanced with all the grace of a cow on a ballroom floor, her brow knitted in a frown.

Connor's jaw tightened, his teeth grinding at Gabrielle's use of the endearment and her maid's offensive nasal tone.

Making a point to remove Gabrielle's hands from his arm, he narrowed his eyes in a silent warning. "For there to be a marriage, Gabrielle, a proposal must come first. And we both know that will never happen. Our arrangement remains platonic and will never change. Do not roam my home uninvited again. Either of you."

He glanced around the room, scrutinizing every detail for signs of disruption, but nothing appeared out of place.

"Don't be so dull, darling." Gabrielle's voice dropped to a silky drawl, as if his words held no more weight than a passing breeze. Brushing his denial aside, she traced a line down his arm with her forefinger. "We'll marry before the year is out, have two children, and live happily ever after, as they say." With a delicate shrug, she reached for his lapel, her gloved fingers brushing the fabric as she flicked away an imaginary speck of dust. "Why shouldn't I stroll through my future home and dream?"

Connor pressed his lips into a thin line and narrowed his eyes. Her tinkling laughter made him want to choke her. God, she could be irritating.

"When I marry, *if* I marry, I will decide the time, the person, and what becomes of my home," Connor spoke in a sharp, clipped voice, hoping she listened this time. "Until such day, you will remain on the first floor, in the room my butler assigns. Should you choose otherwise, I will instruct the servants to deny you entry altogether. Is that clear? We've had this discussion before, and I see no reason to revisit it. You know my feelings on the matter. As well as my insistence you use my name and refrain from over-familiarity. Now, shall we retrieve your coat?"

He extended his arm, the gesture smooth but unyielding.

Gabrielle's blue eyes flashed with fury, sharp as lightning, before a placid smile replaced it. "Of course, darling." Her smooth voice was nothing more than honey over a storm of defiance.

"My name is *Connor*." His irritation surfaced like cracks in stone. No matter how often he rebuffed her endearments, she persisted, as if her will could bend him to her liking.

"Of course, *darling*," Gabrielle repeated, drawing out the word with deliberate insolence.

"Bloody hell." Frustration curled in his chest like a brewing hurricane. How much more forceful could he be about his reluctance to marry?

By the time they reached the foyer, Benson waited with a faint smile as he helped Gabrielle into her coat. The butler's satisfaction flickered beneath his professional demeanor.

"Good day, miss." Benson intoned with a hint of amusement; his aged eyes alight when Gabrielle narrowed hers at him.

Connor escorted her to her waiting carriage with Prudence clumping behind.

Glancing toward the overcast sky, he frowned. Damn her. She had stolen time he didn't have, and now he would be late for his meeting with General Cooper.

At the carriage step, Gabrielle paused, one foot poised on the stool as Connor assisted her. Her gloved hand lingered on his. "Despite your foul mood and unkind words, I shall forgive you." Following her announcement, she gave him a dazzling smile and sank onto the red velvet seat with all the elegance of a queen assuming her throne. "And I will allow you to escort me to the Governor's Ball tomorrow evening."

Connor's brow climbed, incredulous over her boldness. "I have no intention of attending." He informed her in a flat tone. But the steel in his voice slid off her like rain on polished glass.

Unbothered, she continued as though he hadn't voiced his objection. "You must. You gave your word to my father. Do not forget to wear your red waistcoat, Connor." Purring with satisfaction, his name rolled off her tongue like a practiced seduction. "My seamstress poured hours into embroidering the front to my specifications. It would be a terrible disappointment if you failed to wear it. For her…and for me."

Connor helped her maid into the carriage and closed the door, not bothering to answer.

With a final, triumphant smile, she tapped the side of her carriage, and it rolled forward, crunching over the cobblestones.

He stood there, his fists clenching at his sides, wishing he could throttle her. She had been correct. He gave his word to her father, and Gabrielle wasted no opportunity to remind him.

Her unshakable audacity only solidified his resolve to remain a bachelor. Women, he decided, were a vexation he could do without. His scowl deepened as an image intruded on his thoughts, a pair of green eyes and a heart-shaped face refusing to be banished.

Something about Mercy Jackson disturbed his equilibrium in ways he couldn't quite explain. Most thieves would have slammed the door in his face or bolted outright, yet she had done neither. Surprise, indignation, and a flicker of apprehension played across her features before she pulled him into her home with intriguing defiance. Not once during his pointed conversation with her frail aunt had Mercy displayed guilt or repentance. He would stake his finest ship that she intended to trespass on his property again.

Banishing both women from his thoughts with a shake of his head, Connor strode to his chamber to change, his boots echoing against the polished floor. The general awaited his report, and distraction had no place in his schedule.

Minutes later, freshly dressed, Connor saddled his gelding and set out for headquarters. The brisk ride cleared his mind and sharpened his focus for what lay ahead. He bypassed the warehouse in favor of a hidden room tucked behind a bookstore on Fifth Avenue, where the Unified Intelligence Agency conducted its most sensitive affairs.

Striding into General Cooper's office, Connor settled into the chair opposite his commander and recounted the events of the night before. He described his encounter with Mercy Jackson, his suspicions about her intentions, and the troubling appearance of the dull black carriage that vanished like smoke.

As he spoke, he toyed with the end of a pen resting on the desk. The unusual carriage lingered in his mind like a puzzle refusing to align.

"I doubt the carriage holds the answer you seek." General Cooper's rough voice cut through the silence. "If I were the Phantom, I'd avoid theatrics. A new carriage, a pleasant smile, and attendance at social events would better mask my movements. And I suspect he'll be at the Governor's Ball tomorrow night." A thoughtful expression crossed his face.

Connor opened his mouth to protest, but the general raised a hand, silencing him. "I know you detest such functions, but your attendance is critical. The Phantom will be there, keeping you within sight while remaining out of reach. You'll observe, take note of every guest, and we'll sift through them one at a time. We've hunted this shadow long enough to know he won't slip up in obvious ways."

The general leaned back in his chair, propping his polished boots on the desk's edge. A thick plume of cigar smoke curled into the air. "Keep your back to the wall. We know word of the parchment reached the right ears. Your little thief wouldn't have risked breaking into your warehouse otherwise. As for her assessment of your character, I doubt she knows about your affiliation with the Unified Intelligence Agency. Either way, take no chances. We cannot fight this war on multiple fronts and expect to win."

Connor nodded, his mind racing. "If revenge is the motive, Mercy Jackson carries the torch. Her aggression complicates everything. I want the Phantom, not some pretty thief he hired as a distraction. Sending a woman is the act of a coward, and I can't let her disrupt the mission."

The general's eyes narrowed. "Then don't."

The words echoed in Connor's head as he rode home. The command sounded simple, but Mercy Jackson had weaseled her way into his thoughts. When the sun dipped below the horizon, and he strolled up to his chamber, fatigue clawed at his resolve.

Extinguishing the lamp beside his bed, he closed his eyes, but rest eluded him. Visions of green eyes, a heart-shaped face, and untamed curls danced in the darkness, mocking his efforts to dismiss her.

"Damn. Damn. Damn." Punching his pillow in

frustration, he rolled to his other side, determined to dream about something other than her. Another hour passed before sleep claimed him, though her image lingered, a specter refusing to be ignored.

Chapter Six

Mill Springs, Kentucky, January 1862
The echoes of our victory under General George
Thomas at Mill Springs still hang in the frigid air. We
struck a hard blow to the Confederacy in Pulaski County,
and though pride stirs at this early triumph, the sight of
the fallen haunts me. Connor, my eldest, serves as a
courier between the front and Washington, steady and
sharp. I trust his caution. Max rides under General
Sherman, his letters marked with resolve and rising
esteem in the ranks. Reese serves under Grant, who calls
him "a model soldier." Their bravery humbles me, even
as dread coils in my chest each night with the cries of the
wounded.

At home, Maggie is my anchor. Her devotion, her
tireless efforts gathering supplies for our men, and her
steady stream of loving letters remind me daily of all I
fight for. Our daughter, Madelaine, helps tend to young
Chase, whose wild spirit never tires. I dream of peace, of
my son's return, our home whole again, and Maggie's
warm hands in mine. May God bring this cruel war to a
swift and merciful end. –Major Jonathan Calhan
****

"I want gold-etched dinner plates at our wedding,
Connor, and an ocean of champagne." Gabrielle's eyes
gleamed with the indulgence of her vision. "When I told
Mr. Simpson of my plans, the wretched man dared to

assure me there would be no wedding. He despises me, Connor. After we're married, I shall burn your horrible little accountant."

Connor's brows knitted together, his patience already fraying. "Burn him? You mean fire?"

"Yes. Fire." Dabbing her lips with a fine linen napkin, she signaled for more wine.

"You shall do no such thing. Simpson remains on my payroll and shall continue to do so regardless of your opinion." He leaned back in his chair, the clamor of the Governor's Ball grating against his nerves. He ignored Benson's wise counsel to stay home, allowing the general's insistence to sway him, and now he regretted his decision. Gabrielle's relentless chatter bored him like a persistent drumbeat, and the thought of fleeing to the solace of the balcony tempted him. Yet he knew the futility of escape. Gabrielle would follow him, as unrelenting as the sunrise.

As Gabrielle prattled on about her fantastic wedding plans, Connor fought the urge to reach for a glass of whiskey. Or several. The evening dragged on, every second stretching into eternity.

"Our wedding shall be the event of the year, despite your disagreeable employee."

Connor fixed Gabrielle with a look so sharp it could cut glass. His voice dropped to a low growl, each word deliberate. "If you meddle with my staff again, I refuse to escort you to another event. Your reputation, Gabrielle, will be in your hands."

The steely edge in his tone carried across the room, drawing the startled glances of several onlookers.

Her eyes widened, her practiced composure cracking for the briefest moment. "But you cannot. My father asked you for another three months." She breathed the words as she stared at him, the faintest tremor in her voice betraying her disbelief.

"I can, and I will." He wouldn't budge on this issue. "I have not agreed to his proposal. Mention our arrangement once more, and I shall walk out the door. The prospect of a quiet evening before my hearth holds more appeal by the second."

Her lips pursed into a pout, her arsenal of charms deploying in rapid succession. She cajoled, wheedled, and batted her lashes in a desperate bid to sway him, but Connor held firm. Beneath her porcelain facade lay a manipulative streak he could no longer abide. Were it not for his need to maintain appearances, he would sever their ties without hesitation or regret.

The remainder of the evening unraveled in a haze of emotional theatrics, each turn of Gabrielle's mood testing Connor's strained patience. As he sipped his wine, his eyes scanned the room, cataloging the faces of the men in attendance. Amid the sea of evening wear and polished brass, one figure arrested his attention. A man whose silver-streaked black hair framed a face of stark angles, with a hawk-like nose and gleaming hazel eyes that missed nothing.

Intrigued, Connor approached, his curiosity piqued. When he requested an introduction, the man hesitated, a flicker of unease rippling across his features. "I am General…Jones." His slight pause betrayed a falsehood.

The darting gaze and the shallow intake of breath were the tells of deception. Connor's lips curled into a polite smile, his hand extending in welcome to mask his suspicions. "General." The word carried enough weight to suggest he believed the lie. Although he did not.

The rest of the evening dissolved too quickly for Connor's liking. The room's vibrant chatter and clinking glasses were a blur of sound and motion. The general's veneer of confidence intrigued him, his elusive nature sparking a desire to probe deeper.

After mentioning he moved the parchment to his home, he searched the general's face for a reaction. But the man remained stoic.

Acting on impulse, Connor extended an invitation. "Join me for dinner tomorrow evening at my home." With a warm tone, he cast his net into dark waters to see what he caught. "I must avoid social functions for a time and stay home to guard certain valuable assets."

General Jones inclined his head, accepting the invitation with the faintest hint of reluctance.

Satisfied, Connor turned on his heel, his mind crafting questions he would ask under the guise of civility. To fortify his plans, he invited other acquaintances to dinner, making sure to mention he moved the parchment.

As the time grew late, he informed Gabrielle of his intention to leave.

She made a fuss, until he stated if she didn't get in, he would leave her to ride with her father. The two didn't get on well together, and Connor knew the threat of riding in Francios Blanchart's ancient carriage in full view of New York's elite would put the evening into perspective.

Which it did. She beat him to his carriage by twenty feet. Climbing beside him without so much as a glance in his direction, the air around her bristled with unspoken fury, which her maid amplified with a grunt of disapproval.

The following silence held a sliver of victory, though Connor knew better than to savor it. When they arrived at Blanchart House, Gabrielle fled the carriage without a backward glance, her tears glinting in the gaslight as she ascended the stairs.

Connor exhaled, running a hand over his face. She had an unparalleled knack for fraying his nerves. The general's sharp, practical advice echoed in his mind.

Half a dozen eligible men lingered in his social orbit, each one in need of a wife. With the right maneuvering, Gabrielle could secure a sound match, and he would be free of her theatrics.

"I'm hosting a dinner tomorrow evening." Calling after her retreating figure, he waited for her reaction. "Your father will be there, along with several of my business acquaintances. I expect you to join us. A carriage will collect you at seven. Dinner will be served at eight."

Gabrielle's voice, strong despite her tears, sliced through the night. "Don't bother. I won't come."

Connor remained rooted where he stood, his patience worn thin. "The men I've invited are very wealthy."

Gabrielle froze mid-stride, her hand resting on the brass door handle. She turned, her eyes glittering with curiosity masked by feigned indignation. "They have more money than you?"

"Yes." Although ruthless, cunning, and ambitious, the men he invited were considered formidable in business, but against Gabrielle's arsenal, they wouldn't stand a chance.

Her expression softened, mischief creeping into her features like sunlight breaking through clouds. "I'll come, but only if you apologize." Lifting her chin in challenge, she crossed her arms and tapped her slipper against the stone step.

Prudence glowered beside her, mimicking her mistress's displeasure.

Connor's lips twitched. "I apologize."

Gabrielle's face brightened, and her pout transformed into a radiant, triumphant smile. "Be here at seven sharp. I refuse to be kept sitting."

"Waiting?" He supplied the correct word, but the door slammed, cutting off their conversation. Shaking his head, Connor muttered under his breath, "Women."

The next morning, he arrived at his warehouse and collected his tools to change the locks. Mercy proved they were inadequate, and Connor had no intention of leaving the place vulnerable to less benevolent visitors.

Halfway through replacing the first lock, Jefferson Swift, his manager, approached with an urgent expression. "The general sent word. Another chest has been found, this one in Pennsylvania."

Connor cursed and nodded. "I brought my map home last night in case another thief came calling. Let me speak to Max about finishing the locks, and I'll head there as soon as I retrieve it."

Jefferson gave a curt nod and disappeared into the bustle of the warehouse, leaving Connor to put his tools away and take the stairs two at a time in search of his brother. Minutes later, he swung into the saddle, his horse's hooves kicking up gravel as he urged it into a gallop. The wind tore at his hair, but his focus remained unshaken as he hurried home. Reining in behind his house, he slid from the saddle and looped the reins over the hitching post.

His boots echoed against the kitchen floor as he dashed inside, cutting through the familiar warmth of the house with purpose. Taking the stairs two at a time, he reached his bedchamber and flung open the door, expecting the undisturbed stillness of his private retreat. Instead, the sight before him stopped him cold.

His belongings lay scattered in a chaotic heap on the floor. And there, with her head and shoulders buried in his wardrobe, a rounded feminine figure greeted him, her posterior protruding with unmistakable audacity. Recognition swept over him in an instant. Even from this angle, there could be no mistaking the intruder.

"What in God's name are you doing?" Stepping over his discarded formal jacket, he advanced on the invader.

The rustle of silk drew his attention, and a familiar face emerged, flushed scarlet, eyes wide with guilt. Mercy, her green eyes glinting with a mix of defiance and panic, clutched one of his finest silk shirts in her trembling hands.

"Why…why aren't you at the dock?" She stammered, her voice faltering. Tendrils of hair escaped her prim bun, curling against her damp neck and reddened cheeks. Her chest rose and fell with labored breaths, her composure unraveling before his eyes.

Connor's interest dropped to the heaving fullness of her chest, a discovery he hadn't accounted for when he'd mistaken her for a boy. The realization both irritated and intrigued him. "Let go of my shirt before you shred it."

To his astonishment, she obeyed, the fine silk pooling at his feet. Undeterred, she tugged his velvet vest from the wardrobe and began rummaging through its pockets.

"What are you doing in my home? And more importantly, my bedchamber?" His voice sharpened as he folded his arms, avoiding the temptation to throttle her scrawny neck. "How did you get past Benson?"

Her defiant chin tilted upward, her blush deepening to a shade he might have found charming under different circumstances. "Benson doesn't know I'm here." Her declaration came out in a steady voice despite the turmoil in her eyes. Dropping his vest onto the growing pile of disarray, she mirrored his stance, folding her arms and meeting his glare head-on.

Connor studied her throat, where her pulse fluttered like a trapped bird. "No, of course, he doesn't. Not if you made it up the stairs and into my private quarters without him tossing you out on your backside. I'll have to discuss this lapse with him." His words dripped with disdain, though he found her obvious agitation amusing. "You're here for the parchment." His statement sliced through the thickening tension. "The one you claim ignorance of."

She shrugged, an infuriating gesture of indifference. "I admit nothing. Everything I know about the document I learned from you. I came in the other night to get warm, nothing more."

He barked a humorless laugh, the sound echoing in the room. "Oh? And today? What's the excuse this time? Too cold? Too hungry? Or simple curiosity?" His dry tone made her green eyes snap up to meet his, their fire unmistakable.

"I lost my knife." Delivered in a clipped voice as she bent to retrieve the item from the inner pocket of his navy woolen jacket. Straightening, she waved the article in triumph.

Connor ran a hand through his hair, frustration

surging through him.

Her lies danced with the same audacity as her resourcefulness, and she impressed him despite his fury. "You're lying."

Her brow arched, the corner of her mouth curving in a wry challenge. "Am I? I came for my knife. Now that we've been reunited, I'll be on my way."

His jaw tightened as he fought the urge to seize her by the shoulders. "I could have you arrested." He kept his voice low and edged with a warning. Yet even as the words left his mouth, he had no intention of following through with the threat. He wanted repentance, or remorse, any sign the troublemaker possessed a shred of accountability.

Instead, her eyes sparked with defiance, her chin lifting as if daring him to try. "You could," she conceded.

Connor stared at her, weighing his next move. This woman, with her fire and insolence, stormed into his life like a tempest, leaving chaos in her wake. And yet, for reasons he couldn't yet fathom, the idea of her leaving left him colder than the thought of her staying.

"But you won't." Mercy stared up at him, her voice as steady as a blade. "Who would care for Aunt Charity?" Tilting her head, she waited for his response. "And it is my knife."

Connor stepped back, uncurling his fists to stave off the maddening urge to strangle her or kiss her. Either action promised a certain satisfaction, but neither would answer the questions swirling in his mind. "If you asked for your knife back like any respectable woman, I would have handed it over without hesitation. What truly intrigues me is why you are in my home? I've given you coins and ensured Miss Charity receives care from my doctor, removing whatever leverage your employer holds over you. If you end up in prison for theft, the blame will be on your shoulders. Not mine. If you keep on, it is a matter of time."

Her mouth opened, but he raised a hand to silence her. "Do not insult my intelligence with another lie, Miss Mercy. I know why you came back. But I do wonder how your employer will react when you fail to retrieve the parchment yet again."

The faintest flicker of fear flashed in her eyes, and his gut tightened like a vise. Just as he suspected. He would have her shadowed until she led him to the bastard pulling her strings.

Mercy's lips pressed into a grim line, defiance burning in her expression. "I told you. I came to retrieve my knife. And if I were interested in this mysterious document you're obsessed with, I wouldn't take it for the money. I want nothing to do with your tainted coins. Auntie accepted them, which shocked me as much as your parting with them, you blackguard. Now she remembers you in her prayers, God help me." She lifted her chin, green eyes flashing. "But understand this, Mr. Calhan, I'm made of sterner fabric than Aunt Charity. Your money won't win me."

No woman had questioned his honor with such audacity, and the sting sharpened his anger. His voice dropped, cold and clipped. "Never call me a blackguard again. I allowed your earlier insults to pass unanswered, but showing mercy is an obvious mistake. I don't know you, nor why you're so eager to paint me as the villain in this tale, but hear me well. If I find you anywhere near my family, my property, or my possessions again, there will be consequences. You've insulted me twice, and I demand to know why."

****

Mercy took note of the tick in his cheek and the taut line of his jaw, obvious signs she had gone too far. Letting her temper fly and flinging accusations like arrows might not have been the wisest course, no matter what she knew of his sins. She couldn't be arrested for retrieving her possession. She forgot she left it on his office floor in her haste to depart that night, and when she discovered it in his jacket pocket, she thanked the stars she located the item. But curse the fates for sending him home in the middle of the morning. Another couple of rooms to go through, and she would have left. Instead, he caught her red-handed, rifling through his wardrobe like a common thief. She bit her lip, her mind racing for a plausible excuse.

His mouth tightened further, his stare unrelenting. "Well?" He issued his demand in a tone as sharp as ice.

Mercy drew a deep breath, summoning courage she didn't possess. "Fine." Keeping her voice steady despite the wild beating of her heart. "You win. I came for the document you mentioned. It holds personal value for me." Her mind raced with stories to tell him should he ask. "I lost someone, and the parchment lists those responsible." Uncle Justice assured her the parchment contained the names of the men responsible for her mother's death. Union soldiers ravaged the weak and innocent under the command of Connor's father, Jonathon Calhan.

The words hung between them; a partial explanation offered like a fragile olive branch. She waited, tense and uncertain, for his response, knowing full well she had only begun to peel back the layers of the confrontation looming ahead. The less said, the better.

Connor's expression grew thoughtful. He studied her for long minutes before giving her a curt nod. His hostility dropped like a stone in the ocean. "At last, I receive a bit of truth." Picking up his best woolen dinner jacket, he tossed it on the bed and gave a shrill whistle. "I know the pain of loss, and I shall be lenient this one last time. But I stand by what I said earlier, Miss Jackson. There will be unpleasant consequences if you come near me or my property again. For now, allow me to introduce my butler, Benson."

The old man gave a sharp knock on the door and entered. His expression turned from polite attendance to cold disbelief in seconds. "You whistled, sir?" His voice contained all the warmth of an arctic breeze as he stared at Mercy.

His smile didn't reach his eyes. "Allow me to introduce Miss Mercy Jackson. This is the second time she has broken into my property. Please escort her to the front door and see her out. Oh, and Benson? Have both locks replaced and men stationed by every door. I shudder to think what other unpleasant things this devious young woman has planned."

With a doleful glance at the heap of clothing on the floor, a very unhappy butler gave a stiff nod and escorted her from the room.

"Goodbye, Miss Jackson, and may we never have the misfortune to meet again."

Connor Calhan's deep voice followed her down the corridor, and her chest tightened. Now what?

Her uncle hadn't been pleased when he visited her last evening and discovered she didn't have the parchment. "I will give you one more chance, Niece. Do not let me down again. My source informs me that Connor Calhan moved the parchment to his home for better security after you bungled the job." Her uncle's pepper-black hair glinted in the candlelight of Aunt Charity's drawing room, and the shadows cast dark smudges beneath his eyes, giving him a sinister appearance. Mercy dared not contemplate her punishment if she failed a second time.

Brought back to the present by the butler's icy demeanor, she grimaced when he all but set her outside and slammed the door on her behind. "Goodbye, miss."

Not goodbye. She would never concede the battle until she had the parchment rolled up in her hand.

As she trudged down the cobblestone drive toward the road, two grooms passed her, leading two dappled mares. They touched their caps and continued their conversation.

"Mr. Calhan said to have the carriage ready at six thirty tonight. We are to collect Miss Blanchart at seven sharp and bring her here. The party starts at eight, so we will be busy with horses after. Mrs. Briggs said she would serve us supper at six. Trust me, John, now is the best time to see your girl. You will have all afternoon to go courting. Who knows what time the party will end, and you don't want Mary angry with you."

Mercy didn't hear the reply as she picked up her speed. The good Lord planned to help her after all. For two days now, she had serious doubts. If she hurried through her chores and got Aunt Charity settled for the night, she had three hours of freedom to sneak inside and remove the parchment from under Connor Calhan's nose. There were two rooms she hadn't searched, and they wouldn't take any time at all.

Hope blossomed in her chest like a rose in the sun. As she whistled for a hackney, a smile curved her lips, and she wanted to sing. Everything would be all right after all.

Satisfaction settled over her as she stepped into the carriage and gave the driver one of Connor Calhan's coins to take her home.

It was poetic justice that her enemy's coins paid her way so she could rob him of something more precious than his wealth.

Tonight would be a good night, indeed.

Chapter Seven

Richmond, Virginia, May 1862
Tonight, I discovered a terrifying truth. When I went
to fetch a drink for little Mercy, I noticed light spilling
from Percival's study and crept closer, only to overhear
a shocking conversation. Relaxed among familiar
neighbors, and my brother Justice, who has been missing
for months, Percival spoke of a plot to kidnap President
Lincoln and assassinate him to force the Union's
surrender. I gasped in surprise and came close to
revealing my presence.

Justice's sudden appearance in the corridor forced
me to greet him with feigned warmth, though his
coldness chilled me far more than the war raging
outside. He broke the news of our father's death with
heartless calm.

Grief threatened to betray me, but I dared not falter
under Percival's watchful eye. His fury at my late return
to the room brought harsh threats and a demand I return
to my chamber. I spent a sleepless night, torn between
mourning my father and dreading the evil plan unfolding
under my roof. The knowledge Justice, once kind, now
supports murder, sickens me. Morning came with
Mammy's tea, but no comfort. Thank God, Mercy is too
young to understand the darkness closing in around us.
Even I, a grown woman, cannot comprehend it. –Grace
Bennett

****

Connor's talk with the general didn't go as expected. Frustration churned in his chest as he hurried to the shipping office, hoping this recent discovery would provide him with new information about The Phantom and the Knights. His irritation intensified when he opened the chest and discovered Springfield rifles, stolen from a Union train during the chaos of the Civil War, instead of the bounty he hoped for.

Spreading a weathered map across his desk, he marked the site where the chest had been found and leaned back with a scowl. The pattern he sought refused to take shape. This discovery brought the total to five, each one emerging in places as scattered and peculiar as the secrets they contained.

The first chest came to light in Kentucky, unearthed by a farmer plowing his fields. The second appeared in North Carolina, found by an undertaker preparing to bury a body. The third entered their grasp by sheer accident. A suspected Knight of the Confederacy escaped prison in West Virginia, unwittingly leading a marshal straight to its hiding place. The man believed he had evaded capture, digging up the chest to fund his escape to Asia. His ambitions crumbled the moment the marshal's revolver leveled at his chest, the gold confiscated, and his freedom lost once more.

The fourth surfaced on a Tennessee plantation when an iron plow struck the chest with enough force to make the oxen stumble. Within, the sheriff uncovered gold and yet another letter bearing the defiant mark of the Knights. Each discovery painted a grim picture revealing plans to topple government buildings, foster militias abroad, and reclaim the South through shadowy alliances with The

Phantom's signature branded on every page.

Connor traced the edge of the rifles with his fingers, the rust and grime staining his hands, and disappointment sank like a weight in his gut. This chest contained no note, no clue, nor tie to the Knights or the Phantom. The trail had gone cold. Slamming a fist against the iron-bound crate, he growled through clenched teeth. "Damn it all."

"Precisely my sentiment." General Cooper's voice broke through the silence, his head shaking in weary disbelief. "How did the Governor's Ball fare?"

"Much like this," Connor replied, his tone clipped. "An exercise in futility. However, an unusual guest caught my eye. The man did not mingle and stayed in the corner, observing without participating. Although he dressed and acted the part, he didn't belong."

The general's eyes narrowed. "Trust your instincts. Do you have a plan to learn more about him?"

Connor allowed a faint, sardonic smile. "I invited him to dinner tonight. Along with a few other acquaintances. And Gabrielle." His shoulders lifted in a shrug; the irony was not lost on him. "She refused to attend until I assured her my guests were richer than I." Informing the general of his plans to set another trap, he waited for a response.

General Cooper chuckled. "An eventful evening awaits, then."

"Eventful or disastrous." Connor's mind spun with the possibilities of the night to come.

General Cooper removed the cigar from his mouth, releasing a perfect ring of smoke into the air. His gray eyes lingered on Connor. "I see. And if one of your guests happens to be the Phantom, what's your plan to keep the parchment safe? He could be anyone."

Connor allowed a slow smile to form, though it lacked warmth. "The parchment is hidden where no one will stumble across it. Not even Miss Mercy Jackson, who I found upstairs rifling through my dinner jackets not two hours ago."

"Good God." The general crushed the glowing end of his cigar into the glass dish and let the stub drop. "Word travels fast. Did you have her arrested? I would have."

Connor leaned forward, his body tense. "No. When I confronted her, she claimed the parchment holds the name of the person who killed someone she loves. Tell me, how do I respond when the damned document lists the names of those responsible for *my* father's death, too? I do find it interesting that she knows I moved the parchment to my home so soon. I spread the word last night.:"

The general arched a brow, his expression thoughtful. "And if she returns? The girl has grit. I'll give her that."

Connor nodded, his jaw tightening. "Grit, yes. But that's all I will acknowledge. I made it clear this afternoon that I will have her arrested if she returns. And I doubt she'll slip past Benson a second time."

But Connor's confidence proved misplaced, as the evening would later reveal.

After leaving the general's office, Connor headed straight for the docks. He oversaw the replacement of the locks on the shipping office and ensured every point of entry had been secured. Only then did he return home to prepare for the evening's dinner, his thoughts heavy with suspicion and strategy.

When the clock chimed seven thirty, Gabrielle arrived, although not fashionably late as expected, but on time. Draped in blue silk and an ermine wrap, she stood at his door like a vision conjured from a dream. Or a nightmare. The sight of her, punctual for once, set his thoughts spiraling. Had she been waiting for his carriage? The notion brought a frown to his lips. The world must have tilted while he spoke with the general. And the guests he'd invited, poor, oblivious souls, were unprepared for the tempest Gabrielle's presence promised.

"Good evening." Connor bowed over her gloved hand, keeping his expression neutral. Escorting her to the drawing room, he took his place by the hearth to await the rest of his guests.

As the evening unfolded, Connor moved among the crowd, engaging New York's most notable bachelors and a scattering of other luminaries. His attention, however, remained fixed on the men entering the room, scrutinizing each one. He cast a glance every so often toward the staircase leading to his office, a silent vigil he persisted in until Jefferson Swift intervened.

"Go mingle with your guests." Swift's tone, though light, held determination. "I'll keep an eye out for the Phantom."

Connor handed off his watchful role, offering Swift a brief nod of thanks. Snagging a glass of champagne from a passing waiter, he retreated to a shadowed corner of the room. From there, he surveyed the gathering, his mind as sharp and restless as an unsheathed blade, weighing every face, every word, and every movement against the secrets he sought to uncover.

The moment Gabrielle's heels touched the plush

Persian carpet of the drawing room, she seized a glass of champagne from a passing tray and swept toward the nearest male guest, without a backward glance. Her presence dominated the room like an unchecked flame, her laughter sharp and ringing, slicing through the hum of conversation. To Connor's ears, her laugh grated, her eyes gleamed with greed, and her animated gestures hinted at an appetite far more ravenous than joyous.

From his vantage point, Connor's observation shifted between the grand staircase and General Jones, who lingered among the throng of guests. The general smiled, nodded, and murmured polite agreement with everyone who approached, but not once did he cast a searching glance around the room or slip away under some pretense. Connor's jaw tightened at the man's apparent indifference, his irritation bubbling beneath the surface.

When Max and Lilli arrived, Connor greeted them, noting how they stared at each other with such intimacy they defied the world around them. Their whispers and subtle touches excluded everyone from their private haven. The same golden cocoon of love enveloped Chase and Rose, and again with Reese and Shanna. It surrounded them, a private glow shielding them from the chaos of the evening, and for the first time in thirty-one years, a strange pang gripped Connor, a jealousy he could neither name nor shake.

The night crawled forward, its hours sluggish and heavy. Connor made his excuses and stepped onto the balcony in search of air untainted by perfume and idle chatter. The cool breeze kissed his skin, and for a fleeting moment, he found solace in the stars glittering above.

General Jones turned from the balcony rail, his

expression jovial. "You have an eye for remarkable women. Every lady here deserves a second look."

Connor caught the faint sting of champagne on the man's breath and arched a brow. "If you value your life, I'd avoid looking at my brothers' wives. Reese and Chase aren't known for their forgiving natures. Neither is Max."

The general chuckled, stroking his salt-and-pepper beard with an air of amusement. "I'm neither blind nor foolish. I'm talking about the unaccompanied lady."

Connor's frown deepened. "Gabrielle?"

The general shook his head, his chuckle growing into a hearty laugh. "Everyone knows she's spoken for. I mean the other one."

Connor's lips curled into a dry smirk. "If it's Gabrielle you're after, by all means, court her. You'll have my blessing, and you'll be doing me a great service."

He left his next thought unsaid. Jones would need a spine forged from steel to manage Gabrielle's fire, but Connor saw no reason to warn him. Some lessons, after all, were best learned by experience.

The general shook his head once more, and the gesture sent a fresh wave of unease rolling through Connor.

"Not the Frenchwoman." Amusement tinged his voice. "The attractive brunette with green eyes. She'd make a saint stumble."

Connor's eyes narrowed, his pulse quickening. "When did you see this…enticing mystery woman?" His jaw tightened as he waited for the response, each second dragging like an eternity. If Mercy Jackson dared to break into his home again—

"She climbed from the giant oak over there." The general pointed toward the shadowed tree. "And ran off toward the main road, about fifteen minutes ago—"

Connor didn't wait to hear the rest. He took the stairs two at a time, his chest burning with anger.

"Son of a bloody, rotting bollock!" The sight greeting him in the study halted him in his tracks. The door hung ajar, swinging in the draft. Inside, chaos reigned. Desk drawers had been yanked out and tossed aside, their contents scattered like fallen leaves. Books lay in heaps on the floor, some strewn across the settee in careless disarray. His surveillance halted on the desk where his copy of *The Wealth of Nations* sat open and empty, mocking him.

"She took it." He growled the words as he shot a glance at the window panes swinging wide to let in a biting gust of wind. Fury burned in his throat. How in the hell had she heard about the party?

Crossing to the window, he leaned out into the freezing night air and unleashed a stream of curses in several languages. The oak tree beside the house loomed tall and unyielding, its thick branches brushing the sloped roof. From there, she must have inched her way to the window, which should have been latched but hadn't been.

Benson appeared at his elbow, his face a study of disbelief as he took in the scene. "Who could have done this, sir?"

Connor slammed the window shut with enough force to rattle the panes, flipping the latch as though to seal his frustration. "The same wretched young woman who ransacked my wardrobe earlier today." He bit her name out through clenched teeth. "Miss Jackson."

The cold fury in his voice silenced any further questions from Benson.

Connor turned back to the mess, his mind racing. Mercy Jackson might have escaped, but she wouldn't get far. Not this time.

Benson straightened, his expression a mask of discipline. "But how, sir? I've been diligent in keeping the back door locked." His attention shifted to the window, eyes narrowing with dawning realization. "The window. Molly neglected to latch it after dusting this morning. My deepest apologies, sir."

Connor's sigh carried the weight of his mounting frustration, a sound dragged from the depths of his soul. "We'll need to be careful with this one, Benson. She's clever and bold enough to try anything. But lucky for us, I know where she lives."

"Shall I inform the remaining guests of your departure, sir?" Benson's jaw tightened, and his chin lifted with resolute professionalism, though Connor didn't miss the flash of irritation. Molly would no doubt face a stern lecture before the night ended.

"No. Let them enjoy their dinner, then see them out. Offer my regrets to my brothers, but make it clear I don't know how long I'll be gone."

"Very good, sir." Benson offered a slight nod, asking no further questions. He avoided mentioning Gabrielle, and Connor chose not to bring her up, either. The unspoken understanding hung between them. Her presence, or lack thereof, mattered little in the face of this debacle.

Connor turned, his jaw clenched, the wheels of his mind spinning with grim determination. His hands itched with the thought of wringing Mercy Jackson's neck, without, of course, succumbing to the temptation of killing her.

What a cursed disaster the evening had become.

The thief stole more than one document. She'd stolen his patience, his carefully laid plans, and any hope of salvaging the night. With one last glance at the disheveled room, Connor stalked toward the door, a storm brewing in his wake.

Chapter Eight

Richmond, Virginia, June 1862
Two weeks ago, while delivering a message for
General Cooper, I came upon Union soldiers harassing
a well-dressed woman near the city's edge. Her torn silk
gown and terrified green eyes told me all I needed to
know. Their vulgar threats made their intent clear, and I
stepped in, ordering them back to camp. When
Lieutenant Beil hesitated, I drew my revolver and
threatened court-martial. With reluctance, he obeyed,
and the men withdrew. By God's grace, it ended without
bloodshed.
  The woman, shaken yet composed, refused to share
her name. She spoke of a plantation, her young daughter,
and her yearning to return to family in New York. What
startled me most were her whispered warnings of a plot
to abduct President Lincoln, led by a group called The
Knights of the Confederacy. Though skeptical, I sent
scouts to verify her story. To my shock, it proved true.
And thanks to her courage, we intercepted the
conspirators before they could strike. –Major Jonathon
Calhan

****

The evening unfolded into an unexpected triumph
far exceeding Mercy's wildest hopes. Her muffled but
persistent chuckles bubbled up as she made her way
home, her heart racing with a mix of disbelief and

exhilaration. The parchment lay tucked in her pocket, a prize she had almost given up on claiming.

For agonizing minutes, she scoured Connor's study, her frustration mounting with each overturned drawer and every wasted second. Failure loomed large until her eyes fell upon his well-worn volume of *The Wealth of Nations.* If she wanted to hide something precious, she would have chosen a place as innocuous as the pages of a book, hidden in plain sight, and safe from prying eyes.

Except hers.

Her lips curved into a sly grin at the memory. Mercy had long ago learned to use books for concealment, an effective strategy against Aunt Charity's uncanny knack for unearthing her secrets. Even when the woman wasn't present, her intrusive knowledge lingered like an omnipresent specter.

With steps as quiet as a shadow, Mercy crossed the study, picked up the hefty volume, and tipped it upside-down. The parchment slid free, landing on the desk like a gift from fate. She swallowed a triumphant whoop before tucking the precious document into her pocket and retreating toward the open window.

With practiced ease, she slipped onto the roof, shivering as the cool night air brushed her flushed cheeks. Balancing along the edge, she approached the stout oak tree with its wide-spread branches. Her dress bore the evidence of her daring, streaked with grime and torn at the hem, but she gave it no thought. Victory rendered such trivialities meaningless.

She couldn't help but chuckle at the thought of Connor's reaction when he discovered the parchment was missing. The image of his face twisted in shock and fury brought her no small measure of delight. What an altogether splendid evening at Connor Calhan's expense.

As she descended the oak, her thoughts turned to the treasure now in her possession. Within the folds of the parchment lay the names of her mother's killers. Vindicating her mother's name and uncovering the truth would be rewarding enough, but Mercy had no intention of stopping there. Her ambitions would be fulfilled when the bastards faced justice and she found her mother's gold box.

Mercy imagined the possibilities with giddy anticipation. Aunt Charity chose to donate her gold box to the church, but Mercy had other plans for Mama's. A future brimming with elegance, silk gowns, vibrant petticoats, and satin slippers in every shade imaginable, and a large house awaited. She envisioned living in Manhattan's Upper East Side, its grandeur rivaling her ambitions, where she would host lavish gatherings and turn heads at every social event until some dashing gentleman fell under her spell.

Her lips twitched with satisfaction as she slipped unseen into the night, the promise of retribution and riches sparking like fireworks in her mind. Tonight, she played the part of a thief, but soon, she would step into a life even Aunt Charity's sharp tongue couldn't touch.

Mercy's future unfurled before her like a tapestry of indulgence. She imagined being draped in silks, a child on either side, her household bustling with obedient servants. From the cushioned luxury of her velvet-tufted carriage, she would glide through the streets, nodding with regal air at passersby. She would have a life of effortless grace, finally her own.

Lost in the glow of her daydream, Mercy missed her footing. The branch slipped from her grasp, and she plummeted to the ground with a thud, knocking the wind from her lungs. Sprawled beneath the towering oak, she rolled to her back, drawing in breaths tasting of earth and freedom. The parchment in her pocket felt like a promise, an anchor for the future she only dared to imagine. Her trials would vanish, she thought, as shadows flee the light.

Shaking off the fall, she rose to her feet, brushing dirt from her dress. Glancing upward, she froze, her breath catching when she met a piercing set of hazel eyes studying her with intensity. Framed by black hair streaked with silver, the man stood poised on the second-floor balcony, his expression unreadable. For a long, agonizing moment, he stared down at her, and Mercy's knees threatened to give way.

Bloody buggering hell. She had been caught. Again.

Her heart pounded like a war drum, but the man neither called out nor moved to summon help. Instead, a slow, deliberate smile curved his lips, and he raised a champagne glass in silent salute.

The gesture sent a ripple of fear and disbelief through her. What game did he play? Since she had no intention of lingering to find out, she turned on her heel and bolted, her skirts tangling with her legs as she sprinted down the curved drive. Reaching the corner where her horse waited, she scrambled into the saddle, her legs trembling so hard she came close to toppling off.

Spurring her mount forward, she glanced back once and shouted. "Goodbye, Mr. Calhan! May I never have the pleasure of meeting you again!" The words, borrowed from his barb earlier in the day, tasted both bitter and satisfying. If only she could say them to his face.

But Mercy's triumph crumbled when she stepped into Aunt Charity's cramped kitchen and latched the door behind her. Pivoting, she came face-to-face with her relative.

Clad in her finest day gown, Aunt Charity regarded her with stern disapproval. Her brows furrowed, her lips pressed thin, she moved to the stove and set a kettle of water to boil without a word.

Mercy's stomach sank. She knew better than to ask what soured her aunt's mood. Uncle Justice must have arrived. If she returned home via Stone Street, she would have seen his carriage out front and known to stay away. Now, the reckoning awaited her in the drawing room, where the air would no doubt feel colder than the night outside.

Mercy straightened her spine, for the confrontation she couldn't avoid. But the weight of her stolen victory and the consequences it would bring pressed down on her as she stepped toward her fate.

"Is that you, Mercy?" Her uncle's deep, resonant voice rose from the drawing room, cutting through the stillness.

Mercy paused and drew in a fortifying breath for the battle ahead.

Uncle Justice would no doubt be pleased she acquired the precious document she risked everything to obtain, but his unpredictable nature kept her wary. One never knows what storm might follow in his wake.

"Yes, sir. I'll be right there." Casting a sidelong glance at Aunt Charity as she hung her cloak on the hook by the door and turned to leave.

Her aunt's hand clamped on her arm, halting her retreat. "I know Justice sent you on whatever errand dragged you out of this house tonight." Her aunt spoke in a faint voice. "But mark my words, Connor Calhan is a decent man. I'd wager you broke into his property again, and by the gleam in your eyes, I'd say you succeeded. Well, my girl, I hope you don't live to regret making an enemy of him."

Mercy's jaw dropped in astonishment. "Since when do you care what happens to a Calhan?" Her voice brimmed with incredulity, though she knew the answer well enough. Since Connor's recent visit, Aunt Charity spoke of him with reverence.

Swallowing her frustration, Mercy softened her voice. "I disliked him long before this began. I am on a mission for justice."

"Justice, or *for Justice*?" Aunt Charity's eyes narrowed, her tone cutting like a blade. "Your mother is gone, child, and nothing you do will bring her back. Digging for answers will only stir up hatred and revenge, and those bring nothing but ruin. If it's her gold box you're after, you won't find the truth on the parchment from Connor Calhan's desk, nor in the vile tales your uncle spins. The answer lies in her diary."

Mercy opened her mouth to protest, but Charity raised a finger to her lips, silencing her. She gestured toward the drawing room, her expression unwavering. "One thing you should understand, child. Every story you've heard about my sister's death came from Justice. Only your mother and God know the truth. I once believed Justice's account, as you have, but years of prayer have made me question his version of events."

Mercy stiffened, her throat tightening with indignation. "You would let her killers go unpunished?"

Aunt Charity's serene green eyes met hers. "I leave

judgment to God." Her voice dropped, heavy with conviction. "And you should, also."

The words hung in the air, a challenge Mercy could not accept, as the weight of her choices pressed down on her like a stone.

Fighting to contain the storm of anger and disappointment rising within her took intense concentration. Choking back the urge to lash out, she grabbed the tea tray, containing a mismatched collection of two teacups, a cracked porcelain dish of brown sugar, and a delicate sandwich. Her fingers tightened on the tray as if to anchor her fury. "I'll carry this in for you." She offered through clenched teeth. "And come back for the tea when it's ready."

If she lingered a moment longer, she might give in to her rage. Every fiber of her being rebelled at the meekness her aunt embraced, forgiving what Mercy could never forget. *Mama deserved better.* And by heaven and earth, she would see to it.

She marched into the drawing room, her boots clipping against the polished floor, but halted when her uncle turned from the hearth. His expression, carved in deep lines of disapproval, made her freeze mid-step.

Something, or someone, unsettled him, and worry tightened her stomach.

Dressed in formal linen, his dark hair glinted in the firelight, casting sharp shadows across his face. His gray eyes swept over her with the precision of a blade, cutting deeper with each flicker of distaste. His fists curled at his sides, his composure a taut thread ready to snap.

Mercy forced a smile, although her heart fluttered like a trapped bird. Crossing the room, she placed the tray on the tea table with care. "Good evening, Uncle.

I've brought refreshments." Her voice wavered, betraying the unease simmering beneath her practiced civility.

Uncle Justice regarded her with a thin, humorless smile, his eyes locking onto hers like a predator sizing up its prey. "Were you successful in your assignment?" His voice cut through the air, ignoring her polite overture. "This time?"

"Yes." She managed to answer, though her voice faltered under his scrutiny. Stepping back, she steadied her knees. "I succeeded."

His lip curled, disdain flickering across his face. "I am relieved to hear it. You know how I despise failure. Administering the lash pains me far more than it pains you, but I came prepared to punish another disappointment. How you managed to bungle such a straightforward task is beyond me. I taught you better than this." His interest shifted to the tea tray. "Is *this* the best you can provide?"

Mercy swallowed the lump rising in her throat. "Yes, Uncle. I regret disappointing you."

His frown deepened, carving lines into his stern visage. "And yet, your reckless antics at Mr. Calhan's residence this evening have embarrassed us both. Ripping your gown? Drawing attention to your mission? You were trained to act with precision, to get in, retrieve what you were sent for, and leave without raising suspicion. Your carelessness has put me in a precarious position with my employer. Worse still, I cannot afford the luxury of delay. Mr. Calhan will no doubt come calling, demanding answers, and the return of the parchment. Something my employer will frown upon, and we must be gone before he arrives."

The weight of his words crashed over her, and her mouth dropped open in shock. "You were at Connor's dinner party?" The revelation stole her breath. "And what do you mean, *we* must go? I've no plans to leave this house."

She did, of course. Mercy intended to purchase provisions once her uncle compensated her for the parchment. However, revealing such intentions would not be wise under her current circumstances.

Uncle Justice's scowl darkened, his displeasure sharp enough to send her retreating another step. The air between them grew heavy, each second thick with unspoken tension.

Her mind raced, grasping for a way to navigate the churning waters of his temper without drowning in its wake.

"I did not attend," Justice growled, his eyes narrowing to dangerous slits. "But I am aware of everything concerning that parchment. I have ways of knowing things, Mercy. And right now, I lack the time, or the patience, for any further failures." He stretched out a hand, the demand in his voice sharp as a whip. "Hand it over, girl. We leave now."

Mercy twisted the fabric of her skirt, her knuckles whitening as she summoned every ounce of defiance she possessed. Standing against Uncle Justice felt like staring down a lightning storm. "And who will take care of Aunt Charity?" Her voice wavered despite her resolve. His point about Connor's imminent arrival nagged at her thoughts. Her eyes flickered toward the window, half-expecting to see the towering blond-haired menace charging toward them.

Her uncle snorted, his lips curling into a cruel smirk

as he stepped closer. "That old bat can take care of her own needs. You're coming with me, girl, whether by choice or force. I need you where I can keep a close eye on you."

Mercy opened her mouth to object, but he flexed his fists and his hardened expression silenced her before she could reply.

"I have no desire to be violent." His smooth tone made her shiver with terror. "But if you refuse to submit, you leave me no alternative. And this time, Charity will bear the price of your rebellion."

Her heart sank like a stone, the weight of his threat pressing down on her. He had her cornered, and they both knew it. "Fine." She shouted the word, but it came out as a whisper. "Let me get my cloak."

Aunt Charity stepped into the doorway, her face pale, her back rigid with unspoken fury. Her expression, a mixture of indignation and worry, made it clear she heard every word. Placing the teapot on the tray with deliberate precision, she turned to Mercy, her tone brittle but steady. "Do as he says, Niece. Fetch your things while I serve my brother his tea. And don't fret about me while you're away. Young Thomas will stop by every day."

The mention of Thomas softened the moment. The boy, injured in a carriage accident and now walking with a stick, adored Aunt Charity for nursing him through his recovery. Living only a few houses away, he visited whenever he could and performed small chores in gratitude.

Justice's voice cut through the room like a blade. "Five minutes, or you know the consequences." He sat on the threadbare settee, his posture radiating authority, as he accepted the cup of tea Charity handed him with a smug nod. "And before you go, I will take the parchment."

His interest shifted to Aunt Charity, the threat unspoken but clear, and Mercy's stomach knotted. She longed to study the document and uncover its secrets before surrendering it, but the cold glint in Uncle Justice's eye left no room for argument. Her hand trembled as she slipped it into her pocket.

"Here." The word tasted bitter on her tongue as she placed the parchment in his waiting hand. Her heart ached with a sense of loss, but she buried it beneath a mask of submission. For now.

Chapter Nine

Richmond, Virginia, June 1862
Tragedy has struck my home with cruel force.
Though I long suspected Percival's cruelty toward our
workers, I never imagined the depths of his depravity
until I learned he fathered Mammy's daughter Emma's
unborn child. Emma died after a difficult labor, and the
baby was stillborn. With Percival away, Mammy and I
prepared them for burial and arranged for their
interment at her family's settlement, far from this
accursed place.

But Percival returned unexpectedly, delaying
Mammy's departure. I took the bodies, escorted by two
male servants, only to be ambushed by Union soldiers on
our return. They killed my companions and threatened
vile harm until a Union officer intervened. I took
advantage of the moment and related my husband's plot
to abduct President Lincoln. Calhan promised to
investigate. I cannot undo the suffering, but I have
prevented greater evil. –Grace Bennett

****

He went after her.

Connor charged into the night, the thundering
hooves of his gelding echoing through New York's dark,
narrow streets. Galloping at breakneck speed after dark
through the city was a first for him, but Mercy Jackson
had an uncanny way of pulling him into the

extraordinary. Damn her audacity. He thought Gabrielle infuriating and stubborn, but compared to the green-eyed thief's unrelenting determination, the French girl was a saint.

His frown deepened as he rounded a sharp corner, urging the gelding to push harder. Mercy's persistence confirmed their suspicions. Someone wanted that parchment enough to hire her, and Connor intended to use the tenacious little liar to uncover who.

Even tonight.

He dodged a lumbering carriage, weaving past another rider ambling along at a slower pace, and directed the gelding toward the Lower East Side. Every second wasted allowed Mercy to slip further away or, worse, hand the parchment to whoever employed her. Connor clenched his jaw. He had no intention of letting that happen. He planned to be there for the exchange and ensure every guilty party faced justice.

Yet, as his thoughts churned, her face lingered in his mind, heart-shaped, her lips curving with lies, her emerald eyes flashing with defiance. Damn it, Mercy tested him at every turn. He would rather avoid pressing charges against her, for one reason: her aunt. The care and devotion she showed the older woman seemed genuine, and one of the few truths she'd told since their paths crossed three days and a lifetime ago.

One question gnawed at him. Did her persistence in obtaining the parchment stem from love for someone lost, as she claimed? Or was this another deception?

Mercy and her aunt spoke of him and his family with an unsettling familiarity. Did they know the truth about him and his father's murder? Had she wielded the knowledge as a weapon, seeking his sympathy to further

her cause? The thought burned hot, demanding a deeper investigation when time permitted.

For now, his focus narrowed. The gelding pounded down the final street, his pace unyielding, until Connor reined in before the ramshackle cottage Mercy called home. Sliding from the saddle, he tied the horse to a weathered fence post, his movements precise and deliberate.

Striding toward the front door, his boots striking the ground with authority, he raised a fist and rapped the wood.

Hard.

The sound reverberated in the quiet night. A challenge laid bare. Mercy Jackson would answer him, one way or another.

Rethinking his approach, Connor slipped around the cottage and stood by the kitchen door. If he knocked at the front, Mercy would slip out the back. He knew her well enough to anticipate her evasion tactics. This time, he intended to catch her off guard and gain the upper hand in their maddening game. For once.

Minutes ticked by in silence, broken only by the occasional rustle of leaves and the faint sounds of the city in the distance. Wood smoke and coal ash swirled around him as the bite of the evening nipped his nose and cheeks. He remained poised, tension coiling in his muscles.

Then the kitchen door creaked open, not with the stealth of Mercy's escape but with the deliberate movement of someone far more composed.

Aunt Charity stepped into view, her silver-gray hair catching the moonlight, a wry twinkle in her eye, and a knowing smile curving her lips. "She drives you mad, doesn't she?" Charity's tone brimmed with quiet amusement.

Connor straightened, his lips pressing into a tight line, and shook his head. He couldn't deny it. Mercy Jackson had a talent for fraying his patience like no one else. "And how did you know I'd be waiting back here?"

Charity's smile widened. "Because I've lived with Mercy for ten years, and I know how her mind works." She leaned against the doorframe and smiled. "I used to try catching her off guard, just like you're doing now, but it never worked. This is only the beginning of Mercy's special brand of lunacy. She'll run you in circles until you're as dizzy as a mouse in a round room, scrambling for a place to hide."

"I see." He scanned the warm, inviting glow of the kitchen behind her. The comforting scents of tea and freshly baked bread drifted toward him, and his gut clenched. Mercy wasn't here. The emptiness hummed in the air, undeniable. "And where is Mercy now?"

Charity stepped aside, gesturing for him to enter. "Come in, Mr. Calhan. We'd best discuss this in private."

Connor hesitated, his instincts urging him to stay on the move, to hunt Mercy down before her trail grew cold. But something in Charity's demeanor tugged at him, and he stepped through the doorway into the snug kitchen.

His attention caught on Charity's temple, where a swollen red lump marred her otherwise composed features. His stomach twisted as he took note of her slight sway against the doorframe, her weight shifted to one side.

"What happened?" The question came out sharper than he intended, as he moved to her side, his hand steadying her thin elbow. With gentleness, he guided her to a high-back wooden chair at the small table in the center of the room. "Please, sit. You look like you're about to collapse."

Though every instinct screamed at him to chase after Mercy and throttle the truth out of her, he forced his mind to focus. He needed answers, and he wouldn't get them if Charity collapsed. For now, finding out what transpired and where Mercy went took precedence over his rage.

"I've been waiting for you," Aunt Charity said, her tone steady but weary. Folding her hands in her lap, she clasped her fingers with an air of resolve. "Once I've said my piece, I'll retire to my bed. You'd best get settled, Mr. Calhan. This will take a few minutes, but it must be said."

Her chest rose and fell as she drew in a deep breath, and Connor watched the transformation. The same impenetrable mask Mercy wore to shield her emotions now settled over her aunt's lined face. Charity's voice softened with the weight of her words. "I took Mercy in after her mother passed. God rest her soul. I cannot fathom what the poor child endured. She came to me nine summers old, shy, and hollowed out with grief. She would sit alone during the day, staring out the window for hours without a word. Whenever I asked her a question or gave her a task, she would look at me with those big, empty eyes and nod. She obeyed, but she never smiled. She never spoke unless I forced an answer from her.

"At night, the demons came. Her screams would pierce the silence, dragging me from my bed. I would hurry to her chamber, desperate to comfort her, but I didn't know how. That first year, I prayed more than I ever had in my life. Having no children of my own, adjusting to a little one underfoot took time. And Mercy…" Charity hesitated, her voice faltering for the first time. She brushed a stray wisp of gray hair from her forehead and sighed. "The girl carried a pain no child should bear. Soul pain. Losing a parent so young leaves wounds that never truly heal."

Connor shifted, the mention of such loss striking an old chord. He knows too well the ache of losing a parent, though he was grown when his father met his end. The reminder tugged at his sympathy, but urgency clawed at his mind. Every second Mercy remained unaccounted for, the parchment slipped further from his grasp.

Charity cleared her throat, her voice firm again. "I have one sibling left, Justice. He came north after the war and offered to spend time with Mercy while I volunteered at the parish. She liked him, and the two found solace in each other. My brother had a way of coaxing her out of her gloom, of reaching her in ways I could not. For a time, I thought of him as a blessing and thanked the good Lord for returning my brother to me when I needed him most."

Her voice wavered as she pulled a kerchief from her sleeve, dabbing at her forehead and cheeks. Connor sensed an unspoken shadow beneath her words, a bitterness creeping into her gratitude. He leaned forward, catching the subtle tremor in her hands.

Though her story interested him, another part of him wrestled with impatience. The document, Mercy's whereabouts, and the enigma of her true motives pressed heavy on his mind. But for now, he waited, sensing that Aunt Charity had not yet reached the heart of what she needed to say.

"As the child grew, Justice took her on outings, and they would return in good spirits, laughing and lighthearted. I thought nothing of their games or the places he took her, until the year she turned sixteen."

The older woman's hands tightened around the kerchief in her lap as she lifted her eyes to meet Connor's. "That year, I found a diamond necklace hidden among her undergarments. The morning newspaper reported those very jewels stolen from a society dame's estate." Charity's voice faltered for a moment before she continued. "On that terrible night, I uncovered truths I never dreamed possible. I discovered I didn't know my brother at all, and did not understand the depth of his depravity. But the worst of it, what broke me the most, was discovering his determination to teach Mercy every sinful trick and deception he knew. He turned my sweet girl into a liar and a thief, right under my nose."

Her breath hitched, and she brushed a hand across her temple as if to soothe an invisible wound. "When I confronted him, he struck me so hard I spent the next week confined to bed. I learned then Justice would stop at nothing to get his way."

Connor listened, every fiber of his being taut with tension. The implications hit him like hammer blows. "Your brother groomed her to do his thieving, and he's the one who paid her to rob me."

Charity nodded; her face lined with guilt. "Yes."

"Who pays him?" The question burned on his tongue; the answer so close he could taste it. If she spoke the name, it could confirm everything and prove that Justice worked for the Phantom. He forced thoughts of

Mercy's complicity from his mind, at least for now.

Charity shrugged, her shoulders sagging. "I know nothing of his partners or dealings. He doesn't confide in me, and I don't ask. I prefer ignorance over bearing the weight of his sins."

Connor's expression hardened, his jaw flexing. "The bruise on your head. Justice gave it to you." The statement hung between them.

Charity gave a short, reluctant nod. "But he hurts her more. I know he uses the lash on her. I've seen her bloody bedclothes, no matter how she tries to hide them. Mercy thinks she conceals her pain from me, but I see it. And I lie awake at night, helpless, wondering how to protect her. I am no match for my brother, and neither is she."

Visions flashed through Connor's mind of a younger Mercy, her small hand dwarfed by Justice's as he taught her to steal and deceive. The image shifted to something darker. Justice, wielding a lash against Mercy's fragile back, her screams swallowed by the walls of this very house. Molten rage surged within him, his hands curled into fists as he imagined the man striking both niece and sister with the same merciless cruelty. What kind of monster could inflict such torment?

Charity's voice pulled him from the storm raging in his mind. Her clear, steady regard fixed on him. "Mercy has endured more than most could bear. I hope that when you find her, you will exercise restraint and grant her mercy. She wouldn't have done any of this had I known Justice's true nature and shielded her from him instead of encouraging their bond. The only excuse I can offer is that his games brought back her smile."

Connor exhaled, the weight of her words pressing

against his chest. He didn't have time to dwell on her regret; every passing second allowed Justice and Mercy to slip further away. He forced his tone to steady. "You aren't to blame for this, Miss Charity. I promise you, I'll bring her back unharmed. But I need to know where they've gone."

Charity straightened, imbued with resolve. Her eyes searched his face, her expression unflinching. "I believe you'll do the right thing despite being a Calhan."

Her frankness caught him off guard, but she didn't pause. With a small lift of her chin, she gave him what he needed. "To Richmond."

The name hit him like a bolt of clarity. Richmond. Virginia. The pieces began to align. The gold chests unearthed in bordering states, his father's ambush in the same region. Everything pointed back to Richmond. His chest tightened with urgency as his gut told him the answers he'd sought for so long lay buried there, entwined with the very man he now hunted.

"Thank you, Miss Jackson." Connor kept his voice measured as he suppressed the urge to question her disdain for his family name. There would be time for answers later when the pressing matter of Justice and Mercy had been resolved.

He turned to leave, but before he could take more than two steps, Aunt Charity caught his sleeve, her grip firm. "Some might call me a traitor for trusting you with their destination. But I believe you're a gentleman. You must catch them before Justice does any real damage."

Connor nodded, his expression resolute. "I intend to."

Before either could say more, a knock echoed from the front door. Charity's posture stiffened, her head tilting toward the sound. "Mercy refused to leave unless Justice sent someone from the parish to assist me. He…expressed his irritation when she went upstairs to change. But he sent for help, and I expect that's who's here. Go out the kitchen door while I deal with my visitor."

Connor didn't need further prompting. With a curt nod, he strode to the back door, his movements swift and purposeful. Outside, the crisp night air bit his face as he rounded the cottage and untied his horse.

Justice. The name churned in his thoughts like poison. The man carried none of its meaning but deserved a generous portion delivered straight to his hide. Any man who raised a hand against a woman forfeited the right to be called a man. Coward. Snake. Lily-livered bastard. Those were the titles Justice earned.

He vaulted onto his horse and urged it into a gallop, tearing through New York's streets with a singular focus. At the agency, he left a brief note for General Cooper detailing his pursuit. By the time he returned home, he had composed an apology to Max, explaining his sudden departure on urgent business. After a hot meal and packing fresh clothes into a satchel, he ordered his carriage to the train depot.

Settling into his seat aboard the train, Connor leaned back, his hat tipped over his eyes as he propped his boots on the opposing bench. A fourteen-hour ride stretched ahead of him. Once the train reached full speed and the distance from New York widened, he would begin his search for Uncle Justice and Mercy. Whether they took this train, a carriage, or horseback, Connor didn't care. He would find them and follow their trail straight to the Phantom.

If they traveled any other way than by train, he would beat them to Richmond.

Half an hour into the journey, Connor stood and stretched. Moving through the train cars with deliberate ease, he scanned each passenger, his eyes sharp and searching. Reaching the final car, he stopped at the partition separating the regular seating from the private compartments. A pair of railway employees stood at their posts, ensuring no one crossed the threshold without a first-class ticket.

Connor sighed, frustration knotting in his chest as he retreated to an empty seat near the end of the train. From this vantage point, he could watch the corridor leading to the private cars. Propping his feet up again, he settled in, his determination unwavering.

The rhythmic clack of the wheels on the tracks and the gentle sway of the train did little to soothe the tension roiling in his chest. His eyes remained fixed on the corridor, his mind turning over the challenge ahead. Amid hundreds of travelers, how would he find one brown-haired, emerald-eyed thief? The odds were daunting, but his determination didn't waver.

His jaw tightened, hardening with resolve. He would track her down, no matter what the cost. By week's end, Mercy Jackson would be in custody, even if he had to kick in every door in Virginia to make it so. No one escaped Connor Calhan when he set his mind to finding them. Not Justice. Not Mercy. And certainly not The Phantom.

****

Mercy jolted awake, her breath catching as her eyes searched the darkness for something familiar. The rhythmic clatter of wheels on the tracks filled the air, and the faint sway beneath her made her stomach churn. "Aunt Charity?" Groggy and uncertain, she sat up, and the world tilted, sending a wave of nausea crashing over her. The sharp blast of a whistle cut through her haze.

"You're awake." Uncle Justice's nasal sneer filled the small space. "I wondered for a time if you planned to sleep the entire trip. I made up my mind to give you five more minutes before waking you with my cane. Charity isn't here, *Voleuse.* We left her back at that miserable little cottage with the rest of the rubbish."

His words sliced through her confusion, and the memories returned in a rush, standing up to him, his threats, and then finding Aunt Charity on the floor, her temple swollen and bruised. Rage boiled inside her, and she demanded they send for help. But then came a blinding pain, followed by darkness.

How long have they been traveling? The car around her remained shrouded in shadows, the blinds drawn tight against the light of day. She pieced together enough to realize they were in a private compartment.

"Don't call me a thief." Venom strengthened her voice stronger than the pounding in her head. "Even in French. I don't like it." Sliding further into the corner, she braced for his response. Uncle Justice hated defiance, but she no longer cared.

"You *are* one." He gave her a smug grin. "And my employer finds you…intriguing. He asked about you during our last conversation, and I decided to bring you along." His sneer grew more pronounced. "Hastened by your inept bungling. I might add. I cannot afford to leave you at Calhan's mercy while I deliver the parchment. But heed my warning. When we reach my employer's home, remain silent, and let me do the talking. The colonel is far less patient than I. This meeting will mean bigger jobs and better pay. Mark my words, girl. We'll make a fortune."

Mercy's stomach twisted, but not from the motion of the train. "I don't want to do any more jobs for you or your employer." Keeping her voice low and steady, she studied the older man sitting across from her, his rotund frame filling the seat. The games she once found amusing now filled her with revulsion. But they were never games, she realized with a start, not with Justice. "You struck Aunt Charity the moment I went upstairs to change."

Her uncle shrugged, his face a mask of indifference. "She had it coming with her holier-than-thou attitude. I don't take orders, and I don't tolerate disobedience."

Mercy stared at him, disbelief turning to cold fury. "I did as you instructed," she challenged. "Aunt Charity stood up to you, didn't she? She told you to leave me alone."

His expression hardened, his eyes narrowing to dark slits. "What happened between my sister and me is none of your concern."

His evasiveness said it all.

"She asked because she cares." Mercy glared while keeping a tight rein on her rage.

Justice's eyes gleamed like black coals, smoldering with restrained fury. "As do I." His voice dropped to a growl. "Now, stop this insolence. I have been very patient with you, but if you continue to challenge me, I'll remind you of your place with my whip. No more talk of my dear sister."

The threat settled in her chest like a stone, heavy and cold. Mercy bit back the sharp retort poised on her tongue, knowing that goading him further would make matters worse. Instead, she leaned back, forcing her lips into a smile she didn't feel. Distraction became her only option.

"Did you read the parchment?" Keeping her tone light, she hoped to distract him from the violence she read in his eyes.

The dark atmosphere suffocated her, pressing down like a weight. Rising, she pushed aside the heavy drapes, and sunlight flooded the small compartment. The warmth and brightness offered a fragile reprieve, and she smiled, letting the light ease some of the tension knotting her shoulders. If nothing else, she could hold on to this sliver of defiance, this brief moment of control.

"Close the damn drapes." Uncle Justice snapped, his voice sharp as the crack of a whip. "Are you trying to blind me?"

Mercy's eyes flew to his, her lips tightening in defiance. "We need light to make sense of the figures on the parchment."

"I don't." Straightening in his seat, he glared at her until she relented, her shoulders stiff as she drew the heavy fabric across the window. The compartment sank into darkness again, oppressive and stifling.

"You promised to let me study the document once we had it." Resentment flared, making it impossible to suppress the edge in her voice.

His black eyes turned cold and unyielding. "When I decide, and no sooner. And watch your tongue when you speak to me."

The air in the car reeked of leather, coal smoke, and his overpowering cologne. The combination stung her eyes and made her stomach churn. Swallowing the nausea rising in her throat, she wrapped her arms around her middle and shifted her approach. "Why did you force me to come if I irritate you so much?"

"I already told you." Tapping his cane against the floor in a sharp rhythm, he scrutinized her as if she were a puzzle he could no longer solve. "What happened to you, Mercy? We used to have such fun when we worked together. But ever since I sent you to that God-damned Calhan warehouse, you've been acting strange."

Mercy braced under his probing stare. "I've never been caught before. The idea of going to jail doesn't appeal, Uncle. If something happened to me, who would take care of Aunt Charity?"

Justice narrowed his eyes, waving a dismissive hand in her direction. "You're so damned obsessed with that old bat, it's chapping my hide. Nothing is going to happen to you."

Pressing her lips into a thin line, she continued. "Things didn't feel fine when I stood there, face-to-face with Connor Calhan's fury. Tell me, Uncle, if I went to jail, would you bail me out?"

The question landed like a stone between them. He shifted in his seat, his weight creaking against the leather. "Of course." He answered, but the words were clipped and hurried.

His expression grew bored, betraying him. Mercy clenched her fists. As she suspected, he lied. A cold knot of anger and disappointment tightened her chest. Her uncle would leave her to rot if it suited him.

Shifting her approach, she forced her tone into something calmer, less confrontational. "Please, Uncle, let me see the document. I need to know who else is responsible for my mother's death."

Justice grunted, his tone dismissive. "Connor Calhan and his father killed your mother. That's the end of it. There's nothing more to tell."

Tilting her head, Mercy studied him, her mind buzzing with disbelief. "That's not the story you told me when I first came to live with Aunt Charity." Keeping her voice low and calm, she continued. "You told me Union soldiers on patrol with Connor and his father shot her. Every man in that patrol is said to have died that day except Jonathon Calhan, who remained in bed until he died five days later. Mama was found dead in the neighboring plantation's cotton field the next morning. Which means either someone else killed my mother, or Jonathon had soldiers with him not listed in his patrol. I will find out who shot her."

Justice turned his head to glare at her, his eyes darkening into black, gleaming pools of anger—and something else. Fear, perhaps? The realization unsettled her, but she didn't look away.

"Hear me well, girl." His voice turned to a low, threatening growl. "The Calhans killed your mother. There is no one else."

A chill crept down her spine at his tone. She knew the story too well, the words etched into her memory like scripture. Other children grew up with fairy tales and nursery rhymes; her bedtime stories began with, *The day the Calhan bastards and their soldiers killed your mother…* Her uncle shifted again, for the third time, his bulk restless on the cramped seat.

She studied him as he checked the revolver tucked into his belt, fumbling with the weapon as though his fingers refused to obey. The sight ignited a flicker of suspicion. *He's scared.* Frowning at the absurdity of the thought, Mercy pressed her advantage, her voice growing firmer. "Mama deserves justice. I will uncover the truth and see her murderers pay for what they did. You told me last week the names of the soldiers riding with Jonathon Calhan's patrol are listed on that parchment. If one of them survived, I will find him. I have every right to know who played a part in her death."

Justice's sudden roar made her jump, her heart leaping into her throat.

"Why can you not drop this subject?" Bellowing, his voice cracked like a whip in the cramped car. "The Calhans are responsible. I will hear no more! Do you understand me?" By the time he finished, his voice had dropped to a low, venomous whisper, more terrifying than the shouting.

Mercy nodded, stiff with fear.

His intense expression pinned her in place until she squirmed like a mouse caught beneath the shadow of a hawk.

She didn't dare say another word.

A tense silence stretched between them, broken only by the relentless clack and rumble of the train wheels. The sound mirrored the frantic rhythm of her heart as the train car swayed.

The weight of ten years pressed down on her, the same gut-wrenching tale he repeated each time he visited, now settled like a stone in her stomach. The answers she sought for so long remained just out of reach.

"All right." She relented, her tone calculated to convey submission. For now, she would let it rest. But her uncle's violent outburst only strengthened her resolve. The truth was written on that parchment, and

Mercy swore to find the answers she sought, no matter the cost.

Chapter Ten

Mississippi River, July 1862

Major General Halleck now commands the Union Army, and though some praise his success in St. Louis, Fort Donelson, and Shiloh, others question his leadership and ignore his orders. Still, I place my trust where our commander-in-chief does. As we march south, I carry thoughts of Maggie and the family with me. Though I saw them briefly at Christmas, I will never grow used to their absence. I pray daily for their safety, and for Connor, Reese, and Max, though I've had no word of them in weeks. I trust God to guide them, as I once did when they were boys.

Tonight, I ride to Richmond with an urgent dispatch and orders to await a reply. While there, I'll check on our Southern informant, whose bravery has spared many lives, including President Lincoln's. She remains one of our greatest assets. I must keep this brief, for when the moon rises, I ride. –Major Jonathon Calhan

****

They arrived in Richmond just as the morning sun burned through the mist, the train screeching to a halt like an impatient beast. The bustling platform swallowed them whole, a tide of bodies surging around crates and shouting porters.

Mercy pressed close to her uncle like a reluctant shadow. He repelled the crowd as though he were a moving fortress wall, his presence grim but effective. "Move." Barking his order, he hurried across the platform without glancing back. "Someone might recognize us."

He strode toward the waiting line of hackney carriages, his coat flaring with each determined step.

Mercy hesitated for a heartbeat, clutching her skirts. "Who would recognize us? We don't know a soul in Richmond."

Justice stopped short in the middle of the platform, his glare cutting through her words. "Do you ever think, girl?" His sharp voice drew curious glances. "The demon. Calhan. One train out of New York every twelve hours. If he knows where we're headed, where do you suppose he'll look first?"

Her breath hitched, and her hand flew to her mouth. "But you paid for a private car—"

"To keep him guessing." The edge in his tone made her stomach churn. "Never mistake me for a fool, Mercy. That's a luxury you can't afford."

A hackney carriage clattered to a stop before them, the driver tipping his hat. "Where to?"

Justice leaned close, his scowl deepening. "How much?"

The driver scratched his head, squinting. "Depends on the destination, sir. Where to?"

Mercy's glanced back toward the train, and her breath caught. A towering man with blond hair and a face like carved stone stepped onto the platform, his eyes scanning the crowd with unsettling precision.

"Dawson Hills Plantation." Without another glance, Uncle Justice climbed into the carriage and bellowed at the driver. "Double the fare if you take every back road you know. Triple if you get us there without trouble. Now move."

"Aye, sir." The driver whistled and snapped the reins.

Mercy scrambled in after her uncle, the door slamming shut as the carriage jolted forward. She barely had time to settle before glancing over her shoulder. Her heart sank.

Connor shoved his way through the crowd, his icy glare fixed on the space where they'd stood.

"Turn here." Justice barked, hammering on the roof. The coach swerved, throwing Mercy against the leather seat. Her bruised backside throbbed as the wheels clattered through narrow streets, the driver's sharp whistle cutting through the chaos like a blade.

For an hour, the world blurred into a maze of twisting cobblestone roads and muddy tracks. Mercy gripped the seat to stay upright, but the carriage pitched and rolled as though fleeing for its life. When they finally rumbled up a long, curved drive and stopped before an imposing house, her lungs ached with relief. But the respite proved fleeting.

Her uncle's shoulders tensed beside her, and his eyes flicked to the road behind them.

"This is an important occasion, Mercy, and I will not have you making a fool of me. While we are here, you will keep silent. I will do all the talking. The colonel is a man of precise manners and considers it a grave insult for a woman to join the conversation." Uncle Justice's sharp tone echoed in the cramped carriage.

Mercy's mouth twitched, but she smothered her reaction, keeping her eyes fixed on the worn leather of her gloves. He delivered the same patronizing command at least fifteen times since she had awoken in the stifling train car. If he uttered the phrase *women should be seen and not heard* one more time, she would scream.

"Yes, Uncle." She kept her voice flat and unemotional.

Satisfied, he adjusted his grip on the polished head of his cane, the furious tap of his boot against the floor revealing his impatience.

Mercy tilted her head, studying him. Justice's rigid posture and darting eyes betrayed something more than his usual arrogance. Colonel Dawson must hold leverage over him, something critical, and no doubt illegal.

Her curiosity lingered, but she didn't have a chance to press further before the hackney door swung open. A deep, sonorous voice cut through the crisp morning air. "Welcome to Dawson Hills Plantation."

A liveried servant, dressed in scarlet velvet, stepped forward with a practiced air. He placed a stepping stool on the ground and extended his gloved hand toward Mercy with impeccable formality.

Unused to such courtesy, she leaned forward, hesitating for a moment before reaching out to take his hand. But before her fingers could graze the glove, Uncle Justice shoved past her with deliberate force, sending her tumbling back into the leather seat.

"Wait for your betters to leave first, girl."

Mercy bit the inside of her cheek to stifle her sharp retort. She learned long ago to keep out of her uncle's way when he sought to impress.

Justice stepped down with exaggerated precision, smoothing his black linen jacket and brushing the invisible lint from his sleeves. Without turning back, he barked out his orders. "Do not make a sound, Mercy.

Follow three paces behind, keep your face down, and for God's sake, don't embarrass me."

Accepting the servant's outstretched hand, Mercy stepped down, simmering with unspoken defiance.

The sight before her stole the breath from her lungs. The sprawling plantation house loomed, its whitewashed façade glowing in the pale morning light. Wide verandahs stretched along the front, supported by towering pillars, their shadows dark against the pristine walls. Black shutters framed the windows, and intricate iron railings gleamed with frost. Red maple trees bowed under the weight of snow-crusted branches, their tips brushing the upper story. Ice-covered flower beds bordered the lower level like frozen jewels, and a crimson carpet unfurled across the stone steps, leading to massive oak double doors flanked by two scarlet-uniformed guards standing at rigid attention.

The grandeur pressed against her chest like a weight. Yet something in the air, a faint echo, or a half-formed memory, made her stomach twist. A fleeting image raced across her mind, too distant to grasp but potent enough to leave a chill in its wake. Anxiety tightened her chest, and perspiration prickled along her hairline despite the winter air.

Mercy studied the grounds, her pulse quickening as her eyes darted to every shadow and every movement. Something felt wrong, very wrong. The heavy stone in her belly settled deeper, and her instincts bristled with warning.

"Remember what I said," Uncle Justice hissed under his breath, his cane tapping against the stone steps as he strode toward the grand entrance.

Mercy bit back a sigh. She had no intention of

drawing unnecessary attention, so he needn't worry. "Yes, Uncle," she murmured, lacing her tone with enough deference to satisfy him.

The moment she stepped inside, the grandeur of the entry hall made her falter. Gray and white marble gleamed underfoot, polished to a mirror shine. The silk-paneled walls shimmered in the light from an ornate chandelier, its gilded arms sparkling like captured sunlight. The scent of lemon polish mixed with the unmistakable aura of wealth, a cloying, heavy presence demanding reverence. Round and open, the space invited one deeper, as though daring them to get lost in its opulence.

Her brief investigation halted when they were interrupted by the sound of footsteps. An older man in a black livery emerged from the corridor beyond the foyer. His sharp gray eyes stopped short, his frown deepening as he scrutinized her from head to toe.

Mercy flushed under his examination, her instincts whispering her uncle had, as usual, twisted the truth.

"Why is she here, Mr. Jackson?" The man's clipped tone dripped with disdain. "The colonel will not be pleased." His nose rose with practiced indignation, the gesture calculated to make her feel small.

Uncle Justice handed his hat to a younger servant with an air of forced calm. "I had no choice, Jeeves. Calhan knows where she lives. I couldn't leave her behind to be interrogated, could I?"

The man called Jeeves tilted his head, considering. "The colonel will decide what is to be done with her…and with you. Follow me." His icy voice indicated the result would not be pleasant.

Anger coiled in Mercy's chest, hot and steady. She

kept her distance, trailing three paces behind her uncle as instructed. But her mind raced with defiance. If this mysterious colonel thought he could decide anything about her future, he could think again. And as for Uncle Justice's lies, she would deal with him after she got out of this mess.

They passed through the foyer into a gleaming corridor and turned into a saloon draped in muted luxury. Wine-red velvet settees were arranged before a gray marble hearth. Tall, paned windows veiled by heavy burgundy drapes. The room whispered refinement, yet the air felt as cold and lifeless as the marble beneath her feet.

"The lady will remain here." Jeeves' declaration brooked no argument. "Mr. Jackson, you will come with me."

Mercy studied her uncle as she walked to one of the settees.

He refused to make eye contact, his jaw tight, and his retreating figure only deepened the knot in her stomach. He lied all right.

Jeeves gave a curt nod. "A maid will bring refreshments, Miss Mercy. Do not leave this room until I return."

They vanished before she could question how he knew her name, leaving her with her unanswered doubts and rising irritation. For an hour, she sat with her hands folded in her lap, seething at her uncle's lies. Glancing up at the gilded ceiling, her thoughts drifted to Aunt Charity's modest but welcoming home. For all its splendor, this house felt like a mausoleum, beautiful but dead. No warmth, no life. Only an oppressive sense of something unseen, lurking in the corners.

The click of the door startled her, and she turned to see a tall housemaid enter, her movements brisk, a silver tray balanced with practiced ease. The maid's black dress and white apron were spotless, her blonde curls pinned in neat rows, her frown immediate and piercing. "Jeeves said Mr. Jackson brought a visitor, and I did not believe him." The maid's voice carried a faint accent. "But here ye are. The colonel won't be happy."

Mercy stood, brushing invisible creases from her dress. "I have been told."

The maid set the tray down with deliberate slowness, her sharp scrutiny raking over Mercy once more, pursing her lips with distaste. "Yer pretty, just like Jeeves said, but it won't do ye any good. We all know what yer mama did." She planted her hands on her hips, her tone hardening. "Get back in yer fine carriage and go back where ye came from. None of us want ye here."

Mercy's heart leaped at the mention of her mother. The earlier irritation drained from her, replaced by a desperate need for answers. She took a step forward, her voice steady but edged with urgency. "Did you know my mother?"

The maid snorted, a sound bristling with disdain. "Everyone around these parts knows." Tilting her head, she offered Mercy a smug, cutting smile. "But she got what she deserved, didn't she?"

Mercy's spine stiffened, fury blazing in her chest. Every ounce of restraint she possessed kept her from flying across the room and clawing the woman's smug face. Instead, she drew up to her full height and spoke, her voice low and venomous. "I don't know what you're talking about. What I do know is that you work here, and I'm sure you have a million things to do besides taunting me. I may be many things, but forgiving isn't one of them. Say one more vile word against my mother, and I'll rip those curls from your head and toss you out of this room on your backside. I wonder what Jeeves would think then?"

The maid's expression flickered, and the tiniest hint of doubt crept into her defiant glare.

Mercy prayed her threat worked. Servants feared butlers as much as they feared dismissal. But if the smug woman stayed another second, Mercy didn't think she could hold back the storm brewing inside her.

They stared at one another for a long, tense moment before the maid shrugged, sauntering to the door with exaggerated nonchalance. "It won't be long before the colonel gets around to you. And when he does, I'll be watching and laughing. He's been known to kill people who irritate him. And I reckon your being here will irritate him a great deal."

The door clicked shut, leaving Mercy standing in the stifling room, her thoughts spinning. She stumbled to the settee and picked up the porcelain teapot, her hands trembling.

The maid's words lingered like a foul stench. *What did she mean when the colonel got around to her?*

The same dark foreboding churning she experienced earlier returned with greater force. Filling her cup with tea and adding cream and sugar, her thoughts raced. Uncle Justice never acted without a motive, always self-serving, always shrouded in lies. He did not care when Connor cornered her in his warehouse and threatened to call the constable. Which made her wonder why he brought her to a house filled with such animosity?

She blew on the tea, its citrusy aroma soothing her

frayed nerves as she closed her eyes. But the questions gnawed at her resolve. What hold did this colonel have over her uncle? And why did her mother's name seem to hang like a shadow over everything here?

Mercy took a small sip, and the warm liquid trickled down her throat, calming her fluttering stomach. One thing she knew for certain, her uncle lied. He'd dragged her halfway across the country into a web of secrets and deceit, and she wouldn't wait around to see what he planned next.

Setting her cup down with care, she brushed crumbs from her green traveling gown and rose. It was time to take matters into her own hands.

Peeking into the corridor, she found it empty. On silent feet, she slipped out the door, her steps muffled against the polished floor. The stillness of the house sharpened her nerves, making her more aware of her surroundings. Creeping along the hallway, her heart hammering in her ears and her knees shaking, Mercy stopped at the sound of raised voices from a room two doors to her left.

"I delivered the document as you asked. Now give me the God-damned money." Her uncle's voice thundered through the corridor, filled with the sharp edge of desperation.

Another voice, unfamiliar but furious, lashed back. "Why should I pay when the task remains incomplete? I summoned you the moment I discovered Calhan claimed he decoded the list. He and his commanding officer have had *this* document since the war. Without the key, it's worthless. I sent you for the cipher, not the damned list. You betrayed me, Justice."

Mercy froze, the air around her thick with the weight

of their words.

The man's voice dropped to a low, dangerous rumble, and Mercy edged closer, stopping just outside the open door.

"You sent an untrained girl to complete the job I entrusted to you. My instructions were explicit: get in, collect the cipher, and return to Richmond. You failed on all three counts." A heavy silence followed, broken only by the faint clink of glass against wood.

Mercy held her breath, her heart pounding in her ears.

"And now you've brought the girl to Richmond, leading the devil straight to my doorstep. There's a good chance he will recognize me, and I cannot afford the consequences of such an event." The man's tone turned icy. "You violated our agreement, Justice, and you know the penalty."

A chill crept up Mercy's spine as the man's words cut through the air like a blade.

"Calhan knows nothing. He fought in battle, but none of them were in Virginia. For most of the war, he served in intelligence, carrying correspondence from the Union generals to Washington D. C. He wouldn't know you from Adam. The humorous part of this entire story is that Mercy blames *him* for her mother's death." Her uncle's laughter made her grind her teeth. "It's a shame the bastard didn't return sooner to die with his father. Imagine the conversations those two must have had since *he* is convinced Grace lured Major Calhan to his death." A mirthless chuckle followed the statement. "They must truly hate each other."

Mercy's heart jumped up a notch as she digested this latest information. Another lie, and this one would take time to digest. Connor hadn't been in Virginia when her mother died. Frowning, she shook her head, unsure of the proper way to react. One didn't hate another for their entire life, and then one day change their mind. Dizziness washed over her as she pressed closer to the wall for support. Placing the back of her hand over her mouth, she waited for the conversation to continue.

The man grunted in response. "None of this signifies. The fact remains; you failed to bring me the document I requested. And you brought the girl despite knowing how I feel on the subject. You disappoint me, and I should have you shot for insubordination." Icy calm, as though they discussed the merits of crop rotation, the voice continued. "You knew the penalty of breaking your oath. I gave explicit instructions, and you disobeyed me."

Uncle Justice snorted. "Disobey? Insubordination? What is this? We are partners, or did you forget? We both had a hand in the killing, as you well know. You don't want to cross me, Dawson. I know too much. Think what a well-placed word could do to your life and freedom."

Thick silence followed for what seemed like ages.

"Out of curiosity, why did you bring Mercy here when the stakes are so high?" The voice sounded bored now, and the clink of a glass followed.

"I thought you two should meet." Mercy could envision her uncle's shrug. "She would make a wonderful ally where Calhan is concerned. But I changed my mind on the way here and would have left her at the train station, but Calhan followed. I don't know what he's been saying, but she's been acting off since they met." Her uncle stopped, and glass clinked against glass.

If she closed her eyes, she could picture Uncle Justice refilling his glass with the whisky decanter.

"I think he likes her."

Footsteps echoed down the corridor behind her, muffled but deliberate, growing closer before receding to her left. Mercy sidled closer to the door and out of view of the corridor.

"Interesting observation." The voice moved further away, and a chair groaned as the voice sat down. "To be clear, we were never partners, Justice, and you are a fool to come here alone to threaten me." The man's tone slithered around her, laced with fury. "Take the traitor out and shoot him. Then, bring me the girl."

Before Mercy could react, a strong hand clamped around her arm, yanking her forward. She tripped into the room, her breath catching in her throat.

"She's here, sir." Jeeves propelled her forward, his voice thick with disapproval as his iron grip kept her from retreating. "Caught her listening at the door."

She stumbled to a halt in the center of the room, her eyes riveted on the hearth where two brown leather armchairs faced a roaring fire snapping in a black marble hearth. The cream Persian rug beneath the chairs muted the sound of her trembling footsteps. Uncle Justice stood near the hearth, swirling a glass of amber liquid, his face a mask of barely concealed fury. On either side of him stood two burly men in black, their hands flexing as if eager to tear him apart.

Straightening, she turned to study the desk at the far end of the room. Seated behind it was a man whose presence filled every corner. Mahogany brown hair streaked with silver framed a broad brow, piercing blue eyes, and a sharp mustache above a trimmed beard. A jagged white scar slashed across his tanned cheek, its raw line a silent testimony to violence endured. He regarded her uncle with a steely intensity, his expression unreadable.

Mercy's knees trembled, and her mouth turned dry as ash. Something about him made her stomach churn. The cold hatred in his eyes and the way he exuded authority terrified her. She swallowed hard, willing her body not to collapse on the spot.

"You can't." She blurted out her defense in a shaky voice. "Uncle Justice made a mistake, but you can't kill him. You must let him go."

The man's cold eyes shifted to her, pinning her in place. His voice, calm and sharp as a blade, sliced through her plea. "Must I?" He leaned back in his chair, his disdain palpable. "You must be Mercy."

Her name fell from his lips like an accusation, and she shrank under the weight of his stare. He studied her, his disinterest flicking over her as though appraising something insignificant. "I have the parchment, but what I require is a cipher. Not this." He gestured to the rolled-up document on his desk, his tone dismissive.

Mercy latched on to the back of a leather chair to steady her trembling body. Gripping so hard her knuckles turned white, she willed her knees to stop shaking and her stomach to settle.

"A cipher?" She managed to say the words despite her terror. Shooting a glance at her uncle, she glared, conveying her fury. He dragged her into this nightmare with his deception.

But Justice avoided her attempts to draw his attention with a clenched jaw, betraying his guilt.

The man at the desk tilted his head, his piercing

attention unwavering. "Justice did not tell you the nature of the document I sent him to retrieve?"

"No." Confused, she darted another glance at her uncle and frowned. "He instructed me on the location, not the item in question."

The man's lips curled in a mirthless smile. "Allow me to enlighten you. Without the cipher, the parchment is as worthless as a Grayback."

Uncle Justice sent her to collect the wrong document. The room closed around her as the full weight of his words settled.

This stranger frightened her more than any she had ever met, and she couldn't explain why. Something sinister lurked within him, and she wished Mama had named her Caution instead of Mercy. A simple peek around the corner would have been sufficient. She didn't have to stay and inch closer.

"Calhan and his commanding officer claim they have decoded this document and are drawing up arrest papers." The man's smooth voice held threads of menace. Waving the yellowed parchment in his hand like a weapon, his eyes narrowed on Uncle Justice. "For your sake, and hers, I hope they're bluffing."

Mercy's stomach lurched.

Her uncle shifted in her peripheral vision, drawing her focus away from the man behind the desk. Justice's black eyes speared her where she stood. "I sent Mercy to retrieve the contents of Calhan's upper right desk drawer. My contact mentioned multiple papers. My niece delivered one." His smile turned treacherous. "She may have tucked the rest away for leverage. Have you double-crossed me, girl?"

Her chest tightened as the colonel's sharp regard

flicked to her. How typical of Uncle Justice to pin his failures on her. Licking her dry lips, Mercy forced her weakening body to stand tall. "I didn't even know a cipher existed until now. If I had, I would have obtained it with utmost haste."

Trembling from head to toe, she shoved her fear aside and calculated her options. As long as she avoided looking into the colonel's chilling eyes, she could think with a clear head.

Justice's face darkened further. His warning transmitted with clarity. He wanted her to be silent.

The colonel's voice broke the tension like the crack of a whip. "How unfortunate for you both. Take him away."

Mercy's breath hitched as the two men flanking her uncle seized him by the arms and hauled him toward the door.

"Stop!" The word escaped before she could think better of it. Whirling to face the man behind the desk, she lifted her chin in defiance. "I didn't get the cipher from the warehouse because Connor Calhan expected me. Give me another chance, and I'll retrieve it."

The room fell silent, the air thick with unspoken tension. The colonel leaned back, steepling his fingers as he studied her. "Justice knows the rules, and he will pay the price."

"I can pick any lock." To her relief, her voice remained steady despite the fear crawling up her spine. "I'll return within the week."

His sharp blue eyes glinted with mockery. "If you're so accomplished, why the failure in the first place?" His words cut like shards of glass, each syllable laced with disdain. The soft drawl of his southern accent crawled along her nerves, making her wish the floor would swallow her whole.

Mercy squared her shoulders, tilting her head as she met his derision. "Have you ever faced a Calhan?"

"Mercy, be still." Justice's bark went unheeded.

The colonel rose from his chair with the fluid grace of a predator. He crossed the room, his tailored black suit immaculate, his white shirt and blue tie lending him an air of elegance that belied the rot Mercy sensed beneath. He stopped a foot in front of her, and his smile held a wealth of lazy cruelty. "No, I've never had the pleasure. But if I did, he'd be dead."

Mercy bit her lip, nausea surging in her belly. Ignoring the frantic pounding of her heart, she forced her eyes to meet his. Her breath hitched as he reached out, catching a strand of her hair between his fingers.

"You are quite beautiful in the right light," he murmured, his tone a cruel caress. "Are you frightened, my dear? The pulse in your neck is beating like a fluttering bird, betraying you." When his fingers brushed her cheek, she couldn't hold back. The tide broke, and she discarded the contents of her stomach all over his cream Persian rug three times until she had nothing left.

The colonel stepped back, his expression unreadable, while she fumbled for her kerchief and wiped her trembling lips.

"What a delightful guest you've brought to my home, Justice." His deep voice dripped with sarcasm. "I shall...express my gratitude later."

Mercy's cheeks burned as he chuckled, the sound grating on her nerves.

Turning to her, he gave a mocking bow. "I am Colonel Dawson, and this is my humble home."

His eyes lingered on the mess at their feet before sliding to Uncle Justice, who choked and gagged under the weight of the guards' grip.

Dawson's lip curled in disgust as he snapped his fingers. "Get someone to clean this up."

Mercy swallowed hard, her trembling hands clutching her kerchief as the colonel's piercing blue eyes settled on her once more. She'd thought Connor Calhan was her greatest enemy, but now she knew better.

The same hateful maid bounced into the room, her smug expression suggesting she'd been lurking outside, waiting for the summons. Her eyes darted to the mess on the floor, and her smile dropped into a tight, angry line.

"Clean this up." The colonel's tone turned as cold as the gleaming marble underfoot. "And bring more tea for Miss Mercy." His sharp command preceded a disarming smile directed at her. "Come, sit down, my dear, and tell me about this confrontation with Connor Calhan."

Mercy hesitated, her heart thundering in her chest, but the colonel's piercing intensity left no room for argument. Behind her, the maid gathered towels with jerky, resentful movements, muttering under her breath but careful not to defy the colonel outright.

"As Mercy's guardian, I will answer your questions." Her uncle shrugged the men's hands from his arms and stalked toward her.

Her breath caught in her throat at the anger darkening his brow. Resisting the instinct to duck, she stiffened her spine and lifted her chin. Whenever he got angry, he lashed out, and she braced for his blow.

"Justice, stay where you are." The colonel's eyes narrowed, and his tone cracked like a bull whip. "Do not utter another word while I speak with my uninvited guest."

With reluctance, he obeyed, his eyes narrowed on Mercy in warning.

One of the guards placed a leather armchair in front of the desk. The colonel gestured for her to sit, and with trembling legs, Mercy obeyed, perching on the edge of the seat, her spine stiff as a rod.

Under his calculated questioning, she recounted her theft of the parchment and her encounter with Connor Calhan. Her voice faltered several times, but she pushed through, describing every detail she could remember. When her story ended, she sucked in a deep breath, feeling like she had run a marathon under the weight of his unwavering stare.

The colonel steepled his fingers, his expression thoughtful as he turned to her uncle. "I believe I have found a way to salvage the mess you created, Justice. Mr. Calhan has a weakness for Mercy, as you say. I intend to exploit his…interest. Her life may be worth saving, after all."

Mercy blinked, her mind reeling. *Her life?* She hadn't grasped until now how precarious her position was. "Connor Calhan has no weakness, and he doesn't like me at all. He wants to send me to prison."

The colonel's black eyes glittered with dark amusement. "The fact that you are here and not rotting in a cell tells me otherwise. He has a soft spot for you, my dear." His lips curled into a smile chilling her to the bone. "You're like a tabby cat, full of spite and hissing at everything. But in the end, you will do as I say."

He turned back to Justice, his amusement vanishing like a snuffed candle. "I shall keep Mercy as a replacement for your inept informants. She will return to

New York and settle into her new position. As for you…" He glanced at the guards once again flanking her uncle. "Take him to the dome while I consider his future."

"No!" Mercy shot to her feet as the men moved with alarming efficiency, binding her uncle's wrists.

Justice struggled, his voice rising in desperation. "Dawson, hear me out! There is no need for this. I have your best interests at heart. I thought once you met Mercy—"

"I have no wish to hear your excuses." The colonel's smile did not reach his eyes. "You knew the stakes when you swore your oath, and you have remained true…until now. You are no longer an asset." With a dismissive wave, he signaled for one of the guards to bring him a glass of whiskey.

Justice's face paled, his voice dropping into a low growl. "I have stood by you through the worst of it when everyone else failed. Do not threaten me again, Dawson, or I shall reveal—"

"You shouldn't have come alone." The colonel smiled and nodded at his men.

Mercy didn't have time to react before a pistol butt crashed into her uncle's skull.

Justice crumpled to the floor like a sack of stones. Gagged and unconscious, the two burly guards dressed in black dragged him from the room.

"Where are you taking him?" Mercy's voice cracked as she stared after her uncle, her stomach twisting into knots.

The colonel leaned back in his chair, his sharp tone cutting into her. "He is no longer your concern. The better question is what value can you offer to make it worth keeping you alive?"

Her legs wobbled, and she gripped the arms of the chair for support. "There has to be—"

A knock at the door made her jump. Jeeves entered with a grim expression. "Connor Calhan is in Richmond. One of our men brought word moments ago. The bastard followed her, just as Justice predicted."

The colonel's expression grew thoughtful, and a calculating gleam lit his eyes. He leaned forward, clasping his hands. "You begged for your life, Mercy. Are you prepared to pay the price?" His words were soft, almost tender, but their weight crushed her.

Mercy opened her mouth, but no sound emerged. Before she could form a response, blinding pain erupted at the back of her head, and the world dissolved into darkness.

Chapter Eleven

Richmond, Virginia, September 1862
News of the brutal losses at Antietam weighs heavily
on my heart, especially for the mothers and widows left
behind. Percival returned in a rage today, ordered me to
remain upstairs, and locked himself in the study for one
of his secretive meetings. I know he has summoned the
Knights again. They gather to plot whenever the South
suffers a blow. Though Mammy fears I'll be caught, I
cannot ignore what I may overhear. I must do what I can.

My houseboy brought word that Major Calhan has
returned to the area and will remain nearby for a day or
two. He never reveals exact locations, and I would never
betray his trust. I owe him my safety and my dignity after
he risked much to protect me. He is everything a man
ought to be, and if ever I bear a son, I will raise him with
such honor. For now, I have little Mercy, the light of my
life. If Percival's meeting reveals anything vital, I take
comfort knowing Major Calhan is close. –Grace Bennett
****

Connor prowled the streets of Richmond for hours,
his frustration mounting with every fruitless turn. No
sign of the hackney, no trace of Mercy or Justice. The
city, teeming with life, seemed intent on swallowing his
quarry whole. By the time he hailed another hackney and
had the driver drop him at a restaurant in the heart of
town, he was cold, starving, and mad enough to bite a

nail in two. His belly growled like his throat had been cut.

Forty-five minutes later, fed and warmed by a stiff drink, Connor stepped back onto the bustling street. He tugged his hat low over his brow and scanned the fading horizon. The hackney had vanished, but Mercy and Justice hadn't gone far. If they planned to leave Richmond, they would have stayed on the train.

Removing his hat, he ran his hand through his hair and glanced down the street in both directions. He knew where the Union army camped the day his father got shot, and he wanted to scout around a little to see if Justice and Mercy's employer lived nearby, as he suspected. If the employer and the Phantom were the same, this trip would end a decade of hunting. He wanted to catch the bastard so bad; he itched all over.

Glancing up at the sky, he frowned as a hackney stopped beside him. The dimming light would turn to night soon, and he wouldn't be able to search the ambush site as much as he'd like if he didn't get a move on. Still, the chance to see the terrain with new eyes was too important to pass up.

Ten years ago, when the massacre happened, his rage blinded him to everything but grief. Back then, he hadn't known about the parchment or the cipher that sealed his father's fate. Now, armed with knowledge and a decade's worth of hard-earned resolve, he intended to piece together what he missed.

Connor climbed into the hackney and gave the driver his destination, the words tasting bitter on his tongue, the place where it all began.

Settling back against the cracked leather seat, he mulled over the tangled threads of his pursuit. He ticked off the details one by one, like a litany of ghosts refusing to let him rest.

The last time his father spoke to General Cooper, the war had been a living hell on all sides. Jonathon entrusted the parchment to the general for safekeeping, vowing to collect the cipher in a matter of days.

But fate had other ideas. General Cooper went to Richmond, and Jonathon Calhan went to his grave.

Connor's fists clenched as the hackney jostled over the uneven road, the memories as vivid as the day they'd been burned into his mind. His thigh burned as if the metal inside him wanted to relive the past, too.

There were strong doubts within the agency whether the cipher existed at all. But Connor knew his father wouldn't mention it if it didn't, and he figured either his father died before he could collect the cipher, or he hid it somewhere no one would think to search.

Knowing how his parent died, he figured the site of the ambush would be a good place to start. The notion the cipher could be there after all this time seemed farfetched, but after every other rock turned up empty, this one had to have some new clue he hadn't thought of before.

The most intriguing development in his current investigation involved Mercy traveling with her scumbag uncle and the parchment to the very city where his father had been murdered.

Everything traced back to the rumor he circulated about discovering the parchment, revealing the names of the Knights of the Confederacy and the Phantom.

The bastard was here. He knew it.

Five miles southeast lay the spot where his father made his final, valiant attempt to save a woman in distress.

Connor's eyes narrowed as he surveyed the terrain, pushing down the tightness in his chest that always accompanied thoughts of his father. His leather coat and fur-lined hat shielded him from the winter chill as he stared out the tiny coach window. The river, the undulating landscape, and the Bennett Plantation. He checked them off as he passed until he reached his destination.

Tapping on the roof, he signaled the driver to stop and stared at the charred ruins of a once-flourishing property.

Following the surrender at Appomattox, Union soldiers set the plantation ablaze to express their rage over their dead comrades, shot and murdered by Colonel Bennett, Grace Bennett's husband, and the men he commanded.

The place looked like hell. Connor signaled the driver to move on. Rubbing his throbbing thigh with the palm of his hand, he heard again the whistle of artillery shells and the acrid smell of gunpowder. Dread tightened his chest as visions of the dead and dying tied a knot in his stomach.

Even ten years later, the pain and memories of the loss inflicted by the war remained vivid.

When they reached the slough, Connor tapped the roof again.

With a sigh, he stepped from the carriage and paid the driver to wait. Walking north through the foliage, he came to the area where the massacre occurred. Thick brush hid the waiting rebels from his father and his men. They rounded the corner to the prearranged meeting spot, only to be shot from their saddles in a blaze of gunfire.

His father fell first, and another soldier fell on top of him. Wounded, but alive, his father woke sometime late in the afternoon and crawled back to the main road where one of the patrols found him and carried him back to camp. Every man in his patrol died in the ambush but him. The army surgeon took him into surgery and, after ten agonizing hours, declared the bullet too close to Jonathon Calhan's heart. His father spent the next three days in excruciating pain, knowing he would soon die. On the fourth day, he got up against the doctor's wishes and took ink and pen in hand to write to his beloved wife.

General Cooper arrived on the fifth day to discover Jonathon slumped across his writing desk with a sealed letter to Maggie in his hand.

With a heavy heart, the general wrote his letter to Mrs. Calhan, mailed both, and made burial arrangements.

Connor had been the first to respond and the one to bury the dead. His stomach twisted into a knot. Glancing at the lifeless face of the man who fathered him filled him with rage, the bitter taste of injustice, and the deep sorrow of loss. He would never forget the moment if he lived to be a hundred.

Connor pushed the memories aside as he found the graves minutes later and knelt beside the cross bearing his father's name. For long moments, he remained there, allowing his heart to do the talking. Lord, how he missed the sparkle in his father's eyes, the deep timbre of his voice, and the way he slapped him on the back and said, "Good work, son."

"I'm here, Father. It's been a while since we last spoke, but I want you to know I found the bastards who attacked you and your men and put them in the ground where they belong. I've been chasing ghosts for more than ten years, and now I'm hunting the worst of them. The man known as the Phantom. He's a slippery son of a bitch. Every time I get close, he vanishes like an evil spirit into thin air.

"I don't feel like you can rest as you should until I catch the bastard. I know I can't. And Mama will sleep better, too, once I tell her it's finished. She doesn't know I've been hunting the men who shot you down. I haven't told her because she would worry too much. You know how she is about guns, shooting, and things of that nature.

"The boys are doing well. I imagine you know you're a grandpa on several counts. Your other sons have been making babies every chance they get, and they have fine women by their sides.

"Since I can feel you asking, the answer is no, I don't have a wife, nor do I plan to. I have too much work to do, and I haven't found a girl I want to stare at like you did, Mama. I don't think such a woman exists, and even if she did, I couldn't do anything about it until this is done.

"Madelaine's son Jeremy joined the army and could use you looking out for him. Madelaine would be alone except Mama moved in with her, and I have men there keeping an eye on them, though neither one knows. They would ask too many questions, and things would get awkward for me in the line of work I'm in.

"Don't worry about Mama and Madelaine. Last time I spoke with my sister, she mentioned a banker who keeps showing up on her doorstep. I checked him out and he's a decent man. If anyone deserves to find love again, it's her. Mama is having the time of her life fussing over all her grandbabies and talking about how they remind her of you."

Sighing, Connor put his hat back on his head and stood up. "I miss you more than I thought possible, Father. I think about sitting in front of the fire with you and talking things out like we used to. As crazy as it sounds, I felt closer to you while bullets rained down on us and explosions shook the ground we stood on than I ever have. I don't think I will ever be the same man as before the war, but with the Grace of God, I'm a better man for it.

"You have the courage of a lion. I've seen you stare death in the face so many times it shocked the hell out of me when you died for real. I can still see your pale face and unseeing eyes. They gave me nightmares for weeks." Connor cleared his throat and swallowed the lump forming there. Shaking his emotions aside, he stared at the wooden cross bearing his father's name.

"I know you see things better up where you are, and since we can't talk man to man, I came here. I sure could use a nudge in the right direction to catch this last son of a bitch. If you have any tips or something you'd like to tell me, now would be the time."

The scream shattered the stillness, freezing Connor to the spot. His pulse quickened as he realized, with a surge of frustration, he wasn't alone. The scream could be Mercy's.

Without hesitation, he bolted toward the sound, ducking through bushes and trees with as much agility as his aching thigh would allow. Branches scraped at his coat, the fading light casting long shadows across the forest floor. Breaking through the underbrush, he raced toward the main road.

His hackney driver sat rigid atop the carriage, a hand shielding his eyes against the setting sun. Ahead, a farm cart blocked the road, facing the opposite direction. A white-haired man and a rosy-cheeked woman stood beside it, pointing toward the riverbank.

"I think the man is dead." The old farmer's coarse linen shirt clung to his hunched shoulders. He draped an arm around his wife and steered her away from the road. "Poor sod drove his fancy carriage off the bridge. Come away, Gertrude. This isn't something your pretty eyes need to see."

Connor's heart climbed into his throat as he followed the farmer's gesture. His chest constricted at the sight of the overturned carriage partially submerged in the murky river. A glint of black linen caught his eye, and the knot in his stomach tightened. Justice had a black linen suit on earlier today, and the body bore an uncanny resemblance to the bastard.

"Where the hell is Mercy?" Growling under his breath, he scanned the scene. The lack of horses and tracks gnawed at him. He focused on the farmer and his wife, his voice sharp and urgent. "Did you see a young woman nearby?"

The farmer shook his head. "No, sir. Just the carriage and the unfortunate gentleman."

Connor's lips twitched at the "sir." Unused to southern formalities, he never got used to being called sir by anyone but his hired help. He glanced toward the water again, searching for any sign of Mercy.

The farmer's wife shuddered against her husband; her face buried in his shoulder. "It's awful, Henry. I can't bear to think what the poor man went through. Who is

Mercy?"

"Hush, Gertrude." The old man patted her shoulder. "Let me take you home and make you a nice cup of tea." He turned back to Connor, his expression laced with concern. "Want me to send help once I've got my wife home?"

Connor tore his eyes from the river, forcing calm into his voice. "No, I'll notify the authorities and make the arrangements. Thank you for stopping."

The farmer nodded. "Thank you, sir." With a final glance toward the scene, he guided his trembling wife back to their cart.

As the cart creaked away, Connor turned back to the wreckage. His stomach churned. The body in the river belonged to Justice without a doubt. His signet ring gave his identity away. But where the hell was Mercy? The questions pounded in his skull. Why weren't there tracks? And how did Justice end up dead? How did they get separated? Who killed him? If they were together before his murder, how did she escape? Or did she? Was her life in danger? And what now? Did he retrieve the body or scour the banks for tracks?

The eerie silence of the river offered no answers, only the cold weight of uncertainty pressing on his chest.

Undecided, Connor tilted his head back, stared up at the darkening sky, and planted his hands on his hips. "Now what, Father? I need a little more information here."

The river answered with a scrape and a scratch, followed by a heavy thud as the current tugged at the carriage, rotating it toward the center of the rushing water. The gurgling flow bubbled around the submerged wheels, threatening to drag the wreckage further downstream.

Connor frowned, his jaw tightening. As much as he despised Justice Jackson, the man didn't deserve to be lost to the river, his body swept to God knew where. Someone had to retrieve him. Miss Charity, for one, would want answers about her brother's fate, and Connor had no intention of tarnishing his reputation further by walking away from this mess.

The carriage groaned again, the sound of splintering wood cutting through the air. Connor grimaced. "All right, Father. You win. I'll deal with the body first."

The hackney driver approached, stopping just shy of Connor. "Your hour's up, sir. I'll have to head back to Richmond soon. Want me to send someone for you?"

Connor glanced at the rushing water and pulled a gold coin from his vest. He held it out, his expression firm. "How about you help me get the body out of the river, and we go back to Richmond together?"

The driver hesitated, glancing between the icy river, his hackney, and the coin glinting in Connor's hand. With a resigned nod, he agreed.

Neither of them wanted to wade into the freezing water, but someone had to. Two hours later, Connor climbed onto the hackney's driver seat, the strain and cold of the past hour made his leg scream with pain. He cast a sidelong glance at the body now wrapped in tarpaulin behind them.

Justice Jackson's bruised and swollen face bore almost no resemblance to the fastidious, haughty man he'd seen earlier that day.

Connor's chest tightened. *What the bloody hell happened?*

Sighing, he ran a hand through his hair, glancing up

at the sky. "Thanks, Father, for sending even more questions my way. If you could point me toward Mercy and the damn parchment now, I'd be grateful."

His muttered words drew a side glance from the driver, who shifted uneasily. "Who are you talking to?" Suspicion laced his tone, and he glanced upward as if expecting divine intervention to answer.

Connor almost laughed. The man's concern would have been amusing if the situation hadn't been so dire. Mercy could be in real danger, and every second wasted only deepened his frustration. "No one. I'm thinking out loud, trying to make sense of this."

The driver grunted, inching further away but keeping one wary eye on him.

Connor dismissed the man and returned to the gnawing questions clawing at his mind. *Where the hell is Mercy?*

He'd scoured both sides of the river but found no trace of her. The thought of what might have happened tightened his chest. If she'd been caught in this mess, or worse, his failure to protect her would haunt him.

And Justice? Why kill him? Was it because he discovered the parchment's characters were unreadable? Did he pay the price for someone else's frustration? If so, what did that mean for Mercy?

The possibilities churned in his head like the restless river below. Frowning, he leaned forward, urging the driver to increase the pace. If Justice used his head for once, he'd have stashed the green-eyed troublemaker somewhere safe, out of sight, and out of mind. She could be sitting in a hotel room right now, waiting for an uncle who would never return. When she discovered the fact, she'd need a strong shoulder to cry on and a listening ear to share her troubles with. He decided that shoulder would be his.

In the meantime, he'd cover his bases. From his perch, he scanned the passing scenery for any sign of tracks. The fading light made it impossible to see much of anything, but hell, maybe he would get lucky. Maybe his father would come through with a clue from wherever the dead watched over the living.

But neither luck nor his deceased father dropped Mercy into his lap. The sheriff did.

Once they delivered the body to the undertaker, Connor walked over to the sheriff's office to make a report before he returned to the river for another search. If Mercy were alive, he'd find her. If she wasn't...

His insides twisted at the thought, and he shoved it aside.

The sheriff's office was small and dimly lit, with a single desk cluttered with papers and a rickety chair where Connor took a seat and waited. From the other room, a prisoner's shuffling feet and low muttering filled the silence for fifteen minutes before the sheriff appeared.

The sheriff had a bald head, a gray beard, and a wide, easy smile belying the gravity of his profession. At least a foot shorter than Connor's six foot three, he stepped forward, shook Connor's hand with surprising firmness, and dropped into his seat.

"What can I do for you, young man?" His voice carried across the room in a smooth southern drawl.

Connor's mouth twitched. It had been a long time since anyone called him "young man." "I came across a body in the river six miles southeast. I dropped the deceased at the undertaker's and came by to make a statement."

The sheriff leaned forward, his expression sharpening. "A man in a black suit?"

Connor's gut jumped. "Yes."

The sheriff nodded. "An old farmer and his wife came by about an hour ago. Mentioned the accident. Are you the man they spoke to by the river?"

"I am." Connor's instincts prickled, and he felt the conversation turning, the anticipation twisting tighter in his chest. Something was about to happen. He could feel it to the bottom of his size eleven boots.

The sheriff tilted his head, studying Connor's face. "The farmer mentioned you asked about a young woman named Mercy. His niece, I believe?"

Connor's interest perked up like a hound catching a scent. "Yes. She's a…family friend. I planned to search for her as soon as I finished here."

The sheriff leaned back, folding his hands over his stomach. "Well, son, you don't need to search far. I've got a young woman named Mercy sitting in my jail cell right now, contemplating her misguided choices."

Connor resisted the urge to grin. Instead, he sent a silent thanks heavenward. He hadn't had this much luck since Gabrielle caught the flu, and he went to the Governor's Christmas Ball alone. He owed his father an apology.

Still, he knew better than to celebrate too soon. Mercy locked up in a cell meant trouble, and with her, that could mean a host of things. "What did she do?"

The sheriff sighed, his expression clouding with discomfort. "Stole a horse. The penalty's hanging. The owner claims she showed up at his door asking for help. His wife patched her up, and then the girl robbed them blind."

Connor winced. With Mercy, nothing ever went as planned. He didn't want to deal with this kind of problem, but his little green-eyed thief might know where the Phantom lived. And she had an aunt to look after. He couldn't let her hang. "What if I pay the owner fair value for the horse and let him keep the animal? Would that satisfy him enough to drop the charges?"

The sheriff raised an eyebrow, clearly intrigued. "It might. But I have to ask, are you willing to pay that much for the wildcat?"

Connor's brow furrowed. Wildcat? "What else did she do?" Twice he asked, and something told him he wouldn't like this answer any more than he did the first.

The sheriff's lips twitched, a reluctant smirk threatening to break free. "She sent my deputy to the hospital when she cracked a water dish over his head."

Of course, she did. Connor resisted the urge to groan. "And if I pay the deputy's hospital bill, will you drop the charges and let me take her home?"

The sheriff chuckled, his gray beard twitching with amusement. "Will you promise to keep her out of Richmond?"

"Yes." He would tie the little troublemaker up in his parlor if necessary to keep her out of harm's way.

The sheriff leaned back in his chair, rubbing his chin. "If you give me a hundred and fifty dollars for the horse and ten dollars for my deputy, she's free to go."

Connor choked on the price but said nothing. Instead, he pulled out his billfold, cursing Mercy for her expensive escapades. Someone needed to take her in hand and keep her out of trouble.

"There's one other thing." The sheriff said after a

minute.

Connor sighed. With Mercy, there always would be. "What is it?"

"Get her out of here tonight. She's upset the good citizens of Richmond enough." The sheriff stood, ambling toward the door leading to the cells.

Connor frowned. "Is there more?"

"No, but based on what I've seen tonight, you'll have your hands full keeping her out of trouble." The sheriff shook his head, his voice taking on a conspiratorial tone. "When I met my wife, Maryanne, she brought complications by the dozen. Women are nothing but trouble. If you're smart, you'll steer clear. Then again." He grinned and slapped Connor on the back. "Miss Mercy is a mighty attractive female. Can't blame you for wanting to lasso her."

Connor followed, his brow furrowing deeper. "I don't want to do anything but get her home. I promised her aunt I'd look after her. That's the extent of my interest."

"Uh-huh." The sheriff cast a knowing glance over his shoulder. "I told the same lie for about a month after I met Maryanne. Don't fight it, son. Let her have her way. It'll be easier in the end."

"Not this one. Nothing is easier with her. And she's the last woman I would marry." He meant every word from the bottom of his bachelor's heart, until they stopped in front of Mercy's cell.

Her pale, heart-shaped face and wide green eyes met his, her damp tendrils of hair framing her expression. Her dress looked like she had walked for miles in the mud, and her stocking feet were bare against the cold stone floor. Despite her bedraggled appearance, her defiance burned bright, her hands planted firmly on her hips. Her mouth tightened when she caught his eye. The sight of her, so vulnerable yet furious, made Connor's chest constrict.

Bloody hell. She looked like she'd endured a brutal day, and her fiery stare drove the point home. If glares could kill, he'd be a dead man. Running a hand through his hair, he stared, unsettled by the unexpected urge to take her in his arms and comfort her.

The sheriff clapped him on the shoulder with a grin. "Here she is. Why don't you two talk while I speak to the farmer about his horse?"

Forcing a smile, he attempted to ease the tension. "Hello, Mercy."

Her eyes lit with emerald flames, defiance sharpening her features. "Of course, you're the one to find me. The second worst day of my life, and you show up to gloat. But before you ask, I don't have your damned document. Uncle—" Her words faltered, but then she went back to glaring. "Justice took it."

Connor leaned forward as grief, confusion, and then rage chased across her expressive face. Did she plan to weep? Disturbed by the notion, he fumbled for his kerchief. He'd never been good with weeping women, and the idea of this green-eyed spitfire crying terrified him more than her usual defiance.

But before he could offer the handkerchief, she tilted her chin and frowned. "Why are you here? What do you want?" With her hands planted on her hips and her voice laced with suspicion, she resembled the hot-tempered she-devil he knew. "I warn you, if you say one word about me being in jail, I will come through these bars and choke you."

He glanced from her to the heavy bars separating them. "When I told you to stay out of trouble the night we met, I was not issuing a challenge. I meant it as guidance for good health and a long life. Although now, I am curious, is jail everything you imagined?"

Mercy's eyes narrowed to slits and her face turned crimson. "I may be behind bars, but my sins are circumstantial. Unlike yours."

Arching a brow, he studied her mutinous expression. Her condemnation of his character knew no bounds. But her recent loss, coupled with a bloody, traumatic day, earned her a measure of grace, so he said nothing. Justice must not mean as much to Mercy as her aunt believed, or she would be weeping. Studying her mutinous expression and dry eyes, he searched for something appropriate to say. The fact she glared and showed her claws pleased him. The girl had grit, as General Cooper said.

Stepping closer to the bars, he ignored her taunt. "I've come to help you get back to New York."

Mercy tilted her head. "Why?"

He shrugged as if her question meant nothing. "Someone has to tell your aunt what happened, and you need an escort home. How far do you think you will get alone and unchaperoned? You may have a scarred opinion of my character, but I am a man of honor."

Her snort of disbelief echoed around them. "I do not require your help, Mr. Calhan, and I would appreciate it if you get the hell out. I would already be on my way back to New York if this infernal sheriff hadn't stopped me."

He shoved his hands into his pockets, resisting the urge to chuckle, and studied her face. "A trivial matter of a stolen horse and a hanging, I understand. What happened? Didn't your fluttering lashes make an impression on him?" He knew he shouldn't goad her, but her anger could be dealt with, unlike her tears.

Her glare sharpened, and she leaned closer, her voice cutting. "If you want to help so much, make the sheriff release me. Put your powerful Calhan name to use for a noble cause, and I promise you, once we're back in New York, I'll disappear from your life as if we never met."

Connor rocked back on his heels, stroking his chin as though considering her suggestion. He couldn't let her go, of course. She had answers he needed, and someone had to keep her out of trouble. "It's too late for that. You had your chance the night on the docks. You could have ridden away, and I would have forgotten all about you. But you came back, broke into my home twice, and stole from me. I think you owe me."

His eyes wandered, betraying his resolve. Even tired, bedraggled, and mad as hell, she could tempt a saint to sin. Lord, she was beautiful. Disheveled hair framed her heart-shaped face, and her tattered gown clung to her curves like a lover's embrace.

Fury shot from her green eyes like lightning, and for a moment, he nearly forgot the trouble she'd caused him.

"Getting you out of here will cost me a considerable sum of money. What do you have to offer in return?" He hoped she would offer to tell him about the Phantom, relieving him of the necessity to drag it out of her.

Her mouth fell open, color rushing to her cheeks. "Not a God damned thing, you heathen! Didn't you say just two minutes ago that you were a man of honor? How can you even suggest—"

He cut her off, his tone calm but firm. "Hold up. I'm not planning to compromise you, Mercy." A faint shudder ran through him at the thought. "I just want a few honest answers."

Her mouth snapped shut, her eyes wide with shock and indignation. "You don't want to bed me?" Disbelief dripped from every word.

Connor shrugged, amusement tugging at his lips. Of all the things he said, *this* was what she chose to fixate on? "No," he lied. "But don't fret. I'm sure whatever you possess is appealing to most men. I, however, am selective. I prefer women who are truthful, loyal, and possess integrity. Cleanliness and a commitment to regular bathing are also qualities I find appealing."

Her eyes narrowed. "I have those things." Turning her back, she leaned against the bars. "Just because I fell in the mud doesn't mean I don't bathe."

Connor stifled a laugh. "After you stole my property, left the state, and ditched me at the train depot, I would say honesty and integrity are off the list. I spent all day searching for you and my parchment, but you've lied at every turn."

He paused, letting his words sink in before continuing. "I found a carriage accident in the river on my way back to Richmond. I brought the victim into town, and then I walked in here to find you causing problems for the sheriff. Why I'm surprised is beyond me. You've been a pain in my ass since the moment we met. But I do have one question. How did they separate you from your uncle? Or did you run away from Justice, proving my assessment of your character?"

Her eyes flashed with fury, and she folded her arms across her chest, her foot tapping a sharp staccato against the stone floor. "Meaning my lack of loyalty?" Her voice wavered. "The…man we were with lied to me. I had no idea they planned to—" Her chin came up, and she glared green fire. "If I had known, I would have stopped them."

Connor's chest tightened. The bastards must have made her watch, judging from the pallor of her skin. "What didn't you know, Mercy?" He softened his tone, hoping she would consider him a friend…of sorts…and relate the entire event. Any information would be helpful.

Her silence weighed as heavy as a stone before she glanced away.

Some things were better left unsaid, and he understood that.

"Which brings another question to mind." He studied her expression with care. "You didn't say how you got away. Men like the Phantom don't let witnesses walk free."

Mercy's glare narrowed as if he'd just asked the most ridiculous question imaginable. "I *did* mention I can pick any lock." Her chin lifted in defiance. "And we didn't visit The Phantom. We were at a colonel's home. They locked me up in an isolated building near the river…after. I escaped, ran until I found a barn, and borrowed a horse. Well…you know the rest."

Connor studied her, unsure if he believed her story. He stared pointedly at the iron bars between them and raised an eyebrow. "If you're so good with locks, how come you're still in here?"

For a moment, he thought she might lunge through the bars and scratch his eyes out. Instead, she took a step back and glared. "The deputy took my hairpin. In response, I smashed a water dish over his head."

"Of course you did."

Her expression shifted, anger cooling into something bleak and raw, like molten lava meeting an Arctic Sea. "I wish…" Her voice faded. "I should have done something to help him."

Connor sighed and shook his head. He didn't want her spiraling down now. "No, Mercy. If you'd done anything other than what you did, they'd have killed you too."

Her emerald, green eyes locked onto him, searching his face as though looking for absolution. "I didn't know men like him existed. He has the cruelest eyes." Frowning, her expression grew thoughtful. "And there is something about him that frightens me."

Connor's gut twisted. "Did he hurt you?"

"I don't want to talk about it."

Connor cursed. If the bastard touched her, he would hunt him down and kill him. He meant to anyway, but her story added incentive. Gritting his teeth, he pretended to be disinterested. "What is his name?"

"Colonel something or other. He promised he wouldn't kill Uncle Justice for my failure." Her anger returned as she paced her small cell. "He planned to kill Uncle Justice all along."

Her words hit him like a fist to the gut. *Why not kill her, too?* "Give me a name."

Glancing his way, she shook her head. "I do not remember."

Connor narrowed his eyes. He could tell by the way she twisted the sides of her skirt that she lied and had no intention of sharing the information.

He would have demanded an answer, but the sheriff

walked back in. "Well, son, the farmer is willing to drop the charges for an additional fifty dollars or an apology. I figured he was more likely to get paid extra, so I agreed. If you have the money, I will unlock the cell, and you two are free to go."

Connor whistled between his teeth and cast a dark glance at Mercy. "For that sum, I'd better get a hell of a lot of answers." As he removed his wallet, he caught her grimace out of the corner of his eye and smiled. She should be worried. He had been interrogating prisoners for years, and she would be no match for his experience.

Chapter Twelve

Gettysburg, Pennsylvania – July 2, 1863
The battle that began yesterday has proven one of
the bloodiest I've seen in my two years with the Union
Army. At dawn, a chance encounter ignited a savage
exchange with Lee's advancing rebels. Artillery
thundered through the day as our lines crumbled, forcing
us to retreat to the hills. Through the night we waited,
battered but resolute. By morning, we shaped our
defenses into a fishhook formation, and the Confederates
struck hard. Little Round Top, the Wheatfield, Peach
Orchard, Culp's Hill, and Cemetery Hill all saw brutal
combat. Despite staggering losses, we held. Now, I sit on
a knoll, hearing the cries of the wounded and watching
Lee's campfires flicker beneath the sweltering July sky.

My thoughts turn to my sons. Connor rides for
Washington with a dispatch while Max remains
stationed in Port Hudson, securing our position. General
Cooper hopes to recruit Connor into the agency, though
I would not wish this life upon him. Were it not for the
love and steadfast courage of my wife, Maggie, I might
have lost my resolve long ago. I pray for her and our
sons each night, trusting God to keep them safe while this
dreadful war rages on. –Major Jonathon Calhan
****

Connor went for a walk to clear his mind, the cool
night air a welcome balm for his restlessness.

He wanted answers but hesitated to push his unwilling captive too far.

Mercy needed rest after the traumatic day she'd endured. Once she had dinner, her mutinous expression returned as she ordered him from her presence with a pointed glare, declaring if he had a shred of decency, he would vanish from her life forever.

Connor snorted at the memory. They took the last available rooms, and the proprietor roused his wife to fix them dinner. Once they ate and his little green-eyed thief thanked their host for her dinner, she turned on him with the wrath of a thousand dragons, demanding he show her to her chamber.

Releasing another deep sigh, Connor resisted the urge to chuckle over his predicament. Here he stood, the eldest of the Calhan tribe, and a confirmed bachelor in his thirties, loitering outside a hotel, hesitant to return to his room, and the beautiful woman sleeping one chamber over. Shaking his head, he stopped by the wrought iron fence at the back of the property. "If my family could see me now." A loving, close-knit family, convinced that only a wife and marriage could bring fulfillment to his life.

Connor's breath hung suspended in the crisp night air, the chill biting, but invigorating. He already had two women too many, and more complications than he could manage. Gabrielle, who professed undying love for him despite his lack of attraction, refused to accept he would never marry her. And Mercy, who haunted his thoughts with a maddening mix of desire and frustration, demanded he leave her alone, refusing to accept he would get the answers he desired.

Were all women so difficult to get along with?

Strolling back to the bench he passed earlier, he sat. The cold metal pressed against his backside through the wool of his trousers as Connor inhaled the cold crisp air and lifted his eyes skyward.

A shooting star blazed a silver arc across the velvet night sky, as the clear, cloudless canopy sparkled with a million twinkling lights. The most insatiable desire to make a wish took hold of him. Later, he couldn't decide what prompted the sudden display of weakness, the clarity of the quiet night, or the raw plea of his battle-weary soul for peace and the hope of a different life.

Sometimes, he wished for the impossible and thought about what having a wife and children would be like.

Before he could stop them, the words burst from his lips like a child yearning for a new toy on Christmas Eve. "While you're in the mood to grant miracles, Father, will you send me the woman meant for me?"

Snorting, he added, "If she exists." Giving a self-deprecating chuckle over the absurdity of wishing on a star for a woman, with his current problems, Connor cleared his throat and decided a little clarity would be in order. "I'm asking for the one who makes me forget every woman but her, the one woman I want to share my life with. A woman like you found in Mama. Wherever she is, will you tell her to hurry the hell up? The two I am acquainted with now are driving me crazy. The first one won't quit talking and the second refuses to start."

Connor fell silent. The frigid night sky twinkled back as if he hadn't just made the most ridiculous wish of his life, and a slight breeze nipped at his face, but no answer descended. Silence reigned around him, mingling with the darkening shadows. His heart beat low and steady beneath his woolen jacket, and his breath hung suspended around his nose. Alone, and weary to the bone of chasing the Phantom, he drew in a deep breath of arctic air and shook his head as if answering his own plea.

"You're right, Father. Once the Phantom is behind bars, I can consider settling down. No woman in her right mind would want to share the life I lead now. Not with the danger and uncertainty my line of work perpetuates. Once I finish this, we'll talk."

Leaves rustled at his feet, and the scent of burning coal drifted past in whisps as he sat silent appreciating the vivid night sky. Connor's mind returned to his reluctant companion, asleep at the inn.

"Thank you for the help today. I found Mercy, but she is in a bad way." Relating the day's events to the evening sky, Connor shoved his hands into his coat pocket for warmth. Dwelling on the details to draw out the time of his return, a couple of questions came to mind. Why did the colonel let her live when she could identify him? And if the colonel's men killed her uncle in front of her as he suspected, what did they hope to gain?

"He promised..." Mercy's grief-stricken voice tugged at his memory.

They wanted her compliance, but for what?

He shook his head over the situation. Leaning back, he stretched his legs out and crossed his boots. She should have run when he told her to. Now he had one option, to keep her by his side until he solved the riddle and put the Phantom behind bars. Killers didn't allow people to live who could give information or identify members of their organization, and Mercy's life hung by a thread.

Despite his warning, she dove far too deep. With no male family to protect her, he was her only chance for survival.

Connor lifted his head to the crisp night sky and sighed.

Something about the night's stillness brought peace to his soul and strength for the battle ahead. Rising, he retraced his steps to the hotel, hoping Miss Grumpy slept well and rose in a talkative mood. He had a better chance of seeing a nun in a saloon, but a man had to have hope.

****

Mercy snuggled down in the warm bed and smiled. Lord, did this feather mattress feel good! Unlike Aunt Charity's straw ticks.

Strong arms slid around her, and Connor's breath blew against her cheek, so warm and masculine. Fluttering wings filled her belly as she risked a glance at his face. Lord, he was a handsome devil, she admitted. Thick, black lashes framed his mesmerizing azure eyes, and his lids dropped to shield his expression. A day's worth of whiskers grew on his strong jaw and upper lip giving him a roguish appeal. His hard, warm mouth curved in a tender smile.

The heat radiating from his body seduced her, drawing her closer with an allure too potent to resist. His presence promised more than mere warmth. It whispered of solace, safety, and a haven in the storm of her sorrow. Like a firefly mesmerized by the glow of a flame, Mercy couldn't resist the pull, the need to feel the connection of another soul in the face of tragedy.

His touch obliterated every barrier she constructed, leaving her consumed by him, by the raw, undeniable need coursing through her veins.

His warm breath ghosted over her lips, teasing and tantalizing with the promise of his kiss. His hard, lean frame surrounded her, a protective shield against the world. At the same time, the intoxicating blend of his cologne and the sheer power of his presence threatened to undo every inhibition, leaving no space for doubt, no room for hesitation, only the irresistible temptation of his embrace.

Flicking her tongue over her dry lips, she forgot to breathe when his expression deepened. And then his lips were on hers, gliding with exquisite care against her softness.

The world tilted, drawing her into a warm, seductive place, where enemies, guns, murder, and death ceased to exist. She knew only the heat of his body surrounding hers, the thrill of his seeking lips, and the heady scent of desire.

Warm, intoxicating, and male, she traced her lips along his and sighed, startled by the surge of excitement racing through her.

Connor cradled the back of her head, anchoring her to him as he leaned in, his lips exerting a tantalizing pressure as they caressed hers, each movement a dance of seduction and sensuality.

Her stomach tightened, and her breath caught in her throat. Deep blue pools of hypnotic desire enticed her to move closer. Enveloped in the heat of his body, she longed to drown in his embrace. God's truth, he was a heady combination of sensual mature male, and temptation.

The taste of him on her lips made her tremble in his arms. Desire, danger, and tantalizing new waves of pleasure washed over her with each touch. His tongue thrust between her parted lips to swirl around her own, and she moaned with delight. Dear God, kissing a man had to be the most enticing thing she had ever done. And she wanted more. Wrapping her arms around his neck, she arced against him, reveling in the feel of his heat.

He responded with a moan and slanted his mouth over hers in an ever-increasing rhythm. With every stroke, liquid heat filled her belly, and butterflies fluttered in her chest. The teasing pressure of his lips drove her mad in an erotic dance as old as time.

His hands tangled in her hair, holding her in place for his invasion as his kisses grew deeper and more enthusiastic.

All she could think about was his hot, knowing hands and the taste of him in her mouth.

"Connor." His name came out with a breathless sigh. "I want to—"

A knock at the door made her jump. "Mercy. Are you all right in there?"

Connor Calhan.

She sat bolt upright, clutching her bedclothes to her aching breasts. Taking a quick survey of the small bedchamber, her attention returned to the door. Confusion and shame warred in her tight chest.

"Yes. I am…fine." She lied. Her dream replayed in her head, and she shivered in disgust. Remnants of traitorous, vivid desire clung, dragging their fingernails through her mind. Furious, she wondered how her subconscious could betray her on such a basic plane. Connor Calhan had no right to invade her thoughts, let alone her dreams. She must be going crazy. Aunt Charity's Bible verses finally drove her mad. Why else would she dream about the devil and in such…er…compromising circumstances?

"Are you sure? You called my name. Unlatch the door, and let me come in." He spoke against the door jamb and rattled the latch.

"I am not decent." Panic clutched her chest like a too-tight corset. "I will need at least twenty minutes."

The fire on the hearth popped behind her head, and she struggled to sit up.

Silence followed. "I will give you thirty."

His boots thumped on the wooden floor as he walked away.

Mercy blew out a breath of relief. What possessed her to dream such an erotic scenario, and with Connor Calhan of all people? Shivering, she pulled her bedclothes up to her ears and wrapped her arms around her middle. Her mind returned to the dream, and she squirmed beneath her covers.

She had no idea men touched women in such ways until one Sunday she overheard a confession by accident. Shocked, she hurried back to Aunt Charity and the cottage, hoping to forget the harlot's discussion with Father Maloney. Wrinkling her brow, she willed her nausea to calm down, wondering why her mind chose Connor Calhan as her lover.

She might need to go to confession. When she returned home, she would make a point to visit the good father and cleanse her mind of the evil it created last night.

Forcing her thoughts elsewhere, she focused on the conversation she overheard between Uncle Justice and the colonel.

Glancing at the hearth, she bit her lip. Connor hadn't

even been in Virginia when her mother died and had no hand in her death.

The thought would take getting used to.

She had no intention of letting go of her anger toward him. She had harbored the feeling way too long to let dinner and a warm bed sway her opinion. And after tonight's dream, she would keep her distance.

Connor Calhan was still the enemy, and were it not for the colonel's ultimatum, she would pick the lock and find her way home.

"Get close to him. Find out his plans, friends, business, and partners. I want to know everything before it happens, Mercy. Do this and you and your aunt will be safe." The colonel's voice played in her head, and she shivered.

"I won't let anyone hurt you. Or Aunt Charity." Connor promised as he left her outside the door to her rented chamber the night before. His deep voice rumbled as he turned away. "Get some rest, Mercy. I am one door down if you need further assistance."

Mercy closed her eyes and shook her head. One small act of kindness, and she had visions of the two of them kissing.

Embarrassment heated her cheeks. Why would she want to intimate with a man capable of killing in cold blood? A man who hunted innocent men and sent them to the gallows or prison? The colonel wanted her to get close to learn all his secrets, but she had to remain far enough away; tonight's misguided dream never became reality. Her heart couldn't take any more complications, nor could her tentative existence. Connor may not have had a hand in her mother's death, but his father had yet to be exonerated.

Jumping to her feet, she paced in front of the fire. Uncle Justice died because of her failure, and no amount of anger or sorrow could undo it. Her thoughts spiraled back over the events of the tragic day, and her chest tightened as the memories flooded in.

Assuming everything would be all right once she agreed to spy on Connor for the colonel, Mercy waited in the colonel's office for him to address other business, as he put it. When the colonel reappeared and escorted her to the front door, she stepped out expecting to see Uncle Justice. Instead, mounted soldiers waited along with two riderless horses. The colonel waved his hand at a dappled mare and commanded her to mount.

Glancing around, she frowned.

"Where is Uncle Justice?" To her consternation, her voice sounded young and frightened. Mercy turned to glare at the colonel. "I will not move an inch until you answer my question."

The colonel's dark eyes rested on her face as a sardonic smile twisted his lips. "Don't fret, Mercy. We will be with him soon. Now, do as I say."

His soldiers aimed pistols at her head, and she had no choice but to comply. In silent protest, she rode beside the colonel, until a black carriage fell in behind them.

"Ah, your uncle and my men have arrived. Come along, my dear, I have a surprise for you."

They rode for several miles before they stopped at a fork in the road. A wooden bridge sprawled across a wide, angry river off to her right, and the cobblestone road they traversed wound off to her left. "Why did we stop here?"

The colonel turned his dark, soulless eyes in her direction. "Here you will see what happens to my associates who do not follow instructions." Giving a shrill whistle, he waved to his men following the dark carriage. "Pay special attention, girl."

Mercy turned her head and gasped in shock as Uncle Justice appeared, bloody, beaten, and bound to a sturdy stock horse, his face unrecognizable.

"Merciful heavens! What have you done to him?" Her mouth dropped open as she took in his bound hands, gagged mouth, and the bloody mess of his face.

His black suit hung in tatters, and blood soaked the collar of his white shirt. Rage shot from his eyes as he stared at her companion.

"Remove him from the horse and get him into position." The colonel's mount shifted as he gave the command.

Mercy nudged her mare forward, intent on going to her uncle, but a soldier caught her bridle and shook his head, pointing his pistol at her chest.

The colonel's cold voice spoke beside her. "Tie her to the saddle and make her watch from the bridge. She will have the best view from there."

"The best view of what?" Suspicion formed a knot in her stomach, and apprehension sent a shiver of cold sweat trickling down her spine.

The colonel's icy command, given with such relish, made her chest tighten. A fine sheen of terror dampened her brow when the man beside her tied her hands and secured her to the saddle. Only as they positioned her on the bridge facing the rushing water and pulled her frantic relative from his horse did she realize they meant to kill him.

Screaming, she kicked her horse in the flanks, intent on knocking the soldiers holding her uncle aside, until the cool round tip of a pistol pressed against her temple made her cease mid-scream.

"I thought you would enjoy this next part. Don't make another sound unless you care to join your foolhardy relative."

The next few minutes were a blur of horror, disbelief, and panic as the colonel's men tossed a bloody, beaten Uncle Justice into the carriage and secured the door with a rope. Unreality, terror, and helplessness gripped her like a closed fist as she struggled to find a way out of this nightmare.

Driving the carriage to the top of a steep incline, the colonel's men unhitched the horses and sent the vehicle careening down the hill, crashing into the bridge and falling thirty feet over the side, hitting the water with a loud, sickening splash.

Mercy screamed with rage, kicking and bucking against the hands holding her down.

Cracking wood, gurgling water, and her screams filled her head. Gagged and bound to the carriage, Uncle Justice had no chance of survival.

The equipage dipped below the surface, and her scream of rage did little to alleviate the horror she experienced. For several frantic minutes, she searched the surface of the water to see where her uncle had gone, and then a corner of the once luxurious coach appeared amid the torrents of water racing away.

Mercy's stomach heaved in protest, and she retched all over the ground on her left until she had no more left. Blinking back tears, she sat up and stared straight ahead through a haze while she struggled with her composure. Resolve stiffened her spine as shock, denial, and rage warred inside her. One day, she would make the bastard pay for this, she vowed. Choking on her emotions, she glared at the turbulent gray river racing away and remembered her uncle's cardinal rule. *Emotion is a weakness one cannot afford in the face of adversity.*

A cold numbness settled over her as the carriage disappeared beneath the waves a second time.

She and Aunt Charity were the last remaining members of the Jackson family, and damned if she would let anyone change that. Straightening her shoulders, she lifted her chin and stared with unseeing eyes at the scene before her. She would do whatever she must to survive.

A low chuckle beside her brought her back to the present with a jolt. "I believe I have your attention, Miss Mercy. Now that you understand the seriousness of my request, you will send me information on Connor Calhan once a week via telegram. Mishaps and delays will not be tolerated. I will give you one week's leeway and expect my first report in a fortnight. Do not disappoint me as your uncle has or you know the penalty. I will be in contact."

A shiver of terror raced down her spine. She had no choice but to do as the colonel asked or risk losing Aunt Charity.

They locked her in the storage room of a deserted cottage half a mile away, heartbroken, furious, and determined to figure a way out. Revenge and hatred are powerful motivators. Within an hour, she had her hands free and plucked a hairpin from her hair for the lock on the door.

She shouldn't have stolen the horse, but desperation made a person do crazy things. The one thought on her mind had been to get the hell out of Virginia and back to Aunt Charity.

The fire popped, sending a small shower of sparks over the glowing logs, bringing her back to the present.

Boots thumped toward her, and with a cry of alarm, she ran for the screen, determined to be dressed before her enemy returned. For her battle with Connor, she required full-body armor.

Chapter Thirteen

Richmond, Virginia, December 1863
In recent weeks, I have reflected on the horrors of war and the sacredness of freedom. After a Confederate officer requested use of our home for wounded soldiers in January, I could not refuse. Servants converted the ballroom and parlors into wards, and I have since spent sleepless nights tending to broken bodies and anguished souls. The suffering has humbled me beyond words.

Two nights ago, Percival returned and exploded in fury at the sight of our house turned into a hospital. He forced the wounded out within hours and reminded me in a cold voice that I hold no authority on his plantation. That same night, he convened one of his secret meetings under guard, raising further suspicions. Unlike other homes in the area still sheltering the injured, ours now stands untouched, reserved, he claims, for "important purposes." I am certain something sinister unfolds behind closed doors, and I vow to expose it. Freedom belongs to all, and I will not stand idle. —Grace Bennett

****

"I have breakfast. We should hurry if we plan to catch the train back to New York. It leaves in an hour."

"I am almost ready." Lying came easier each time with Connor involved.

The train, New York, and Aunt Charity. Mercy repeated the words. They were worth the price she would pay, getting close to Connor and giving the colonel what he required. She shivered as she hooked the front of her corset.

Answers were what she planned to give to keep him close. But not truthful ones. No, she would give him the ones the colonel wanted him to have and no others.

The previous evening, Connor had been so kind and understanding. Too much so to be real, and she wondered what he hoped to gain. Answers? His gentleness and understanding, though appreciated, were responsible for her dream. And that particular memory she kept chained up in the bottom of her soul where it belonged. Connor was the son of the man who killed her mother, and she would never forgive him.

Mercy's hands were stained crimson with Uncle Justice's blood, and if she had any hope of reaching the ripe old age of forty-five, she had a role to play and information to obtain. With a heavy sigh, she finished dressing and stared at her long braid, wishing for the comfort of a brush, though she knew she had no time for such luxuries now.

Her gown bore tears from yesterday's ordeal, and she lost her shoes somewhere along the way. Tepid water in the small basin beneath an oval mirror would have to suffice for her toilet. As she stared at her reflection, Mercy noted the lines on her brow and around her mouth brought on by yesterday's trauma and the worry of relating the details to Aunt Charity.

How could she tell the older woman her last remaining sibling had died?

"The food is getting cold. Open the door, Mercy."

"All right." When she unlatched the door, Connor entered with a tray bearing two bowls of porridge, two spoons, and a bit of cream.

Mercy's mouth watered.

Setting the tray on the table, he retrieved a hairbrush from his jacket pocket. 'This is for you."

She froze, unsure of what to say. Astonished he would think of her, she stared from him to the brush and back. Narrowing her eyes with suspicion, she asked, "Why?"

Setting the brush beside the basin, he shrugged. "Why not? You look like hell." Dishing porridge into a bowl, he added a splash of cream and walked to the door.

His cheerful comment set her teeth on edge. "And after?"

"There are no strings attached, Mercy. It's a brush, nothing more. Now, get going. I have a carriage waiting to take us to the depot. The ride will take twenty minutes, and I will return to collect you in five."

Half an hour later, Mercy leaned back against the velvet cushion of the last remaining first-class compartment the train offered as the whistle blew announcing their departure.

The elderly woman Connor met at the station and invited to share their car for propriety's sake sat in the corner with her knitting basket by her feet. Gray-haired and curious, she picked up her yarn and settled back for the trip.

Mercy rehearsed the lies the colonel advised her to say in her head. Twisting her hands in her lap, she waited for Connor to settle.

Sitting across from her, he raised a brow and propped his foot on the opposite knee. "And now we talk."

His attention drifted over her heated cheeks and

settled on her lips for the barest second before returning to her eyes. "I want the truth, Mercy."

She had to lean forward to hear what he said and cast a side glance at their companion, who was busy counting stitches.

"Mrs. Patterson cannot hear us. The train wheels make too much noise by the window, which is why I offered her the seat. Now, talk, Mercy." Connor's eyes bored into hers, and she resisted the urge to squirm.

When she opened her mouth, he shook his head. "I am not interested in more deception. Lies will not save your life, or your aunt's, despite what you believe, or any promises whoever killed your uncle gave you. I can keep you alive, but you must trust me. The man or men who employed your uncle are ruthless, as I warned you the night you broke into my shipping office. If they murdered your uncle for failing them, what makes you think they will keep their word to a woman? Whatever they promised you is not worth the price you will pay." His eyes lingered on her face. "It is time you told me all of it."

Mercy looked down at her lap. She had to admit he made a good point. She had to trust him to keep her promise to Mama, but not with the whole truth. If he discovered her true identity, he would have nothing to do with her, and she wouldn't be able to gather the information the colonel required. Taking a deep breath, she told him enough to guarantee his help. "There is a second document which contains a cipher for the parchment. The men who…murdered my uncle believe you have it in your possession."

"And you are to bring the document to them if you want to live? Or did they threaten to harm Aunt

Charity?" His voice, though mild, made her wince.

Connor knew too damn much.

"I have one chance." Swallowing, she blurted the truth through her heartache. "They killed Uncle Justice for failing to collect the cipher. The colonel didn't want the parchment."

Her companion's expression did not change. His blue eyes glittered in the morning sun streaming through the little window of their compartment. "And where am I rumored to keep this all-important document?"

Mercy held her breath. "I am to discover its whereabouts." Glancing up at him through her lashes, she gave him her best impersonation of a distressed lady and hoped to God Connor Calhan had enough gentlemanly qualities to lower his guard.

Connor leaned forward. "Where did you go in Richmond?"

Mercy frowned. Most men were drawn to her helpless act, offering every kind of masculine service they could think of.

This one asked more questions.

"Uncle kept the drapes across the windows. I do not know." Lord, the lie made her tongue burn. Although she did not know the exact location, she knew they had visited Dawson Plantation.

"You left the train depot in a hackney carriage. They are not equipped with drapes." His eyes narrowed. "I grow weary of the lies, Mercy. I am your best chance of living, but I must know the truth. Your and Miss Charity's life depends on it."

She knew well the price she would pay for failure. "We stopped at an alehouse and changed to a private coach, with drapes. I do not know our final destination."

They stared at each other in a silent battle of wills until Connor sighed. "Fine. If you refuse to give me the answers I require, I will find a different way. When we get to New York, I will drop you off at your aunt's house, but understand, if you set foot on my property again, I will have you arrested. I cannot help you if you refuse to cooperate. And although I am loath to report you to the authorities, if you are in prison, you will be safe for the time being."

Mercy stared. "You have no proof of anything beyond my confession, and I refuse to accommodate you."

His smile did not reach his eyes." Your invasion of my private party a few nights ago is documented by an acquaintance who witnessed you stealing the parchment by way of the tree outside my home."

Her heart dropped. The man with the silver hair. Her mind raced with worry. If Connor's guest gave a statement to the police, she would be incarcerated and unable to protect Aunt Charity from the colonel.

He lied. He wasn't a gentleman after all. Flicking her lips with the tip of her tongue, she conceded. "The man we visited had a two-story brick home, and Uncle Justice referred to him as the colonel. He is close to your height with black hair and is very wealthy, from what I witnessed. He does not have your strength or agility and employs an army of servants."

"How old would you guess him to be?" Connor's lids dropped over his eyes, shielding his thoughts.

Her gut told her his question had an underlying purpose, and she decided to tell the truth one more time. "A year or two older than Uncle Justice."

Connor leaned back in his seat, studying her face.

178

"Thank you."

She wanted to scream and shake him. "Well?" She gave him information, and he should return in kind.

"Well, what?" His deep voice grated on her nerves, as did the arched brow accompanying it.

"Where is the cipher? You cannot be that obtuse. I answered your questions, now answer mine." She could tell by his impassive expression; he didn't plan to tell her a damn thing.

"I am curious why the colonel believes there is a cipher." Tilting his head, he studied her face.

"Why wouldn't he? Who would write gibberish without a cipher?" Her mind raced with worry while panic clawed at her chest. He had to give her some clues. The colonel would expect news by the end of the week.

"Someone intent on deception, planning to lead his enemy astray. Have you considered the man who wrote the code, and the person he wrote it for, both knew how to decode the parchment, thus making a cipher obsolete?" Connor lounged back against the soft cushion, straightened his long legs, and crossed his ankles. He looked for all the world like a satisfied man intent on having a nap.

Mercy's heart quit beating and then did triple time. Did Mama do the same thing with her diary? Did she know the code by heart?

"What makes you so sure the person who wrote the code for the parchment is a man?" If she didn't produce a cipher, she would have to have information for the colonel, or she would not enjoy another birthday.

"I'm open to every possibility."

Giving her companion her most beguiling smile, she made her voice breathless and innocent when she asked,

"What do you plan to do when we get back to New York?" If he did not tell her where he hid the cipher, maybe he would give her a tasty tidbit to pass on to the colonel.

Something glittered in the depths of his blue eyes, and a smile played around his beautiful lips. "I plan to check on my shipping business."

Disappointment welled up in her throat. "Is that all you have to say? I answered your questions. Where is the cipher?" The world twirled around her head as her heart picked up speed. Frustration and anger warred inside her. She thought this would be easier. A little smile, a little flirting, and she would have the answers she required. If he didn't cooperate, she would have to spend more time with him than she planned. And that would never do. Biting her lip, she clutched her hands together so tight they turned white against the emerald satin of her gown. He had to tell her something important. He promised.

"You haven't persuaded me yet."

Mercy couldn't breathe. Stiffening her spine, she lifted her chin. She could do this. She survived much worse. "What would you like me to do?" God, the words burned her tongue and made her nauseous.

"Tell me everything. I will not let them hurt you, but you must trust me enough to let me in."

Her heart fluttered in her chest. He asked the one thing she could never do, and as she stared into his sincere blue eyes, Mercy's resolve faltered.

Chapter Fourteen

Winter Quarters, Brandy Station, Virginia January, 1864

Reese and Max have joined me in winter quarters, and though we survive on boiled pork and hard tack, their presence lifts my spirits. Connor has been reassigned to Mississippi until the weather breaks. Our days follow a strict routine: rising at six, drills, weapon inspections, and hand-to-hand combat training. To stave off boredom, the men pass time with banjos, cards, or foraging. My Southern informant continues to be a valuable asset, recently warning us of dangerous Confederate plots. Her husband, a ruthless member of the Knights of the Confederacy, meets regularly with others during the cold season. I've asked her to compile names of those attending these secret gatherings, though I fear for her safety should she be discovered.

With so many soldiers nearby, I advised her to delay sending further messages until winter quarters disband. I thank God daily for preserving my life and the lives of my sons. We have much to lose, but far more to be grateful for. I pray for Maggie and the family's continued safety. –Major Jonathon Calhan

****

Shifting in her seat, Mercy lifted her chin and folded her arms across her chest. "I can take care of Aunt Charity." The words tumbled from her lips, tight and brittle, each one constricting the invisible band binding her chest.

Connor studied her, taking in her rigid posture, her defiant chin, and the tension brimming beneath her composure. "Let's make a bargain." He leaned closer and caught her hands in his firm grasp.

She assessed his hold without making any real effort to break free. Something in the intensity of his stare rooted her in place, a silent force halting her resistance.

"What kind of bargain?" She asked in a whisper, her eyes drawn to the piercing blue of his.

His eyes held hers, steady and sure. "I know someone you care for is tied to this parchment and its secrets. You risked everything to steal it, even your freedom, and in the process, you lost your uncle. The men who killed Justice won't stop. They'll destroy anyone who stands between them and their goal, and they'll do it without hesitation.

"Here's my bargain." He leaned closer, the heat of his presence wrapping around her like a tangible force. "No more lies. Tell me about your uncle's dealings with this colonel and any jobs he might be connected with. In return, I will help you find the cipher, keep you, and Miss Charity safe. You have my word."

The sincerity in his tone sent a flutter through her chest, a hundred wings stirring in her belly. His word of honor, the vaunted promise of the mighty Calhan name, delivered with such conviction it robbed her of breath.

Mercy's tongue darted to wet her dry lips as she wrestled with doubt and temptation. Could she trust him? A devil's deal, to be sure. To place her life, and her aunt's, in the hands of a man she despised, knowing he might unearth the secret she guarded, felt reckless beyond reason.

Narrowing her eyes, she tilted her head and peered into his soul. She couldn't fight Connor and the colonel at once. They were devils of different stripes, and with any luck, they might destroy each other before they did her. But what of the gold box? She needed it to start a new life, beholden to no one.

Her brow furrowed, her thoughts darting to her mother's diary, the puzzle she had yet to solve as Mammy's words echoed in her mind: *"The diary holds all the answers."* But without a way to decode it, its secrets remain locked. But that was another problem for another day.

For now, a bold plan took shape, sharp and daring. If Connor suspected Colonel Dawson's ties to The Phantom, why not lead him to believe they were the same person? A dangerous deception, but one she could wield to her advantage.

"I accept." She murmured the words, her voice steady despite the storm raging within her.

Connor's sharp scrutiny fixed on her, searching for cracks in her resolve. "Tell me about the day you spent in Richmond. You may have seen or heard something useful."

Mercy recounted every detail of her uncle's last day, omitting nothing, except, of course, the pieces she dared not reveal. When she finished, she clasped her hands in her lap and waited for his response.

Connor leaned forward, placing his arms on his knees, his expression unreadable as he absorbed her story. "Colonel Dawson." He mused, his voice low and thoughtful.

"Yes." Mercy's voice cut through the silence.

"Now, what of the cipher? If you share how you came into possession of the parchment but not the cipher, we can unravel the answer together." *And I can be rid of you for good.* Hoping her expression didn't give her thoughts away, she tacked on a sweet smile.

He took her measure with a sidelong glance, and then he recounted the story of his father's death.

Twice, Mercy's lips parted, ready to interrupt, but the quirk of his brow halted her, and she bit back her words, unwilling to explain her knowledge of his father's fate.

Listening with careful attention, she noted the gaps in his tale, missteps, and misassumptions, making her roll her eyes. His narrative, riddled with inaccuracies, fueled the beginning of a dangerous idea.

"Your father handed the parchment to the general before his death, but not the cipher?" Pressing, she kept her tone neutral. "Why would he separate the two?"

The subtle shift in Connor's expression told her he didn't like her question.

Mercy leaned back, folding her arms across her chest. In this game of devils, she intended to survive, and if luck held, to win.

Connor's voice, though calm, contained a subtle challenge. "I would think the colonel knew. My father's contact in the South claimed the cipher would arrive later, but he never received it and died before he could decipher the gibberish."

Mercy grappled with his words, their sharp truth slicing through her thoughts. A cold knot twisted in her stomach, the bitter taste of doubt creeping in. Had Uncle Justice lied about this, too?

"What about you?" Her voice faltered, but she

pressed on, the question burning her throat, wanting to hear him confirm what she overheard in Virginia. "Rumor claims you were there when the…southern lady lured your father into a trap." The words hang in the air like poison, each syllable tasting of death.

He met her intense regard without flinching. "I was on my way back from Washington, D.C., and arrived in time to bury him." His voice dipped, steady yet laced with pain. Clearing his throat, he continued. "Until now, I assumed the cipher didn't exist."

A shiver raced down her spine. Hearing his confirmation didn't make her feel any better.

"If the colonel works for The Phantom, why send us after the cipher?" Her heart pounded in her ears as the possibility took root: her uncle and his lies. Once again. And what about Major Calhan?

He studied her face, his expression thoughtful and searching. "We spread the word we had a way to read the parchment, hoping to draw The Phantom out. Who else would know it existed?"

Her heart sank, the weight of realization pulling her down. "Someone with firsthand knowledge. Either the writer or someone close to them."

Connor nodded. "Exactly. And I'd wager my fastest ship that the person we're hunting is on the list. Colonel Dawson and whoever he's allied with are not to be underestimated. The threat is real."

Mercy swallowed hard, her thoughts racing. Connor's words stirred memories of the past three years. Jobs her uncle took, and promises he made. Were they all connected to the Knights of the Confederacy and The Phantom? Uncle Justice trained her to believe the Calhans killed her mother. With Connor in the clear, the question remained on his father's involvement unless…She tensed. Did The Phantom and the knights kill her mother, too?

Hope flared in her chest at the thought of unmasking her mother's other killers, but doubt overshadowed it. "Even if we find the cipher, Colonel Dawson has the parchment." She fought the knot forming in her throat. The idea of stealing the document back turned her stomach.

Connor's calm smile infuriated her as he released her hands and tipped his hat over his eyes. "Does he?"

Confusion knitted her brow. "You know he does."

Stretching his legs out, he brushed his calves against her skirt, sending a jolt through her. "He has *a* parchment, yes. But not the one in question."

Her heart leaped, first in hope, then in dread. "The parchment we delivered is…a fake?"

Connor tilted his hat back and arched a brow in question.

"The colonel will figure it out soon enough. That's when the real trouble begins." Her breath hitched. The colonel would come for blood. Her blood and Aunt Charity's. Her hands trembled as the enormity of the danger bore down on her. "If the Knights of the Confederacy killed my mother, Uncle Justice knew the men responsible." Anger rose like bile in her throat. He kept the truth from her, let her anguish fester while he withheld justice and the truth.

Mercy closed her eyes as she relived his sharp retort in the carriage when she asked to read the parchment. He never intended to let her see it and used her mother to get her to steal the document for him. But why?

And then she knew. Connor fought in the war, and

with his close connection to his father, he would recognize her uncle in connection with the knights. The memory of Uncle Justice's cruelty, strikes, and scorn surged to the forefront, crystallizing into a betrayal so sharp it numbed her. He knew who killed her mother and protected the bastard.

Connor's deep voice broke through her thoughts. "I'm sorry Justice hurt you. But men who consort with killers are rarely good men."

Her uncle's voice echoed in her mind: *"Beware of Connor Calhan."*

Mercy lifted her chin, shrugging off the memory. "What else do you need to know?"

"Do you know who The Phantom is?" The question cut through the air, and though he kept his hat tipped, the intensity of his tone made her tense.

"No." She shook her head. "Colonel Dawson is the only associate of my uncle's I've met. He managed the negotiations while I stayed behind." Regret gnawed at her. If she joined him, she might have the names and faces she needed instead of relying on Connor to spot the threats.

Connor patted her hand, sending a shiver down her spine. "What changed this time? Why did Justice bring you along?"

The answer came with certainty, her voice quiet but firm. "You did." His touch soothed her, and she frowned. One did not find solace in the enemy, no matter how attractive they were. Desperate to regain control, she shifted her legs away and turned to stare out the window, her voice steady despite the turmoil inside. "The colonel didn't like Uncle bringing me to Richmond. He knew you'd follow the parchment. And me."

Risking a glance beneath her lashes, she braced for Connor's reaction.

Instead of the anger or disbelief she expected, he tilted his hat back and smiled, his blue eyes meeting hers.

"We will find the men responsible for both our parents' deaths, no matter how long it takes. Together, we'll uncover the truth and make the bastards pay." Connor's voice rumbled low, a vow steeped in iron. He patted her hand again. "Relax, Mercy. It's been a long day. I will keep you safe."

The steady rhythm of the train wheels clacking along the tracks and the gentle sway of the car lulled her restless mind. Sheltered against the soft velvet seat, Mercy sifted through the fragments of the last three years, dissecting every job she and her uncle undertook. A weary breath escaped as a troubling realization took root. Several homes on New York's Upper East Side warranted a second visit for answers.

Against her better judgment, she admitted the truth in silence. Connor Calhan was right. Uncle Justice harbored dark secrets and consorted with ruthless men. The thought stabbed her pride, sharp and unrelenting. She should have run the moment she sensed the shadows creeping into their lives. But then, she had been a child and did not know the depth of her uncle's evil soul.

****

Connor's mind churned with new revelations. Colonel Dawson. The name stirred no memories, and he wondered if the man was a recent addition to the Knights of the Confederacy or an old enemy hiding behind a new alias. Either way, Jefferson would dig into the details once Connor returned to the office.

Beneath the brim of his hat, he glanced at Mercy.

Her long lashes fanned against her pale cheeks, her deep, even breathing signaling sleep. The sight of her so vulnerable tugged at something deep within him.

"You will never face his wrath again." He murmured a quiet promise to the woman who flinched even in her dreams. "Justice is gone. He cannot hurt you anymore."

Mercy stirred when he mentioned her uncle's name, her body trembling. Connor tucked a shawl from the end of the seat over her knees, refusing to explore the overwhelming need to shield her from the demons of her past.

She needed time to process the trauma of the past days and time to find solid ground.

For today, he offered her comfort, a reprieve from the storm raging within her.

Forcing his thoughts away from the woman sleeping across from him, Connor refocused on the matter at hand. The colonel loomed large in his mind, a ruthless adversary who orchestrated Mercy's suffering. Trauma like hers didn't fade overnight, and she would need careful handling if she were to recover.

He resolved to enlist the general's help. Stationing men near Aunt Charity's home seemed prudent. A man as cold as Dawson wouldn't leave loose ends. Mercy's reaction when Connor broached the subject earlier spoke volumes, her flushed cheeks betraying her fear.

The cipher's existence, once a distant uncertainty, now sounded plausible. If Dawson killed for it, the document must have survived the war. Connor's father's faith in its importance echoed in his memory, and tomorrow he would scour old reports, searching for clues he might have overlooked.

Mercy's words resurfaced. The colonel ordered the deaths of two spies.

Connor reviewed every man and woman in his employ; confident none could have betrayed him. But the thought nagged, a shadow refusing to dissipate. Someone close to him gave Justice the layout of his shipping warehouse so Mercy could steal the parchment.

A soft hiccup from his sleeping bundle pulled him back. Her red-rimmed eyes and tear-streaked cheeks told of her exhaustion, even in sleep. Her tears twisted something in his chest, an ache he couldn't ignore. She shed no tears for Justice. Were these tears for her, Aunt Charity, or something he knew nothing about?

"Don't cry." He kept his voice quiet as he brushed a stray curl from her face. "Everything is going to work out."

But even as he spoke, the weight of the unknown bore down on him. And deep in his heart, Connor knew the road ahead would be anything but easy.

Chapter Fifteen

Richmond, Virginia, June 1864
At last, patience has paid off. Last night, the entire group of the Knights of the Confederacy gathered in Percival's study. I feigned sleep and crept downstairs once Mammy came for Mercy. From behind a large vase, I watched thirteen men arrive, including Justice. Tension ran high—Alexander Brown stormed out, followed by Lieutenant Dewheart, who left the door ajar. I caught a glimpse of Percival's safe and my stolen gold box within. The men debated raising an army in Cuba under Spanish rule, with Percival proclaiming their coming victory and America's downfall. Justice stepped into the hall, paused alarmingly close, and whispered, "Grace? I smell roses." I held my breath. He warned me to show myself before Percival discovered my betrayal, then returned to the study and spoke quietly to him.

The cook's arrival bought me time to escape. I slipped back to my chamber, undressed, and pretended to sleep as Percival entered minutes later. He loomed over me and said coldly, "Mind your own affairs, for your health and your daughter's welfare." Though his threat haunts me, I cannot remain silent. The list of names must reach Major Calhan. I will entrust it to a houseboy, for I dare not risk leaving the estate. –Grace Bennett

****

Aunt Charity took a turn for the worse.

The first hint of trouble struck Mercy the moment Connor's carriage halted outside the small, weathered cottage. As she stepped inside, a bitter chill greeted her, cutting through her cloak. No fire crackled in the hearth, no warm kettle steamed on the stove, and the silence pressed heavy, broken only by the creak of the floorboards beneath her hurried steps.

"Aunt Charity!" Panic gripped her chest as she rushed down the narrow corridor toward her aunt's bedchamber. Questions flooded her mind. Had the colonel lied? Had he sent men to silence her aunt while she hurried home?

Throwing open the door, Mercy froze on the threshold, her heart pounding against her ribs. Darkness shrouded the room, and the frigid air seeped into her bones. Her eyes took a minute to adjust before falling on the faint outline of a bent figure buried beneath a mountain of blankets. A loud snore broke the silence, rattling from the depths of the bed.

Relief swept through her, leaving her weak-kneed. "Thank God." Her heartbeat slowed to a steady rhythm as she approached.

A lace-trimmed bedcap peeked out from beneath the feather pillow, and a wheeze punctuated Aunt Charity's slumber.

"Mercy?" A thin, shaky voice emerged from the cocoon of blankets. "Is that you, child, or have I lost the last of my senses?"

Mercy perched on the edge of the bed, her voice soft but firm. "It's me, Auntie. I'm home." She reached out, brushing a stray lock of hair from her aunt's pale face. "Where is Tom? He was supposed to help you while I was away."

Her words held a bitter edge as guilt gnawed at her. Uncle Justice left her no choice, and they both knew it.

Aunt Charity's frail hand emerged, trembling as it clutched Mercy's. "Tom came the night you left, but I haven't seen him since. Something must have gone wrong, or he'd be here." Her explanation dissolved into a fit of coughing, her frail body trembling beneath the weight of the blankets.

Dread coiled in Mercy's chest, her earlier relief evaporating. She made a mental note to ask after Tom at the parish. Sliding an arm beneath her aunt's shoulders, she propped her up, taking care to keep the layers of warmth intact.

Connor appeared in the doorway, laden with logs. He crossed the room and dropped to his knees beside the cold hearth. "I found these outside the back door." His brisk, calm tone soothed her panic. "Why don't you see if you can light the stove in the kitchen and brew a pot of tea? She'll need something warm."

Mercy nodded, her mind swirling with unanswered questions. As she patted her aunt's back, she hesitated, then asked, "Did anyone…visit while I was away?" She had to know if the colonel or his men made contact.

Her aunt's slender hand tightened around hers. "I'm too chilled to talk, child. Let me rest, and we'll speak later." Her words trailed off as her eyes drifted closed, her gaunt face sinking deeper into the pillow.

A lump rose in Mercy's throat, her chest tightening at the sight. She couldn't lose anyone else. Turning away, she wiped away the tell-tale trail of tears down her cheek. Forcing a smile, she kissed the wrinkled cheek. "I'll bring you hot tea, Aunt Charity. Connor is lighting a fire. We'll have you warm and well in no time."

But there was no reply. Her aunt's face disappeared beneath the blankets, leaving Mercy staring at the fragile outline of her frail body.

Slipping out of the room, she made her way to the kitchen. Her hands trembled as she lit the stove, the frigid air biting her cheeks. Staring into the growing flames, Mercy bit her lip. She would disappear if it were just her and find a remote place where the enemy's approach could be seen for miles. Here, in the tangled streets of New York, the advantage belonged to the colonel.

But even in the face of danger, she knew she could never regret staying for Aunt Charity. Sometimes, her aunt's smile or a softly spoken word bore such a striking resemblance to her mother that Mercy's heart ached with both love and longing. She would hold onto those moments as long as she could, no matter the cost.

As the kettle began to steam and warmth crept through the small kitchen, Mercy closed her eyes, seeking a fleeting moment of peace. The sharp whistle of the kettle pulled her from her thoughts. Pouring hot water into a teacup, she added dried elderflower and fennel, a soothing blend to ease her aunt's strained breathing. Placing a dried biscuit alongside slices of cheese and apple on a small tray, she turned toward her aunt's chamber with a determined step.

When she walked through the doorway, Mercy paused. Connor sat at Aunt Charity's bedside, holding her frail hand in his. His voice, low and steady, carried an unmistakable weight, and the shock on her aunt's face revealed the gravity of his words.

"And what of Mercy?" Aunt Charity's voice trembled, rising an octave as her thin fingers clutched his much larger hand. "Is this madman after her, too?"

Mercy hovered in the doorway, heart pounding, until Connor glanced up and motioned her forward.

"He wants what she can find out," Connor explained, his voice edged with steel. "That's why he hired Justice to steal the parchment from me. He will kill anyone in his path, including you."

The older woman fell silent, her face pale and drawn, as Mercy set the tray on the bedside table and offered the steaming tea. Aunt Charity's hand trembled as she accepted the cup.

"I always feared Justice would be the death of me." Aunt Charity murmured, her words tinged with sorrow. *"An unrepentant sinner is the devil's servant, bringing ruin and despair to all he touches."*

The quiet pain in her voice cut Mercy to the core. Swallowing hard, she forced a steady tone. "We won't give Colonel Dawson the chance to harm us, Auntie. I would sooner die."

"Unacceptable," Aunt Charity snapped, her sharp eyes locked on her niece. "Your mother would never forgive me if I allowed harm to come to you. I gave her my word to protect you, and I shall keep it."

Her focus shifted to Connor, her frail yet commanding presence formidable. "And you, young man, what do you plan to do to keep my niece safe?"

Connor leaned forward, his tone steady and reassuring. "This is a dangerous game, Miss Charity, and I won't pretend otherwise. As long as Mercy holds something the colonel desires, he won't harm her. For now, her task is clear. Find the cipher. I have my work to do, and once I complete it, I'll determine our next steps. Until then, I'll stay close, and my men will keep watch over this house. You have my word."

"Colonel Dawson." Aunt Charity spoke the name, as though tasting its weight. "It's a peculiar name. Years ago, I heard of a man with the same name who started a rebellion in Cuba. The government sent troops to kill him on sight, but I never heard how it ended." Her brow furrowed in thought. "My sister, Mercy's mother, kept a diary, also written in code. I suspect the names of her murderers are listed there. In her last letter, she mentioned The Phantom in the most chilling terms. I believe he had a hand in her death. Does the name mean anything to you, young man?"

Connor's expression remained neutral, but Mercy took note of the slight tick in the pulse at the base of his neck. She alone knew the name stirred him.

"May I read the letter?" His quiet tone relayed all the importance of a discussion about the weather, as he smiled down at her aunt.

Panic clutched Mercy's chest, and her teeth began to chatter. A letter from her mother? Aunt Charity never mentioned she had one before. Why now? And if Connor read it, he would know the secrets she fought so hard to keep.

"I would allow you to if I still had it." Aunt Charity's response brought both relief and frustration. "I mentioned the letter to Justice during his first visit after Mercy joined me. He asked to see it, but later claimed it slipped from his hand and fell into the hearth, burning to ashes."

Mercy's breath caught, her emotions a storm within her. Relief coursed through her, but frustration burned hot. She couldn't read it either and wanted to howl her disappointment.

"Interesting," Connor commented, his tone low and thoughtful.

Mercy glanced at him, uneasy with the sharp intelligence in his eyes. What conclusions had he come to? With any luck, her secrets would remain safe, for now.

"Is The Phantom connected to my brother's death?" Aunt Charity's voice, sharp and resolute, shattered the stillness. No longer huddling beneath layers of bedclothes, she sat upright, her back pressed against the headboard. The tea and biscuits worked their magic, but the intensity in her eyes, glued to Connor's face, revealed something more than restored strength. Both her frail hands clasped his forearm as if he were her lifeline.

The room, now brimming with warmth from the hearth, stifled Mercy. She couldn't decide whether the discomfort stemmed from her recent encounter with the colonel or the dread of her secrets unraveling. Either way, she prayed for a burst of arctic air to clear her mind.

"Yes, he is involved." Connor's voice carried the weight of certainty tempered by caution. "I believe Colonel Dawson works for The Phantom. Though, to be truthful, I have met neither man, and my suspicions remain difficult to prove." Rising, he added, "I must be on my way. You should rest, and I have research demanding my attention. I bid you good evening, Miss Charity."

But her aunt held onto him for a heartbeat longer, her grip firm despite her frailty. "It is a sin to say so, but I thank God Mercy broke into your warehouse. Knowing you're protecting her eases my mind, and I am grateful you brought her home from Virginia. We owe you our debt of gratitude, Mr. Calhan." Aunt Charity's demeanor sharpened. "But before you go, I have a favor to ask."

Mercy froze mid-step, balancing the tray in her hands. A frown tugged at her brow. Whatever her aunt wanted, she would find a way to provide it. She disliked being beholden to anyone, least of all Connor.

"Whatever is within my power is already yours." With a disarming smile, Connor paused. Slipping his arm behind Aunt Charity, he steadied her as she adjusted her position. The ease of his movements left Mercy staring, her frustration melting under the sheer force of his charm.

"I need to visit my brother's home tonight." Aunt Charity's voice brooked no argument. "I must retrieve something before any of his unsavory companions hear of his death." Her chin lifted as if daring Connor to deny her.

He hesitated for the briefest moment before offering a respectful nod. "As you wish. Once you're rested, I will escort you."

But Aunt Charity tightened her grip on his arm. "No. I must go now." Urgency colored her tone, raising it several octaves. "I would not ask if the matter were not serious."

Surprise flickered across Connor's face before his features settled into calm resolve. "Then now it shall be." Stepping back, he strolled toward the door. "I'll wait outside while Mercy helps you prepare."

The moment the door shut behind him, Mercy turned on her aunt. "What are you after? Why drag Connor into our private affairs?" Her voice dropped to a hiss. "I want him at arm's length, not pulled deeper into our business."

But her aunt would not be swayed. "I must collect

Justice's box. As the last of my siblings, it belongs to me by right." Her tone hardened, brooking no dissent. "I cannot risk Colonel Dawson or any of Justice's vile friends finding it first. Nor will I risk you going alone into Justice's den of iniquity. We will make use of Connor Calhan while we can."

Mercy sighed, resignation pulling at her shoulders. When Aunt Charity set her mind to something, no force on earth could deter her. She helped her aunt into a loose gown and carefully brushed out her hair, her thoughts consumed by the box. The whereabouts of her mother's box haunted her for years. The missing link to her mother's past, as it were.

An hour later, Connor opened the door to Uncle Justice's study and led Aunt Charity inside. The chill in the air bit Mercy's cheeks, but her focus remained on the ornate mantlepiece where Aunt Charity removed a gleaming, jewel-encrusted gold box.

The object radiated elegance and wealth, while the intricate oval centerpiece embossed with the initials "JJ" caught fire in the lamplight.

Connor let out a low appreciative whistle.

"These boxes," Aunt Charity began, cradling the treasure, "were commissioned by our father, Ebenezer Jackson, from Chaumet, the great jeweler. He ordered one for each of his children. Mine went to church as a gift. Justice displayed his here. And my sister's…" Her voice faltered, emotion flickering in her eyes. "My sister's box disappeared when she married and left for the South, taken by her husband. It hasn't been seen since."

Mercy's chest tightened at the mention of her mother's box, the mystery of its disappearance weighing heavier now than ever. She glanced at Connor, whose calm demeanor betrayed nothing, though she caught the subtle flicker of interest in his eyes.

The box flashed in the lamplight, its significance palpable. The family believed her mother's box had been lost for good during the war.

But Mercy knew different. Her mother, in a final act of rebellion, slipped into her husband's office one fateful night, and reclaimed the box. Wrapped in a coarse sack, hidden from prying eyes, and entrusted to Mammy, the box traveled far, cradled alongside Mercy as they fled into the shadows. Her mother's act of defiance remained Mercy's most sacred secret; one she guarded with silence as impenetrable as the night her mother died. Until the day she held the box in her hands, no one would know the full truth.

"No one knows what happened to my sister's box. Although there have been disturbing stories." Aunt Charity's voice softened with remembrance as she ran her fingers over the ornate lid. "We hope her diary will reveal what happened to her and her box."

Mercy's pulse quickened as she ushered her aunt and Connor from Uncle Justice's study before another family secret could escape Aunt Charity's lips. To her relief, Connor said nothing, guiding her aunt to the waiting carriage with the same quiet composure that unnerved her all evening. He offered a curt nod to Uncle Justice's scowling staff before entering the carriage.

"I believe your visit is timely, Miss Charity," Connor assured her once they were settled. "From the expressions Justice's staff wore, I am convinced the box would have vanished before sunrise had you not retrieved it." His gentleness with her aunt and the careful way he helped her into the velvet-pillowed seat, tugged at Mercy's heartstrings.

She scowled, unwilling to acknowledge how he undermined her defenses. Watching the two of them across the carriage, she noted how Aunt Charity leaned into his side, her thin fingers clutching his tawny, muscled forearm as if he were her kin. He gave every comfort he could provide without hesitation, tucking pillows behind her and pulling the butter-soft blanket from beneath the seat without being asked.

Mercy rolled her eyes toward the heavens. "I thought velvet pillows were the devil's tools, unfit for any God-fearing person lest they corrupt the soul with sinful indulgence."

Aunt Charity wrinkled her nose, not bothering to make eye contact as she nestled deeper into the cushions. "They are. But the Bible says nothing about enjoying a Calhan's velvet temptations."

Mercy snorted. "I see. His soul is already in question, so why not revel in his bounty of sins?"

"Precisely." A small smile hovered on her aunt's lips.

Connor arched a brow, his tone playful. "Since the night is frigid, may I tempt you further with an ermine blanket? My sins are legion."

"Ah, yes. I would be delighted," Aunt Charity replied with a dramatic sigh.

Before Mercy could respond, Connor had her aunt swathed in the additional comfort of the luxurious blanket, tucked snugly against his side. Despite Aunt Charity's strict simplicity, she couldn't resist the allure of fine things. Within moments, her head bobbed against Connor's arm, and soft snores filled the carriage.

Relieved her aunt relaxed enough to sleep, Mercy turned her attention to the streets as they sped toward the Lower East Side. The scent of wood smoke filled the air as gas lamps cast flickering shadows across the cobblestones, and the carriage wheels rumbled home. But the familiar sights and smells weren't what caught her attention. A dull black carriage, reminiscent of a hearse, trailed behind them at a deliberate, unsettling pace.

She stiffened, her breath catching. Turning her attention toward Connor, she whispered, "Friends of yours?"

He met her inquiry with a sharp, assessing stare. "No."

Connor rapped on the carriage roof with his cane in a deliberate series of taps, quick, then slow, then quick again. His grip on Aunt Charity tightened, his jaw set, and Mercy's unease grew.

"Arthur will lose them," Connor assured her, his voice low to avoid disturbing Aunt Charity. "He's well-practiced at such maneuvers."

Mercy nodded, glancing back at the shadowy carriage as their own picked up speed. The rhythmic clatter of hooves grew louder, and the streets blurred past in a haze of gaslight and darkened shopfronts.

True to Connor's word, by the time they reached the Lower East Side, the ominous black carriage no longer trailed behind. Their journey concluded without further incident, but Mercy's pulse didn't settle until Connor carried her slumbering aunt into the cottage and laid her on the bed.

He stepped from the room without a word, leaving Mercy alone to watch over her aunt. She lingered for a moment, the unease from their shadowy pursuer still gnawing at her. Somewhere in the night, unseen eyes were watching, and she knew the reprieve wouldn't last.

Aunt Charity's voice startled Mercy. "I think God will make allowances for that one, despite what Justice claims. Now, hand me the box, girl, and go thank Connor for overseeing the situation." With a deep sigh, the older woman burrowed beneath her bedclothes, disappearing into the depths of her feather pillows.

Mercy couldn't suppress a wry smile. Aunt Charity would thank the devil if he appeared with a glass of spiked punch to quench her thirst.

A shiver raced down her spine as she escorted Connor to the door. Dare she trust this man whom she had grown up loathing, and whose gentle care for her aunt chipped away at the iron bands guarding her heart.

Stopping beside the door, she took a steady breath. "You mentioned research earlier?" Grasping for something, anything, to relay to Colonel Dawson, a snippet to buy more time, she hoped Connor would comply without coercion.

His smile made her pause, melting her weakened defenses. "I will keep you safe, Mercy." His voice softened, yet his eyes danced with amusement as he rubbed his chin and tilted his head, his blue eyes resting on her flaming cheeks. "Tell Dawson I have letters and reports written during the last battle in Virginia to review. With any luck, I'll find something I missed, which will lead me to the cipher's current location. Now I know The Phantom's roots trace back to Richmond, my focus will be there. When you send your telegram, be sure to let him know I'm coming for him."

Before she could summon a reply, Connor leaned

forward and pressed a swift, maddening kiss to her lips before the door clicked shut behind him, leaving her stunned and shaken.

Chapter Sixteen

Washington, D.C., July 1864

Earlier this month, Confederate forces reached within five miles of the capital. Thanks to a timely warning from my Southern informant, we assembled Union forces in time to repel the attack. President Lincoln came under fire while observing the battle, though he escaped unharmed. By God's grace, the threat has passed, and calm has returned. On my way south, I paused to spend a night with my beloved Maggie. Though I spared her the full truth of war's horrors, her presence was a balm to my soul.

Connor and Max remain in the thick of it, faring as well as can be hoped. I've heard nothing of Reese for over two weeks, though I hide my worry from Maggie. Despite the bitter cold, hunger, and sorrow around us, I cannot bring myself to complain. My sons and I still live. When I kissed Maggie goodbye, a shadow whispered I might never see her again, but I forced it away. I choose hope. Love, light, and better days wait ahead. Until then, we endure—and place our faith in God's hands. –Major Jonathon Calhan

****

Connor strolled down the cobbled street, a low chuckle rumbling in his chest. Miss Mercy Jackson intrigued him. Her soft lips and rounded body drove him mad, and her mind played cat-and-mouse games with his. He knew she would have to feed the colonel some tidbit to keep him at bay, and yet she refused to ask. He didn't have time to see if she planned to seduce him into talking as he hoped and gave her just enough to seem credible while revealing nothing of consequence. Another day and another time.

In truth, his focus lay elsewhere. Back at his office, the satchel containing the last few months of his father's letters awaited. With his focus on Richmond, any irregularity in those reports might hold the key to locating the cipher and uncovering the truth his father died for.

The parchment Mercy stole and delivered to Justice had been a clever counterfeit, altered to serve as bait. The original remained locked in the general's safe, untouched and guarded until they could decipher its secrets. Neither he nor the general trusted anyone else with its location.

Hours passed as Connor pored over his father's correspondence, the flickering lantern light casting shadows across the room. The scent of aged paper and ink filled the air, each letter a step closer to unlocking the mystery.

At three in the morning, his eyes burned with exhaustion. Blowing out the lanterns, he collapsed onto the bed, succumbing to a dreamless sleep.

Knocking at the door roused him far too soon. Benson's muffled voice broke through the haze of sleep. "Sir, there has been an accident."

Connor bolted upright, heart slamming against his ribs. Throwing the bedclothes aside, he barked, "Come in, Benson. Tell me what happened."

God, if anything happened to Mercy or Aunt Charity after he left, the colonel wouldn't live to see another sunrise.

Benson entered, his usual composure tinged with gravity as he placed a tray laden with breakfast and tea on the side table. "Francois Blanchart has been found, Sir. Authorities discovered his body floating in the East River early this morning. Miss Blanchart awaits you in the west drawing room."

Connor's heart, tight with dread, eased, and he released a long breath. Relief flooded him. Thank God.

"She is…agitated, Sir."

"Understandably so." Connor dressed quickly, shrugging into a cream linen shirt and fawn breeches. He slipped on his brown jacquard vest with gold embroidery, its intricate pattern gleaming in the morning light. As he pulled on his tall boots, Benson fussed with his cuff links, his precision as steady as ever despite the somber news.

Straightening his collar, Connor squared his shoulders and headed for the drawing room, his mind racing through the implications of Blanchart's death.

"Sir, she is…more so than usual." Benson's droll tone stopped Connor mid-stride on his way to the door.

Turning back, he tilted his head in surprise when Benson extended a pistol toward him. "You may require this."

Connor's eyes narrowed. He disliked the tone, and he liked the implication even less. Taking the pistol, he tucked it into his belt, its weight a subtle reminder of the confrontation waiting downstairs.

Descending the stairs with measured steps, he entered the west drawing room.

Gabrielle Blanchart stood before the window, her back rigid and unmoving. She wore a pale blue silk gown, her hair swept into an elaborate updo adorned with white ostrich feathers and a smart blue hat perched amid the curls. Her tailored jacket hugged her curves, creating the enviable hourglass silhouette coveted by women of her station.

Connor moved to the hearth; his posture relaxed, but his mind alert. "Good morning, Gabrielle. To what do I owe the pleasure?"

She turned, her lips curling into a feral smile. "Revenge. Justice. And hatred. All for you, Connor Calhan." Her voice dropped to a chilling pitch. "I came to kill you."

Connor's brow lifted. "Before I've had my breakfast?"

The transformation startled him. The poised, genteel lady of fashion turned to a rabid she-dog radiating raw, unrestrained fury. Her narrow eyes glittered with malice, her nostrils flared, and her mouth pressed into a thin, cruel line.

"Close the door, *darling*, so we can be alone." She dropped her pitch, although her tone remained razor-sharp. With one hand tucked inside an ermine muff, she gestured with the other toward the door.

He studied the muff. The way she clutched it, awkward and tense, piqued his suspicion. "I believe the door is fine as it is."

Her lips pulled back, revealing white teeth in a predatory snarl. The vein in her neck pulsed a visible testament to her mounting rage. "You misunderstood me. Close the damn door, or I'll shoot you in the heart."

The muff lifted, and Connor caught a glimpse of the barrel of a Derringer tucked inside.

"My finger is on the trigger." Her voice trembled as

she shifted her weight. "I will not hesitate to fire."

Connor inclined his head, his expression calm. "Close the door, Benson."

The sound of the heavy oak door clicking shut echoed in the room. Connor's eyes never wavered from Gabrielle's face as he leaned against the mantel. "You seem quite out of sorts this morning, Gabrielle. Did you not eat either? I will have Benson bring us a tray, and you can explain why you've entered my home armed and full of murderous intent."

A scream of fury burst from her lips, sharp and piercing, making his ears ring. "I do not want to eat, you smug, conceited bastard! I want to kill you. I did everything right. I cried, I cajoled, I offered my body, and I played the victim until I wanted to vomit. And still, you refused to do the one thing I wanted!"

Taut and ready to spring, she held her posture stiff, and her shoulders squared while she eyed him like a caged animal.

Connor arched a brow, his tone unperturbed. "This is about marriage?"

She stomped her heeled slipper so hard she almost lost her balance. "No! This is about *my life*! Mine, Connor Calhan. I should be in Paris, married to Pierre Lefevre, living the life I deserve. But because of you, because you refused to cooperate, my father is dead."

Connor pieced together the fragments of her tirade. "Pierre Lefevre? The man who wronged you and left you to face scandal alone?"

Her laugh, sharp and bitter, cut through the room. "There was no scandal, you fool. I fabricated the entire story to get close to you so I could gather information." Her eyes blazed with venom. "What did I do to deserve this? God, when I think of all the times I begged you to take me to your bed, I feel sick."

Connor's lips curled into a faint, humorless smile. "The sentiment is mutual, Gabrielle. Please, do continue. I'm eager to uncover the root of this outburst."

Resting his forearm on the mantel, he studied her with detached patience while he waited for her to continue.

Her tone sharpened, cold fury gleaming in her eyes. "We were nothing when we came here. Just another poor immigrant family scraping by, desperate for work. No one would hire a man who spoke broken English. We were destined for the workhouse until Colonel Dawson came along. At first, his offer seemed heaven-sent. He gave us money, bought Papa ships, and set us up on the docks." Her smile didn't reach her eyes. "Right beside you."

Her voice dipped, trembling with anger. "All I had to do to repay him was spy on you. I gave the colonel maps of your warehouse, detailed your movements, and searched for some damned parchment. But every time I got close, either you or your bloody butler got in my way. Then the colonel sent someone else to finish what I couldn't, and now my father is dead. I will never forgive you, Connor Calhan."

The pieces clicked together. All the times he'd caught Gabrielle wandering through his home, rifling through his possessions, all made sense now. And Mercy. Her unerring ability to find her way to the second floor and his desk, despite never having stepped foot in his building before. Connor strolled over to the drink trolley, splashing whisky into a glass. His movements were deliberate. Rolling his shoulders, he prepared for what came next, knowing his nonchalant demeanor infuriated her, as he intended.

"Get back by the hearth and don't move unless I say." Her voice trembled, betraying her fear.

Connor hid his smile.

Gabrielle claimed to know him better than anyone. And she should be terrified.

Replacing the stopper in the bottle, he swallowed the fiery liquid and grinned. His mother always said he had a problem with authority. And he agreed, especially when the figure in question was a woman who couldn't hit the linear side of a stationary train.

"And your father?" He kept his tone casual, though his eyes never left her face. "What did he get for his part in this charade? Other than dead?" Tossing back the rest of his drink, he poured another measure and strolled back to the hearth, ignoring her trembling hands and the Derringer she clutched in her muff.

Her eyes bulged with fury. "The ships, you fool. The God-damned ships! But you fixed that too, didn't you?"

"I have no idea what you're talking about." Swirling the amber liquid, he raised his glass. "If something happened to Francois's ships, I wouldn't know. I've been busy. You know what kind of a man the colonel is. I would look in his direction for someone to blame."

Her rage boiled over. "Don't you understand? Both of my father's ships were set on fire last night. We've lost everything." Her voice cracked, and she flung her free arm wide, spewing hate-filled threats ranging from crude to impossible. But one struck a nerve.

"I will find your little green-eyed witch and make her pay—"

"If you so much as look in her direction, I'll snap

your neck in two." His voice dropped, flat and cold as death.

The threat struck true. Gabrielle stepped back, her eyes wide with fear.

"Don't feel bad, *darling*." Connor drawled to give more emphasis. "You played the part of the deranged lover well. Almost convincing enough to earn my pity. If I had a heart, I might have married you off to a cousin. But something about you never felt right."

Her face twisted, and her hand began to rise, trembling. "Neither do you. No decent man is so cold, so cruel, and I've come to end it now."

"Agreed." Connor moved like lightning. With a flick of his wrist, he sent her muff flying across the room. Before she could blink, his hand closed around her throat, pinning her in place.

Her wide, terrified eyes locked on his. "What are you going to do to me?"

"Nothing." He kept his grip firm but restrained. "Benson?"

The door swung open, and three officers strode in, followed by Benson, whose beaming smile bordered on smug.

"However, these fine gentlemen are here to escort you to a private cell where you'll await trial as a traitor." He gave a nonchalant shrug before delivering the final strike. "Let's hope the judge sees you before the colonel finds you."

Her bravado crumbled like a castle made of sugar in the rain. "You can't do this. If he discovers I'm alive, I'm a dead woman. Please!"

Her sobs filled the room, but Connor didn't waver. Her pleas slid off him like water off of stone.

"Take her away." Stepping back, he dismissed her with a wave of his hand.

As the officers escorted Gabrielle from the room, Connor turned to Benson. "Send word to Richmond. Let the colonel know Miss Blanchart has been arrested."

"You cannot do this." Gabrielle's eyes, wide with terror, brimmed with tears as her trembling voice echoed through the room. Her desperate sobs and pleas clawed at the air, but Connor remained unmoved.

"I might have allowed you to leave my home a free woman despite your threat to end my life." His eyes narrowed on her pale face. "But you made the mistake of involving Mercy."

Gabrielle dropped to her knees, almost toppling the officers. "I swear on my mother's grave, I'll leave the country. You'll never see me again. Please, Connor, let me go."

Her tone caught his attention. For once, she didn't whine or pout. Her wide eyes and trembling lips were real, laced with terror.

His mouth tightened. "I will give you one chance." He kept his voice cold as ice. "If you are still in the United States by morning, I will deliver you to the colonel in Virginia. And trust me, Gabrielle, he won't extend the same mercy."

Her face drained of color, and she stumbled as the officers hauled her to her feet.

Connor didn't move or speak as they led her from the room. The heavy door closed behind them, leaving a thick silence in their wake. Good riddance.

Ringing the bell, he informed the housemaid he required breakfast before any more complications in his day arose. Connor crossed to the hearth as the maid hurried away, resting his forearm on the mantel. The fire crackled and popped, its warmth doing little to dispel the chill settling in his chest. He couldn't afford distractions, not with Colonel Dawson looming, and the cipher still out of reach.

And not with Mercy Jackson occupying too much space in his thoughts.

Chapter Seventeen

Richmond, Virginia, July 1864

After weeks of eavesdropping outside Percival's study, I've learned a shadowy figure known only as "The Phantom" leads the Knights of the Confederacy, though his identity remains hidden. I've finalized a coded system to communicate with Major Calhan and await the right moment to send my next message. Last night, I returned to my chamber to find Percival near the spot where I hide my diary. My heart stopped, fearing he might assert his marital rights, a thought made more loathsome by what he's done to the enslaved women. Instead, he only asked about Mercy, kissed my cheek, and left.

The war creeps closer to our doorstep, and I fear for Mercy's future. Tonight, The Phantom is expected at a secret meeting, and I plan to hide behind the corridor vase to record the names of those in attendance. Justice's chilling look today made me suspect he knows I leaked information about the train robbery and hidden gold. But my tip helped defend Washington from Jubal Early's assault, and though some may call me a traitor, I place my faith in God's mercy. With Mammy's help, I will encode and deliver the names to Major Calhan. Since Emma's death, Mammy has been my only true ally. – Grace Bennett

****

"Well, I'll be double damned." General Cooper

leaned back in his leather seat and shook his head when Connor finished his report. "This Colonel Dawson is a resourceful man. He has coins to pay for ships and connections to set up a shipping company in the same location as his victim. And he does so with such aplomb, no one thinks anything of it. Logic suggests our colonel has access to a chest of gold coins to make such a purchase. I find it interesting Miss Mercy's aunt thinks she heard of a man in Cuba with the same name. If he is the same man, we know why we were unable to locate The Phantom following the war."

Connor nodded. "I will have Jefferson check into this and see what we can find. There may be people in Cuba who know something useful."

"I agree. What do you plan to do about the cipher?"

"You were the closest to Father. Is there any other place or thing we haven't examined?" Connor tossed the question out, hoping the general would remember something.

But the general shook his head. "You know the story. You were there to witness the carnage of war. Things were lost and destroyed. Homes were burned, possessions stolen, virtue lost, and lives snuffed out. No one was safe during those dark times. Everything Jonathon had in his possession at our post outside Richmond has been scoured and categorized. He died in his nightshirt after writing his letter. I am sad to say, we may not have the one thing keeping Mercy and her aunt alive. If the colonel is willing to risk coming to New York to kill Francios Blanchart, he can get to her, too."

Connor had the same thought. "I know." Silence filled the office. "I have more reports of Father's to go over at home. God willing, something jumps out at me this time around. I plan to swing by and check on Miss Charity on the way."

As soon as he came down the street, he could tell something was amiss. The air hung heavy, laden with an unsettling stillness. His horse's hooves clip-clopped along the cobblestones, the only sound in the empty lane.

Connor pulled on his reins, his pulse quickening. Stopping outside the little cottage, he froze. No smoke curled from the chimney, and no candle lit the interior. The door hung by the top hinge, and nothing moved. Swinging down from the saddle, he assessed the scene with practiced eyes. No blood or signs of struggle in the yard.

Connor's heart slammed into his ribs when he pushed the door aside. Broken dishes and furniture littered the floor.

"Mercy!" God, if the colonel came for her while he spoke with General Cooper, he would tear Virginia apart until he found the bastard and rip his throat out.

Striding through the small domicile, he stepped over more broken pottery and pieces of furniture. Someone tore the settee to shreds and ripped open the threadbare cushions. His chest tightened as he hurried to the end of the corridor.

Kicking Miss Charity's bedchamber door open, he ducked when a fire poker missed his head by a hair.

"Mercy?"

Claws came from behind the oak door to scratch his eyes out, and he caught both small wrists with one hand. "It's me. Are you hurt? Where is Miss Charity?"

Wild-eyed and furious, Mercy glared at him as if she didn't understand his questions.

"Whoever did this to your home is gone. You're safe

now." He dropped his voice to a soothing whisper as he tugged the terrified woman into his embrace.

"Connor?" The fight drained from her, and she clutched his sleeves like a lifeline. "I thought…and Aunt Charity. What if they got to her? I couldn't let them hurt her." Swallowing, her voice grew stronger. "There were two different men. Maybe more. They were looking for something, and they said the most horrible things. I thought we would die…"

"Hush. I'm here now. You're safe." He tucked her head under his chin. "Where is Aunt Charity?"

"I am here." An old gray head bobbed up from under the bed. "And I will thank you to let my niece go. She isn't a plaything to be mauled." The thin older woman brushed dust and cobwebs from her pristine white night rail, stopping to glare at Connor. "Well?"

Connor chuckled. "If you want us to part, I suggest you take the matter up with Mercy."

The terrified bundle in his arms had a death grip on him until Aunt Charity snorted and demanded she let him go.

Stepping three feet away, Mercy's face turned crimson as she patted her lopsided chignon with shaky hands. "I…wanted to ensure he came to assist us and not lure us from our sanctuary. It will not happen again." Her chin rose, but her expression lacked her usual defiance.

Aunt Charity shook her head. "From where I stood, it looked less like a test and more like you dove into his arms, hoping for the best."

Mercy's face filled with color.

He rolled his eyes. "And did I pass the test, or should I reenter the chamber with more flair?"

Her embarrassment gave way to fury. "You passed.

If not, you would be trussed up like a Christmas goose at my feet."

Aunt Charity sniffed. "Please, Mercy. You could not truss a goose without singeing your eyebrows, and I would have had to finish the job. You would have fainted at the first sight of the stuffing."

Conner's lips twitched as he studied Mercy's face. She could pretend to be tough, but they both knew she bluffed. "What happened?"

Aunt Charity answered. "We were getting ready to retire when the outer door burst open, and men stamped into my house. We could hear the furniture breaking and someone dropping all my dishes and cursing. Mercy slid the lock across the door and stuffed me under the bed. I thought about arguing, but she suggested that if we kept quiet, the ruffians damaging my belongings might not know we were here." A deep sigh, followed by a shudder, shook her thin body. "I allowed her to have her way because her suggestion had merit."

"Did you recognize them?" Connor's attention shifted back to Mercy.

"No." Gripping her hands together in front of her, she shook her head. "They were upset they didn't find whatever they came looking for."

He surmised as much by the mess they made of Miss Charity's home. "Did they mention what?"

"No. Just that the article in question is quite valuable, and they were certain Auntie hid it somewhere in the cottage." Mercy's chin lifted. "I could have dealt with the situation."

"Of course." Giving her a small smile, he glanced from the two frightened women to the destroyed corridor and shook his head, knowing he had one course of action.

The idea had occurred earlier when he spoke to Gabrielle, and now he had no choice. "Is there a rider close by? I wish to send for my carriage."

"The parish is home to several young men who would be happy to earn a coin or two." Mercy frowned. "Why do you want your carriage? I am sure the villains are miles from here by now. They heard your horse and assumed you were an officer."

"I plan to take you to my home where you will be warm, comfortable, and safe. A dozen capable men in my employ ensure my home is villain-free. Don't shake your head, Mercy. Think about Aunt Charity. What if I hadn't come? The locked chamber door is a dead giveaway that the room is occupied. Do you think you could defend both you and your aunt from two or three ruffians with a fire poker?"

Her frown intensified. 'I don't want to go to your home. Think of my reputation."

"I invited Aunt Charity as well. Your reputation will remain spotless. Think about what would happen if you stayed and they returned." He tilted his chin at the older woman who had a valise open on the bed and a meager pile of threadbare belongings beside it. "You may not want to come, but there you will both be safe."

Her aunt folded her small pile of clothing with rapid, shaky hands. "He is right, you know. If he hadn't come along, we would have been hurt or killed. The doors are not on the hinges, and the night will be long and cold. You may stay if you like, Mercy. But I plan to go home with Connor and sleep in a warm bed." Tucking a thin chemise inside the bag, she snapped it closed. "I'm not willing to risk my life if they come back."

Mercy's drawn-out sigh came from the bottom of

her tattered boots. 'Fine. But I don't have to like it."

Aunt Charity glanced at her. "Judging from the way you were clinging to Mr. Calhan, you won't dislike it either."

Connor didn't wait to hear anymore as he strode for the parish. An hour later, he opened the door to his best guest chamber and carried Miss Charity inside. "I hope you will be comfortable. Ring the bell by the bed if you need anything. My staff will be happy to assist you."

The older woman beamed and snuggled down under the down comforter the second he set her down.

Mercy would take a bit more convincing. But either way, they would both stay where he could keep an eye on them.

"I don't want to be here." Mercy's lower lip extended at least an inch, and Connor smiled.

"You will be safe, and I have extra men on the way. No one will come in or go out without my knowledge." Somehow, the thought of her snuggled in his guest chamber made him breathe easier. "Get some rest. Dinner is at eight in the dining room. I will have the Benson wake you. I will see you in the morning."

He turned after taking two steps. "One other thing. While you are a guest in my home, please respect my privacy. You may access all the books in my library and enjoy the amenities of my home, except for my office. I cannot have my papers disrupted."

Her glare would have melted a lesser man.

Changing the locks would do no good, and he could only hope she would respect his wishes. Closing the door to his study, he turned up his lamp and put Mercy out of his mind. Pouring a generous amount of whisky into his glass, Connor sighed and opened the satchel with his father's papers. He had a lot of reading to do before he could find his bed.

****

Mercy stared at the closed door, uncertain whether she should laugh or cry. Connor knew she planned to learn his secrets, and thought asking her to stay out of his study would suffice? Shouldn't he be bolting the door, worried she would find out about his family's dark past? She already knew, of course, but he didn't know that.

She didn't want to be here. Not in his house, not under his roof, not wrapped in anything that bore the scent or signature of Connor Calhan. And yet, in the face of real terror. When ruffians destroyed Aunt Charity's home, threatening violence, Connor had not felt like the enemy, but the only thing standing between them and ruin. She had not seen a murderer. She had seen shelter.

A yawn took her by surprise, and she turned to study the guest room. White and gold furniture with a cream floral bed covering. Long golden drapes hung before floor-to-ceiling windows. A gilt-edged wash basin and mirror adjacent to a white marble fireplace crackling with heat. A shiver of delight ran through her before she could stop it. Such luxury should be available to everyone, and for tonight, she would enjoy the sins of the Calhans.

Even if she detested admitting how much comfort she found for those scant few minutes in the strength of Connor's arms.

She must have slept because the next thing she knew, a knock came at the door, startling her.

Opening the oak panel, she discovered a shy housemaid who informed her she had come to help her dress for dinner. Since she had nothing to change into, the maid brushed and plaited her hair before leading the way down the wide, polished stairs.

After eating a delightful meal alone in Connor's elegant dining room, the housemaid asked if she would like a bath.

The steaming water soothed her tired muscles and fed her soul while the shy housemaid rubbed rose-scented soap on her skin and hair. Silk undergarments and a silk night rail were provided by a dour-faced housekeeper who informed her the articles of clothing belonged to Connor's sister Madelaine, who left them following her last visit.

Never had such luxury caressed her skin, and Mercy stroked the fine garment with the tips of her fingers. What would it be like to own such a luxurious article of clothing? She couldn't imagine the sinfulness of such extravagance and wallowed in pure delight, determined to enjoy the moment to the fullest. Snuggled beneath the silken coverlet on the massive bed, Mercy sighed in utter bliss.

The next thing she knew, the shy housemaid drew back the glorious golden drapes as sunlight poured into the elegant bedchamber.

"The master sent breakfast up to you." Placing a tray of fresh fruit, fragrant tea, fresh cream, sweet butter, tart jelly, and crusty slices of bread on her knees, the shy housemaid bobbed a curtsy. "My name is Callie. Please ring the bell if you need anything."

"Of course. Thank you." Mercy had never eaten in bed and studied the loaded tray with delight. She may have to reconsider Connor's offer if she enjoyed such luxuries on a regular basis. Pausing with a fresh strawberry halfway to her lips, she frowned. She had to obtain some juicy tidbit for the colonel before evening and send it off at the telegram office. If her luck held out, Connor would be at the shipping office, and she could search his study without interruption.

Excited at the prospect. Mercy finished her breakfast in record time and rang the bell for Callie to help her dress.

Benson glowered down his nose at her when she stepped into the corridor. "Your aunt awaits you in the dining room, Miss Mercy. If you will follow me."

Mercy's lips twisted. "Of course." She would have to find a way to sneak into the study without Benson's knowledge. But then, she enjoyed a good challenge, and fooling the over-observant butler would sharpen her skills.

Aunt Charity beamed with pleasure when Mercy entered the dining room and took her seat at the long table. "Isn't this lovely, child? I do believe the bread was freshly baked this morning. I haven't had such flaky crust and creamy butter since my childhood. You must have some." Nibbling at a slice of bread slathered with butter and jelly, the older woman smacked her lips with satisfaction.

"I ate in my chamber earlier. It is indeed a delightful breakfast." Mercy studied the older woman. They should eat like this every day, and when she found her mother's chest, they would. But first things first. "I am not feeling well, Auntie. I think I will go back to my chamber and lie down if you will excuse me?"

"Of course, my girl." Aunt Charity had a mouthful of fresh strawberries and cream, and Mercy couldn't be certain the older woman knew what she said. A blissful expression crossed her aunt's face as she closed her eyes and relished her food.

Determination stiffened her spine as she slipped out of the dining room door and hustled across the empty corridor to Connor's study.

Benson's light step whispered toward her from the kitchen, and Mercy slipped into the salon off to her right. She had time to step behind the drapery before Benson peeked inside. His all-seeing eyes swept the room and peered beneath the settees.

Mercy held her breath and waited. Several intense minutes passed before the butler departed and closed the door behind him, muttering something about having ladies underfoot.

After waiting another ten minutes for good measure, she swung the door of Connor's study open and stepped into the masculine room still fragrant with the clean, spicy scent of his cologne.

Her stomach twisted in a knot as memories of his quick kiss flashed across her mind. She had not been able to breathe for several minutes afterward. "Stop it. I am here to get information, Nothing more." Her sage words of wisdom fell on deaf ears when she caught sight of the long table along one wall covered with pages of masculine handwriting.

Mercy picked one up, and the knot in her stomach tightened. Every single page before her widening eyes had been written by none other than Jonathon Calhan, the man responsible for her mother's death.

Terrified and excited beyond words, Mercy devoured the first letter and reached for another.

The first few she read with disbelieving eyes as Jonathon recounted his experience of the war. She wanted to yawn with boredom until a page further down the table caught her eye. Her mother's name leaped from the page, wrapping around her heart like a vice.

The woman allowed me to escort her to a fork in the road and no farther… I followed a safe distance behind until she turned in at her gates. To my astonishment, the gentle lady I rescued is Colonel Percival Bennett's wife, Grace. I have not been as surprised since Maggie O'Leary agreed to be my wife, and I spent the ride back to camp in deep contemplation. Could I trust the notorious Confederate Colonel's wife? Did she give me information to lead us all into a trap? Did her husband send her to ensnare us with her big green eyes and pretend allegiance to President Lincoln and the Union? I did not know, and the truth remains to be seen. –Major Jonathon Calhan.

Mercy stared at the parchment, unable to comprehend what she read.

Jonathon Calhan protected her mother?

Her heart lodged in her throat, and her hand shook so hard, the words blurred. She knew the Calhans and most of the Union army blamed her mother for Major Calhan's death, while the Confederates considered her mother a traitor who received her just recompense for her treasonous deeds.

But she hadn't considered the fact Major Calhan and her mother had more to do with each other than the fateful afternoon Jonathon got shot and the following day when they found her mother's body. What else didn't she know?

Setting the parchment down, she reached for another when deep voices filled the corridor.

Her breath came fast when footsteps clattered on the tile floor and stopped outside the study.

Without considering her actions, Mercy scooped up the next four letters, rolled them up, and stuffed them up her full sleeve.

She had two seconds to school her features before the latch jiggled, and the door swung in.

Nose to chest with Connor, she adopted a nonchalant stance when his eyes swept over her, darted to the table, and then swung back, "I see you had a profitable morning." His intense scrutiny narrowed on her face. "I asked you to stay out of my study, and yet here you are. If I am to discover the cipher, my papers must remain as I leave them. They cannot be mixed up and shuffled because I have them organized in a specific manner. Finding the document is of equal importance to us both, and I would expect you to do everything in your power to aid me in my search, not this."

For some reason, his disappointment hurt worse than Uncle Justice's whip. "I apologize." Crossing her fingers and her eyes at the same time, she hoped God and Connor would forgive her, for she had no intention of respecting anything. She learned more about her mother in the last hour than in her previous nineteen years.

She would discover the truth about her mother's murder, clear her mother's name, and find her gold box, if they were the last things she did on this earth. And Connor Calhan had best beware.

Chapter Eighteen

Richmond, Virginia, August 1864
Percival's fury grows with each Union victory,
especially after Admiral Farragut's capture of Mobile
Bay. He no longer hides his secret meetings, and his
associates shout vile threats late into the night. I retreat
to my chamber with Mercy, barring the door and using
a quilt to muffle the sounds. Though supplies grow
scarce and deserters roam freely, I suspect Percival's
men remain behind not to protect me, but to keep me
under watch. Still, their presence deters looters for now.

Tragically, the houseboy I sent to Major Calhan
with the list of Knights was found dead in the cotton
fields. Though Percival's men blame deserters, my heart
tells me otherwise. I fear he suspects my connection to
the Union officer. The Knights show no mercy to Union
or Confederate, man, or child. My father could never
have known that by marrying me to a Southern
gentleman, he cast me into a living hell from which I
cannot escape. –Grace Bennett
****

Mercy read the journal entry and sank back against
her pillows, her heart hammering in her chest. Her dear,
brave mother risked her life to help the Union Army and
Connor Calhan's father. In all the years Uncle Justice
talked about her mother and her death, he never
mentioned she knew Jonathon Calhan. How did the

major go from praying for her mother's safety to being involved in her murder?

Something didn't add up.

Biting her lip, Mercy glanced at the closed door. She had to get back inside Connor's study and read the rest of his father's letters.

In the last three days, she had secreted away two dozen pages of his journal, learning a great deal about the war and the Calhans. Most of which surprised her. She never thought about having siblings, and reading accounts of the siblings through their father's eyes made her realize how much she missed out on.

One could be forgiven for thinking they were a large, loving family interested in each other's success and accomplishments, and not the cold, ruthless, power-hungry people she thought them to be for years.

Mercy wrapped her arms around her waist and sighed. How wrong she'd been about the Calhans. When she thought of all the horrible things Uncle Justice laid on Connor's broad shoulders, she wanted to weep.

Not because her uncle blackened his character, but because she believed him.

Connor surprised her every day with his attentiveness to Aunt Charity. The dear woman did nothing more than express a desire for something, and it appeared. Marveling at the patience and gentleness Connor exhibited to her aunt, she experienced a twinge or two of some unknown emotion. It could not be jealousy because she would have to care for that to be the case. But anger? Connor provided all the things Mercy wished she could and couldn't. Nodding, she agreed with her decision. Dissatisfaction made her chest burn and gave her the insane desire to shriek at Connor, demanding he hold her arm, too.

A short rap sounded on her door before her maid hustled in with a large box tied with a red ribbon. "This came for ye a moment ago." Glancing at Mercy as she put the parcel on the table, she closed the door and hurried to the bed. "Shall we see what the modiste sent or order yer bath first?"

"Modiste?" Bewildered, Mercy shook her head. "I don't even know one, much less order something. There must be a mistake."

Callie grinned. "No mistake. There are more boxes downstairs from the dressmaker. Mr. Connor ordered them for ye. The footmen will bring them up after yer bath. Shall we see what's inside?"

Four of the loveliest hats Mercy had ever seen lay nestled in a bed of tissue paper. A jaunty rose silk one with a long ostrich plume, a small woven bonnet with a circle of delicate roses around the brim, a navy-blue silk perched hat meant to be worn at an angle on the front or top of the head, and a green silk hat with a matching lace veil trimmed with small white roses.

She couldn't breathe as she ran her fingers over the soft, silky fabrics and down along the delicate feathers.

"There are gowns to match and new undergarments, stockings, and shoes. Ye will look like a princess when we get ye all dressed." Callie's smile widened as she drew the curtains around the bed. "The footmen are coming with the tub.

Mercy's mouth gaped as boots shuffled in, and the heavy brass tub slid to the floor in front of the marble hearth. Part of her wanted to refuse such an expensive gift, and the other part of her, the part that always wondered what silk felt like, won.

An hour later, she stood with her arms outstretched as Callie hooked the front of her new silk corset. Delicate pink buds trimmed the bodice, and new whalebone molded her figure into a perfect hourglass. Silk chemise, silk pantalets, and silk stockings slid against her delicate flesh with the tantalizing brush of sin. Lord, did she love the feel of soft fabric.

Callie tied silk petticoats around her waist and topped them with a bustle. A dozen gown boxes littered the room, and Callie lifted one glorious creation after another from the delicate tissue they were packed with. "Which day gown do you prefer, the pale pink, the mint green, or the sky blue?"

Running her fingers over the pleated bodice of the rose-colored gown, she sighed. "This one."

The gown fit her like a lover's caress and swished around her ankles as she turned to stare at her reflection in the long-looking glass. No one would guess the beautiful young woman with the pink cheeks and shining eyes was Mercy Elenna Jackson, daughter of a notorious southern colonel.

High-necked with a pleated bodice, long tight sleeves edged with delicate lace, an elegant bustle above a sophisticated pleated train trailing behind. She could have stepped from a page in *Godey's Lady's Book*.

"Miss Mercy, ye are beautiful, and yer figure is perfect. Mr. Connor will have a tough time keeping the suitors away." Callie twisted her hair into a chignon and used extra pins to keep her heavy masses in place." Now yer ready. I think I will peek from the upper floor when Mr. Connor gets a good look at ye."

"Why?" Mercy's stomach twisted. Connor paid for all of this, and she really shouldn't allow such a thing, but her vanity got in the way. What would it hurt to dress in silk for one day?

Strolling down the stairs, Mercy couldn't resist smiling as her skirts swished around her ankles. Wool didn't swish. It dragged.

"You're not that daft, are ye? He fancies ye. I can tell by the way he watches ye. Most men don't know their heads from their arse, but Mr. Connor knows everything about ye." Callie's candid remark made her freeze.

Not everything. And she would go to the ends of the earth to make sure he never did.

Connor rose to his feet when she entered the breakfast room, and the gleam in his eye when he assessed her from head to toe made her flush. Slow, heated, methodical, and knowing, his hooded interest hovered over her breasts, dropped to her hips, and then rose to meet her eyes with such passion, her knees knocked together.

"Good morning."

His deep voice brushed over her like a caress.

"You are very lovely this morning, Mercy." Holding out her chair, he leaned down as she sat.

Warm breath whispered across the nape of her neck, smelling of citrus and sandalwood, as he adjusted her chair.

When his hands settled on her shoulders, desire slid down her spine, sending tingling sensations to every part of her body. Shaking her head to rid her body of its fascination with her host, she spit out the first thing that came to mind.

"I shouldn't accept such an expensive gift. What could have possessed you to order so many clothes? I have no wish to be beholden and shall return all but this gown. I do not need fancy clothing, and once I find my mother's box, I will repay you." She could have bitten her lip when the words slipped out. She didn't need Connor to know her business.

His eyebrows rose as he straightened and resumed his seat. "Do you know where she may have put it?"

"If I did, I would have it already and would no doubt be living in a large luxurious home of my own." Indicating she wished for a cup of tea, she shot him a glance." You didn't answer my question. Why would you order so many clothes and go to such an expense? What is it you want from me?" Narrowing her eyes on his face, she waited for his answer with a tight chest. She knew what she wanted from him, and since reading his father's journal, doubts crept in. She had to find her mother's killer, clear her mother's name, and find the box. None of that changed despite Connor Calhan's beautiful blue eyes and handsome face.

A wry grin twisted his lips." I give them without strings attached. I expect nothing in return." Holding up a hand when she opened her mouth to argue, he said, "Let's just say I could do without one more gilded carriage this year. The surplus…wealth allows me to provide you and your aunt with warmer clothing."

Her heart beat high in her throat. She accused him of buying gilded carriages and ignoring the poor, the first night they met, and embarrassment heated her cheeks. Connor's giving nature appeared in Jonathon Calhan's journal on more than one occasion. "Then I thank you. You are most kind." Frowning, the other part of his comment infiltrated her conscience. Her and her aunt?

"Kindness has nothing to do with it. I wanted to, and

so it happened. I will hear no more about it. Enjoy the clothing, Mercy. I have no use for them."

They were interrupted by Aunt Charity's grand entrance in a black silk day gown, complete with black fitted gloves and spectacles hanging from a bejeweled chain around her neck." Good morning, child." She looked chipper as a June bug and happier than she had been in years.

How had he convinced her penny-pinching aunt to wear the expensive silk gown?

Connor shrugged as if reading her mind and rose to his feet. "I learned long ago, silk, flowers, and good food are the way to a woman's heart. Please excuse me, I have work to do and visitors to attend." With a stiff bow, he left the room.

Mercy stared after him. Did his mother respond to those things, or did he reference other women? Gabrielle perhaps? Ignoring the tightness in her chest and her need to shriek her discontent, she whirled on her aunt. "Did Connor buy you more than one gown?"

A slow smile crossed the older woman's face as she lifted a teacup to her thin lips. "I have not been so warm or so well fed in years, Mercy. *And God is able to bless you abundantly, so that in all things at all times, having all that you need, you will abound in every good work.*"

Mercy rolled her eyes when she recognized the Bible quote. "I thought the bible only allowed suffering and punishments. Since when is abundance and wealth considered saint-like?"

Her aunt's green eyes shifted to her face. "The quote has been there the whole time. I didn't change a thing."

"What did Mama's last letter say?" Changing the subject to safer and more important grounds, Mercy bit her lip, holding her breath that this time, the older woman would answer the question.

Aunt Charity set down her fork. "I thought I would give you the letter when you got older, and I never should have let Justice read it."

"Auntie, please." She knew her tone begged, and she didn't care. Reading Jonathon's journal gave her an insatiable need to know the truth of what happened between Jonathon Calhan and her mother. With any luck, she could figure it out before Connor discovered who her parents were. The more she read about Colonel Bennett, the more she rejoiced she had no memory of him. And the more she thanked her mother for protecting her from his evil.

Aunt Charity folded her napkin. "She mentioned her fear of your father and wrote if she didn't arrive within a fortnight of sending you, to fear the worst. The Phantom and your father were responsible for many innocent deaths on both sides of the war, and she feared for her life. Grace didn't know how far these men would go to seek vengeance and sent you to me to protect."

Taking a long sip of tea as if for strength, her aunt continued. "Percival found a document in her chamber and threatened her, or she wouldn't have been so frantic to get you away from there. I have long suspected The Phantom is responsible for her death and your nursemaid, Mammy's, as well. In her letter, Grace mentioned she took her box from Percival's safe, and if anyone knew where the box went, it would be Mammy."

Mercy couldn't breathe.

She had memories of Mammy holding her and saying everything would be all right. For the first few years, Mammy would come to visit on the anniversary of her arrival, and then, when she turned fifteen, her visits stopped. A new thought flashed across her mind. Mammy died the same year Uncle Justice moved to New York.

Coincidence? Not if he read her mother's letter.

Uncle Justice demanded to see her mother's diary the first week they went out together. She didn't think much of the matter...until now. Anyone reading the diary would know how much Mammy meant to her mother and how close the two women were.

A shiver raced down her spine. In her heart, she knew Mammy died protecting Mama's secrets.

Whatever happened, she must find a way to decipher her mother's diary.

Rising to her feet, she kissed Aunt Charity's cheek. "Please excuse me. I have something I must see to."

"Of course, dear. I will be in the north salon reading if you need me." With a wave of her hand, her aunt resumed her breakfast.

Mercy frowned. The older woman would be brushing up on her Bible quotes, no doubt.

Slipping down the corridor, Mercy paused outside Connor's study. Two male voices came from within, and she pressed her ear against the panel to hear better.

"Where else could it be? I have gone over everything again, and I can find nothing more than I did before."

She came close to falling on her face when the door opened without warning.

"Do come in, Miss Mercy. You can help us solve the riddle of the missing cipher. I suggest taking a chair by the hearth where you will be more comfortable." Connor's eyes were hooded, so she couldn't see his expression. He didn't seem surprised or angry that he caught her listening to their conversation.

She sat on the edge of the chair and folded her hands, careful not to make eye contact.

An older man with a long curling mustache sat in the other leather chair in front of the hearth, sipping amber liquid from a glass. His gray eyes wandered over her from head to toe. "Ah. Now I understand your hurry to get home. You failed to mention what a beauty your little thief is, Connor." The general's deep voice held a note of amusement.

Connor ignored his remarks. "Mercy, allow me to introduce my commanding officer, General Cooper."

Mature, kind, and charming, the older man stood to shake her hand while he smiled into her eyes.

Gentle hands and kind eyes won her over, and she found she couldn't work up the energy to be offended by his remark. "How do you do? If you explain the whole situation, I can add some insight." Bracing against the dreaded story of her mother as the villain, she plastered a serene expression on and listened while the general relaxed in his chair, sipping his drink.

Connor related the events as he knew them, while she ground her teeth with irritation, and the general nodded in agreement.

Running his hand through his hair, Connor sighed. "I have gone over Father's papers countless times, and I cannot find any new clues as to where he would hide a cipher if one existed."

Mercy's mind ran rampant. "Except the letter to your mother. Have you ever examined it? If I had a husband I loved as much as he loved your mother, that's where I would send it."

The silence in the room made her glance up. Both men stared at her as if she had grown another head.

"I won't ask how you know so much about my parents since I know you have been stealing sections of my father's journal from my study to read at night. But you do make a good point." He searched her face. "I have not asked my mother about her letter, nor have I examined it. Shall we visit her?"

"Me?' Her voice came out in a croak. She wanted to scour his study in his absence, not meet the family. Glancing toward the general to see his reaction, she met his nod of approval.

"Quite right." The older man set this glass on the table by their knees and rose to his feet. "Let me know how it turns out, hmm?" He left a moment later.

Connor rang the bell and ordered his carriage from a hovering Benson. "Shall we?"

Taking her elbow, he led her from the room and locked the door behind him. As he sent a footman upstairs to collect her new cloak, it occurred to her, he hadn't locked his study before this. Did he want her to read his father's papers?

Shifting her feet, she met his amused expression. "What is so funny?"

"I am amused you thought I didn't know you've been in my study. Especially when you consider how we met."

Mercy wanted to kick him in the shins. "Why not invite me in then?"

Connor's grin widened. "What's the fun in that? You claim to be good with locks, and you're persistent if nothing else. This new lock is proclaimed to be tamper-proof, and I want to evaluate its effectiveness. Besides, there isn't anything in my father's letters your colonel would be interested in."

He had a point. If they were offered to her, she wouldn't have read them. Irritated that he understood how her mind worked, she frowned. "How could you know that?" Taking her cloak, she threw it over her shoulders and tied the ribbon.

"The colonel fought in the war. Did you learn anything in my father's letters to support your idea that my mother has the cipher?"

"No. But it makes sense." Mercy chewed on this added information. Of course, the colonel fought in the war. From what she learned in Virginia, he knew Uncle Justice for years. He may have even known her father. Another shiver raced down her spine as she accepted Connor's hand into the carriage.

"It will be all right. My family is very likable. You'll see."

Chapter Nineteen

Richmond, Virginia, September 1864
Victory at Mobile Bay and General Sherman's
success in Atlanta have turned the tide of war in our
favor. I thank God for Connor, whose bravery as both
courier and soldier earned high praise from Sherman.
Max fights in Missouri and Tennessee, where even small
skirmishes carry deadly consequences. Every report
brings trembling hands, relief for my sons' safety, and
sorrow for those lost. A letter from Maggie lifted my
spirits; she writes that Madelaine and her boy contribute
to the war effort while her husband, James Baker, serves
under Grant in Virginia. Their beauty and grace draw
notice wherever they go, making their distance harder to
bear.
My Southern informant's latest message carries
grave news. She fears her husband has intercepted a
letter exposing the Knights of the Confederacy. Despite
the risk, she remains determined to uncover the traitors
she believes have Union ties. Her courage is unmatched,
but I urged caution, too much is at stake. Like Maggie,
her convictions run deep, and while her efforts have been
invaluable, I dread what may come if she is caught. I
pray God protects her and all of us in these uncertain
days. –Major Jonathon Calhan

****

Connor's family was more than likable, and

Mercy's conscience pricked her as she thought of all the things she believed about them for years.

"Mother, this is Mercy Jackson, the young woman I mentioned who lost her uncle in a recent tragic event. She and her aunt are staying with me until it's safe for them to go home."

Connor's mother, Maggie, had graying hair, laughing blue eyes, and a welcoming smile. She invited Mercy in without batting an eye or asking awkward questions. She accepted Connor's sparse explanation as if he invited strange young women into his home every other week.

Kissing Connor on his cheek, she reprimanded him for not visiting more often. "We live fifteen minutes away, not fifteen miles." Her laugh wrapped around Mercy's heart as a faint memory of her mother flashed through her mind. They would have been friends; she thought with a jolt. Both women were loving mothers, fierce defenders of their families, and tempered with the heartache of loss.

His sister Madelaine swept her into a hug and slipped her arm through Mercy's as if they had known each other for years. Leading her through the oak front door and into a spacious entry hall with marble floors, pale floral silk walls, and a cream plaster ceiling, she turned right into a mauve and red salon. The house had a warm, inviting atmosphere, and before Mercy knew what happened, she sat on a red velvet settee before a massive marble hearth with a cup of tea at her knees, and Connor squeezed in beside her.

Maggie and Madelaine sat opposite them and joked as they passed out cake with the tea.

"I have a question, Mother." Connor leaned

forward, resting his elbows on his knees.

Mercy squirmed as his hard thigh pressed into hers and the heat of his body enveloped her with his unique scent of citrus and sandalwood. Butterflies took flight in her belly, and she wrapped both arms around her middle to hide her nervousness.

"Oh?" Maggie set her tea down and folded her hands in her lap. Her gaze drifted to Mercy's face before resting on Connor. "Is this about the…er…recent events with Francios Blanchart and his daughter?"

"No." Connor shook his head. "It's about Father. Do you have his last letter, and may I read it?"

Maggie paled and then nodded, rising to her feet. "Of course. If you will give me a minute." She disappeared down the corridor as Madelaine rose to her feet.

"I apologize for leaving during your visit, but I am meeting Mr. Beaumont for luncheon at Delmonico's." She flushed red when Connor raised an eyebrow. "He sent an invitation around yesterday, and I accepted."

Connor nodded. "He's a decent man. You have my approval. And this time, I hope you find what you're looking for, Maddy."

A flash of surprise crossed her face. "You investigated Mr. Beaumont?" Her hands gripped the back of the chair as she stared at Connor.

"Of course. If he exhibits an interest in our sister, he can expect her brothers to take his measure." His matter-of-fact tone said she should expect nothing less.

"Of course." Madelaine recovered and stepped forward to kiss his cheek. "Thank you, Connor. But I am a grown woman and can make my own decisions."

"And I accept that until some man breaks your heart,

and then I will kill him unless one of my brothers gets to him first." His grin said she could argue all she wanted, but facts were facts.

With a long sigh of defeat, Madelaine bid Mercy farewell. "I hope to see you again soon. Take good care of my brother. He is one of a kind." She swept from the room before Mercy could disillusion her about the nature of their relationship.

Maggie returned a moment later. "If you will excuse us, Mercy?"

Her eyes flew to Connor, and he nodded. He would speak to his mother alone. Hiding her disappointment, she nodded. "I shall sit here and enjoy this wonderful tea. Thank you, Mrs. Calhan."

"Call me Maggie." The blue-eyed woman smiled as she led her son away.

Mercy waited all of two minutes before she tiptoed after them. If Connor's mother had the cipher, she should know about it. Voices came from a door left ajar on the other side of the corridor. On silent feet, she crept closer and kept her back against the wall, stopping a foot from the door.

Maggie sat in a leather chair before the marble hearth facing Connor. She held a yellow envelope toward him. "Jonathon mentioned a man would come asking for his letter. I never expected it to be you. I thought General Cooper or one of the other men Jonathon worked with would be the one." With a shaky voice, she continued. "I know the importance of what you ask. You follow in your father's footsteps." Her statement hung between them, understanding flashing across her face. "You have since the day he died. And after all of this time, you never told me."

"Yes." Connor took the letter with a firm hand. "I meant to tell you once it ended, and I caught them all. But to do so, I need a cipher to decode the list Father gave to General Cooper before his death." With short, terse sentences, he explained about The Phantom, the Knights of the Confederacy, and the colonel.

"And you believe these men, not the southern woman, bear responsibility for his death?" Maggie's voice trembled, her eyes misted as she turned to the hearth, the flames reflecting her unspoken grief.

"Father's journal mentions Grace Bennett." Connor kept his tone steady but taut. "And the story of her and her daughter's life being in danger. In a different entry, he speaks of meeting his 'Southern Informant' on the same day he promised to meet Grace. It never occurred to me until I met Mercy that the women might be the same person. Grace promised to deliver a cipher, the key to the list a house boy brought him weeks before. Whether the cipher even existed, or Grace Bennett knew more than she claimed and orchestrated a masterful ploy to lead Father and his men to their deaths, no one knows. What we do know is we never found a cipher. And this letter is the one thing he carried that I haven't dissected a dozen times. There has to be a clue." Connor turned the yellow missive over in his hands.

Mercy bit the inside of her cheek, nearly drawing blood to keep silent. She wanted to scream that Grace Bennett would never harm a soul, let alone plot the massacre of Union soldiers. But speaking now would betray her presence and expose her eavesdropping. Her lips would remain sealed.

"And Mercy?" Maggie touched Connor's sleeve, her voice laced with skepticism. "Why bring her here?

This is family business."

Connor inclined his head. "I agree. But I cannot leave her out of my sight."

He recounted their first encounters, painting a vivid picture of Mercy clad as a boy, climbing trees and picking locks.

From her spot beside the door, she seethed, her cheeks flushing with indignation. Yes, she *did* those things but hearing them laid bare before Connor's mother made her wish the floor would swallow her whole.

Her attention snapped back when Connor mentioned her name again.

"Someone murdered Mercy's mother." His voice softened. "She believes the list holds the name of the killer. I cannot seek justice for Father and deny her the same. She has as much right to the names on the list as we do. And something about the way her voice changes when she speaks of her mother, and the way her eyes shimmer with unshed tears, tugs at my heart. She's like a newborn lamb, lost and vulnerable. I know what it's like to lose a parent, and God knows what I would do without you, Mother. Mercy has no one but an elderly aunt…and me." He paused. "I gave her my word I would help her find justice."

His words hung in the air, heavy with conviction.

Maggie said nothing, but the flickering firelight caught the glint of emotion in her eyes. Silence stretched, thick and unyielding, as the gravity of his vow settled over them all.

Mercy's jaw dropped. *Weepy?* Her? Over Mama? The nerve. Newborn lamb, indeed. Crossing her arms over her chest, she shot a glare down both corridors to make sure no one discovered her presence.

Connor's voice continued, steady and resolute. "I could turn her over to the constables if I wanted. It's well within my right. But I choose to help her."

His mother's lips curved into a soft smile. "I see."

She wanted to roll her eyes. *No, you don't see.* Neither of them did. To understand her predicament, they'd have to know the full truth, and that was something she'd never allow. Yet the realization she wanted them to like her struck like a bolt of lightning, Correction, she wanted *him* to like her.

The thought sent heat rushing to her cheeks, then a cold chill to her spine as she grappled with its implications. Once, she sought to unmask the Calhans as the villains Uncle Justice painted them to be. But after reading Jonathan's journal, doubts gnawed at the edges of her convictions.

Connor unfolded the letter, his brow furrowing as his eyes scanned the page. Slipping his fingers back into the envelope, he removed another note.

"I'll be double-damned." His deep voice dripped with disbelief.

"Connor!" His mother gasped, clutching her bosom. "Do not blaspheme in my home. I know you say such things, but you *will not* use them in my presence."

Chuckling, he leaned forward, sweeping her into a warm bear hug. "I'm sorry, Mama. Truly. But I cannot believe you had this the entire time."

Mercy's pulse thundered in her ears. *The cipher.* He held it in his hands, as sure as she stood by the library door. Her breath quickened, her knees trembling. Now she knew it existed, she could retreat to the salon, finish her tea, and devise her plan.

"Yes." Maggie gave an apologetic shrug. "But I had no idea of its importance, or I would have told you years ago. It's gibberish to me."

Connor grinned, his tone thick with gratitude. "Mother, I love you. Thank you for keeping it safe. Now, I can unravel the truth of what happened the night Father died and who's to blame."

"Will you let Mercy see it?"

Maggie's question stopped Mercy mid-step. She pressed her ear closer to the door, straining to catch his reply.

The silence stretched long and tense before Connor spoke. "Of course. But not until I've read it and made a copy. I can't risk her stealing it and delivering it to the colonel before I've deciphered the list."

Mercy's lips tightened, and a frown crept over her face. *As if I would!* Yet a traitorous voice in her head whispered that indeed she *would* if it meant protecting Aunt Charity.

Connor's footsteps approached. "I should check on Mercy. She could have gotten into all kinds of trouble while we've been talking."

Panic flared. Mercy darted across the corridor, slipping into the salon mere seconds before the thump of his boots echoed against the marble.

She snatched her tea, draining the half-filled cup in one gulp. Picking up a sandwich, she nibbled on its corner, praying her flushed cheeks and erratic breathing wouldn't betray her.

But her resolve hardened. She *would* get that cipher. She *would* make a copy for her mother, for Aunt Charity, and for her future.

There could be no other way.

****

Connor stepped into the room, his eyes catching the telltale flush on Mercy's cheeks and the rapid rise and fall of her chest. Her pulse all but echoed in the air, and her trembling hands betrayed her nerves. He sighed from the depths of his soul. *Of course, she listened at the door.* How foolish of him to think she'd stay put and drink her tea while he and his mother discussed the cipher.

"Are you ready to return?" His sharp and unrelenting scrutiny flicked over her too-casual posture and feigned nonchalance.

Her eyes widened enough to betray her surprise before she recovered. "Of course. I hope you found what you were looking for." Her smile widened, sweet and disarming, and his heart skipped a beat despite his effort to remain unaffected.

"No." Lacing his tone with disappointment, he waited for her reaction. "And now I'll have to scour Father's journal again to see what I missed."

The lie dangled in the air like a baited hook, and Mercy's eyes narrowed, a flicker of anger flashed across her face so brief he might have missed it if he hadn't been paying attention.

"I'm sorry to hear such woeful news." Keeping her tone measured, she shrugged as if the conversation meant nothing. "I hoped we'd find a solution today. Could I help with the journals? Another set of eyes might catch something you overlooked."

She placed her plate on the table, rising gracefully. Turning to his mother, who stood just behind him, she offered a warm smile.

"Thank you for a delightful tea, Mrs. Calhan. The sandwiches are the best I've ever tasted, and the lemon cake is divine."

Before Maggie could respond, a thin man with graying hair and an unmistakable air of superiority swept into the room. His sharp eyes raked over Mercy, assessing her from head to toe with the precision of a jeweler inspecting flawed gold.

"I see." Speaking at last, he kept his tone clipped and inscrutable as he turned to Connor with an air of self-importance. "I shall get started at once, Master Connor."

Connor's smile brightened at the sight of the man. "Giles! What are you doing here? I thought you'd be in Chicago, hovering over Shanna. I heard she's expecting again."

Giles's nose tilted an imperceptible inch higher. "Indeed, she is, but Master Reese has her well in hand. I sensed I would be needed here, and by the looks of things, I arrived just in time."

He frowned, his brows knitting. "What things?"

Giles shook his head with exaggerated patience. "I never believed that ridiculous business with you and the French girl. Miss Shanna, of course, would become most distraught whenever I argued the point. But now—" He straightened, his gray eyes glinting with smug satisfaction. "Now, I shall win our wager."

The frown deepened. Giles had come into his sister-in-law Shanna's life when she inherited Delaney Estates in Chicago, and he'd remained an uncanny fixture ever since her marriage to Reese. Giles had a knack for predicting every wedding, baby, and emotional entanglement in the Calhan family, to both their consternation and delight. And he *never* lost a bet.

Rubbing the back of his neck, Connor glared at the man. "Giles, we don't need your wagers right now."

"Perhaps not, Master Connor," Giles replied, his thin lips curling into the barest hint of a smile. "But I suspect you'll soon find my instincts are impeccable."

Connor had a good laugh when Giles predicted his brothers' weddings and offspring, but now, he resisted the urge to run a finger inside the tight neck of his shirt. "What wager?"

"Well, your marriage, of course. I shall begin right away." Giles gave a small smile and turned to depart.

"There isn't going to be one. Gabrielle returned to France and her lover. How could you not know?" He alone would decide his fate and did not rely on the older man's predictions like the rest of the family.

Giles' eyes softened, and he patted Connor's shoulder. "I have known all along." His eyes searched Connor's face. "Many men find love later in life and survive. You come from a strong family, so do not worry." With a nod, he turned on his heel and addressed Maggie. "Thank you for allowing me to stay for the last two days. I am done here and must return home. Miss Shanna will be delighted with my news. I will send the invitations when appropriate."

Maggie nodded, her expression thoughtful. "Of course. Please let me know if you require any help. I am delighted with the news."

"I will take my leave." Connor snorted, and clutching Mercy's hand, dragged her from the room.

"What is wrong? What is happening?" Her wide eyes and hesitant voice made him slow his pace. He explained about Giles and the family's belief in his predictions. Stuffing her into his carriage, he ordered the driver to take them back to his home.

"I don't understand. Why are you upset? If he

predicts the future, I think you should be happy to know." Clasping her hands in her lap, she gave him a quizzical look.

His mouth twisted. "Do you? Well, what if I told you Giles is planning our wedding? He thinks we shall be wed soon and is making the preparations once he is back in Chicago with Reese and Shanna."

Mercy's mouth dropped open, and Conner had the immense satisfaction of knowing for the first time in their unpredictable relationship, he made her speechless. At last.

Chapter Twenty

Richmond, Virginia, November 1864

My heart aches as I reflect on the past weeks. I finalized the list of Percival's Knights of the Confederacy, confirming Justice's deep involvement. His cruelty makes him unworthy of any place in Mercy's life. After their last meeting, he cornered me in the corridor, gripped my arm, and threatened exposure. I reminded him I remain mistress of this house and escaped to my chamber, shaken. The next night, I found Percival burning parchment in my hearth. I feared he had discovered my message to Major Calhan. His cold warning that if I defy him again, Mercy will grow up motherless left me numb with dread.

Thankfully, my new code protected the list. But his discovery of my diary has made me more cautious than ever. In secret, I've begun helping our staff escape north through the Underground Railroad, starting with young women and children most at risk. As I imagine their arrival in a free land, I find myself longing for such a future of my own. –Grace Bennett

****

The silence of the house pressed down on Mercy as she opened her chamber door. The kind of stillness found only in the hour before dawn, when everything slept. She had no reason to be awake, but sleep fled hours ago, chased off by restless thoughts of the cipher.

She meant to fetch a shawl she left in the drawing room earlier and to search the study without fear of interruption. But as she neared the open door to the drawing room, she stopped.

The fire was still lit, and Connor sat in his favorite chair, shirt sleeves rolled to his elbows, hands laced together, and head bowed. His right leg stretched before him with the boot off, and the stocking rumpled. Deep lines of pain etched the sides of his mouth and brow.

She didn't speak at first. Just studied the way he grimaced as he worked the muscles of his thigh. Stunned to see him so vulnerable, she didn't know if she should continue into the room or withdraw.

His jaw tensed, and his hand trembled as he massaged his leg.

Without thinking, she crossed the room and stopped beside him. "An old wound?" It was the only explanation that made sense for a man as fit as he was.

Connor did not look up, nor did he act surprised by her presence. "Yes." Hoarse and curt, he continued to work his thigh.

"Aunt Charity has nerve pain so severe she cannot sleep, at times. The body remembers pain even after the moment passes. So, does the mind." The urge to touch him shocked her, and she tucked her hands behind her back to keep them away from mischief.

His jaw tightened, but he did not send her away.

"For a moment, I thought the pain came from your leg alone, but I think it's more." Mercy could not imagine going to battle and wondering if today you would die. Or witnessing your friends and companions' deaths.

His head came up, and he glanced at her, tired, raw,

and vulnerable in a way she had not witnessed before. He was not angry, or guarded, but…haunted. "It is both the leg and the noise in my head. Sometimes, I hear the blast. I feel the heat, and I smell the blood."

"Shrapnel?" She imagined all sorts of accidents in relation to his wound.

Connor nodded. "Too deep to remove. Some days, I forget it is there. On others, I cannot move." His long fingers turned white as he worked, and Mercy stared, imagining his muscled thigh riddled with shrapnel.

Sympathy stirred where suspicion once ruled, a slow, aching warmth blooming in her chest which frightened her far more than the grim details of his wound. She looked away, unsettled by the way her heart twisted at the sight of his pain, so raw, so unhidden. He was not the monster she believed him to be, not the cold, calculating threat she'd sworn to resist. No. He was flesh, blood, and sorrow.

"Auntie drinks sherry when she gets 'the shooting pains' as she calls it." Her expression softened as she studied the sheen of sweat on his brow and the tension carving deep lines into his features. "And I rub her legs."

Connor glanced up, arching a brow. A spark of challenge ignited behind his weariness. "Are you volunteering to massage my thigh?"

Low and edged with amusement, his voice wrapped around her like smoke. Heat licked up her neck, and she dropped her eyes, struggling to summon a composed answer, one that didn't betray the wildfire he sparked inside her.

"Or is that particular kindness reserved for your aunt?"

Mercy snorted and crossed her arms. "You don't

limp enough to pass for family." Mockery clung to her words, brittle and forced. But her traitorous eyes lingered, drawn against all good sense to the defined line of muscle beneath the fabric of his breeches. How she itched to touch him, to ease his agony, to kiss the line of his jaw until he forgot the pain.

Desire clawed at her resolve, merciless and hot. She clenched her arms tighter. This could not happen. Not with him. Not without unraveling everything she fought to hold together.

Silence stretched between them, thick, taut, and perilous.

Then his eyes found hers. "I am not jesting."

Molten heat pooled in her belly, stealing the breath from her lungs. Her knees threatened to give beneath her as her mind betrayed her, envisioning the stroke of her hand along his bare thigh. Temptation and lust hit like a blow. God help her, she wanted him.

"Damn." The word slipped out, quiet and carrying a wagon load of weight. He was the last thing she needed, and the one thing she craved. Distance and a stern talk with her libido were in order.

Snatching her shawl, she turned and fled for the door. "You should have stayed a monster," she muttered. "This would be so much easier."

Had she looked back, she would have seen the war raging in his eyes, frustration, desire leashed by restraint, and something else. Something mirroring the chaos twisting in her chest.

When morning light stretched across the floor, cool and unwelcome, Connor left.

Mercy burst from her chamber to prowl the house like a restless shadow with too much heat in her veins.

Her heart still raced from the weight of his scrutiny and the way his voice curled around his wicked invitation.

She should have ignored him, should have laughed at the suggestion, and slammed the door on her way out. Instead, she ran, clutching her shawl like a shield with her heart thudding and need simmering beneath her skin. As if she did something shameful….

Focus. She needed to find the cipher.

Wandering from room to room, her frustration mounted with every empty drawer, untouched shelf, and unyielding cabinet. "Where did he hide it?" Hissing under her breath, she slammed a drawer shut. The sharp crack echoed through the room. "I am no closer to finding the damn thing." And far too close to losing control.

For now, the colonel seemed satisfied with the bits of information she'd managed to provide about Connor, which offered her a brief reprieve. But she knew it wouldn't last. She *had* to find the cipher.

Jonathon Calhan's journal haunted her, its entries churning like butter in her thoughts each night. If what he'd written was true, then the implications were staggering. Someone other than Major Calhan killed her mother. Which meant:

One-Her mother's true murderer walked free for years, watching and smiling over her failure to bring him to justice.

Two-She had been wrong about the Calhan family.

And three-She owed Connor Calhan an apology.

The first two truths tasted like bile, bitter and unbearable. But the third loomed like a mountain she didn't think she could climb. Not after last night. Not after seeing him vulnerable and human. She preferred the cold, arrogant, untouchable man, making him easier to hate and easier to use. If she were intelligent, she would keep her distance.

Which was not a possibility in her current predicament with the colonel. Still, she couldn't ignore the flicker of warmth stirring her desire when Connor looked at her, or the ache in her chest when he spoke in his deep, rich voice, making her mission all the more impossible. The closer she got, the more tangled the lies became, and she feared the truth would destroy them both.

And yet, she wanted to go back, yearned to stroke his heated flesh, and kiss him for real…

Mercy spun on her heel, scanning the rows of books along the east wall, shoving all thoughts of Connor aside and focusing on the task at hand. His father's journals filled her with an unbearable ache to understand her mother's tangled history, to uncover the answers eluding her at every turn until she wanted to scream.

Her eyes flicked to the lower drawer of Connor's desk and froze.

The drawer.

Dropping to her knees, she tugged it open, and her breath caught in her throat. A safe rested in the bottom drawer, gleaming like forbidden treasure.

With trembling fingers, she turned the dials. The first cylinder clicked into place. *Twenty-two.*

A rush of satisfaction flooded her chest, but the sound of the front door opening and closing shattered the moment.

Male voices echoed down the hall.

Connor. Not again.

Her heart leaped into her throat. He returned and not

alone.

Scrambling to her feet, Mercy glanced around the room, desperate for a place to hide.

Footsteps approached too fast. She had just enough time to slide behind the heavy velvet drapes before the door swung open, and Connor strode in with General Cooper close behind.

Pinned in her hiding spot, Mercy's pulse thundered in her ears. She held her breath, praying neither man would notice the faint sway of the curtains or hear the hammering of her heart.

Connor's voice sliced through the silence. "Now we go over everything again."

General Cooper grunted. "Time is a luxury we don't have, Calhan. If this cipher leads us to the truth, we must act."

Connor's voice carried a sharp edge of frustration. "I've deciphered the full list. There's no connection between the names on the parchment and Colonel Dawson. I thought we had him dead to rights, but I'm missing something."

Mercy winced from her hiding place. His disappointment mirrored the relentless frustration plaguing her own fruitless search for answers.

"Let me take a look." General Cooper settled into the leather chair opposite Connor's desk with a loud creak. "Maybe I can spot something you've overlooked."

The sound of boots walked around to the other side of the desk and paused.

Mercy's breath hitched, her heart pounding so hard she feared they might hear it. For two agonizing seconds, she thought he had discovered her.

"Mercy's been in here."

Her stomach twisted into a knot. *How does he know?*

"I can smell her perfume," Connor explained, followed by the sound of shuffling papers. "She has been searching for my hiding place but has not discovered the safe yet. Or if she has, she has not had a chance to open it."

General Cooper grunted in acknowledgment. "Justice Jackson was a member of the Knights of the Confederacy? Does Mercy know?"

Connor's sigh filled the room as his footsteps crossed to the drink trolley. The clink of glass against crystal and the splash of liquid punctuated the silence. "If she didn't before, she does now." His voice shifted, edged with calm authority, sending shivers down her spine. "Come out from behind the drapes, Mercy."

Her stomach dropped. She wanted to vanish, to become invisible, but there would be no escape. *Why can I fool every other man but him?*

Schooling her features into a practiced smile, she lifted her chin and stepped out from behind the velvet curtains. She strolled into the room as though she had every right to be there, even as her insides churned. The knowing smiles exchanged between the two men made her grimace.

"How do you know Uncle Justice joined them?" Her heart raced as the revelation settled over her.

Connor arched a brow. "His name is on their list. Sit down. I planned to send for you anyway. I have a few questions." He gestured to the chair beside General Cooper, his invitation leaving no room for refusal.

Mercy sank into the buttery leather chair, folding her trembling hands in her lap. Glancing across the desk, her interest caught on a yellowed parchment, and her mind buzzed with unanswered questions.

"How many of Justice's acquaintances have you met or can recall?" General Cooper asked, turning the document in his hands.

"None, other than Colonel Dawson." She kept her voice steady despite the storm brewing inside. "Uncle Justice managed the men and made the deals. He would stop by later to fill me in on the details."

As they spoke, her eyes darted back to the cipher. *A=D, B=J, C=K*...The letters seared together in her mind. Another few minutes and she'd have several of them memorized.

Connor cleared his throat, pulling her attention to his sardonic smile. "There's no need to strain your neck to read the cipher."

Her cheeks heated as their eyes locked. "There isn't?" Glancing down, she tilted her head to catch a few more pairings: *D=O, E=Q, F=S, G=J.*

"No. It won't matter now. The list is decoded, and there's no connection to Colonel Dawson. What I don't understand is why he's so determined to get his hands on it."

His dark blue eyes pierced hers, searching for something beneath her calm exterior.

Mercy's mind churned as she analyzed his words. If Colonel Dawson wanted the list, then the cipher held secrets she hadn't yet uncovered, and Connor might not have.

"And he made sure whatever Uncle Justice knew died with him." Mercy's frown deepened. "They fought the day we were in Richmond. Uncle Justice mentioned he knew...things."

"Things which got him killed." Connor leaned against the edge of his desk, his long legs framing her crossed ankles. His steady gaze locked on hers. "Let's go over the day again. There may be something else you can recall."

For the next hour, Connor and General Cooper questioned her. To her surprise, Mercy found she no longer wanted to keep the horrors of that day a secret. Uncle Justice lied. Major Jonathon Calhan and his family were nothing like the cold, ruthless murderers her uncle painted them to be.

She believed every word Major Calhan wrote about Connor and his heroism in the face of adversity. He learned to kill in war, but he mastered the art of gentleness and kindness at the hands of his father.

She studied Connor's face as he scribbled notes. The afternoon sunlight streaming through the long-paned windows turned his blond hair gold. A shadow of whiskers dusted his jaw, giving him a roguish air, and her stomach fluttered.

The iron band of distrust gripping her heart for so long loosened and disappeared.

When he glanced up, their eyes locked. The air between them thickened, and her pulse quickened under the weight of his stare. He remembered last night, too.

"Is there anything else?" His voice, low and rich, wrapped around her like a warm embrace, sending a shiver through her despite the heat of the room.

There's plenty.

She stared at his firm mouth, and licked her too dry lips. She remembered her dream and the shocking things he'd done with his mouth. The way his arms felt around her, his lips trailing fire across her skin. Her limbs trembled with the memory of his touch, of his hot mouth closing over—Did real men do those things, or had her mind conjured a unicorn?

"Mercy?"

The room tilted. She startled, jerking back as General Cooper's hand landed on her shoulder.

"What?" She blinked as if waking from a dream.

Both men stared at her, their expressions a mixture of confusion and concern.

"Is there anything else you can remember?" Connor's eyes darkened as he studied her, lingering on the frantic pulse beating at the base of her neck.

"No." Her tongue felt like wool, and her knees were as sturdy as wet paper. The butter-soft chair beneath her kept her from melting into a puddle on the floor. Twisting the seams along the sides of her dress, she thanked the heavens her skirts masked her pitiful weakened condition.

Connor's lips curved into a knowing smile. "Thank you for your help. We will talk later." His voice dipped as he added, "I believe your aunt wishes for your company in the salon."

Two pairs of male eyes fixed on her as though she were under a microscope. Damn.

Frowning, she focused on his words. "What?"

Connor arched a dark brow, gesturing toward the door with an open hand. "If you will excuse us, the general and I have matters to discuss."

Mercy hesitated. She wanted to stay and hear the rest of their conversation, and his command grated against her pride. "I've told you everything I remember." She lied. Lifting her chin, she glared despite the guilt creeping up her neck. *Except for her real name and who her parents were.*

Before she could protest further, Connor's large, warm hand closed around her elbow. He lifted her to her feet and guided her to the door.

His voice dropped to a low murmur as they walked down the corridor. "I know remembering the day Justice died is traumatic. I wouldn't have asked, but we must find the colonel."

They stopped outside the drawing room door. He turned to her, studying her with quiet intensity. "I hoped there would be something you could recall to help us track the bastard down."

His fingers brushed her cheek with the lightest touch, and she shivered to the tips of her satin slippers. His warmth had a magnetic pull that left her weak and breathless.

One long finger stroked the side of her cheek, drawing her like a warm fire on a frosty winter night. "I…?"

His lips hovered an inch above hers, and she stared at him, needing his touch as much as she needed air. If he leaned forward the tiniest bit, she would know whether his kisses tasted as good in real life as they did in her dreams.

Understanding flashed across his face a second before his lips took possession of hers. "God, Mercy. Don't look at me like that."

His lips touched hers, soft, warm, and gentle, shattering something inside her. Molten lava flowed through her veins and settled in her belly. Her breath hitched, caught between surprise and longing as her world melted around that single point of contact.

Her mind emptied of all thought, snuffed out by the

hush of his nearness and the pure, exquisite sensation of his lips moving against hers.

Her heart thundered at his nearness, and a sigh escaped, half gasp, half surrender. She had not meant to respond to his advance, but her lips moved, parting beneath his, drawn by some ancient instinct beyond her control.

Connor slanted his mouth over hers, drawing her shaking body into his heat. Delving deep, he stroked along her tongue and drank from her mouth like a man tasting the nectar of the gods. Butterflies flew in her belly as his hands molded her hips against him. Heat spiraled through her as she wrapped her arms around his neck and clutched him close. Every aching, trembling stroke of his tongue sent thrills of delight through her as she squirmed to get closer.

"Mercy?"

Aunt Charity's high-pitched voice crashed over her like a dunk in the Atlantic. Jerking away, she sucked in rapid, shallow breaths and swallowed. "I'm coming." Guilty heat crept along her cheekbones as she risked a glance at his face.

His expression gave none of his thoughts away. Leaning close, Connor kissed the end of her nose. "I knew we would be good together. We will talk later."

The dark sensual promise in his eyes made her stumble as she hurried into the salon.

Her conscience burned as she sat with Aunt Charity. She should have spurned his advance instead of clutching him closer, should have pushed him away instead of kissing him back.

Her first kiss, stolen in the corridor of Connor Calhan's Upper East Side mansion. Her face heated.

She knew what Aunt Charity would think of her actions and sighed. Her lips still tingled from his kiss and the warmth of his breath caressing her cheek. And God help her, she wanted to kiss him again.

Chapter Twenty-One

Richmond, Virginia, December 1864
The past few weeks, we have blockaded Confederate ports, crippling Southern supply lines, and hastening the end of this bloody conflict. General Sherman's march from Atlanta to Savannah carved a ruthless path through Georgia, leaving devastation the Confederacy will not soon forget. President Lincoln's re-election strengthens our resolve. His victory secures the continuation of the war effort until we achieve unconditional surrender and the abolition of slavery. We have come too far and lost too much to falter now. My son, Connor, has witnessed more death and hardship than most men yet retains his spirit and vigor for the cause. I am proud to call him my son.

My Southern informant has secured a complete list of The Knights of the Confederacy, revealing their true identities and their elusive leader, The Phantom. Twice she has come close to being discovered, and I have urged her to guard her safety more closely. With winter upon us, we depart soon for quarters, and communication with this courageous woman must wait until spring. May God grant us His mercy in the months ahead. –Major Jonathon Calhan

****

Mercy didn't discover how much she looked forward to his promise of talking later until she sat alone in her room after dinner with disappointment tugging at her chest.

Connor and the general left hours ago and hadn't returned. When they didn't appear for dinner, she tucked the memory of his kiss away and focused on the enticing opportunity to search his study undetected.

Calculating how much time she would require to slip into Connor's study and make a copy kept her occupied until Aunt Charity's chamber door closed for the night with a thud.

Mercy nibbled on her bottom lip as she surveyed the empty corridors. He said the decoded list didn't tell him more than he already knew. This meant the code held no value for him, other than a sentimental one for being one of the last objects his father held before he died.

Which made her guilt over sneaking into his study less oppressive.

An hour later, she sat back on her heels and stared at Connor's safe. Never had she dealt with such a complicated mechanism, and failure weighed heavy on her shoulders. Connor could walk in at any moment, and she had no intention of being caught. Again.

A deep sigh escaped as she turned to go. But her attention caught on a sheet of parchment tucked beneath a large book on his desk. Lifting the book, she picked up the sheet of parchment and smiled.

She plucked a pen from a nearby stand and a fresh sheet of parchment with quick, fluid movements. Dipping the tip in the ink well, she wrote. *A=D, B=J, C=K, D=O, E=Q, F=S, G=T...*

Ten minutes later, she climbed the stairs to the second floor with her contraband rolled in one hand. Elation put a bounce in her step. Tomorrow, she would wire the colonel and inform him she had his cipher.

Once she returned to her chamber, she kicked off her slippers, sank onto her bed, and stared up at the cream-gilded ceiling. Guilt over what she planned to do plagued her, and she spent a good hour arguing with her conscience. Although Connor dismissed the decoded list as worthless, the fact she stole into his study and copied the cipher made her squirm. She promised, and until now, hadn't worried about breaking her word to a Calhan.

The end had to justify her actions. She meant to use the cipher to barter for her and Aunt Charity's lives, and he must understand the importance.

Her chest grew heavier, and she sighed as her inner voice argued with every justification she produced. All she knew about the Calhans she heard from Uncle Justice. A tapestry woven of lies.

Although Major Calhan's journal proved enlightening, she yearned to decipher her mother's diary and learn the truth. There were questions she wanted answered. Beginning with the real name of her mother's murderer. But one truth she could not deny, Major Jonathon Calhan had no hand in Mama's death.

A thought flickered, wild and sudden, sparking her into motion. She stumbled to her feet, with her heart pounding, and lunged for the bedside table. Her hands trembled, clumsy but determined, as she aligned the cipher against the cryptic script of her mother's diary. Her breath hitched, shallow, and ragged when the first words unraveled.

Mercy froze. Her pulse thundering in her ears as she read the revelation:

Two weeks ago, I finished the list of Percival's

Knights of the Confederacy secret society. I must confess I am shocked, and yet not surprised, to discover Justice wields authority in their sinister little cult…

Her fingers hovered above the delicate pages, trembling under the weight of what she uncovered. Did her mother truly pen this coded message? A jolt of realization fueled her frenzy, and she worked with no thought of time, decoding line after line until two pages lay bare before her. Her vision blurred, and her thoughts spiraled into chaos.

Connor's warning echoed in her mind, no longer whispers but thunderclaps of truth. Uncle Justice not only knew The Phantom but also joined their cult as a ruling member of The Knights of the Confederacy. A man who instilled terror in her mother's heart.

Anger burned hot in her veins as she slumped back in her chair. Staring into the crackling fire, memories of Uncle Justice's cruelty flooded back. His merciless treatment of Aunt Charity, his callous disregard for anyone who dared defy him, and the cruel comments he made about her mother.

Clenching her fists, the truth struck her with brutal clarity. She had been blind, and her judgment clouded by lies. And yet, despite her accusations and venomous words, Connor took her and Aunt Charity into his home and offered them his protection.

The flames danced before her, the flickering light a reminder of her resolve. Mercy sat battered by revelation but unbroken, ready to confront the tangled web of betrayal binding her past.

Her mother knew and trusted Connor's Father. The thought astounded her. Mama invented the cipher to sneak information to Major Calhan to aid the Union cause despite the danger of discovery.

Her heart twisted as she stared at the thick diary before her. Too many secrets and truths lay hidden between those pages for her to quit now. With renewed determination, she pulled out a fresh sheet of parchment and applied the code to the next page.

At midnight, Mercy closed the diary and rose to her feet. With shaky hands, she removed her gown and donned her night rail. She had half a dozen pages deciphered and thought she might be sick.

Her father, Colonel Percival Bennett, had been an evil, vindictive man, and she thanked Aunt Charity's God she had no memory of him.

Fatigue and raw emotion overwhelmed her as she slid beneath the silken bedclothes and closed her eyes. Tears ran unheeded down her cheeks as she rolled to her back and stared up into the darkness. "Thank you for taking care of me, Mama." The words were inadequate to describe the well of emotion filling her bosom. Wishing she were older and a bigger help did no good when her mother repeated her gratitude for the blessing of holding her while she slept.

"I will find whoever took you from me, and see they receive justice."

The nightmares started at three in the morning.

Mercy cuddled in her mother's soft embrace as a deep voice threatened to lock them inside the hot chamber with no water or food.

"You were supposed to stay upstairs, Grace." A hard voice rang in her ears. "The child is so...vulnerable without you here. I would hate for something to happen to her while you are prying into things you shouldn't."

She strained to see the dark figure looming over her,

certain the figure meant to end her life. Her mother no longer held her, and the figure bent closer. She screamed with terror.

"If you hurt her, I swear by all that is righteous, I will kill you." Her mother's voice rose in volume.

The darkness settled over her, making it difficult to breathe. Danger and death dampened the air as she struggled to free her arms for defense.

The bedclothes wrapped around her legs as she tossed and struggled to gain her freedom. And the man with the black eyes who haunted her soul after she came to live with Aunt Charity returned. This time, more vivid, eviler, and more terrifying.

Screaming as loud as she could, she shoved against the bulky black figure. "I swear to God if you touch me or my mother, I will cut your heart out."

"Your mother?" Large hands gripped her upper arms. "Wake up, Mercy. No one is here but me."

The deep voice made her hesitate. She knew him. "Connor?" She froze, heart hammering in her chest, and every muscle coiled tight.

His hand, rough and warm, rested on her arm where he soothed her from her nightmare. She should have pulled away, but the memory of their kiss flared like a living thing.

"Yes. Wake up and talk to me. What frightened you?" His deep, steady voice calmed her pounding heart and lit the darkness inside her chamber. The demons that tormented her fled.

"I dreamed a man held me by the arm and refused to let go. He had dark eyes and the most terrifying smile." Mercy swallowed. "He haunted me for months after I came to live with Aunt Charity, but I have not dreamed of him for years." Shivering with remembered terror, her body betrayed her, tilting toward him.

"Who, Mercy?"

Frowning, she searched for a name. "I don't know. He's...familiar...but not someone I know very well. He knew my mother."

Connor's warm breath blew against her cheek. "Did he hurt you?" His tone said he would tear the man apart.

"No. But I remember being terrified he would." She swallowed. "Whenever I dream of him, I cannot breathe, and the air smells like...death. My feet are planted in the ground, and as he gets closer, my heart beats so fast I feel faint. I wake dripping with terror."

Connor's expression grew more thoughtful. "Do you remember anything particular about him that could identify him? Such as a scar?"

She searched her memory. "No."

Connor's deep voice grew thoughtful. A pregnant pause followed. "Could this nightmare be your father?"

Mercy shook her head. "I do not think so. I would have known if he were my father. Other men were there all the time, attending meetings and things."

Connor froze. "You remember meetings?"

Her breath caught in her throat. She planned to keep her identity a secret, and if she said more, he would figure it out. "My father commanded a squadron of soldiers. They came to our home all the time. The servant would make me hide whenever riders appeared, whether Union or Confederate. Both were apt to plunder in the name of the war." Her shiver started at her toes and worked up her spine.

Connor caught one hand in his and squeezed. "Hush. You are safe now."

His thumb brushed her skin in a faint, single stroke, shattering her defenses as a lifetime of standing alone, yearning to be held and loved, crashed into her chest. She froze, her heart slamming against her ribs, the urge to flee warring with the deeper, hungrier ache rising within her. Every muscle tensed, desperate to resist the pull of desire, and yet her body betrayed her, inch by trembling inch, leaning into his warmth. A strangled breath caught in her throat, thick with both need and terror. Before she could master it, a soft, broken moan slipped free, baring the depth of her surrender. Clutching the bedclothes in her fists, she struggled to summon anger or pride to shield her from the tenderness unfolding between them. When she dared lift her gaze to his, she found no mockery there, but a quiet hunger mirroring her own.

The air between them thickened. Large warm hands drew her close, caressing her arms and dipping to draw lazy, heated circles on her back, removing the remnants of her resistance.

When his forehead dropped to rest against hers, she drew a shuddering breath, aching to be held without war or hatred between them. Mercy needed Connor's touch like a parched mouth required water.

She shuddered as the first brush of his lips caught hers, tentative, searching, a question half-asked. She should have recoiled, reminded of all the reasons this was foolish, dangerous, and wrong. But the night clung to them like a conspirator, and when his hand cupped her jaw, rough thumb stroking the corner of her mouth, she melted against him.

His kiss deepened, moving over her lips with devastating tenderness, as though he feared she might vanish if he pressed too hard. Trembling with emotion, she clutched the front of his shirt, desperate for an anchor in the storm he unleashed inside her.

A low moan rumbled in his chest, raw and unguarded, tearing through her last thread of caution. She answered with a soft, yielding gasp, and in the space between heartbeats, the world outside ceased to matter.

He pulled her closer, into the hard, trembling line of his body. And her heart threatened to jump from her chest. Restraint thrummed through him, evident in the way he remained rigid, unwilling to take more than she offered, even when his body betrayed the depth of his longing.

Somewhere in the haze of her senses, she knew this could not, must not, go further. And yet, when he pressed his forehead to hers once more, their breath mingled, their hands tangled in each other's clothing, she made no move to break away.

Pulling back, Connor stiffened. "I should—"

"No."

For one stolen moment, they belonged to each other, not to the past, and not to the world that would tear them apart come morning.

Connor stayed still, his breath a raw, uneven tremor against her skin, every muscle in his body strained to give her the chance to pull away.

"Please...don't go." She did not want distance. Not tonight. Not after all the cold, lonely nights she spent building walls against a world that had never been gentle.

The seconds ticked by, and then Connor stripped off his shirt, slipping beneath the bedclothes. Their mouths met in hungry, wild kisses as he stretched out beside her and took her in his arms.

Shy, tentative, and desperate to touch him, she slid

her fingers along his chest, feeling the wild beat of his heart against her palm. His hand, which had remained frozen on her hip, flexed once and then, emboldened by her touch, swept up her back in a slow, reverent stroke, sending shivers racing through her.

Their mouths met again, this time without hesitation, and the kiss grew hungry, deep, like a thirst neither could quench. His hands roamed over her with aching tenderness, as though he sought to learn her form and worship her body, not simply possess her.

Mercy responded with fervor, wrapping her arm around his neck, and she opened her mouth for his assault.

Their kisses turned wild, hot, and demanding as his hands grew bolder, tracing over the contours of her body through the silk night rail she wore. She wanted more, wanted him everywhere, around her, beside her, over her, and inside her.

Heat bloomed low and insistent in her belly as her need for closeness burned away fear and memory alike. She did not remember removing her night rail, only the desperate need to feel more of him, solid and real beside her.

When his lips traveled down the curve of her throat, she tilted her head back with a trembling sigh, surrendering to his caress, and no longer caring about past betrayals, about the rules of society, or the fear that would return at dawn.

"God, you are beautiful."

His words set her on fire. All that mattered was the way he touched her, as if she were precious. And when he whispered her name against her skin, hoarse with need, she let the last of her defenses fall. If only for tonight.

Her heart leaped, and liquid heat poured into her belly when he cupped her buttocks and held her against the length of his shaft.

"Yes…" Her voice sounded strange to her ears. The feel of his heat pressing into her made her squirm with anticipation. "Connor…"

He groaned in response. Clad in tight black breeches, he took a deep breath, his chest glistening in the dim light of the fire as he rolled Mercy to her back and nudged her thighs open. "I'm here, baby." Settling between her legs, he gathered her closer and kissed his way back down her neck, nipping and licking until he reached the frantic pulse pounding at the base of her throat.

"Your heart is beating like a runaway horse." One hand slid up to cup her aching breast, and she cried out when he squeezed her fullness.

"God. Yes. You make me feel so…" She ended in a cry of delight as he took her straining nipple between his thumb and forefinger, rolling the hardening pebble into a stiff peak.

For several glorious minutes, she reveled in the feel of his hand on one breast, and then its twin while she writhed beneath him.

Connor rocked his hips into hers, and she shuddered as his shaft pressed deeper.

"I want to taste you, Mercy." His deep voice grew harsh as she arched back, squeezing her eyes closed in delight.

Past thinking about anything but the feeling of him touching her, she nodded. "Yes." Her breath came fast, and her mouth dried in anticipation. "Please." She needed the pleasure he could give her. Required it like she needed air to breathe.

Catching the waistband of her pantalets, he paused. "Tell me now if you want me to stop. Once I feel you naked against me, I don't know if I can."

Naked against me. "Don't stop. I want to—"

Her pantalets came off, and he settled back against her pelvis, his hot lips closing over one aching nipple. She cried out and gripped his shoulders as waves of desire washed over her. Her legs spread wider, and she arched against his hips, astonished at the way his body made her feel. Hot, wanton, and delirious to experience more, Mercy wrapped her legs around his hips, gasping at the friction his heat created.

Connor tugged her other nipple into his mouth before dropping his hands to cup her bottom. Holding her tight against his grinding pelvis, Mercy thought she would go mad if he didn't touch her…there.

Every tug on her nipple sent a fresh wave of liquid heat to her secret place until she squirmed in discomfort. "Connor…please touch me."

A rush of cool air brushed over her as Connor rose, dropped his breeches, and then settled back over her, nudging her thighs wide apart. "Is this what you want?"

One long finger probed her tender flesh between the soft folds of her femininity, and she gasped with pleasure when he penetrated her. "Yes. Oh God, yes."

Mercy opened her eyes and met the full weight of his intense scrutiny.

His expression darkened as he slid his finger back out and plunged forward. "Do you like this?"

She whimpered in response, too caught up in the friction he created as he increased the tempo.

She bucked in response, thinking about his thick shaft jutting out from his slim hips hovering above her quivering belly.

He had to enter her soon or she would die of anticipation. Although his fingers gave her pleasure, she knew his manhood would send her to an unimaginable realm of ecstasy.

Burning with passion, she wrapped her hand around his stiff shaft and stroked him, wanting to feel the velvet strength of his desire.

His breath came out in a hot rush, and he jerked back as if burned. "I won't be able to stop. God, your hand feels good. I don't want to hurt you, Mercy."

She frowned. "Did I do something wrong?"

His cheeks were flushed, and his dark eyes glittered as he stared at her. "No. I like what you did too much. I won't be able to go slow if you touch me like that."

Mercy smiled and trailed her fingers down the side of his shaft, marveling at the way he shuddered in response. "You want to mate with me as much as I want you to." Marveling at her power over him, she repeated her caress, closing her hand around his stiffness and stroking him.

"More. God, you drive me crazy. The sway of your hips, the dip of your waist, and the fullness of your breasts have made me wonder what you look like naked. I need to be inside you, Mercy." Connor's mouth slanted over hers as he dipped his fingers inside her one more time. "You're so wet for me." Shifting his hips, he centered the swollen head of his arousal at her opening.

She thought she had died when he slid inside and stopped. Never in her wildest dreams had she imagined mating with a man could feel this good. Arching against him, she lifted her legs higher and gasped as he slid further inside.

"Don't move." Connor's hoarse voice warmed the side of her neck as he shuddered in her arms.

"I want…I need, please, Connor."

He complied with a surge, seating his shaft inside her.

Mercy cried out when her virgin barrier ruptured and gripped his shoulders in panic. "You're hurting me."

"There is pain the first time, and I'm sorry I hurt you. It will feel better in a minute." He kissed her eyes, and then her nose, before taking her lips in a gentle, seductive rhythm. Coaxing and deliberate, he teased her until she arched against him once more.

Slipping his hands between their joined bodies, he stroked her slick folds and the sensitive nub hidden within until she shuddered against him, gasping with pleasure.

"Let me love you, Mercy." With gentle rocking motions, he slid back and then thrust into her liquid heat, stoking her passion into a burning inferno.

Panting for breath, and mindless to all else but the pleasure of his touch, she lifted her hips to meet each thrust, delirious with delight, her pain forgotten. As the pressure built, she responded with more abandon, wrapping her legs higher and clutching his back as he brought her to the peak of ultimate fulfillment.

Oh God, oh God." Her chant filled the night air as she soared high in the pinnacle of his embrace, caught in a whirlwind of delight, pleasure, and glorious gratification. Her world split apart, and she fell through a glittering abyss of pure bliss, floating on a wave of contentment.

Connor found his release a moment later and sank against her, slick, wet, and satisfied.

Elation, joy, and euphoria burst from every part of her body as she sank back to earth, secure in Connor's arms.

Their combined labored breathing hung heavy in the air with the scent of their lovemaking. The fire crackled and popped, bringing Mercy's awareness back to the present. She never imagined bedding being so personal or so satisfying.

****

Rolling to his side and tucking her against him, Connor sighed. "How are you feeling?"

Mercy stretched and snuggled closer to his broad chest. "Wonderful."

He smiled at the top of her head, and as their ardor cooled, his mind raced with all the implications of their joining. He hadn't planned to bed her when he woke to her screams. Reality settled over him like a damp mist. What if he gave her a child? Frowning, he stared at the top of her head. He couldn't relieve her of her virginity and then pretend nothing happened.

"If you plan to make a speech about being obligated to me, save your breath. I have no interest in marriage. I have plans for my future that don't include being tied to some man."

Connor stiffened, shocked by her nonchalant attitude. Why wouldn't she want to get married after what they experienced together? "I took your innocence." Is this how all the women he took to his bed felt when he explained he had no interest in acquiring a wife?

"I had to lose it sometime, and I chose you."

Shrugging, she continued as if they were discussing the tides. "I shared my body with you for a few minutes to chase away my nightmare. You did a marvelous job, and I feel much better now. Thank you for your participation, but I have no further need for your services. Please leave before someone discovers you here, and we are forced into a situation neither of us wants."

Astounded and unprepared for rejection, he gaped while his mind raced with bewilderment. He didn't know how to respond. "My…services? What if you carry my child?"

Mercy gave another dainty shrug, infuriating him. "Yes. We will discuss the matter when and if such a thing occurs. Until then, I am weary and would like to get some rest."

She dismissed him with a wave of her hand and a healthy yawn.

For a tense moment, he stared down at her, speechless. Snapping his mouth closed, Connor rose from the bed and tugged on his discarded clothing. "We will speak of this later. But rest assured, you will marry me. I am a gentleman, and an honorable one." He would be damned before he let some green-eyed pain in the ass keep him from doing his duty.

"I will marry no one. I have explained my views on the subject and do not foresee changing my mind." Her voice drifted off as she turned her back and tugged the coverlet over her head, ending the conversation.

"We shall see." Slamming the door closed behind him, Connor stalked away to his chamber, furious that Mercy couldn't see the predicament he put her in. Or how he tried to right the wrong with his offer of marriage. But Mercy hadn't considered Aunt Charity. If she wouldn't comply with his wishes to wed, he would enlist the older woman's help. She would make sure her niece had a ring on her finger and a man's protection long before any babe made an appearance.

The thought made him rest easier. Until he closed his eyes and relived the most exciting sexual encounter he'd ever participated in. His back would be sore for days from her nails scoring his flesh while she writhed beneath him, and her soft moans of pleasure filled his senses. Mercy would be his, one way or another.

Chapter Twenty-Two

Richmond, Virginia, March 1865
Twice during the harsh winter, I caught Percival rummaging through my private papers, but my coded writing has kept my secrets safe. I know the identities of all the Knights and their leader. Recently, Percival dragged me into his study to berate me. There, I saw my gold box on his desk. Smiling, he taunted me with my father's gift. "Your father paid a ransom to make this box for you, and now it sits in my safe holding the seeds of your destruction. When we win the war, I shall travel to New York and bury the box beside him, with your heart nestled inside. After all these years, the box holds as little charm for me as you do."

Desperate to confirm a connection between Percival and the Knights, I overturned the box. The seals inside bore the emblems of the Knights, The Phantom, and Percival's family crest. Clutching the box, I fled into the corridor, but Percival overtook me and struck me down. My fear turned to anguish when I saw Mercy peeking through the staircase rails. The devastation in her eyes remains etched in my soul. I vow to deliver the list of the Knights to Major Calhan, even if it costs me my life. I have arranged to meet him two nights from now, while Percival is away in Richmond. I will not waste this chance to bring the Knights to justice. –Grace Bennett
****

Mercy didn't sleep for the rest of the night.

How could she contemplate marriage after all the history between their two families? If Connor discovered her true identity, he would hate her as much as she hated him all these years. What would he have done if she had accepted his proposal and ended with "*By the way, my real name is Bennett. The woman you believe lured your father to his death is my mother.*" Snorting, she punched her pillow and rolled to her back to stare at the ceiling.

No, she would finish deciphering her mother's diary, find the gold box, and disappear. With the box, she could purchase a house, provide for Aunt Charity, and live on her own terms.

"And if you are with child?" The voice in her head asked.

"I will have enough money to take care of the child, and Connor need never know. It is a far kinder fate than succumbing to his charm and agreeing to be his wife. Not when such bad blood exists between us."

At four in the morning, she gave up trying to sleep and rose to don her dressing gown. Lighting her candle, she spent the next four hours deciphering the diary.

She learned more about the war, her father's violent nature, and his mistreatment of his women servants than she cared to.

Horrified, she tucked the diary away and slid between the covers a few minutes before Callie entered the chamber to help her dress.

Half asleep and weary from her long night, she sent the maid away and slept until noon. Dreams of Connor invaded her slumber and stirred her awake. He transported her to the stars last night, and although she enjoyed every moment, they must never share the same bed again. Connor Calhan's seductive smile, gentle touch, and caring nature had the power to destroy her. Sighing, she pushed thoughts of him aside and spent the rest of the day going through the diary.

Connor knocked on the door when she refused to come down for dinner. "Let me in, Mercy."

He wouldn't leave until she satisfied all of his questions. Sighing, she slid the diary under her pillow and rose to unlatch the door.

His gaze swept over her, tracing every curve with an intensity that weakened her defenses. Her hair, her face, her heaving bosom, and then his eyes locked with hers. "Are you all right?" His concern hit her square in the heart.

All day, she read entries contradicting everything she believed about her mother, Jonathon Calhan, and Connor. Her mother's account of her father and Uncle Justice chilled her to the core.

They murdered innocent men, women, and children, and used the war to further their crimes. Her father had one true love: power. And he never wasted an opportunity to use it or acquire more.

She could understand Connor's determination to catch The Phantom. For if any soul existed who was more evil than her father, it would be he.

Regret, remorse, and sickening details made her queasy most of the day until she longed to rush into Connor's arms and beg for his forgiveness. Jonathon Calhan and Connor fought for their country with honor, courage, and the hearts of patriots, while her father fought with cowardice, cunning, and deceit.

When she thought of the things she accused Connor of and said to him, she wanted to melt into the floor. As the sun sank behind the forest of houses between her and the horizon, she discovered she had fallen in love with him.

Somewhere between stealing into his warehouse, his gentleness with Aunt Charity, and her mother's revealing entries, she found the man her heart yearned for.

Connor would keep her safe, love her beyond her wildest dreams as he did the night before, and give her the family she never had. If only things were different.

Now, staring at him through the crack in the door, Mercy's heart ached with remorse. She had to convince him she didn't care before he destroyed her. The pain of his rejection when he discovered her parentage would be unbearable. "Yes."

"Why do you stay in your chamber? I have been worried about you." His dark eyes burned into hers, and her knees weakened.

Fluttering wings filled her belly as she stared into his eyes. Hours before, she kissed those lips, stroked his chest, and shared her most secret place with him while he carried her to heaven and beyond.

Imagining his reaction when he discovered her true identity, she gave him a cold smile. "I made a copy of the cipher and sent it to Colonel Dawson today. I made a deal with him, and now it is fulfilled. Aunt Charity and I are safe and will leave your home tomorrow. By then, I should have confirmation the colonel received my telegram."

His blue eyes narrowed. "I forbid you to leave. If you learned nothing else, your time with the colonel should have convinced you he is not a man of honor. He will break his word to you with as much speed as he did

Justice. You are not safe unless you are with me."

Giving him a delicate shrug, she continued. "We shall see. As I mentioned last night, I have no further need for you." Cold and sick at heart over the lies she told, Mercy studied his face.

"You do, and you damn well know it." His gorgeous eyes flashed blue fire before he stepped back, his features carved in marble. "You will be my wife. There is no other way." Turning on his heel, he strode away without another word.

"No." Waiting until he disappeared from view, Mercy closed the door and secured the latch. A sob escaped as she leaned against the oak slab, hoping the pain ripping her apart would cease, but instead, it intensified.

She broke her own heart and used Connor to do so. On wooden legs, she crossed the room and resumed her translation.

At three in the morning, Mercy closed the diary and slumped over the secretary where she sat.

Good Lord God Almighty. Stunned, angry, and in awe of the woman who birthed her, she focused on breathing until her anger dissipated, and she no longer felt faint.

With shaky hands, she pushed her hair from her eyes and stared at the fire. Her mother gave her life protecting her and fighting for her country. Braver than the boldest soldier, with the courage of a lion, she did everything she could to combat evil and preserve innocent lives.

The day before her mother's death, she went for a ride as was her custom and discovered several of her husband's soldiers following her. Cutting across the field, she returned home to find Colonel Bennett waiting in the stable. "I do not think it wise to leave the plantation anymore, my dear. Unspeakable things happen to women during war, and I could do nothing to stop an attack with you so far out of my sight." Stepping close, he twisted her arm behind her back and shoved her against the barn wall. "I should hate to have something terrible befall you should you choose to ignore my warning as you have in times past."

His threat sent a shiver down her spine, which she hid by coughing with as much gusto as she could summon. "You are hurting me, Percival."

He loosened his hold with a chuckle and placed a hand on either side of her head, pinning her in place.

Swallowing, she continued. "I strive to be obedient, husband, and am saddened you think otherwise." A horse whinnied, and she turned her head, glancing at the group of soldiers approaching. "Thank you for sending men to look after me while I ride. Although I do not venture off the plantation, I appreciate your concern for my safety."

Colonel Bennett's breath stirred the hair at the nape of her neck, and she could not disguise her shiver.

"I am aware of your activities, my dear. Do not deceive me again, or you will breathe your last."

Mercy closed her eyes. Her mother knew she had one chance to get the cipher to Major Calhan, and if her husband discovered her missing, she would die in the process.

Courageous to her last breath, she packed a satchel for Mercy and delivered her to Mammy with specific instructions on how to get to New York without being discovered.

Mercy remembered Mama kissing her and asking her to be a good girl for Mammy, promising to join her at Aunt Charity's in a week. Then she gave a heavy, woven sack to Mammy and told her to guard it, and Mercy, with her life.

She never saw her mother again.

And now, she knew the truth about what happened. Sick to her stomach, Mercy retched into the chamber pot until she had nothing left. Afterward, she wiped her face, curled up on her bed, and wept until dawn.

Only one mystery remained: the location of her mother's gold chest.

She supposed her mother would give instructions or some kind of clue to guide her, but when she reached the last journal entry with no mention of the chest, Mercy groaned aloud.

"Why does it have to be so complicated?' And then, she knew. The poem on the back of the diary would lead her to the chest. Mama took every precaution in case Uncle Justice or her father came seeking the box. They would have to solve the riddle to find it.

And so would she.

Beneath the watchful oak it lies,
Where father's whispers kiss the skies.
Amid the roses' tangled maze,
A treasure sleeps in twilight's haze.
Seek not the stone of strength and pride,
Though there the weary oft confide.
A cradle rests, a treasure keeps,
Where love eternal softly sleeps.
Yet seek not far, but turn within,
The treasure lies where love begins.

Stumped, she studied the words until the page grew blurry, and she had to stop.

Tired to the bone and sick to her soul, Mercy slid

beneath the comforter and drifted off to sleep.

****

Her cries woke him from a deep slumber, and he threw back the covers to rush to her rescue.

"As I mentioned last night, I have no further need of you." Her shallow words, delivered in such an icy tone, did little to slow him down. After an hour of stewing over the matter, he concluded Mercy said the words, hoping to put some distance between them. The connection they shared when making love frightened her as much as it did him. If the truth were known, he would have said much the same thing in times past to avoid any entrapment created by expectations, real or imagined.

But with Mercy, things were different. Her quiet, selfless words absolved him of any obligation, while the fire they shared struck him to his core. He didn't feel trapped, hunted, or obligated to do a damn thing. They shared desire, pure, unrelenting, and irresistible.

And God help him, he wanted more. He wanted forever.

Being with Mercy, seeing her every day, and learning about her quirks were no small moments in time, but the very essence of his days. She consumed his thoughts from dawn until the deepest hours of the night. Several times this past week, he discovered he stared at her in the same peculiar way his father used to look at his mother, and he had to laugh, shaking his head.

"You always knew, didn't you, Father?" He murmured to the ceiling before diving back into his father's journal, searching for clues. Yet even as he turned those pages, his thoughts would drift back to her, and the way she made him feel.

Last night, when he took her in his arms, the sheer

rightness of it shattered every pretense, silencing the cautious voice of his conscience. What followed had not been mere passion, but pure transcendence. The most unforgettable union of his life.

And he craved it again.

Now, as he approached Mercy's door, her cries grew louder and more insistent.

Slipping the key into the latch, Connor stepped into her chamber and latched the door closed behind him.

On silent feet, he approached the bed and shed his clothing, sliding in beside her to draw her rigid body into his arms.

The second he touched her, she turned into his embrace like a lost kitten in a thunderstorm and snuggled close to his heat.

Shivering and mumbling, Mercy wrapped both arms and legs around him, welcoming him into her bed.

They made slow, sweet love until she trembled in the afterglow of her release, still holding him tight against her.

Connor kissed the top of her head and cleared his throat, hoping to discuss what happened between them. But even as he formed the words, her soft breathing told him she'd fallen asleep.

Over the next week, Mercy ignored Connor during the day, delivering scathing remarks and sweeping from the room as soon as he entered giving him no time to speak.

Refusing to accept Mercy's rejection, his resolve hardened with every breath he drew. She might deny him with trembling words, but her heart spoke a different language, and he would not let her slip away. When her cries shattered the stillness of the night, he rushed to her side, finding her trembling in the darkness. Without hesitation, she opened her arms to him, pulling him into her bed with such desperate, searing passion every doubt disappeared. She clung to him, needing him, trusting him, and Connor knew with fierce certainty, they were meant to be together, in every way that mattered.

They made tender, passionate love, while she begged for more, pleading with him to stay. At the end of every night, she clutched him like a lifeline, as if she were afraid this would be the last time they would come together, and she would lose him forever. Her icy demeanor would return as soon as the sun rose, and they would repeat the cycle.

But he understood how her mind worked.

She enjoyed being with him as much as he enjoyed being with her, and it terrified her. Mercy lost everyone she cared about except for Aunt Charity, and she believed she would lose him too if he got too close.

On the eighth day, Connor had enough and decided to act. As he left General Cooper's office, he recited how he would word the most important conversation of his life. Somehow, he had to convince Mercy that they were made to be together, and he refused to take "no" for an answer. Mercy Elenna Jackson would be his wife. There could be no other alternative.

He hadn't traveled more than a block before a familiar, dull black carriage came into view and followed him.

Connor stopped his horse and waited as the carriage drew alongside him and halted.

The driver jumped from his seat and approached with a bow. "My master would like to speak to you."

Connor's hand closed around the butt of his pistol,

tucked in the back waistband of his trousers. "Where is your master?"

"Here." The driver opened the carriage door, and he glanced inside, curious to see who owned the mysterious carriage.

Surprised, he tilted his head in greeting. "Good morning, General…Jones." The man with the silver streak in his hair, who witnessed Mercy's escape from the tree outside his home the night of his dinner party. "Please explain why you accost me during my ride."

The general gave him a half smile. "If you care to meet me at fifty-eight Broadway, all will be explained."

"Now, why would I do that?" Connor arched a brow and stared into the man's black eyes. After his last encounter with Gabrielle, he reassessed every acquaintance to see if any more traitors had infiltrated his life. Besides Mercy, of course.

"Because, Mr. Calhan, I wish to discuss a mutual acquaintance without fear of being overheard. You know a man named Colonel Dawson. He is a person of great interest to me and my country. The Spanish Consulate is the one place I know where our conversation will be private."

Excitement tightened Connor's gut. This man had information. He could feel it. "You are Spanish and not an American general as you pretended?"

The general tilted his head. "The government of Cuba has sent me to locate Colonel Dawson. He holds significant importance to us."

Connor narrowed his eyes. "How so?"

A slight smile twisted his lips. "Shall we meet in half an hour? Tell the soldiers at the gates, General Del Ejército Ruiz wishes an audience with you."

He'd be double-damned. Aunt Charity's informant told the truth.

Inclining his head in agreement, Connor guided his mount back a step as the driver closed the door and the dull black carriage rolled away. A high-ranking general in the Spanish army was the last person he suspected of owning the vehicle.

His gut told him General Jones wasn't who he pretended to be the night of the Governor's Ball.

Intrigued by the summons to speak in the consulate, Connor turned Adonis' head around and rode back through town, circling to enter Broadway from the south, close to the entrance of the Spanish Consulate.

The soldiers at the gate allowed him inside and escorted him to a masculine office on the upper floor with a sweeping view of the city. Connor sat on the leather armchair in front of a large oak desk and waited until the general arrived.

Twenty minutes later, they were alone with a decanter of wine and two glasses.

General Ruiz took a sip of his wine. "You are probably wondering why I gave you a false name to get invited into your home."

Connor shrugged. "Not really. You wanted to investigate my connection with General Dawson, and you couldn't do that with your real name, rank, and nationality." The red wine in his hand slid down his throat like liquid silk, delighting his palate with its spicy, robust flavor. "I understand the need for secrecy. However, I do wonder why you were in the Lower East Side before you approached me at the Governor's Ball."

"Ah. You wonder what I know of Miss Mercy and Miss Charity Jackson. Allow me to set your mind at ease, my friend. I am not a danger to the ladies. I followed their male relative, Mr. Justice Jackson, and grew curious about who he visited in such a poverty-stricken area. For a time, I suspected Colonel Dawson might be hiding there, but soon discovered my error. Mr. Jackson robbed, stole, and killed for the colonel and involved Miss Mercy as much as her aunt would allow. Which did not amount to much, I am thankful to say. She is beautiful and quite clever, as you discovered. Tell me, what did she rob from your home? I have been most curious."

Connor explained about the parchment, the cipher, and Justice's death.

Silence filled the room. "You are certain Miss Mercy does not know the location of the colonel's home?"

Connor's head came up. "Justice made sure of it. Otherwise, the colonel would have killed her too."

"If she is lying?" General Ruiz studied him. "What will you do?"

He wondered the same thing, but shook his head in denial. "Why would she protect the man who murdered her uncle before her eyes?"

A slight smile touched Ruiz's full lips. "No reason." He finished his wine and set the glass down. "And if you are correct in your assumption, Colonel Dawson is your Phantom?" Opening the lid of a decorative tin on his desk, he removed a fat cigar.

"He is mine to kill." Staking a claim on the bastard, Connor downed the contents of his glass. "I suspect The Phantom ordered my father's death, and I have scoured the country for him for years. When I find him, I will kill him."

"Not if I find him first." Sniffing the length of the

cigar, the general raised a brow at Connor. "My compatriots have a special ending in mind." Snipping the end of his fat smoke, he lit it and took a drag. "For what he did to my country and my people, he deserves to die a painful death."

Connor declined when the general offered the tin. "Tell me what happened."

An hour later, Connor shook his head and leaned back in his seat. The tales of treason, treachery, and death rivaled his list of crimes for The Phantom. "I understand your desire to capture the villain."

Colonel Ruiz nodded. "He may well be The Phantom as you suspect. Spain has declared him an enemy and issued a death warrant. I am the man they sent to bring him to justice." Blowing a perfect O of smoke into the air, the general smiled. "I asked you here to strike a bargain. Alone, we have half the chance of finding the man. Together, we have better odds."

"What do you propose?" Now he knew for certain Colonel Dawson had been out of the country when The Phantom's crime spree declined, and they could find no trace of him. His conviction the two were the same man grew.

"Collaborate. We have the same purpose, albeit different endings planned." His resolve never wavered.

"On one condition. Whatever you find, whatever you suspect, whatever she may be involved in, Mercy is mine." He hadn't liked the speculative gleam in the general's eyes when he asked if she lied, and he'd be damned before he let the general get close enough to ask.

"Agreed."

Chapter Twenty-Three

Richmond, Virginia, March 1865
I received a note from my Southern informant
requesting a final meeting in the slough. Fearing for her
life after her houseboy's brutal murder, she carries
urgent news. She plans to send her daughter away with
their nanny, Mammy, to protect her from her husband's
wrath. When I questioned whether he would harm his
own child, she answered grimly, "Then you, sir, do not
know my husband." As a father, I cannot fathom such
cruelty, but war has shown me not all men are created
equal. President Lincoln's inaugural address called for
reconciliation, and I pray we reach it soon.

General Grant's siege of Petersburg tightens its
grip, and General Lee's forces crumble with low morale
and heavy desertions. Max reported safe outside
Petersburg, Connor is returning from Washington, and
Reese marches with General Sherman through North
Carolina. I sit by the fire, counting my blessings, though
my heart aches for Maggie and home. Tomorrow, I meet
my informant one last time to collect the cipher she now
uses to shield her messages. With God's grace, the South
will soon surrender, and we can begin to heal—both as
a nation and as a family. –Major Jonathon Calhan

****

Connor closed the journal and stared out the dark
window into the night.

With the cipher, he could read the cryptic entries he had no way of understanding before. Grace Bennett did not orchestrate his father's death as he supposed. She risked her life for the Union cause and changed the course of the war.

The army and General Cooper would be astonished by the news because, since the war, Grace Bennett's name had become synonymous with traitor. The knowledge she did not kill his father had him shaking his head and frowning. Who did then?

There had to be a connection between Colonel Bennett, Colonel Dawson, and The Phantom. Nothing else made any sense.

The War Department had several rosters of Confederate soldiers, and he would borrow one tomorrow. Perhaps a name or a date would jump out at him and give him the required information.

Blowing out the candle, He lay on his bed until Mercy cried out.

But this time, when he took her in his arms, she knew the name of the man who tortured her in her dreams.

"Let me go, father. I will never forgive you for hurting my mother." Her frightened voice tightened a vice around his chest.

Holding her close, he kissed the top of her head. "You have nothing to fear, Mercy. Your father died years ago and will never hurt you or your mother again. The archives list his death as May of 1865. One month after Lee's surrender at Appomattox."

Mercy responded with a deep sigh and surrendered to his kisses with a moan of pleasure.

The night passed, and morning came too soon.

Connor stepped from the bed and dressed in the early morning light. He hated leaving before she woke, but he had her reputation to think of, and until she wore his ring on her finger, they must be careful.

Glancing down, his chest tightened. God, she was beautiful with her hair tousled from their vigorous and satisfying lovemaking. Her face flushed with sleep drew his attention, and he bent down to kiss her velvet cheek.

As he did so, a piece of parchment peeking from under her pillow drew his attention.

A sheet containing the same gibberish code as the list of the Knights of the Confederacy slid into his hand.

His glance skated over the document and skidded to a stop. Astonishment, anger, and understanding marched through him with rapid progression.

And then it all made sense.

Grace Bennett, Colonel Bennett, and …Mercy.

By God. She was Grace Bennett's daughter. Stunned, he stared at the sleeping woman as he digested this new piece of information. Dissatisfaction and anger followed. After all they shared, and all they had been through together, she hadn't trusted him enough to tell him.

How could she keep such monumental information secret?

Her mother, the diary, the box, Mercy's determination to steal the parchment, and her equally focused effort to find the cipher raced through his mind. God, what a fool he'd been. How could he not see it?

The family names alone should have been his first clue. Grace, Justice, Charity, and…his eyes slid to the naked beauty before him…Mercy.

Her nightmares made so much more sense. A

conversation he had with Aunt Charity came to mind and gave him pause. Justice blamed his father, Jonathon Calhan, for Grace's death and convinced Mercy to do the same.

She hated his father as much as he nurtured a dislike for her mother. Connor ran a hand through his hair and groaned. God, what a mess.

In reality, an unknown assailant murdered both. Connor shifted his weight as he pursued another notion.

Did she know about the connection between their parents? Or had she discovered the nature of their relationship the way he had, through his father's journal?

Irritated, he shook her shoulder, not wanting to wait until another midnight encounter to get an answer. "Why didn't you tell me you were Grace Bennett's daughter? Why don't you trust me? Whenever I think we have moved beyond lying, something else comes to light. Of all the deceptions you have told, keeping your identity a secret is the hardest to bear. I have extended mercy to you repeatedly, and yet you continue to deceive me. How can I love a woman I cannot trust?"

"What?" Mumbling in her sleep, she turned, exposing a soft white shoulder.

"Why didn't you tell me? Or were you planning to continue the deception until the day we wed?"

Her eyes snapped open, and she stared up at him. "What are you talking about?" Sitting up, she glared. "Did you say wed?" She searched his face, and her eyes dropped to the damning parchment in his hand. "Oh God, you know." Terror beaded her brow as she tugged the bedclothes to her chin. Lord, even her earlobes looked guilty.

"Yes. And I wonder what else you have kept from

me." Frowning, he shook his head. "We need to talk, and I don't have time this morning." Running a hand through his hair, he swore. "Bloody buggering hell. Someone is going to have to tell my family." He paused. "And my mother."

"I'm…sorry." Her whisper circled him and fell to the ground.

"So am I. She isn't going to like what I have to say, and hearing the truth will be difficult for her to bear." Shaking his head, he closed the door behind him.

He had an appointment with the library at the War Department, after which he planned to meet with General Ruiz and discuss any new findings about Colonel Dawson. Then a long, hard talk with Mercy would sort out a few things before this went any further.

****

Mercy opened her eyes and stretched, wishing she could stay in her perfect dreamland a little longer. Sitting up, she frowned when her attention caught on the piece of parchment lying across the small table beside the bed.

Her heart knocked against her ribs. She hadn't dreamed of the conversation after all. Connor found the page she deciphered last night, and he knew the truth.

She was Grace Bennett's daughter.

"We need to talk…" His deep voice played in her head as she twisted the strings at the neck of her night rail around her finger. *"Someone is going to have to tell my family…And my mother. She isn't going to like what I have to say."*

His frown said the talk wouldn't be pleasant.

Her heart twisted like a knife in her chest. "What am I going to do?" The ceiling had no answer, and neither did the window bursting with sunlight.

He hadn't been happy with the news about her parentage, or the fact she kept the information secret. He would kick her out of his house and life. How could he want anything to do with her after all the lies she told, the times she broke her word, picked the lock to his study, and read his private papers?

"I prefer women who are truthful, loyal, and possess integrity." Connor's list of requirements taunted her, and a tear slipped unheeded down her cheek. She did and said those things for one reason, to find her mother's killer.

Once she didn't mind what Connor thought of her, but now...

Callie arrived at her door with a welcoming smile. "Good morning, Miss. A note came for you this morning. Benson said to wait for you to wake before bringing it up."

Mercy dashed the tears from her face and pushed her broken heart to the back of her mind to deal with later. No one could know how much Connor Calhan meant.

Lifting her chin and plastering a serene smile on, she waved Callie forward. "Who is it from?"

"I don't know, Miss. An errand boy arrived with it earlier this morning."

Which meant someone other than Conner sent it. Unsure if she should be relieved or more nervous, Mercy plucked the paper from the silver tray with shaking hands and read.

Meet me tomorrow morning at Delmonico's at ten sharp. Come alone and do not be late. -Col Dawson

She shivered to the bottom of her cold, bare feet, and clutched the bedclothes in her fists.

What could he want? She kept her end of the deal and sent the cipher. According to their bargain, she and

Aunt Charity were free.

Frowning, she hugged her knees to her chest and stared at the split in the drapes where sunshine streamed into her chamber. Now she thought on the subject, she hadn't received any messages from the colonel in over a week. She had been so busy with her mother's diary and its revelations; he slipped her mind. Dread tightened a knot in her stomach. The very devil would be more welcome than he.

The colonel's demand to meet couldn't have come at a worse time. She knew everything, and without Connor's protection, she would be an easy target. As he pointed out a little over a week ago. Mercy's mind raced with possible avenues of escape and stopped.

The box.

Once she found the little gold chest, she could collect Aunt Charity and move somewhere far away. Somewhere, neither Connor nor the colonel could find them.

"Help me dress." She had little time to waste.

Half an hour later, she sat at her secretary and read her mother's poem again.

Beneath the watchful oak it lies,
Where father's whispers kiss the skies.
Amid the roses' tangled maze,
A treasure sleeps in twilight's haze.

The first four lines were clear. Mercy scribbled "Grandpa and Roses" on the page, her mind racing.

Seek not the stone of strength and pride,
Though there the weary oft confide.

Aunt Charity had much to say to her father when they visited his grave. Those lines weren't tough. But what in thunder did the last lines mean?

A cradle rests, a treasure keeps,
Where love eternal softly sleeps.
Yet seek not far, but turn within,
The treasure lies where love begins.

Pressing her lips together, she chewed over the words. The chest had to be buried beneath the roses planted on either side of her grandfather's headstone.

She sat bolt upright, her heart hammering against her ribs. "Quick, see to my hair. Order a carriage and fetch a shovel."

Ignoring Callie's startled expression, Mercy tucked her mother's diary under her pillow, the last page left open like a silent sentinel.

She could do this. There *had* to be a God watching over her, for He had sent her this perfect escape when she needed it most. With the chest, she could evade the Colonel's schemes, whatever they were, and free her and Aunt Charity from his grasp. And she could leave Connor's home before he tossed her out.

Excitement thrummed in her veins as she slipped on her cloak and descended the stairs an hour later. Her breath caught as she entered the sitting room to face Aunt Charity.

Her plan would work. The treasure awaited. And with it, freedom beckoned.

"I will be gone for two hours or so." Mercy's words hung in the air, but Aunt Charity paid no attention.

Waving a hand in her direction, her aunt smiled without looking up. "Have a wonderful time, dear. Take one of the maids with you."

"Of course, Auntie." Mercy pressed her lips together, stifling a sigh. She remembered Aunt Charity taking her to Trinity Church Cemetery when she turned fourteen. For reasons known only to Aunt Charity, that year she placed a candle and a small knot of flowers on Grandpapa's grave.

Now, half an hour later, Mercy's heart thundered against her ribs as she accepted the groom's hand and stepped down from the carriage. Her knees trembled, but her resolve held firm.

Her grandfather rested beneath the sprawling oak tree at the center of the cemetery. She spotted the familiar landmark the moment she glanced up.

"This is it." Her breath misted in the crisp March air. Her mother's diary revealed the seals belonging to the Knights of the Confederacy and The Phantom were hidden within the chest. With those, Mercy could expose her mother's true killer.

General Cooper would be the one to help her once she unearthed the chest. The decoded diary entries would forever clear her mother's name, dispelling any lingering rumors of treachery during the war. Mama's bravery and sacrifice would be recognized, just as they deserved.

Of the three tasks Mercy had set out to accomplish, this would complete her journey.

She walked forward, her boots crunching against the gravel path as she passed elaborate headstones until she reached the one she sought.

Ebeneezer Phinneas Jackson
June 1, 1800 – May 2, 1862

Blood-red roses flanked either side of the headstone, their blooms vivid against the stark gray stones surrounding them. Mercy let out a shaky sigh, satisfied she found the right place. Angling the shovel's blade into the earth, she began to dig.

The freezing wind tugged at her cloak as she

worked, her breaths coming in short, determined puffs. Thank goodness for the thick leather gloves. Without them, her hands would be numb from the chill.

Unused to physical labor, she paused to straighten, rolling her shoulders to ease the ache. Glancing up, she froze.

A shadow shifted, and from behind the thick trunk of a nearby tree, a figure emerged.

"Well, well, well. My patience is paying off after all this time." The voice, deep and venomous, sliced through the quiet, and Mercy's blood turned to ice.

She clutched the shovel tighter, swallowing the knot of fear rising in her throat. With a slow, deliberate motion, she lifted her eyes to meet the sneering face of the man she dreaded most.

"Hello, Father."

Chapter Twenty-Four

Richmond, Virginia, March 1865
In an hour, I leave to meet Major Calhan for the
final time. The South's defeat is inevitable, Percival,
furious at the loss of his slaves, vows to make the Union
and President Lincoln pay. Many of our servants have
been freed by my hand and sent north through the
Underground Railroad. If Percival discovered my part,
he would kill me without hesitation. But I have one last
act before seeking asylum in the North. I must deliver
Major Calhan the cipher to decode my messages,
revealing the identities of the Knights and Percival's vile
crimes, including the stolen Union gold that funds his
schemes. If I fail, innocent lives will be lost.

Before I left, I kissed my angel goodbye, placing her
into God's and Mammy's care with a prayer for mercy.
I entrusted Mammy with Papa's chest, wrapped in
coarse cloth, giving strict instructions to hide it if I did
not return. Inside the box lies not only its jeweled
treasure but the seals of the Knights, the Phantom, and
the Bennett family, evidence enough to put Percival
behind bars for the rest of his life. I pray I survive this
day to hold my daughter again, far from this place. If not,
may the truth outlive me and justice be served. –Grace
Bennett

****

Connor strode into General Ruiz's office and

dropped into a seat.

The general poured a glass of brandy and slid it across the desk. "We must discuss the terms by which the United States will surrender Colonel Dawson to the Spanish army." He took a long sip of his drink, savoring it before continuing. "The people of Cuba demand justice."

Connor shook his head. "There will be no surrender. Colonel Dawson will stand trial and face execution in the United States for his crimes."

Ruiz's lips curled into a sly smile. "Her Majesty, Queen Isabella, offers fifty thousand gold coins for his extradition to our custody."

Connor leaned back, the leather creaking beneath him. "No deal."

The general's smile sharpened. "You misunderstand. The Spanish Crown lays claim to Colonel Dawson. Her Majesty signed his death warrant. I am under direct orders to locate him and see the execution carried out."

Connor's attention flicked to the parchment on the desk. The royal insignia glinted in the light, drawing his attention. Sitting upright, he snatched the document and began reading.

By the Grace of God and the Constitution, Her Majesty Queen Isabella II, Sovereign of Spain, to All Loyal Subjects and Authorities of the Realm:

Be it known and declared:

Whereas Percival Edward Dawson Bennett, a subject of foreign origin, has been duly tried and convicted by the Court of Her Catholic Majesty's Realm...

The name leaped off the page like a spark igniting a

powder keg.

Percival Edward Dawson Bennett.

"Bloody hell." Connor's heart climbed into his throat. He sat frozen for a moment before the realization hit him like a thunderbolt. "I have to go home."

His mind raced. A note arrived for Mercy that morning, requesting a meeting tomorrow. Which meant Dawson was in New York. Did Mercy know the truth about him? God help him, he had to find her before Dawson did.

General Ruiz arched a brow. "So, you concede?"

"Hell no." Connor jumped to his feet. "But we can argue later. Colonel Dawson is in New York."

The general rose, his movements unhurried but deliberate. "Fetch my cloak." Snapping his fingers at his side, he turned to Connor. "I take it this involves your green-eyed lady?"

Connor ignored him, already heading for the door. "My butler, Benson, will fill you in. I don't have time to explain."

As he strode down the corridor, Ruiz's amused laughter followed him. "Ah, love, how it complicates everything!"

Connor arrived home in record time, bursting through the door and taking the stairs two at a time.

But Mercy's room was empty. Callie glanced up, startled, when he stormed inside.

"Where is she?" He scanned the room before his attention caught on a piece of parchment lying on the small secretary.

Callie wrung her hands. "I don't know, sir. She asked for a carriage and a shovel."

"A shovel?" Connor's chest tightened. "Why?"

"I-I don't know." Callie retreated a step. "Is she in trouble?"

Connor's jaw clenched as dread coiled in his belly. Mercy was in danger, and he didn't have a second to waste. His eyes darted to the poem and the scribbled notes, his gut tightening. Forcing his voice to remain steady, he said, "I believe she's on a treasure hunt, nothing more. Do not be alarmed." He sounded far calmer than he felt, his heart hammering harder with every passing second.

She had gone to dig up her mother's gold chest. If Dawson, or rather Colonel Bennett, discovered where she went and what she sought, he would kill her.

Callie wrung her hands, her brow furrowed. "I've been worried about her, sir. Miss Mercy didn't act right this morning. She hid her face so I couldn't see she'd been crying. Then she took out her mother's diary and wrote the poem on the parchment. After that, she perked up. But if you say there's nothing wrong, I'm relieved."

She gave him a faint smile and resumed tidying the room, though Connor could see the worry still etched in her features.

"Her mother's diary?" Connor swept the room with a quick glance and stopped on a leatherbound book peeking from beneath Mercy's pillow.

Callie gave a nervous laugh. "She tucks it there when she wants to hide it from someone. I don't know why. It's the first place I'd look."

Connor retrieved the diary, flipping through its worn pages as his mind raced. "Where is Miss Charity?"

"In the salon, playing chess with Benson." Callie smoothed the comforter. "They've got a wager on who's the better player."

Connor nodded and left, taking the stairs two at a time. He found the two in a heated chess match.

"Where are your parents' graves, Madam?" Struggling to keep the urgency from his tone, he cleared his throat. "The information is vital, and time is of the essence."

Miss Charity glanced up, startled, her expression shifting to concern. "Mercy asked me the same question not an hour ago. What's happening?"

"I don't have time to explain, Miss Charity." Connor softened his tone as her face paled. "Suffice it to say, she's gone to the wrong place and is in danger."

The older woman's hands trembled as she grasped the arms of her chair and rose to her feet. Her voice, though steady, quivered with a dark thread of emotion. "Her father is here, isn't he?"

Connor nodded.

Miss Charity swallowed hard and gave him clear, precise directions, her voice cracking as she finished. "I knew the tidings of his death years ago were false, and my instincts are never wrong. Bring my niece home, Mr. Calhan."

Connor met her command with a determined nod. "I plan to."

Turning to Benson, he barked out orders. "Lock the house and ensure everything is secure in case the colonel strikes. See Miss Charity to the secret room and stay with her until I return."

"Yes, sir." Benson straightened, his eyes narrowing on the door, and his jaw tightened with tension. "The bastard won't get past me."

"Good man." Turning on his heel, he strode out, his grip tightening on the diary as he prepared to face whatever lay ahead.

Benson knew his responsibilities and would keep Mercy's aunt safe.

Connor took three of his best men and raced toward the graveyard. His heart pounded with urgency as they sped across the terrain, the freezing air biting his face. Every second counted.

When they arrived, he swung down from his horse, tying the reins to a low-hanging tree limb. His attention caught on two figures facing each other a good distance away.

Mercy and a man.

His blood ran cold.

Signaling to his men, he gestured toward the surrounding gravestones. "Spread out. Approach from different angles and stay sharp. The colonel may not have come alone."

His men nodded, their faces grim as they melted into the shadows.

Connor crept forward, each step careful and silent. His eyes stayed locked on the man facing Mercy, his every instinct screaming to act.

"What are you doing here?" Mercy's voice carried in the still air, calm yet tinged with defiance. "If you wanted to pay respects to my grandfather, you only had to ask. I'd have told you where to find the grave." She shrugged, her expression shifting into one of innocent detachment. The same look she used when bluffing her way out of trouble.

Colonel Dawson stood five feet away from her, dressed in black and radiating menace. His glacial stare pinned her in place, and his low, venomous voice carried through the silence. "Don't play games with me, girl.

You know what I want."

Connor's breath hitched when he caught sight of the weapon in the colonel's hand. A surge of terror slammed into his chest, chilling him to his core. For the first time in his adult life, he knew the true, paralyzing fear of death.

At this distance, he could do nothing. If the colonel pulled the trigger, there would be no time to reach her. The thought clawed at his sanity, and for a moment, he faltered. Cold sweat trickled down his spine as he realized how much Mercy meant to him. She had breached his defenses, the walls he erected with such care, and claimed a place in his heart.

If anything happened to her…

Connor's jaw tightened as he pushed the thought away. *Focus. Analyze. Act.*

Wishing he could take back every harsh word he said this morning, he forced his mind to calm. There could be no other outcome than victory. No world existed without Mercy safe in his arms.

Drawing his firearm from his belt, with practiced ease, he analyzed the scene before him, studying the colonel's stance, his focus, and the way his weapon wavered.

Connor inched closer, his movements calculated, his pulse steadying with each step. There would be no failure.

****

"And I sent your precious cipher a little over a week ago. I should think you'd have it by now." Mercy kept her voice light, though it was one of the hardest things she'd ever done. Every fiber of her being screamed to run, to hide, to escape the icy menace in Colonel

Dawson's eyes.

His expression hardened. "The cipher no longer does me any good, as I'm sure you're aware. You've had ample time to decode Grace's diary, and now you're here to dig up her box." His icy stare swept the graveyard, and a cold chuckle rumbled from his chest. "She was clever. Too clever for her own good. I never would have thought to search the graveyard, as she rightly guessed. I've turned over every other place she had access to, including Charity's ramshackle cottage, and found nothing."

Mercy's hands tightened on the shovel as her heart raced. "Those were your men the other night?" Her voice wavered despite her effort to sound calm.

"No." He sounded conversational. "They were Justice's friends, hoping to get their hands on his treasure. The old bat must have known they'd come sniffing around. I planned to surprise you, but with Calhan following you like a lovesick fool, I had to wait."

Mercy shifted her weight, her mind racing. There *had* to be a way out of this. Her grip on the shovel tightened, the wooden handle grounding her even as fear threatened to take over.

Colonel Dawson's chuckle sent a chill down her spine. "Do I frighten you, my dear? You should know Mammy fought like a wildcat. Even under…persuasive methods, she refused to reveal what she knew."

Mercy's stomach lurched. Bending over, she retched until she had nothing left.

When she finished, she leaned against the oak, trembling and too weak to stand alone. Three feet away, the colonel's smile twisted into amusement as he studied her.

"Grace had the same reaction when she got upset." Cocking his pistol, he nodded toward her feet. "I figured she left details on where she hid the damn box in her journal, and once you got your hands on the cipher, you'd figure it all out. It was pure genius to send you after the damned thing, although Justice warned me you were out for vengeance. A shame he isn't here to enjoy this moment with me."

Mercy's mind reeled, but she forced her voice to remain calm. "I have no idea what you're talking about. I came here to take a cutting from the rosebush to plant at home." She stepped back, flicking her tongue over her dry lips, feigning indifference. "I thought you planned to meet tomorrow, not today."

His smile darkened. "I scheduled the meeting for tomorrow to see if you were as much of a coward as your mother. And I was right. You planned to run, just like she did."

Rage flared, driving away her fear as her chin came up in defiance. "My mother had more courage than you'll ever have. She's the reason you failed to kidnap President Lincoln and why the Union supply wagons never fell into your hands. At Sharpsburg, she is the one who informed the Union army of Southern strategies. She fought a better war than you ever could and outsmarted everyone, including you and Uncle Justice."

Dawson's expression twisted into a malevolent grin, chilling her to the core. "Then why is she dead?"

Mercy froze, the words burning like a slap in the face.

"She wasn't as smart as you think." Dawson stepped closer, his grin widening. "You see, I discovered her treasonous activities and took appropriate action."

Mercy's breath hitched. Her vision blurred, and her throat felt like sand. Conviction burned her stomach like a potent poison. "You killed her?" With a mouth as dry as the Sahara, she forced the words out.

"In a roundabout way." He gave her a satisfied grin. "I punished her, and Justice finished the job. Shot her dead."

Mercy staggered; her knuckles white on the shovel as she clung to it like a lifeline.

"Now." Dawson gestured at the ground. "Get digging, unless you want the same treatment."

With her heart lodged in her throat, Mercy bent to take another scoop of dirt. Her arms shook like leaves caught in a storm, and she forced her mouth to suck in a steady breath. Her father's horrific revelations poleaxed her, leaving her teetering on the edge of despair. But she couldn't crumble. Not now. She had to focus. She had to survive.

The shovel struck metal, and she froze.

"There it is." The colonel's cold chuckle sent shivers down her spine as he waved the pistol in her face. "Lift it out and open it."

Her trembling hands obeyed, and she brushed away the clinging dirt to reveal the delicate details etched into the chest's sides. Something didn't feel right. Her stomach churned as she unfastened the latch and lifted the lid.

Oh Lord, God above, have mercy.

"This isn't Mama's." Her voice cracked with disbelief. The chest held only trinkets, ropes of fake pearls, tarnished rings with gaudy imitation jewels, and a handful of worthless Confederate graybacks.

"There's nothing here." Shaking her head as if

trying to wake from a nightmare, she swallowed. "Nothing but costume jewelry and useless bills."

She glanced up at her father, her eyes wide with shock and fear.

"What do you mean, you fool?" The vein on the side of his neck bulged as his mouth twisted with fury. "How could this not be Grace's chest?"

He rushed forward, and Mercy's instincts took over.

She bent low, dropping the chest, her fingers catching the shovel handle in a death grip. With every ounce of strength she could muster, she swung it upward, knocking the pistol from his hand.

The weapon fell to the ground. Without hesitation, she swung again, the shovel's edge connecting with the side of his face. The colonel stumbled, a cry of rage escaping his lips as he toppled backward.

Mercy didn't wait to see if he got up. She turned and ran as if the very devil were chasing her. Dodging trees and weaving between headstones, she zigzagged to avoid being an easy target.

Behind her, the colonel's furious cry split the air, followed by the sharp report of a pistol. A bullet whizzed past her and hit a tree with a sickening thud.

An arm came out of nowhere and wrapped around her middle, yanking her off her feet. Two seconds later, they pulled her against a warm, solid chest.

Panic surged until the familiar scent assaulted her senses. Relief and confusion tangled in her breathless voice. "Connor! What are you doing here?"

His grip tightened. "Saving you."

The sound of running feet pounded the ground behind them. Mercy gripped Connor's arms, her voice trembling but resolute. "We have to go. Now."

Chapter Twenty-Five

Richmond, Virginia, March 1865
In an hour, I will meet my Southern informant for the last time. She has been a tremendous asset to the Union cause, and whispers of surrender grow louder as hundreds of Confederates desert daily. In desperation, the Confederate congress has passed legislation to enlist enslaved men—an irony not lost on any thinking man. General Lee prepares to evacuate Petersburg and Richmond; the end is near. If the Southern Army had half her courage, we might have lost. I intend to thank her properly today, for no one deserves greater honor.

Still, unease weighs heavy on me. A dark feeling clings to the future, and I cannot shake the fear she confided. She insists we meet so she can deliver the cipher, and I will not abandon her now. I informed General Cooper of my intent, naming her for the first time, and once the war ends, I will see she receives the recognition she deserves. I must go; my riders await my command. –Major Jonathon Calhan

****

"He doesn't know which direction you went. We're safe for the moment." Connor glanced down at her. Leaning forward, he kissed the tip of her frozen nose, a fleeting gesture of reassurance. "I came to rescue you, but you did it on your own."

His tone carried a note of pride, but before she could

respond, he stiffened.

"Stay here with Jefferson while I arrest the colonel."

Before she could protest, he disappeared from view, leaving his warehouse manager, Jefferson, at her side.

Mercy's protest died in her throat. She swallowed her panic, knowing any sound might give away her position.

The graveyard fell silent. Mercy's breath stilled as she strained to listen for the faintest sound.

A crunch of boots to her right. A twig snapped to her left.

Her pulse quickened. Peering around the tree, she spotted Colonel Dawson, or rather, Bennett, creeping forward, his pistol raised. He moved like a predator, using a large oak tree for cover as he prepared to launch a surprise attack.

Connor emerged from the shadows, holding a gold chest in one hand and his pistol in the other. His calm, authoritative voice rang out. "Is this what you're searching for?"

Dawson froze, his eyes narrowing as they locked on the chest. Stepping into the open, his glare sharpened. "Where did you find the real one? Give it to me, and I'll let the girl live."

Connor tilted the lid open, revealing the contents. His voice remained steady. "This box and its contents belong to Mercy. I'm here to make sure she receives them and lives to put them to beneficial use."

Dawson's lips twisted into a snarl. "I could shoot you and take the chest."

Connor ignored the threat, studying the man with calculated disdain. "You wouldn't make it two feet. My men have you surrounded. But it's not the box you're after, is it? It's what's inside. Isn't that right, *Colonel Bennett*?"

For a moment, Dawson faltered. He glanced around and paled. Connor's men were on his left, his right, and behind him with their weapons ready.

Then Dawson's sneer returned. "You think you've got me all figured out, don't you? Did you know—"

"That Mercy is your daughter, and you're The Phantom? Yes." Connor's voice hardened to steel. "Or were you referring to how you orchestrated my father's death as well as Grace's? And why you killed Justice after all these years? Couldn't risk a witness to her murder, could you?"

Dawson stiffened, though he masked his reaction with a careless shrug. "A witness is irrelevant now. Years have passed since the woman died. I sent my men to follow her and kill the Union bastard she met with. We were at war. No one cares what happened to the traitor. She got what she deserved."

The callous words ignited Mercy's fury. Her vision clouded with rage, and a low growl escaped her throat.

In a swift, fluid motion, she struck Jefferson in the throat, forcing him back and gasping for air. "Thank you." Snatching his revolver from his stunned hand, she dodged between headstones and trees, emerging in the open, and taking up position ten feet away on her father's right. She lifted the revolver, her hand steady despite her pounding heart. "I'll see you in hell for what you did to my mother."

Mercy meant to graze him, but before she could fire, Jefferson tackled her from behind, knocking the gun from her grip.

The colonel seized the opportunity, lunging forward

to knock Connor's pistol to the ground. His other hand grabbed the chest, sending three heavy metal seals clattering to the ground at their feet.

Connor dove for his weapon, rising, his right leg buckled as Mercy regained her footing and rushed toward her father.

"Mercy, no!" Connor's voice snapped like a whip, followed by a string of curses as he straightened his right leg and lunged forward, his face etched with pain.

But his warning came too late.

Dawson dropped the chest and dove for Mercy.

The sharp crack of a revolver echoed through the graveyard, halting everyone in their tracks.

Mercy spun, her eyes locking on Connor, searching for any sign of injury. His face went pale, his expression stunned as he stared back, one hand gripping his right thigh.

Then the colonel dropped to the ground at their feet, moaning in pain.

Mercy whirled to see who fired and froze. Her breath caught as she recognized the man with the silver streak in his hair, standing fifteen feet away, holding a smoking revolver and smiling.

"There is only one way to deal with this bastard." The man's calm, controlled voice boomed in the deafening quiet. "I didn't aim for his heart. We still need to discuss the details of our agreement. For now, he'll be incarcerated at the Spanish Consulate." Tucking his revolver into its holster, he strode forward as police officers, led by General Cooper, filled the cemetery.

"Not so fast, General Ruiz." General Cooper stepped forward, barking orders at his men. Turning, he dismissed the general. "We'll take it from here."

Two officers hauled Dawson to his feet and cuffed him while General Cooper rocked back on his heels, puffing his chest with authority.

"Colonel Percival Edward Dawson Bennett, you are under arrest for murder, treason, attempted murder, attempted kidnapping, and robbery, along with any other crime I can think of." He gave Ruiz a curt nod. "We'll have our discussion after the courts make their decision."

The general narrowed his eyes, his lips pinched in irritation. He glanced at the thirty officers surrounding him and gave a stiff nod. "As there's nothing I can do at present, I'll make my departure."

With a swirl of his cloak, Ruiz disappeared into the trees as the police led the colonel away.

"I'll make you pay for this." Dawson's sinister promise sent a chill down Mercy's spine.

Connor stepped between Mercy and her father, his voice as cold as death. "You will not get the chance. Say another word, and I will kill you now."

The officers hustled Colonel Dawson away before he could respond, shoving him into a waiting police wagon. General Cooper clapped Connor on the back. "We've got him, my boy, and we'll make sure he never sets foot outside of prison again. Come along, men! Let's get this bastard to the station and locked behind bars."

The other men dispersed, leaving Connor and Mercy alone by her grandfather's grave.

She stared at Connor's broad back as he waved off the remaining officers. Her heart hammered against her ribs like a too-tight drum. When he turned to face her, she bit her lip and bent to retrieve the cloth-wrapped objects in the grass, not daring to meet his eyes.

Unwrapping one, her trembling hands revealed a

seal bearing the symbol of a knight. "The Knights of the Confederacy."

Connor crouched beside her, retrieving the other two seals and unwrapping them. He held them up for her to see. "We have him now. This one is The Phantom's seal, and this one is the Bennett family seal. With these and Grace's diary, Dawson will never see the light of day again."

Mercy swallowed hard, her voice barely above a whisper. "Where did you find my mother's chest? The poem said Mammy buried it here."

Connor smiled, stepping closer. His hands clasped her upper arms, pulling her into his embrace. "No, the poem said:

A cradle rests, a treasure keeps,
Where love eternal softly sleeps.
Yet seek not far, but turn within,
The treasure lies where love begins.

"At first, I thought your mother meant your grandfather's grave, too. But then I asked, 'Where does love begin?' My love begins with you, Mercy. And I realized you were digging in the wrong place. Your grandfather loved your mother, yes, but his love began with your grandmother."

Mercy stiffened, struggling to process his words. "Your…love?" Disbelief laced her tone. How could he say such a thing after what happened this morning?

"Indeed." Connor's voice dropped, thick with emotion. "This afternoon's events frightened me more than the bloodiest battle of the war. How could you be so reckless, walking into such danger? I asked you to stay with Jefferson, where you'd be safe. When Colonel Dawson pointed his revolver at you…" He shook his head, his voice breaking. "I couldn't breathe. My heart dropped to my feet, and I shook with rage. Never take such chances again. I couldn't bear the pain of losing you."

Before she could respond, his lips captured hers, urgent and unyielding. At first, she struggled, disbelief warring with the raw intensity of his kiss. Then, her resolve melted, and she surrendered to the warmth of his embrace.

When he broke the kiss, she stared up at him. "You went to my grandmother's grave? I'm not even sure I know where she's buried. How do you?"

Connor brushed a strand of hair from her face, his lips grazing her temple. "I asked Aunt Charity. Your grandmother is interred in a sepulcher on the west side of the graveyard. Her family was wealthier than your grandfather's, and they buried her in their family crypt as befitting her status."

Mercy sighed, shivering as relief mingled with the heat his touch ignited. The feel of his mouth on her neck and the gentle scrape of his teeth on her earlobe made her burn to be alone with him. But there were still questions she needed answered.

"How did you know where I went?" Leaning against him, her body trembled as the adrenaline drained from her. "Or discover Colonel Dawson, my father, and The Phantom are the same man?"

Connor wrapped his arms around her, his warmth anchoring her as her teeth chattered. "Let's get you somewhere warm, and I'll tell you everything. Shall we go home?" With a smile, he picked up the chest, replaced the seals, and closed the lid.

Home sounded like heaven, and she nodded her

agreement. "Yes, please. There is nowhere else I would rather be."

Later, they sat in the salon with the door open to assuage Benson's sense of propriety.

After relating the details of his appointment with General Ruiz and the discovery of her father's full name on his death warrant, he leaned toward her. "I read your page this morning." Lifting her chin, he stared into her eyes. "I want to apologize for the angry words I said. I love you, Mercy, with all my heart and soul, and when I discovered you didn't trust me enough to tell me the truth about who you were, it crucified me. We are meant to be together, and for our marriage to be successful, we must be honest with one another."

Her breath caught in her throat. "Our marriage? What about your mother and your family?" Her knees knocked together like loose chimes in a windstorm. "You said she shouldn't be pleased with the news of my parentage."

Connor searched her face. "No. My mother will be distressed. She blamed your mother for her husband's death. She will be even more distraught when she discovers you are Grace's daughter. She will want to welcome you into the family and will worry that you will feel awkward after all the secrets. My father kept the name of his southern source a secret for fear your mother would be shot or hanged if she were discovered. He never even revealed her identity to General Cooper. On the day of his death, my father told the general he planned to meet Grace Bennett and help her and her daughter. Frightened for their lives, the southern woman convinced him they would be killed and asked for his help. General Cooper didn't know she was my father's informant. My father is the only one who ever met with her. And when General Cooper returned and found his best men dead from an ambush, he assumed your mother lured him to his death.

"I didn't discover Grace, and his southern informant was the same person until we visited my mother and found the cipher. Father revealed his source's name in a separate letter written in code and tucked inside the cipher."

"It really is over, isn't it?" She smiled up at him, and for the first time since she could remember, she felt free. Her mother's good name would be restored with all the documents they had. The gold chest sat at her feet, and her mother's killer had been arrested. Everything she set out to do the night she broke into Connor's warehouse happened. Her promise to Mama had been fulfilled.

"Yes, my love. The nightmare is over." He kissed her with gentle, soothing kisses.

A cool draft swept past carrying the scent of lemons and…sandalwood? The same scent Connor used, but…different. More mature.

Mercy glanced up and found Connor gazing at the ceiling.

"All right, Father. I know I promised. You've done your part as we agreed, and now I will do mine." Dropping to one knee, he picked up Mercy's hand and gave her such a heated stare, she flushed.

Did he plan to…?

"Mercy, from the moment I first laid eyes on you, my heart became an uncharted sea, drawn by the compass of your smile, steady and true. You are the lighthouse in my storm, the anchor holding me fast in turbulent waters, and the gentle tide that carries me to peace.

"My love for you is as boundless as the ocean and as eternal as the waves kissing the shore. With every sunset that dips below the horizon, I see a promise of a new dawn, of adventures yet to come. Adventures I want to share with you.

"Mercy, you are the captain of my soul, and the keeper of my sails. Together, we've weathered squalls and basked in calm waters, and there is no ship I'd rather be aboard than the one we've built together. You make even the darkest nights sparkle like moonlight dancing over the waves.

"Today, I kneel before you, offering you my heart as my most precious treasure. I ask you to be the navigator of our shared journey, to chart a course with me through life's endless seas. Let's cast our anchors together, build our harbor of love, and explore the depths of this world and the next.

"Will you, Mercy, be my first mate, my partner, my one true love for every tide and tempest to come? Will you sail with me into forever?"

She stared at him, unable to believe he meant to marry her. Mama must have heard her whispered plea in the wee hours of the morning because Connor, bent on one knee, asking for her hand after knowing the truth about her, had to be the most miraculous event she ever imagined. With her heart in her throat, she whispered. "Yes."

How could her dark, uncertain world turn into something so bright and promising in the space of one afternoon?

Connor rose to his feet and caught her to him, smiling with joy. "My darling." And then his lips were on hers as he swung her around.

For long moments, they clung together, caught up in the joy of the moment, until Benson cleared his throat from the door. "Sir, would you care for tea?"

Connor lifted his head and grinned. "I much prefer wine to celebrate our good news."

"Wine it shall be, sir. May I offer my sincere felicitations?" Snapping his fingers, he sent a footman to the kitchen for wine.

"Thank you, Benson." Glancing down at Mercy, he arched a brow. "Shall we tell Aunt Charity the good news?"

Her heart leaped with joy as she nodded in agreement. Two hours, a broken heart, and an unexpected proposal ago, she stood in the cold graveyard anticipating the need to sell her mother's precious chest so she could relocate, believing she lost Connor forever. And now she stood in the circle of his embrace with her sights on her future and her demons behind her. Glancing at her new fiancé, she leaned forward. "I cannot wait to be alone with you." Tilting her head toward the over-observant butler, she gave him a rueful smile.

Connor's eyes darkened as he inspected her from the top of her shining hair to the bottom of her leather soles. "Soon, my love." Tilting his head, his eyes flashed with passion. "I used to be fascinated by the lump you made with your beautiful hair and how it would slide off your head to land above your right ear. Now, I wish to pull the pins and run my hands through your silken tresses and breathe in the lovely fragrance of your skin. I have a terrible need to hold you naked, my darling, and kiss every inch of your silken body." Glancing toward the door, he sighed. "But first a toast, and then on to our respective bed chambers to put Benson's mind at ease."

She nodded, knowing he would come to her when the house grew quiet and transport her to paradise with his lips and body. Anticipation and pure bliss radiated from her smile as she turned to accept the crystal glass. For the first time in forever, the future glowed with promise.

Chapter Twenty-Six

Dearest Mercy,

If you are reading this letter, my fears have become reality, and I am no longer with you.

Your father will never forgive me for taking my chest from his safe or for stealing his seals.

It is my hope that a decoy chest will aid you if he comes for the box. The seals will ensure he pays for the innocent lives he took with such little regard.

I instructed Mammy to hide the real chest in a different location. Reread the last lines of my poem located on the back page of my diary, and you will understand. My chest is my gift to you, my darling, so that you may live the quality of life you deserve. I will love you forever.

Learn from my mistakes, dearest, and never allow any man to control you. Do not compromise, my dear. No man is worth the price you will pay.

Although nothing can make up for the lost time we should have had together, I sent you to Charity because she is a good woman and will take care of you. Not as I would have, of course, but as second best. For her home is the safest place I could think of to hide you until after the war.

I have no doubt Justice and Percival will track Mammy down, and I have warned her to take precautions. They are not to be trusted, for to do so is utter folly.

Your father is clever, but not more so than I.

Know that I am with you wherever you go. Although I am not there in form, I am there in spirit. I shall be the whisper of the wind in your ear, and the light of the sun on your beautiful face. In my heart, I see you as a grown woman, loved and in love with a wonderful man. He shall be everything you desire and more, despite what you've been told. I love you forever, my daughter. –Mama

****

The Calhan family welcomed Mercy with open arms and murmurs of condolence for her mother's death. They listened with equal measures of surprise and respect over a cozy family dinner held at Connor's home as he related the tale of their father and Grace Bennett.

Shanna, a breathtaking blonde married to Connor's second-youngest brother, Reese, rose to her feet and hugged Mercy as close as her burgeoning belly would allow. "My mother has been the greatest source of comfort in my life, and I cannot imagine living without her." Leaning back, she grinned. "I must confess I am not surprised about your sudden engagement. Giles has been rushing about ordering flowers, selecting fabrics and patterns for different wedding gowns, and fussing with cakes since the day he returned from New York a few weeks ago. He really is the best."

Max, the brother, just younger than Connor, rocked back on his heels and mouthed, "I told you so," and grinned when his pregnant wife, Lilli, a striking brunette, nudged him in the ribs.

Lilli hugged Mercy next and confided she lost her mother at the tender age of nine years as well.

Chase, the youngest brother, and his wife Rose, a

short, pretty woman with curly chocolate-brown hair, made their introductions and scooped her into an embrace. "Welcome to the family."

Connor's mother, Maggie, took her in her arms and kissed both her cheeks. "Bless you, my dear, for the traumatic losses you have endured, and thank you for making my son happy."

Madelaine, Connor's sister, whom she met on her previous visit, grinned and proclaimed her perfect for their oldest sibling. "He's grown into such an irritable old man. He needed you to come along and stir up a little dust."

As the evening progressed, Mercy studied the family from beneath her lashes. They were nothing like Uncle Justice said. They were loving, warm, and inviting. The brothers stood in front of the fireplace, drinking glasses of port and teasing each other. All four topped six feet, had broad shoulders, and striking blue eyes like their mother. Except Chase. His eyes were a deep whiskey-colored brown.

Their wives sat on the settees surrounding Mercy, discussing the latest activities of their children, and catching up on family news. As Mercy sat there, surrounded by the once-hated Calhans, a deep sense of peace, love, and tranquility settled over her, and she knew without a doubt this was where she belonged.

She cast a glance at Aunt Charity, who sat beside Maggie deep in conversation about Grace, her diary, the cipher, and the letter her husband sent the day of his death. When they announced their engagement, she never turned a hair and nodded with satisfaction. "My sister would approve."

Mercy believed she would, too, and smiled. Her

mother's unique scent of roses and hyacinths wafted past Mercy, and she glanced up to find Connor staring at her.

Tilting his chin toward the outside doors, he smiled and extended his hand.

Moments later, they strolled around the corner out of sight of the dining room and clung together in a heated kiss that quickly turned carnal.

"Have I mentioned how delighted I am that my brother Reese married Shanna? When she inherited her family estate, Giles came as part of the package. If not for his scheming and planning, our wedding would have to be postponed for at least three weeks to a month. Since he visited New York, he has been busy preparing. Everything is in place for tomorrow, and I owe the man a debt of gratitude."

Mercy flushed as Connor gripped her hips and held her against his hardening member. "I wish my family would leave now that we've had dinner and made introductions. I wish to be alone with you."

"What would you have done if your family rejected me because of who my parents are?" Her breath came fast, and her knees turned to pudding as his hot mouth devoured the side of her neck.

"They wouldn't. Calhans may be many things, but cold-hearted we are not. Kindness, forgiveness, and love are the basis of our core family values." Grinning, he moved lower to kiss the tops of her breasts pushed high by her corset. "And more than one has confessed they are happy I did not fall in love with Gabrielle. She did not fit in at all."

"But I picked the lock on your warehouse, broke into your home, stole your parchment, and lied to you about everything. You were right about me not possessing any of the qualities you desire in a wife." She sounded breathless and shy to her ears, and flushed.

Connor lifted his head and stared down into her upturned face. "Yes, you did the things you mentioned, but they mean nothing when considering the reasons behind your behavior. I have broken into houses, picked locks, stolen important papers, and lied to find my father's killer, too. It took me a bit to see I had no right to stand in judgment when I am guilty of the same crimes. When I look at you, my darling, I see a beautiful woman willing to shovel dung in hell if it helped her ailing aunt, a dutiful niece who did dubious things at the request of her uncle, and a doting daughter risking her life to find her mother's killer. You have shown strength when others were weak, courage when there was no hope, and faith when you had no one." Sincerity shone from his eyes, and the last of her inhibitions floated away as if they never were.

Thinking back on their conversation when he gave her his list of requirements for a wife and pointed out her shortcomings, she grinned. "And I bathe on a regular basis."

Chuckling, he kissed the tip of her nose. "Little did I know the peril I brought into my life by granting you mercy the first night we met."

She froze. "I do not understand. What peril has befallen you?" Frowning, she stepped back to inspect him.

His grin widened. "Love, my darling. Amour has seeped into my blood, taken my heart hostage, and bound my soul in chains of desire, leaving me powerless against your intoxicating allure. I love you, my darling, more than I thought possible."

"Are you two going to stand out here all night or come inside and share your newfound love with the people who care the most?" Max leaned against the corner of the house and grinned. "I don't want to be the brother who says, 'I told you so,' but…"

A chorus of voices shouted, "We told you so, Connor."

Mercy sighed with delight as he slipped an arm around her waist and followed Max back through the double doors where the rest of the family waited. The second she stepped inside and met their happy smiles and good-natured teasing, she knew she had come home at last.

Epilogue

They were married in the family church and spent their honeymoon in Italy. When they returned, one month later, they discovered the courts refused to punish Colonel Dawson for crimes committed during the Civil War. The blank amnesty issued by President Johnson in July of 1868 for all former Confederates protected him from prosecution. Except for the crime of treason. And although Colonel Dawson sought the downfall of the United States Government, they had nothing to tie him to the crimes but three-decades-old seals which had been out of his care since the war.

The court took the position that anyone could have taken them and used them to implicate Colonel Dawson and absolved him of all charges involved.

Although the courts ordered the colonel to serve another thirty days for his part in the attempted abduction of a senator, they refused to convict him for lack of evidence.

"Following the war, President Lincoln sought peace and reconciliation with our southern neighbors. You should do the same." Pounding his gavel and dismissing the court, the judge returned to his chambers, and the guards led a smiling colonel away to his cell.

Mercy sat stunned when General Cooper paid them a visit to their home and related the details. "He cannot go free...."

The general shook his head. "He shall not. I have invited General Ruiz to join us if you are amenable. He waits without."

The four held a closed-door meeting that lasted a full fifteen minutes. When the Spanish General emerged, his satisfied expression would have made the devil nervous.

Two nights later, while the prison guards dealt with a suspicious explosion on the outskirts of the prison wall, Colonel Percival Edward Dawson Bennett escaped.

Authorities could not comprehend how the colonel managed to unlock his cell door, evade four guards stationed in the corridor, walk undetected through several long corridors, and exit the building. From there, he crossed the compound without being seen and slipped through the heavy metal gate. Someone from outside must have been waiting, for no one witnessed any carriages or horses at that time of night.

Only three men had master keys: the commandant, the warden, and General Cooper. Since all three were loyal, honest, dependable men, with strong alibis, the investigators were stumped.

"They call him The Phantom with good reason."

The only evidence they were able to compile came from one of the other prisoners, who mentioned seeing a strange black carriage the night of the escape.

"Dull and black with no shine as if it belonged to a mortician." The man could relate no other details and kept commenting on its bleak appearance until the investigators gave up.

A week later, Cuba announced they found and executed Colonel Edward Dawson for treason and other related crimes. The country held a two-day celebration in honor of the occasion.

A month to the day of Colonel Dawson's execution, a magnificent basket of flowers appeared on Connor's doorstep. The card contained one word.

"Gracias."

Mercy smiled and passed the card to Connor, who nodded. Together they accomplished what neither one could alone. They caught their parents' killer and delivered him into justice's hands. The precious gold chest had a place of honor over the hearth in the salon, and The New York Times, along with The Boston Herald, ran the story of the southern lady who aided the Union Army during the Civil War and saved Abraham Lincoln from abduction.

Mercy had everything she vowed to accomplish, plus a loving husband and soon-to-be father. Placing her hand over her blossoming belly, she smiled up at the night sky, knowing her mother could rest easy now.

As for Connor, he retired from the Unified Intelligence Agency and spent his time overseeing Calhan Shipping and his wife's happiness. They lived long, happy lives and had two daughters, Love and Patience.

"Because they are the two we were missing." Mercy would explain when asked about the name choices. "And now, we are complete."

Until Connor stepped outside one night to talk with his father, staring at the night sky.

Mercy heard the first part of his discussion and closed the door with a laugh.

"Father, I want to thank you for sending Mercy to me and making me see that marriage and love aren't what I thought they were. And I'm damn grateful. But while we're on the subject, I've been meaning to have a talk with you about Madelaine. Something must be done…"

A word about the author…

I am a romance author, history lover, and eternal dreamer. I write stories filled with passion, danger, and unforgettable characters who fight for love no matter the odds. When I'm not lost in the past or tangled up in plot twists, you'll find me surrounded by roses, happily stitching away at embroidery, knitting, crocheting, or quilting something beautiful by hand.

I have a big, loud, and wonderful family that keeps me grounded and inspired. I'm also a firm believer in chasing dreams, and I'm currently checking off items on my ever-growing bucket list, because life is too short not to live it fully.

Writing has been one of the greatest joys of my life. I love creating heroines with fire in their hearts, heroes worth swooning over, and stories that take readers on an emotional journey. Thank you for being here. I hope my books bring you as much joy as I had writing them.

www.ingramcontent.com/pod-product-compliance
Lightning Source LLC
Chambersburg PA
CBHW060940030726
47503CB00003B/675